W9-AYA-161

"ENTHRALLING."
Charlotte Observer

"ELECTRIFYING."
**Dr. Henry Lee,
forensic criminologist**

"REMARKABLE."
Houston Chronicle

"A KNOCKOUT."
Lansing State Journal

"A HARROWING RIDE."
New York Times
bestselling author Jerry Bledsoe

Resounding praise for
CARVED IN BONE

"**A** superb mystery novel—well-plotted, filled with memorable characters, based on accurate forensic science and written with . . . flair and literary sensibility . . . the novel, in fact, is in Cornwell's league, high praise indeed."

Houston Chronicle

"**S**keletons—literal ones and many figurative ones— are the foundation for a compelling first novel from Jefferson Bass. *Carved in Bone* introduces a captivating protagonist and is full of obscure, fascinating forensics. Bass effortlessly manages the difficult task of making the living characters much creepier than the dead ones—he's a fine new talent."

Stephen White,
New York Times bestselling author of *Missing Persons*

"**A** creepy, knockout debut crime novel . . . Full of rich and sometimes stomach-turning forensic detail, this smoothly crafted crime novel has a surprising, satisfying conclusion."

Lansing State Journal

"*Carved in Bone* brims with terrific forensic detail . . . the real deal."

New York Times bestselling author Kathy Reichs

"*Carved in Bone* isn't the typical murder mystery based on fantasies. It offers terrific forensic details and the science of solving cold cases. It is electrifying, provocative, and full of surprises."

Dr. Henry Lee, author of *Cracking Cases*
and *Henry Lee's Crime Scene Handbook*

"Percolates with wit, gentility, and scientific savoir-faire . . . alive with verve and charm . . . Engrossingly entertaining."

James Starrs, author of *A Voice for the Dead*

"*Carved in Bone* has a unique corpse, solid science, quirky humor, and a lovable protagonist . . . Very human, down-to-earth characters."

USA Today

"Bass makes a successful first foray into fiction . . . The pacing and action bode well for this crime series."

Publishers Weekly

"*Carved in Bone* is what you've been waiting for. Jefferson Bass pulls readers right into an engrossing case that combines suspense, humor, and humanity even as it teaches the lessons of science . . . Move over, Kathy Reichs. The Sherlock Holmes for bones has arrived."

Katherine Ramsland,
author of *The Forensic Science of C.S.I*

"This gripping tale . . . is like a harrowing ride on a twisty mountain road."
Jerry Bledsoe, *New York Times* bestselling author of *Bitter Blood* and *Before He Wakes*

"Fantastic forensic detail and an engaging hero make *Carved in Bone* an intriguing, entertaining novel. Jefferson Bass brings an authoritative, compelling new voice to the forensic mystery."
Jeff Abbott, *USA Today* bestselling author of *Panic*

"A gripping murder mystery that will take you from the colorful—and often terrifying—backwoods of Tennessee into the high-tech world of forensic science."
Emily A. Craig, Ph.D.,
Kentucky State Forensic Anthropologist and author of *Teasing Secrets from the Dead*

"Successfully combines a fascinating mystery, a delightful course in 'how to examine a skeleton,' and the intrigues of the Tennessee moonshine backwoods!"
Michael M. Baden, M.D., former Chief Medical Examiner, New York City and author of *Remains Silent*

"Southern-fried forensics . . . It does taste good going down."
Kirkus Reviews

"Cliff-hanging dramatic scenes . . . enthralling . . . Please deliver a second novel soon, Jefferson Bass."
Charlotte Observer

Books by Jefferson Bass

CARVED IN BONE

Coming Soon in Hardcover

FLESH AND BONE

ATTENTION: ORGANIZATIONS AND CORPORATIONS
Most Harper paperbacks are available at special quantity discounts for bulk purchases for sales promotions, premiums, or fund-raising. For information, please call or write:

Special Markets Department, HarperCollins Publishers, 10 East 53rd Street, New York, New York 10022-5299.
Telephone: (212) 207-7528.   Fax: (212) 207-7222.

CARVED IN BONE

A BODY FARM NOVEL

JEFFERSON BASS

HARPER

An Imprint of HarperCollinsPublishers

This is a work of fiction. Names, characters, places, and incidents are products of the author's imagination or are used fictitiously and are not to be construed as real. Any resemblance to actual events, locales, organizations, or persons, living or dead, is entirely coincidental.

HARPER

An Imprint of HarperCollins*Publishers*
10 East 53rd Street
New York, New York 10022-5299

Copyright © 2006 by Jefferson Bass, LLC.
Excerpt from *Flesh and Bone* copyright © 2007 by Jefferson Bass, LLC.
ISBN: 978-0-06-075982-7
ISBN-10: 0-06-075982-8

All rights reserved. No part of this book may be used or reproduced in any manner whatsoever without written permission, except in the case of brief quotations embodied in critical articles and reviews. For information address Harper paperbacks, an Imprint of HarperCollins Publishers.

First Harper paperback printing: January 2007
First William Morrow hardcover printing: February 2006

HarperCollins® and Harper® are trademarks of HarperCollins Publishers Inc.

Printed in the United States of America

Visit Harper paperbacks on the World Wide Web at www.harpercollins.com

10 9 8 7 6 5 4 3 2 1

If you purchased this book without a cover, you should be aware that this book is stolen property. It was reported as "unsold and destroyed" to the publisher, and neither the author nor the publisher has received any payment for this "stripped book."

To the faculty, staff, and graduate students of the University of Tennessee's Anthropology Department, who made the Body Farm possible . . . and to Patricia Cornwell, who made it famous

Prologue

I PICKED UP THE hunting knife with my left hand and tested its heft, then shifted it to my right hand to compare. Golfing and batting, I'm a lefty, but I grade papers and dial phone numbers with my right. The knife felt more at home there, too. Okay, I thought, add "stabbing" to the list of right-handed activities.

The nude man lay facedown in the woods, the Tennessee sun filtering through the trees and dappling his back. Kneeling beside him, I slid my left thumb along his spine, feeling for the gap between his fourth and fifth ribs, just behind the lower chambers of the heart. Having found the spot, I set the tip of the hunting knife there—it snagged in the soft flesh—then leaned in and began to push. It took more force than I'd expected, and I found myself using both hands, plus some weight. Once the blade was deep into the muscle tissue, I cocked the handle to the left, skewing the blade in the opposite direction, toward the man's spine. It wasn't angling as sharply as I wanted, so I leaned harder. Still no go. I sat back and considered whether there might be some other angle of attack that would land the tip of the blade in his right lung. As I contemplated the weapon jutting from the bare back, a black-and-white SUV, blue lights strobing, roared up and slid to a stop on a concrete slab in front of me. A young deputy leapt out, his eyes wild and his face a battleground of warring impulses.

I held up my left hand, keeping a tight grip on the knife with my right. "You reckon you could hang on for just one second?" I asked. "I'm not quite done with this." Grunting with the effort, I gave the handle one final sideways shove and bore down with all my weight. As my victim jerked and skidded from the force, a rib broke with the sound of a green tree branch splintering. The deputy fainted dead away, his fall cushioned by the corpse I knelt beside.

1

FIVE MINUTES HAD PASSED since the deputy's eyelids first fluttered open, and he still hadn't spoken, so I figured maybe it was up to me to break the ice. "I'm Dr. Brockton, but I expect you know that," I said. He nodded weakly. According to the bar of brass on his chest, his name was Williams. "This your first visit to the Body Farm, Deputy Williams?" He nodded again.

"Body Farm" wasn't my facility's real name, but the nickname—coined by a local FBI agent and given title billing in a bestselling crime novel by Patricia Cornwell—seemed to have stuck. Cornwell set only a brief scene of the novel at my postmortem-decay research lab at the University of Tennessee, but that one scene—along with the facility's catchy nickname and macabre mission—must have been enough. As soon as the book hit the shelves, the phone started ringing and the media descended in droves. The upshot is, millions of people know about the Body Farm, though few of them know its boring but official name: the Anthropology Research Facility. Unlike some of my colleagues, I don't care which name people use. To paraphrase Shakespeare, a Body Farm by any other name would still stink.

A lot of people wonder what an anthropologist is doing with dozens of rotting human corpses scattered across (and beneath) three acres of Tennessee woods. When they hear the term "anthropology," they think of Margaret Mead and her sexually liberated Samoans, or Jane Goodall and her colony of chimps, not physical anthropologists and their calipers and bones. But the rise of forensic anthropology—using the tools of physical anthropology to help solve crimes—seems to be elevating the profile of the bone detectives. It's amazing what you can learn about murder victims by studying their skulls, their rib cages, their pelvises, and other bones. Who was this person who was cut into pieces and hidden in a junkyard? What's the age, race, sex, and stature? Do his dental fillings or healed fractures match X-rays of missing persons? Is that hole in the skull from a gunshot wound or a golf club? Was he dismembered with a chain saw or a surgeon's scalpel? Finally—and here's where my facility has made its greatest mark over the past quarter-century—judging by the degree of decomposition, how long has this poor bastard been dead?

Of course, when word gets around that you've got dozens of dead bodies in various states of disrepair, all sorts of interesting research questions come your way. That's why I now found myself kneeling over a corpse, plunging a hunting knife into his back.

I looked down at my "victim," the weapon still jutting from the oozing wound. "I'm running a little experiment here," I said to the shell-shocked deputy who had caught me *in flagrante delicto*. "Despite the knife in his back, this fellow actually died of a coronary—halfway through a marathon." Williams blinked in surprise, but I just shrugged in a go-figure sort of way. "Forty years old, ran every day. I guess you could say his legs just outran his heart." I waited for a laugh, but there wasn't one. "Anyhow, his wife took some of my anthropology classes here at UT about twenty years ago, so when he keeled over, she donated his body for research. I'm not sure if that says good things or bad things about the marriage."

Williams's eyes cleared and focused a bit—he seemed to be at least considering whether to smile at this one—so I kept talking. The words, I figured, gave him something to latch on to as he hauled himself out of his tailspin. "I'm testifying in a homicide case that's about to go to trial, and I'm trying to re-produce a stab wound—what the medical examiner's autopsy called the fatal wound—but I'm not having much luck. Looks like I'd have to violate a couple of laws of physics or metallurgy to get that blade to follow the path the ME de-scribed." His eyes swiveled from my face to the corpse and back to me again. "See, the ME's report had the blade enter-ing the victim's back on the left side, then angling up across the spine, and finally veering sharply into the right lobe of the lung. Can't be done. Not by me, at least. Between you and me and the gatepost, I think the ME botched the autopsy."

I had propped the deputy against the trunk of an oak tree. By now he looked like maybe he was ready to get up, so I peeled off a glove and hauled him to his feet. "Take a look around, if you want," I said, nodding toward a cluster of clothed bodies at the edge of the main clearing. "You might see something that'll help you with a case someday." He considered this, then took a tentative glance around the clearing. "Over there, we've got a decomposition experi-ment that's comparing cotton clothing with synthetic fab-rics. We need to know if certain types of fabric slow down or speed up the decomp rate. So far, looks like cotton's the winner."

"What difference would it make?" Ah: he *could* talk!

"Cotton holds moisture longer, which the flies and mag-gots seem to like. Keeps the skin nice and soft." He winced, clearly regretting the question. "Up the hill in the woods," I went on, "we've got a screened-in hut where we're keeping the bugs away from a body. You'd be amazed how much the decomp rate slows when bugs can't get to the corpse." I turned to him. "One of my students just finished a study of cadaver weight loss; guess how many pounds a day a body can lose?" He stared at me as if I were from another planet. "*Forty pounds* in one day, if the body's really fat. Maggots are like teenage boys: you just can't fill 'em up."

He grimaced and shook his head, but he grinned, too. Finally. "So you've got bodies laid out all over the ground here?"

"All over the ground. Underneath it, too. That concrete slab you just parked your Cherokee on? Two bodies under it. We're watching them decompose with ground-penetrating radar." He spun toward the SUV, looking all panicky again.

"Don't worry," I laughed, "you're not doing them any damage, and they're not coming after you for parking on 'em." I felt an urge to goose him in the ribs and yell "*boogedy-boogedy-boogedy!*" as I might have done with a skittish student, but I resisted. "Just relax, son. Take a deep breath—or maybe not so deep, now that I think about it. Look at all this as research, not as dead people." I paused for effect, then delivered my dramatic closing argument. "What you're seeing here is forensic science in action." With that, I reached down and wrenched the knife from the back of my research subject with a flourish. The blade popped free with a wet, sucking sound. A blob of purplish goo arced toward the deputy and plopped onto his left shoe, where it quivered moistly.

This time, I caught him before he hit the ground.

2

DEPUTY WILLIAMS, STILL LOOKING like he'd seen a ghost, threaded the Cherokee through the maze of UT Medical Center parking lots that bordered the Body Farm. "I make a good neighbor for the hospital," I joked to Williams. "If you're late to work, you have to park out by the Body Farm, so all the hospital employees get to work a half-hour early." Judging by his expression, if he worked there, he'd be clocking in an hour or more before his shift.

Leaving the hospital complex, we merged onto a six-lane highway and crossed the Tennessee River on a soaring span of concrete. To our right, the bridge offered a panoramic view of UT's main campus, sprawling along the river's north shore for nearly two miles. To our left, the view ranged from dairy cows on the near shore to mansions on the opposite side, lining the upper shores of Fort Loudoun Lake.

Fort Loudoun—locals call it "Fort Nasty" for its cornucopia of pollutants and sewage—is one of a string of dammed reservoirs along the 650-mile length of the Tennessee River. The Tennessee actually begins just a few miles upriver from the Body Farm, at the confluence of the Holston and French Broad rivers. For a brief stretch through downtown Knoxville and past the university, the river runs narrow and brisk. Then, just past the concrete bridge Williams and I crossed, the Tennessee makes a sweeping

left-hand turn, where it slows and broadens, domesticated by
Fort Loudoun Dam, forty miles downstream. The inside of
this big bend is occupied by a UT cattle farm; the outside, on
the northwest shore, by the estates of Sequoyah Hills,
Knoxville's richest neighborhood. The mansions' views
across the water to the rolling cattle farm are stunning, but
they come at a price over and above their jumbo mortgages:
on torrid days, if the air's drifting slowly from the east,
Knoxville's finest homes are bathed in the pungent aroma of
cow manure, overlaid—very faintly and very rarely—with a
hint of human decomposition.

Williams angled to the right where the highway inter-
sected Interstate 40, dumping us into the traffic crawling
through downtown Knoxville on I-40 East. Inching along
through the latest in a seemingly endless series of interstate
"improvements," we had plenty of time to admire Knoxville's modest architectural skyline—a couple of thirty-story
bank towers, a hulking Presbyterian hospital, a few cereal-
box-shaped UT dorms, and the "Sunsphere"—an empty
relic of the 1982 World's Fair that looked like a seventy-foot
golden golf ball balanced on a two-hundred-foot structural-
steel tee. But once we cleared downtown, traffic thinned and
the buildings dropped behind us, replaced by the rolling
foothills and the sharp spine of the Great Smoky Mountains,
backbone of the Appalachians. The Appalachians defined
the entire eastern border of Tennessee. And Cooke County,
Tennessee, defined—or at least personified—Appalachia at
its most rugged.

Officially, the man who had sent Deputy Williams to fetch
me, Tom Kitchings, was Cooke County's sheriff. In reality,
though, he was its sovereign. The title "Lord High Sheriff"
had never been used in Tennessee, as far as I knew, but that
term seemed to sum up Kitchings's position in his mountain
stronghold.

With its forested hills and tumbling streams, Cooke

County was one of Tennessee's most beautiful places. It was also one of the wildest, in every sense of the word. Buttressed by the rugged border of North Carolina to the east and Great Smoky Mountains National Park to the south, Cooke County was a legendary refuge for moonshiners, bootleggers, and other sundry scofflaws. Its rugged topography, tight-knit clans, and serpentine roads had kept the law at bay long after most of Appalachia had acquiesced in its own taming. Well into the era of television, the Internet, and mountaintop condos, Cooke County had hung onto a frontier mentality—the Wild South, I guess you might say—where rough, redneck justice was the only sort of justice whose arm was long enough or strong enough to reach back into the hollows and up to the mountaintops.

But all that seemed to change when Tom Kitchings took over.

Kitchings himself was a product of Cooke County—there was no way an outsider could ever get himself elected sheriff of the most clannish, insular enclave in a clannish, insular part of the state. There had probably been a Kitchings in Cooke County for as long as there had been a Cooke County, maybe longer. But Tom Kitchings was not your stereotypical hillbilly. He'd played high school football, though that part wasn't surprising; the school was so small, every able-bodied boy was drafted to play, and they played with a vengeance. Other East Tennessee schools dreaded playing away games in Cooke County. Members of the visiting team—including my son, Jeff—invariably limped home with sprained ankles and bloody noses; some returned sporting fewer teeth than they'd gone up there with. Kitchings, though, was not just a thug in pads; he was a gifted athlete. He ran tailback for Cooke County High, and he was good enough to win a scholarship to UT during a period when UT had its pick of the best athletes in the Southeast. He looked to be on the fast track to the NFL—he rushed for a thousand yards his sophomore year and twelve hundred the next. But his college career and his football career ended seven minutes into the first game of his senior year in front of 90,000 fans in Neyland Stadium, when an Alabama linebacker slammed into his left knee and shredded the ligaments.

Kitchings had hobbled home to Cooke County and dropped from sight. My son—who tracks UT players the way daytime TV fans track soap opera stars—said Kitchings was rumored to be drinking a lot, but that was all he was able to tell me. Then, six or eight years later, Jeff showed me a story in the sports section reporting that Kitchings was alive and well and had found his life's calling as a lawman, helping tame the wild denizens of Cooke County.

The taming didn't always go smoothly. Some years after Kitchings joined the force, his boss, the sheriff, was killed in a moonlit shootout on the edge of a two-acre marijuana patch. Pot, outsiders seem surprised to learn, is the number-one cash crop in Cooke County, followed quite distantly by tobacco. Marijuana grows tall in the cool and moist mountain air; in fact, Cooke County pot supposedly packs more punch than the crops from Mexico or Colombia, say my law enforcement colleagues. It doesn't take a big patch to bring in good money, and the county's roadless ridges and hollows give farmers the kind of privacy once prized by moonshiners. But every now and then, somebody's pot patch gets busted, and sometimes somebody gets shot, though it's not usually the sheriff.

In a special election held to fill the post, Kitchings outran his opponent—a local undertaker—as easily as he'd once outrun would-be tacklers. Since then, he'd spent a decade bringing the sheriff's office into the modern era. With the money seized in a spate of drug busts, he bought a fleet of new vehicles: SUVs that could handle the rutted roads threading the county's hollows; off-road ATVs that could cross swollen streams and reach hillside pot patches; even a

helicopter from which he could survey his mountain king-
dom from on high, with his brother, Chief Deputy Orbin
Kitchings, a former army chopper pilot, at the controls.

Despite his success, and despite the passage of nearly
twenty years, Tom Kitchings had never fully gotten over his
football injury. He still carried a slight hitch in his step and a
fair-sized chip on his shoulder. He'd gone about as far as he
could go in Cooke County, but that was leagues away, literally, from NFL stardom.

I didn't actually know any of this firsthand. Everything I
knew about Tom Kitchings came from UT fans like Jeff and
law enforcement colleagues like Art Bohanan, a criminalist
with the Knoxville Police Department. Unlike every other
sheriff in East Tennessee, Kitchings had never consulted me
on a forensic case. Not that I minded. Judging by things I'd
heard from Art, getting involved in Cooke County cases was
a lot like snake-handling: it was an act of faith that violated
all the dictates of common sense—and it entailed a damn
good chance of getting snakebit. According to Art and others at KPD, it was not entirely clear which was more ven-
omous in Cooke County, the bad guys in the battered
pickups or the good guys in their SUVs and aircraft. Nothing was certain; anything was possible.

I had plenty of time to ponder these things as the Cherokee bored east on Interstate 40, traversing the broad valley
of the French Broad River. Then, just before I-40 plunged
into the heart of the Appalachians, Williams whipped the
Jeep down an off-ramp, skidded left onto a county road, and
began threading curves that made a corkscrew seem straight
by comparison.

The road had a solid yellow center line, but Williams drove
as if both lanes were his alone, wandering from one edge to
another. "Is this one way?" I asked, knowing it wasn't, but
hoping he might take the hint and stick to the right lane.

"One way?" He laughed easily. Now we were in his territory, not mine. "Naw, but you got to straighten these curves or you'll never get where you're going." By way of demonstration, he took both hands off the wheel, and the Jeep barreled straight ahead for a hundred yards, while the center line whipsawed beneath us. "It's easier at night, when you can see the other cars coming." He drifted left to hug the inside of a tight curve. "Unless they got their lights off. One or two nights a year, we get a bad head-on wreck long about here."

I switched to pondering that for a minute, but as the road grew more tortuous, my pondering shifted to another alarming topic: how many more curves could I take before I threw up? Not many, I realized, as sweat began beading on my forehead and premonitory saliva filled my mouth. I rolled down the window and thrust my face out into the bracing air, panting like a dog. It helped, but not enough to offset our continuing roller coaster ride. I pulled my head back inside. "Listen, I hate to do this," I said, "but I've got to ask you to stop. I'm getting really carsick."

He looked startled, as if he'd never heard anything so ridiculous. Carsick? On this fine road? It was the look a camel might give a parched human in the Sahara. *Thirsty? Didn't you drink some water just last week?*

A pained expression worked its way from his mouth up to his eyes; then he shook his head once. "Sheriff said he needs you right away. Reckon we better keep on a-keepin' on. Just hang out the window there and let fly if you need to."

As if on cue, I did. Flecks of vomit spattered the gold star painted on the door. I pulled my head back in. "It's not that simple," I rasped. "It isn't just vomiting. I've got Ménière's disease—vertigo—and I'm about thirty seconds from getting a dizzy spell that'll last for days. Trust me, if that happens, there's no way I'll be able to do whatever the sheriff needs me to do."

He cursed under his breath, but he hit the brakes and we crunched to a stop on the shoulder beside the tumbling Little

Pigeon River. Two minutes later, we were under way again. This time, we kept to our side of the blacktop, and the tires had ceased to squeal. That's because this time I was driving.

"I can't believe I let you talk me into this," Williams muttered. "Sheriff's gonna be mad as hell."

"Not as mad as he'd be if I had to lie down in a dark room for three days," I said. "Maybe it won't be so bad." I rolled down the window to dispel the acrid scent of vomit.

Ten minutes later, we rounded yet another curve, and suddenly—for the first time since we'd dived off the interstate—I could see for more than a hundred yards ahead. The road ran straight and level for half a mile, bringing us into Jonesport, the county seat. The town occupied what must have been the one patch of level ground in all of Cooke County.

Hunkering in the center of the town square was the courthouse, a two-story structure that appeared designed to repel a military siege. Laid up in thick slabs of rough-hewn granite, its façade was broken by only a few small windows, all of them barred, and by a mammoth ironclad door that could have shrugged off a medieval battering ram. I'd seen prisons that were flimsier. Prettier, too.

"That's a mighty stout courthouse you've got there," I observed.

"Old one burned down back in the twenties," he said. "Fellow was in jail, his kinfolks was trying to get him out. There was a shootout, then a fire. Reckon they didn't want that kind of thing happening again."

"Fellow get away?"

"No sir, he didn't. First he caught a bullet, then he burned up. Thing is, he shouldna oughta been in jail in the first place. It was a goddamn frame-up from the get-go."

"You take a strong interest in local history," I said.

"That piece of it, anyhow. Fellow was my granddaddy." He pointed. "Park here."

As I eased the vehicle into a diagonal slot in front of the courthouse, I sensed a presence beside me. I glanced out my open window and saw a khaki-clad belly hanging over a pair of olive-drab trousers; a .38 dangled from a gun belt. Then a face leaned in at the window. "Williams, what in holy hell is going on here?"

I thought it best to speak right up. "Sheriff Kitchings? This is one smart deputy you've got."

Both men stared at me in astonishment. I plowed ahead, full speed. "I got sick as a dog on the way up here. I was on the verge of passing out when your deputy remembered an article he'd read about motion sickness. Asked me if I'd be willing to try driving a spell, see if that helped." Kitchings looked from me to Williams and back again. "Fixed me right up. Lucky thing, too—if it hadn't, I'd've had to lay under that tree over there for a week till my head quit spinning."

I could see a question forming in the sheriff's mind—something about his deputy's medical library, I suspected—so I shifted gears before the discussion could take a bibliographic turn. "Sheriff, I don't remember having you in any of my anthropology classes at UT," I said. "Should I?"

He blushed and shook his head, suddenly a student being quizzed by a professor again. "Uh, no, sir, I never got around to taking anthropology. I did come to your class once, though. The time you showed slides of that fireworks explosion."

An illegal fireworks factory in southeastern Tennessee had gone up with a bang one day, hurling thirteen people—in half a hundred pieces—through the roof of the barn where they were mixing gunpowder with pigments. It was a gruesome accident, but it was also a fascinating forensic case study, a homespun mass disaster. Before showing slides of the carnage to my classes, I always warned students a week in advance that the pictures were horrific, and I gave them the option of skipping class—that one class out of the whole semester—without penalty. Invariably, the day of the slide show, the lecture hall was jammed—standing room only, including dozens of students who weren't even taking the class. The first time it happened, I was surprised; after that, I knew to expect it. If I were smarter, I'd have charged admission every year, then retired early and rich.

"That was an interesting case," I said. "I think we finally got everybody put back together right, but when we first stacked up all those arms and legs, I wasn't sure we'd be able to."

Williams was safe now, I guessed, so I cut the small talk. "What can I do for you, Sheriff? Your deputy here said it was mighty important, but he didn't say what it was."

"There's a body I need you to look at."

"I kinda figured that. Is it in the morgue?"

"Morgue?" He snorted. "Doc, the closest thing we got to a morgue up here's the walk-in beer cooler at the Git-'N'-Go." He and Williams shared a laugh at the image of a body laid out atop cases of Bud Light. "The body's still where we found it at yesterday."

The look of alarm on my face made him smile. "Don't you worry—another twenty-four hours in that place ain't gonna hurt it none." He winked across me at Williams, and Williams laughed again, this time not so much at what Kitchings had said as at what he *hadn't* said. Williams laughed with the relief of a child who'd come home from school expecting a whipping and gotten a cookie instead. At that, I smiled, too.

3

"OKAY, BOYS, SADDLE UP and move out." Kitchings swung a leg over his mount, and Williams and I did the same. I hit the ATV's starter button and the Honda engine purred to life. They'd offered me a choice: double up with Williams or ride solo. I'd ridden with Williams once today, and I hadn't much liked it, so I opted for a machine of my own.

I had never driven an all-terrain vehicle before, but I'd seen kids tearing along highway shoulders and across fields on them, so I figured there couldn't be much to it. There wasn't, at least on flat ground. The throttle was a lever on the right handgrip that you pushed with your thumb, just like the Honda jet ski I rode once at a colleague's lake house on Fort Nasty.

The sheriff's ATV had a hand brake for the front wheels and a foot brake for the rear—just like the English three-speed bike I pedaled to campus back during my own graduate student days. So far, so good. The gearshift was an oddly placed pair of buttons on the left handgrip—my first few shifts lurched comically—but after a few uneventful laps of the courthouse parking lot, the sheriff seemed satisfied that I'd make it back in one piece from wherever it was we were headed.

The serpentine road we'd taken into Jonesport was a superhighway compared to the track we followed out of it. It started out as a lane of gravel, turning off the highway a half-mile south of town. The first time we crossed the river, we did so on a sagging wooden bridge. The next four times—or was it five?—that we forded it, the current piled up against the balloon tires of the ATVs. Before long the single lane of gravel gave way to a pair of parallel ruts, and soon those turned into a single muddy gully. Our progress, as we lurched and fishtailed upward, was excruciatingly slow—which was the only thing that kept me from getting sick again. The ATV had seemed simple to handle on the road. On the trail, it was a whole different beast. Keeping my balance and maintaining control required half-sitting, half-crouching, in a posture that I could tell was going to send my academician's thighs and buttocks into fits of agony. But every time Kitchings and Williams looked back to see how I was faring, I gave a quick thumbs-up, trying not to look completely clumsy and panic-stricken as I made my grab for the handlebars again.

Gradually a limestone cliff reared out of the mountainside, and the trail, such as it was, edged close to its base, at times running beneath overhangs framed by towering hemlocks and glossy rhododendrons. At one such overhang the officers slowed, turned toward a cleft in the rock face . . . and then plunged into the bowels of the earth. I sucked in my breath, gritted my teeth, and plunged in after them. Okay, I didn't actually plunge—crept, more like it—but I followed. The key point is, I followed, finding the switch for the headlamp just as the last glimmer of daylight dwindled behind me.

The floor was surprisingly smooth and level—dry sand in some places, packed mud in others. The headlights of the ATVs fell away into nothingness, which told me we were in a huge subterranean chamber, the blackness so thick you could almost touch it. Then, after a distance that I had no way of estimating, glistening walls began closing in upon us, and we entered the bed of a subterranean stream. It was a foot deep, perhaps six feet wide, and straight as an arrow, following some precise crease in the layers of bedrock. When the passage widened again, Kitchings and Williams turned the vehicles up out of the streambed and stopped. They killed their engines and cut the lights, so I did the same, and we sat in utter darkness.

No one said a word. The water gurgled softly past. My ears adjusted to the quiet, as my eyes might have adjusted to dim light, had there been a single photon to latch on to. Gradually I began to hear another sound underneath the stream's noise, a sound that was musical, haunting, and human: unmistakably, I heard the laughter of small children.

"Do you hear . . . ?" I began, but I couldn't even bring myself to finish the question.

"The kids. Yeah." It was Kitchings. "Spooky, huh? I've been told two different things by people who know this cave. One is that it's just some weird echo from the stream. The other is that it's the spirits of Indian children."

He must have sensed my confusion, because he continued, "This cave is on land that was sacred to five separate tribes. Even when they were at war, they could mingle here in peace. Powerful magic, they say. When I'm out in the daylight, I believe in the science. When I'm in here in the dark, I believe in the spirits."

He flipped on a flashlight, and when he did, the laughter died in midnote. Opening a cargo box bolted to the rear of the ATV, he fished out three powerful lanterns and a jacket that read "D.E.A." in big letters across the back. "Here, you better put on this heirloom drug-bust jacket, Doc; you're liable to catch pneumonia in here." I waved it off, but he handed it to me anyhow. "I'd hate to be remembered as the sheriff who killed Dr. Brockton," he said. As I put it on, I realized I was already shivering.

We trudged up the side of a sloping basin, ducked into a

side tunnel, and soon emerged into another chamber. The rest of the cavern had been a dull grayish-brown, but these walls sparkled—practically blazed—with the fire of millions of crystals. Quartz, I guessed, though they seemed as brilliant as diamonds. A mammoth stalagmite, also sheathed in crystals, filled one side of the chamber.

A narrow cleft separated the stalagmite from the wall. Kitchings nodded toward the crevice and played his light over the opening in a go-here sort of way. I edged my way in. It was a tight fit—I wondered how the sheriff had wrangled his beer belly through it—but then it opened up into a small, glittering grotto. Laid out on a rock shelf along one side was a body—the most remarkable human corpse I'd ever seen. I stared, and blinked, and stared again.

The sheriff had been right. A day—or a month, or even a year—would have wrought little change in the striking corpse laid out on a rock shelf in that glittering grotto.

I had seen adipocere many times before. The term is Latin; it translates literally as "grave wax," and that pretty much sums up what it is and where it's found: a greasy, tallowlike material that forms when fatty flesh decomposes in a damp environment. Bodies buried in damp basements or crawl spaces under houses often have adipocere on them; so do floaters—bodies found in Tennessee's abundant lakes and rivers—with most of the adipocere centered along the floater's waterline. But the dozens of basement bodies and floaters I'd seen bore scant resemblance to the specimen laid out on the stone ledge before me. At first glance the corpse had appeared shrouded in adipocere, but as I studied it, I realized that what I was seeing wasn't a surface coating, but something much rarer. The body's soft tissues had been completely transformed into adipocere—almost as if Madame Tussaud had placed a waxen mummy here as a private exhibit for me alone. The clothing had apparently crumbled away, its residue incorporated into a dark layer that began at the corpse's neck and continued all the way down to the rotting leather at the soles of the feet.

The Smithsonian possessed a similar corpse, that of Wilhelm von Ellenbogen, who had been dug up in the course of moving a cemetery more than a century ago. The Mutter Museum in Philadelphia—home to some of the most bizarre medical and forensic oddities on the planet—had his female counterpart, whom they nicknamed "the Soap Lady" because of adipocere's chemical kinship to soap. But those were misshapen and repulsive compared to the eerily preserved corpse before me. It was not an image of repose, mind you—the eyes stared blindly and the mouth gaped in an eternal scream—and yet despite the grotesque expression, there was something oddly beautiful about it.

I started forward, then caught myself and called out, "Have you all been in here?"

"Just far enough to see the body. Didn't want to disturb the scene before you got a chance to look at it."

"Good man. I wish more of your colleagues would be so careful."

I took out the 35-millimeter camera I'd brought with me from Knoxville. Early in my career, one of the smartest cops I ever worked with gave me a piece of advice that sounded equally apt for crime scene photographers and ruthless bank robbers: "Shoot your way in and shoot your way out," he said, and I'd been doing it ever since. Standing in the opening to the crystalline grotto, I started with wide shots from eye level, to establish the scene as a whole. Then I squatted down and shot across the floor of the cave at a low angle—another photography trick he'd taught me—to cast shadows that would throw footprints into sharper relief.

The flash was too quick and bright for me to see what it was getting, so I played the flashlight beam across the floor. The unevenness made it hard to tell for sure, but I thought I saw prints leading toward the body. I zoomed in on what seemed to be the best ones and fired off shots from several angles. Then I turned my attention and my lens toward the body.

I approached, slowly and circuitously, taking photographs every time I moved more than a few feet. I'd started with a fresh roll of 36 exposures—slides, as always, because a carousel tray was easy to carry into a classroom or a courtroom, and the film's resolution was still far better than any digital image. You could project a good slide on a movie theater screen and it'd still look crisp; try that with a digital image and it would turn into some murky Impressionist rendering of a crime scene shrouded in fog. Besides, the one occasion when I'd tried using a digital camera, every picture I snapped erased the one before, so I left that crime scene with just one photo, a close-up of a stab wound. But I had read that the last Kodak carousel slide projector had rolled off the assembly line a year or so back, so I knew my nondigital days were numbered. "Progress, hell," I muttered.

"What's that, Doc?"

"Sorry, just talking to myself in here. Y'all come on back."

They squeezed through the crevice into the grotto. Williams, who was skinny as a stray dog, slipped through easily. Kitchings required considerable time and effort. He turned sideways, his arms raised, for the first part. Then, when he reached the narrowest part of the passage—"Fat Man's Squeeze," the gap would be called if this were a commercial cave tour—he reached down, cupped his hands under his belly, and squished it upward like some gargantuan breast in a cyclopean Miracle Bra. I knew I shouldn't, but I couldn't resist: I raised the camera and pressed the shutter.

He yelped when the flash seared his eyes. "God*damn!* What the hell?"

I grinned. "Just making sure I document everything at the scene."

"Document my ass. Looka here, Doc, forensic legend or not, you show that picture to a soul, and I figure any jury in Cooke County would call your death justifiable homicide."

Williams piped up, "Could be, Tom, but to beat the rap, you'd have to show the picture to all twelve of 'em." He chuckled at the notion.

"Well, shit. That complicates my damn plan, don't it? I reckon maybe I better just confiscate the doc's film."

"I wouldn't lose any sleep over it, Sheriff," I said. "I think I had the lens cap on anyhow."

When they were both standing beside me, I asked, "Mind if I take a picture of your feet?"

They looked puzzled for a moment, then the light dawned. Kitchings held Williams's shoulder to steady himself, then raised one boot sole toward me for a photo, followed by the other. Next, Williams braced on Kitchings and I photographed his feet, too. Finally, I handed the camera to Kitchings and had him snap mine. It was unlikely to come up in court, but I didn't want some defense lawyer claiming that what the prosecution presented as a ruthless killer's footprints were actually an inept anthropologist's.

The only things I'd brought from Knoxville besides my camera were a pair of latex gloves, a small tape measure, and a pocketknife. I opened the pocketknife and set it on the rock shelf, then donned the gloves and picked it back up. Using the tip of the blade, I gently picked at the adipocere in the region of the cheek. As I suspected, underneath was nothing but bone. "Can't tell the race from the skin," I said, "because there's no skin left."

Williams spoke up. "Got to be white. We don't have black folks up here. Not after sundown, anyhow." He snickered. "Not if a black man values his life."

I leveled a look at the deputy. "Then again, if a black man was to have car trouble or get lost up here when the sun went down, this might be just the sort of spot he'd wind up in, mightn't it?"

"Leon, you dumbass hillbilly redneck," Kitchings spat.

Williams blinked and looked away, his jaw muscles twitching hard.

"You're probably right, I'm pretty sure it's a Caucasian," I went on. "The hair looks straight and blond, and the mouth structure is textbook Caucasoid—see how vertical the teeth are?" I touched the tip of the knife blade to what was once the upper lip, just below where the nose had collapsed, then swung the flat side of the blade down across the lips, resting it on the greasy chin. "If this individual were Negroid, the teeth and jawbones would angle forward, and this straight edge wouldn't touch the chin."

I pulled out the tape. With Williams holding one end gingerly, I measured the corpse. "About five feet eight," I read. "Allowing for postmortem shrinkage of the cartilage, could've been another two or three inches taller than that in life. Just from the stature, I'd have guessed male, but from the facial features, the small skull, and the wide pelvis, I'm thinking female. Any guesses? Any women—tall women—missing in Cooke County?"

They thought awhile before Kitchings broke the silence. "Not that I know of. How long you reckon she's been here, Doc?"

"Between the cave and the adipocere, it's hard to say. Caves are cool, and it doesn't look like the flies and maggots ever got to her. So it could have been a long time—I'd say years rather than months, maybe even a whole lot of years."

"Well, that's gonna mean going back through the files quite a ways, then," Kitchings said. "Might take awhile. Some of the files aren't too good, either. The ones since I took office are okay, but the older ones are a mess."

"Well, see what you can find," I said. "There might be

some folks who'd remember right off. Didn't I see some old-timers whittling on a bench outside the courthouse? You'd be amazed what guys like that can tell you."

"Well, I'm not sure I'd put too much stock in the memories of those guys, but I'll ask. What else can you tell me about her?"

"Not much right here, right now. I need to get the body back to the Forensic Center at UT Medical Center and process the remains," I said. "Clean off the tissue, study the bones closely. Then I can tell you how old she was, how tall, what race. We'll take X-rays, look for healed injuries that might show up in somebody's medical chart, try to find dental records. If we get lucky, we'll find out who she was and maybe even how she died."

"That would be lucky," he said. But he didn't say it with the hearty conviction you'd expect from a sheriff with an unidentified murder victim on his hands.

While I took a few final photos, Kitchings and Williams retrieved the body bag and the litter that were lashed to the back of the deputy's ATV. I unzipped the bag, bunched the opening under one side of the body, and gently worked the corpse up off the rock and into the bag. Then I zipped it up and we slid it off the rock ledge and into the litter. We hauled it back to the vehicles, where the officers retied it to the rear rack. The rack had been designed to haul beer coolers and deer carcasses, but it would serve to haul a body. The added weight, though, rocked the vehicle back on its haunches, making the headlight angle upward. As we retraced our route back to the mouth of the cave, I heard Williams curse more than once as he thumped into unseen rocks in his path. When we emerged, squinting, into the afternoon light, he faced a different challenge. On the trek up the mountain, the empty litter had been lashed lengthwise, projecting several feet off the back of the deputy's ATV; now, weighted with the body, it was crosswise, and the six-foot litter was wider than many parts of the trail. Whenever the trail necked down, Williams was forced to execute a series of tricky, needle-threading maneuvers, which he accompanied with a volley of curses.

By the time we'd bumped down the mountainside and rumbled to a stop behind the courthouse, the sun was slipping behind a ridge, and my thighs and buttocks were burning from their hours of shock-absorber duty. The courthouse whittlers were long gone. Night fell early in the mountains, I realized, and I wondered if that had anything to do with the darkness that seemed to dwell within many of the souls who inhabited these shadowy hills and hollows.

Williams drove me out of Cooke County at a funereal pace. Maybe it was the body in the back of the Cherokee, maybe it was my earlier bout of sickness; whatever the reason, I was grateful. On the winding river road back to I-40, I watched for onrushing headlights, but there were none. I also listened for the squealing tires and screaming engine of someone desperate enough to run this road without lights, but we were the only car around. With each passing mile, the isolated town and the remote cave seemed to fall away, not just into the distance but into some other time and dimension. It reminded me of Brigadoon, the mythical village said to materialize in the Scottish Highlands for just one day every century. But I knew, despite my wish to the contrary, that the places I had just visited were not about to vanish for a hundred years. They would revisit me in far less time, I was sure, and with far less charm.

4

I DIRECTED WILLIAMS TO THE garage door that led into the Regional Forensic Center, which was housed in the basement of the University of Tennessee Medical Center. An imposing tower inhabiting a bend in the river just across from the main campus, the hospital complex hovered over the wooded hillside that was home to the Body Farm.

The Regional Forensic Center, which shared space with the hospital's morgue, was one of five forensic centers in the state. The others were in Nashville, Johnson City, Chattanooga, and Memphis, the cities that anchored the state's midpoint and its northeast, southeast, and southwest corners. Although Knoxville wasn't nearly the size of Memphis or Nashville, our forensic center was the newest and the best of the bunch. The forensic center in Memphis—a city with five times as many residents and fifteen times as many murder victims—was half the size of this one and consisted of little more than one large, dingy autopsy room and an undersized cooler. Ours, on the other hand, had a walk-in cooler the size of a three-car garage, two clean, well-lighted autopsy stations, and a third station in its own room, dedicated to cleaning the ripest of human remains. The decomp room, as everyone called this room, owed its existence to me and the Body Farm. It was outfitted with electric burners and steam-jacketed kettles for simmering bones; laundry-sized sinks for scraping and scrubbing them clean; and industrial-strength garbage disposals for grinding up whatever came loose from my parade of decayed murder victims and rotted research corpses. The only amenity that was lacking was an underground conveyor to ferry my bodies out to the Farm and back.

A video camera at the loading dock tracked our arrival, and as Williams backed toward the building, the garage door rolled upward to let the Jeep enter the loading bay. As I clambered out into the bay, an interior door opened and Miranda Lovelady emerged, rolling a gurney to the back of the Cherokee. Miranda was a graduate assistant in the Anthropology Department's forensic program. Instead of grading sophomore exams and checking for plagiarized papers, like a typical graduate assistant, we had put Miranda to work defleshing corpses and cataloguing bones. She couldn't have been happier.

Miranda helped me wrestle the body bag out of the SUV and onto the gurney. Williams watched warily from the far end of the garage bay. As I latched the vehicle's back door, he practically leapt into the driver's seat. "Reckon I'd better head on back," he said. "We'll be in touch. Thanks, Doc."

"Glad to help," I said. "You drive careful, now."

"Always."

As he idled out of the garage bay, his brake lights added a rosy overtone to the floodlights illuminating the concrete, the corpse, and Miranda. I paused to admire the effect. On most people, I'd noticed, a scrub suit hung like a tent. Miranda's scrubs, on the other hand, somehow accentuated her curves. How she managed to look so shapely in such a shapeless garment was a mystery I found endlessly fascinating.

She interrupted my reverie. "Whatcha got here, Dr. B.?"

I reminded myself why we were here. "You're gonna like this case, Miranda. A body from a cave in Cooke County. Most extensive adipocere formation I've ever seen."

She nodded appreciatively. "Cool. You ready to bring it in, or you wanna take some pictures first?"

"Let's take some pictures."

She ducked back inside, then reemerged a moment later wheeling a portable X-ray machine, which inhabited a small office just down the hall. I had learned, from years of experience, that X-rays could reveal remarkable things hidden in burned or decaying flesh: a bullet lodged in a skull or chest cavity; a cut in a rib or vertebra; a pacemaker or orthopedic device that could be traced back to a manufacturer, a surgeon, or even a patient. But I had also learned, from a memorable chewing-out, never to show up in the hospital's radiology unit with a reeking corpse in tow. I suspected that even if the Forensic Center's budget hadn't covered the cost of a portable unit, the radiologists themselves might have gladly dug into their own pockets to keep me and my rotting friends at arm's length.

"This is case number twenty-three for the year," I reminded Miranda, though clearly she already knew, because she handed me a radiographically opaque tag she'd prepared for the X-rays. The tag included the last two digits of the year, followed by the case number. In my first few years as state forensic anthropologist, I'd never gotten out of single digits—it was probably 1990 before I needed a number as high as 90–10. During the past decade, though, I'd gradually edged up through the twenties and into the thirties.

We started at the head and worked our way down. We would try to match the cranial X-rays with antemortem dental X-rays from missing persons—if we could find any missing folks who fit the description of our body. In addition, we'd search the films for any signs of skeletal trauma, such as fractures or cut marks, or radiographically opaque material such as lead. Even if a bullet has passed completely through a body, it often leaves a telltale smear or splatter inside the skull or on a rib.

I worked the film cassette under the body bag in the region of the head, and Miranda snapped the exposure. As I slid the cassette out and held it up for her, she took it in her left hand, swapping it for an unexposed cassette that she handed me with her right. We worked wordlessly; having done this dozens of times before, we could have performed this macabre dance in our sleep.

After X-raying the head, we took films of the chest, the abdomen, and finally the pelvis. Besides showing us the bones, the pelvic X-rays would also reveal any metallic objects that had been in the pockets of the clothing. Although the clothes themselves had rotted—a hint that they were all cotton, and therefore pretty old—the adipocere in the region of the hips and thighs might well contain small objects that had been in the pockets.

While Miranda stashed away the X-ray machine, I wheeled the gurney into the cooler. Miranda called out, "Aren't we processing this one tonight?"

"It's pretty late. How about tomorrow? Like the sheriff said, one more night ain't gonna hurt this one none. Besides, I've got to be in court early tomorrow for a hearing in the Ledbetter murder."

"Oh, you mean the case where you're going to destroy the medical examiner's career and put a cold-blooded killer back on the streets?" I winced, but she grinned and wagged a finger at me. "You're doing the right thing, you *know* you are—he should have retired years ago, and he totally blew that case. Go home. Sleep the sleep of the just and the competent."

Only after I emerged onto the barren loading dock did I remember that my truck was parked a quarter-mile of asphalt away, over at the Body Farm, where I'd left it fourteen hours ago. I sagged in dismay and sudden fatigue.

The one thing I needed most was a good night's sleep. But that was also the one thing I was least likely to get.

5

MY TRUCK SAT ALL alone at the far corner of the hospital parking lot. By day, the Body Farm's weathered, wooden privacy fence—an eight-foot screen that shields the corpses from sightseers, and shields squeamish hospital workers from the corpses—blends into the woods. Now, under the glare of the sodium security lights, it shone a garish yellow-orange.

Unlocking the cab of my truck, I turned back toward the hospital and waved at the surveillance camera mounted high atop the roof. I doubted anyone was scrutinizing the monitor that closely, but just in case, I wanted the campus police to know I appreciated their round-the-clock vigil over my unorthodox extended family.

At this time of night, almost eleven, the highway was practically empty as I crossed the river and swooped down the Kingston Pike exit. Kingston Pike—Knoxville's main east–west thoroughfare—grazed one edge of the UT campus. If I turned right at the light at the bottom of the exit ramp, I would traverse the lively six-block stretch called "The Strip," which was lined with crowded restaurants, noisy bars, and inebriated students. Turning left instead, I made for the quieter precincts of Sequoyah Hills, where I threaded my way along the grand median of Cherokee

Boulevard for half a mile before diving off into the maze of dark, quiet streets that led to my house.

Most Sequoyah Hills real estate was unaffordable on a college professor's salary, or even ten professors' salaries. The riverfront homes had especially astronomical prices, some of them selling for millions. Here and there in the wealthy, wooded enclave, though—like patches of crabgrass in the lawn of an estate—persisted small pockets of ordinary ranch houses, split-levels, even a handful of rental bungalows fronting a tiny park. It was in one such pocket, thirty years before, that Kathleen and I had found a charming 1940s-era cottage. White brick with a stone chimney, a slate roof, a yard brimming with dogwoods and redbuds, and an only slightly ruinous price tag, it looked like a postcard-perfect place for a pair of academics to settle down and start a family. And it was. Then, suddenly, it wasn't.

Instead, it now hung around my neck like a millstone, and tonight—as always—I fished out the key with a sense of foreboding. The deadbolt slithered open, the door swung into silent darkness, and I knew it had been a mistake to go home. My footsteps clattered on the slate foyer with all the warmth of frozen earth shoveled upon the glinting lid of a steel coffin.

I showered off the mud and grit of Cooke County, and I tried to steam away the ache in my thighs and shoulders. Then—with a mixture of sinking hope and rising dread—I crawled into my unmade bed.

After hours of tossing, I finally slept, and I dreamt of a woman. In the way that is common in dreams, she was a generic, unspecified woman at first, doing something generic and unspecified. Then she looked at me, and suddenly she looked quite specific and very afraid. A hand reached out and stroked her cheek. Then it slid downward and closed around her throat. The woman, I now saw, was my wife, and the hand, I now realized, was my own. A look of pleading filled her eyes, and then a look of sorrow. And then her eyes turned to empty sockets, and her mouth to a vacant oval. But I was the one who gave voice to the scream. "Kathleen!"

Heart pounding, sweat and tears flowing, I awoke—as I had every night for the past two years—to find myself alone in the bed. Alone in our bed. No—alone in *my* bed. My empty, lifeless bed in my empty, lifeless house in my empty, lifeless life.

6

THE DISTRICT ATTORNEY, ROBERT ROPER, gave me a rueful nod as I headed toward the witness stand, ragged and bleary-eyed. I'd testified as a witness for Bob in half a dozen murder cases, but today I was testifying for the other side, hoping to demolish his charge that Eddie Meacham had murdered Billy Ray Ledbetter.

As a forensic anthropologist, my obligation is to the truth, not to prosecutors or police. In practice, speaking the truth usually means speaking for murder victims, and often that means testifying for prosecutors. Not this time, though. This time, I was speaking for Billy Ray Ledbetter, and I was convinced he hadn't been murdered by his friend Eddie. But speaking that truth—at least, on behalf of the defense attorney who had roped me into this—was going to stick in my craw so tight I might need to be Heimliched right there on the witness stand.

The bailiff rattled off what I assume was the routine swearing-in question—I wondered if he dabbled in auctioneering on the side, such was his speed—and I assented. Then Burt DeVriess stood to question me, and I felt my hackles rise.

I reminded myself that I was here as a witness for DeVriess and his client, but it wasn't easy to suppress years of animosity. In almost every East Tennessee murder trial in which I'd testified for the prosecution, DeVriess—nicknamed "Da Grease" by local cops—had served as defense counsel. The guiltier you were, and the more heinous your crime, the more you needed Grease. At least, that's the way things seemed. Serial rapists, child molesters, drug kingpins, stone-cold killers: the dregs of humanity—or inhumanity—were Burt DeVriess's bread and butter. I had faced him from the witness chair a dozen times before, and his cross-examinations had never failed to enrage me. Some of that anger was a natural response to the legal system's adversarial structure, which I didn't much like. It was maddening to do a meticulous forensic exam, then hear it challenged and undermined by the sort of careerist witnesses widely known as "defense whores": *Yes, theoretically, I suppose it's possible, as Dr. Brockton claims, that the skull fracture might have been caused by the bloody baseball bat found beside the body. However, in my expert opinion, the fracture more likely resulted from the impact of a large, anomalous hailstone . . .*

Although I resented that sort of far-fetched second-guessing, I wrote it off as a necessary evil. But what I couldn't forgive or forget was the way DeVriess would skillfully impugn my professional and personal integrity in the slyest, most underhanded of ways. His favorite tactic was to pose an outrageous question that would be struck down immediately . . . right after it had been etched indelibly in the jurors' minds. *"MISTER Brockton, did you slant your findings to fit the prosecution's theory, the same way you did in the such-and-such trial three years ago?"* ("Objection!" "Sustained." "Withdraw.") Every time I squared off against DeVriess I knew an exchange like that was coming, but every time it did, I still got sputtering mad. Which was, of course, was exactly what he wanted.

So given how thoroughly I despised the man and his tactics, why on earth was I about to testify for *his* team at a murder hearing? Because he had played me like a fish yet again, this time reeling me over to *his* side of the courtroom. It had happened a few weeks before, when he invited me to lunch—"to bury the hatchet," he said—and sure enough, throughout the meal he was gracious and conciliatory, praising my research, praising my students, apologizing for his aggressive defense tactics. Then, during dessert, he cast the bait. He had a case he'd appreciate my advice about, he said, because it involved the most baffling forensic mystery he'd ever seen. He posed a series of innocent-sounding hypothetical questions about skeletal structure and sharp trauma— "When a person is stabbed, the knife blade can leave marks on the bones it contacts, can't it? Can it leave metal particles from the blade, or residue from a sharpening stone? How much variation is there in the shape of the spine? What about such-and-such?" He paid rapt attention to my answers, then posed incisive follow-up questions. "Yes, but if the knife had a thin, flexible blade? If the victim had curvature of the spine?" After it was too late—as I lay flopping in his creel—I realized that he'd been setting the hook during that entire chocolate-fueled dialogue. Da Grease, clever bastard that he was, had appealed to both my scientific curiosity and my sense of justice. As he settled the tab, he concluded with a litany of troubling allegations about the autopsy Billy Ray Ledbetter had received at the hands of Dr. Garland Hamilton, the Knox County medical examiner. I, DeVriess had insisted, was the only hope for saving poor, innocent Eddie Meacham.

He was putting me in a delicate position. As an anthropologist, I'm not technically qualified to determine cause of death; in Tennessee that's a call that can be made only by a physician with a specialty in forensic pathology—and, what's more, by a pathologist who has been officially appointed as a medical examiner, a position that marries medical expertise with law enforcement powers. In the normal pecking order of the academic and forensic world, a forensic anthropologist with a Ph.D. was considered a rung below a medical examiner with an M.D. On the other hand, there were certain areas in which my expertise far surpassed the medical examiner's, and one of those was skeletal structure and geometry. In addition to studying thousands of human skeletons and hundreds of corpses—including scores of mangled, murdered ones—I had also spent a year teaching human anatomy to medical students. So if a man's life hinged on whether or not a knife blade could thread a zigzag path through the human back, spine, and rib cage, I felt confident that my skeletal research and anatomical knowledge more than equaled Dr. Hamilton's medical degree.

"Off the record, Dr. Brockton, I'm gonna level with you," Grease had leaned in and confided. "The vast majority of my clients are probably guilty of the crimes they're charged with." Golly, what a news flash *that* was. "Eddie Meacham is not. He did not kill Billy Ray Ledbetter. He's being railroaded by an incompetent, impaired medical examiner—and by a prosecutor who doesn't want to humiliate the ME and compromise his other cases. And for the sake of that, they're willing to send an innocent man to prison for life. That's wrong, and if I've learned anything at all about you over the years, Dr. Brockton, it's this: you stand for the truth. Period. I'm begging you, set aside your personal feelings about me and speak the truth about this case and this sham of an autopsy. Eddie Meacham needs your help."

God, he was good. For years I'd loathed him—today, settling into the witness chair, I loathed him still—but sitting in that restaurant a few weeks ago, I couldn't help admiring his skill and what appeared to be his passion. I also couldn't resist his plea to exercise my best judgment and do whatever I thought was right. Flattery? Probably. But wasn't it possible to be flattered *and* right?

And what was right, I came to decide as I studied Dr.

I gave him a smile I hoped was reassuring. "It's okay. You're just doing your job the best way you know how."

He squeezed again. "I . . . meant about Kathleen. I should have said something a lot sooner, but I just didn't know what to say. I'm so, so sorry."

I tried to speak but found I could not. I looked away, extricated my hand, and fled.

7

AN HOUR AFTER THE walnut-paneled door of the Knox County Criminal Court closed behind me, the stainless-steel door of the cooler at the Regional Forensic Center opened before me. The room was as familiar to me as my own kitchen, and I felt just as much at home here. No: I felt *more* at home here, I realized, remembering the hours of pacing I'd done last night, trying to escape the painful loss of Kathleen. Here, at least, I was in control; here, death was always close at hand but never close to home; here, only anonymous strangers stared at me with lifeless eyes.

I extricated the gurney that held the body of my cave-woman, as I'd begun to think of her, and wheeled it down the hall to the decomp room. Parallel-parking it against the wall, I butted one end against the side of a big stainless-steel sink and latched the cart into place with a pair of large metal hooks that clipped onto brackets on the face of the sink.

At that moment Miranda—fetching in a fresh set of scrubs—walked in with a tray of instruments: scalpels, probes, scissors, tweezers, and, although I doubted we'd need it, a Stryker saw. The Stryker autopsy saw is a truly ingenious power tool: its fine-toothed oscillating blade can lop off the top of a skull in a minute flat, but if it grazes your fingertip by mistake, it delivers nothing worse than a tickle, without so much as nicking the skin. I've used one hundreds of times, and every time, the first thing I do is press the chittering blade to the heel of my hand, just to appreciate anew the ingenuity of the design.

"Playing with your favorite toy, I see," said Miranda.

"Simple pleasures for simple minds. You ever notice how similar this blade's motion is to an electric toothbrush?"

"Ouch, man," she said. "Quick way to lose some teeth."

"I know, you wouldn't want to get the two confused. But I wonder which came first, the toothbrush or the saw?"

"I think the egg came first," she said. "Then the chicken. *Then* the autopsy toothbrush."

"Okay, I get it, you're over it," I said. "You got the X-rays?"

"Across the hall in the lab. Be right back."

Ratcheting the zipper of the body bag down, I marveled once more at how thoroughly the flesh had been transformed into the waxen features of a mummy. In some cultures, a corpse in this condition would have been considered an "incorruptible"—a holy relic or saint, perhaps capable of working miracles. A shrine might be established, to which the sick and the maimed would flock by the thousands in hopes of being made whole again. And all because of a trick of fat, moisture, and temperature. But then again, who was I to dismiss it as a trick? Maybe it was more than that. After all, here she was, almost perfectly preserved, just waiting to be found. Waiting to be identified. Waiting patiently to tell her story and ask for justice. If it *was* a trick of chemistry, it was a mighty slick one.

Normally the first step would be to remove the clothing from the body, but the garments had decayed to rotted shards enmeshed in adipocere. As the adipocere came off, so would the bits of fabric. I would start at the head and work my way down.

My eyes drifted to the neck, and something just below it caught my gaze—a slight bulge at the top of the chest. Just then Miranda brought in the X-rays. "Look," I said, "I think she's wearing something around her neck." She leaned in and we both studied what appeared to be a flat, oblong pendant hidden beneath a veneer of adipocere. Whatever chain or cord it had once hung from had long since crumbled to a greenish-white line of oxide encircling the waxy neck.

"Oh, that," she said. "I saw that on the X-rays." There was an odd note in her voice. On the surface, she sounded nonchalant—practically bored—but underneath, she was almost quivering with excitement. I waited. After a tantalizing pause, she added, "That's not all I saw on the X-rays." She switched on a light box on the wall by the door and slipped one of the films into place. Her head blocked my view.

She turned toward me, still blocking my view, then, with her eyes locked on mine, leaned sideways to reveal the image. "Holy Mary Mother of God," I breathed.

"Well, that's probably not how you should word it in the report, but it is worth noting."

"Let's get to it."

We turned back to the gurney and the waiting corpse. The hair mat had slid backward on the skull, shifting the hairline back to the top of the head. Despite being matted with adipocere and discolored by mold, the hair still showed traces of its original fineness and straw-blond color. The ears were mostly gone—with no bone to support them, they had gradually collapsed and merged with the waxy tissue of the scalp. The face looked almost masklike: the adipocere had separated slightly from the underlying bone, creating an eerie effect, as if a skeleton were masquerading as a mummy for some bizarre costume party of the dead. Although the lips were parted in an eternal scream, the teeth were tightly clenched. The eye orbits were filled with lumpy disks of wax, which stared blindly up at me, at Miranda, and at the harsh fluorescent lights that had taken the place of the cave's velvety blackness.

The gurney had a lip of stainless steel running completely around its edge, as well as a screened drain near its foot. With the cart latched in place, the drain hung directly above the sink—a morbid but inspired design feature suggested by the person who'd cleaned more decomp spatters off walls and floors than anyone else in the world: me. A spray head, a twin to the one in my kitchen at home, hung from a bracket on the wall. I turned on the water, keeping the volume low but cranking the heat up almost to scalding. The adipocere's texture was somewhere between wax and soap. Hot water would melt it like a cake of Ivory in a Jacuzzi.

Working gently, I played the water back and forth across the face. At first there was no effect—the adipocere was cold and almost rock-hard—but gradually it softened and sagged, then began to run, dripping greasily through the drain and down the sink. In the cave, and even when I had unzipped the body bag just moments earlier, I'd noticed almost no odor, but as the hot water began dissolving the adipocere, it unleashed the stench of decomp, mixed with acrid overtones of ammonia.

In less than a minute, the lump that had been the nose was gone, exposing the nasal openings in the skull. It didn't take much longer for the zygomatic arches, the cheekbones, to emerge through the molten cheeks. The maxilla and mandible, the upper and lower jawbones, appeared next. As the connective tissues attaching the mandible to the skull gave way, I held the bone in place with my left hand until it was completely free, then gave it to Miranda, who turned and placed it on a counter lined with absorbent surgical pads. When I finished washing the adipocere off the bones, we'd do an initial examination of the entire skeleton to determine the race and estimate the stature and age. Then Miranda would simmer the bones in a vat of hot water (seasoned with a dash of Adolph's Meat Tenderizer and a bit of Biz laundry detergent to nudge the process along), followed by a gentle scrubbing with a toothbrush to remove any remaining tissue.

Having exposed the bones of the face, I directed the spray at the sides and top of the head, gradually peeling the hair mat off the skull, like some bizarre aquatic scalping. As the mat peeled free, I continued rinsing to remove the scalp residue. Miranda lifted the soggy tangle of hair, squeezed out most of the water, and set it on the pad to dry.

That's odd, I thought as I studied the upper jaw. The woman didn't have any upper lateral incisors; she was missing the two teeth that should have flanked her "two front teeth." I didn't see any extra space between the central incisors and the canines, nor any signs that the jawbone had filled in any gaps. So it wasn't that she'd lost them; she'd never had them in the first place. Anomalous absence of teeth, as it's called, is pretty rare, but it does happen. I kept quiet, waiting to see if Miranda would notice. If she did, she didn't mention it.

With the mandible removed, the top of the spinal column was now visible. I directed the spray onto the first and second cervical vertebrae to expose them fully. The first vertebra is little more than a ring of bone—a spacer or washer, basically; it's the second vertebra that actually bears the load of whatever weighty matter causes the human head to tip the scales at roughly ten pounds. "Okay, let's remove the skull," I said. Miranda nodded and moved into position at the end of the table.

Grasping the skull with both hands, she tilted it back slightly to widen the joints between the vertebrae. I took a scalpel from the instrument tray on the counter and eased it into the space between them, working it back and forth to sever the remaining bits of cartilage holding them together. The gap widened, then the skull pulled free in Miranda's hands. She held it over the sink to drain for a moment, then took it to the counter and set it down. I shut off the water and followed.

We studied the skull in silence for a while. "Tell me what you see," I said to her, as I had said to students hundreds of times before over the years. Miranda took up the skull and took up the challenge.

"Well," she began in a careful, formal tone, "the skull is gracile, very smooth. The eye orbits are sharp-edged and the brow ridge is minimal"—here she paused, rotating the skull—"and so is the external occipital protuberance at the base of the skull. Clearly female, in my humble opinion."

"Mine, too." I smiled. We were almost mocking each other, and our skeletal Socratic dialogue, but not quite—certainly no more than we were mocking ourselves and our own tendency toward scientific stuffiness. "What about race?"

"The mouth structure is orthagnic—strongly vertical—so it doesn't appear Negroid. No appreciable occlusal wear, so she didn't have an edge-to-edge bite, and the incisors are definitely not shovel-shaped. That probably rules out Native American or Asian, though to be sure, we should put the skull measurements into ForDisc." ForDisc—short for "Forensic Discrimination"—was a UT-developed computer program that used skeletal data to calculate, with great precision and accuracy, an unidentified person's age, race, sex, and stature. Miranda took a final survey of the face and mouth. "Yup, she's textbook Caucasoid, I'd say."

"I'd say so, too. How old would you say she is?" This was a trick question, but Miranda didn't hesitate more than a nanosecond.

"Approximately twenty years, ten months, five days, and seventeen-point-two minutes," she rattled off. I stared at her, dumbstruck, and she laughed. "Gotcha. You know I can't tell till we see the clavicles and pubic symphysis." She studied the zigzag seams in the skull. "The cranial sutures aren't obliterating yet, so she's young. Third molars haven't erupted, but that doesn't mean much—she might be one of those highly evolved people whose bodies know that wisdom teeth are a waste of good calcium." She tilted the skull backward to study the seams in the roof of the mouth. "The maxillary sutures are beginning to fuse, so she's adult, not subadult. But I can't say if she's eighteen or twenty-eight until we deflesh the clavicles and the pelvis." She paused, then added, "Not that you asked, but I can also tell you that the skull shows no obvious signs of trauma, blunt or sharp. She has three unfilled cavities, suggesting either low socioeconomic status or limited access to dental care. Probably both, if she grew up in Cooke County. And she has no lateral upper incisors, probably because of a genetic anomaly rather than tooth loss—the maxilla shows no resorption of bone, which we'd see if an empty socket had gradually filled in." God, she was good! Miranda was going to make a spectacular forensic anthropologist, if she didn't get lured away by some smart medical school first.

"Great start," I said, "let's move on." Miranda set the skull down on the counter and we returned to the headless corpse. As I began cleaning the remaining cervical vertebrae, we both leaned in closer. Miranda saw it first. "There." She pointed with a gloved finger. A small, curving bone, about the thickness of a wishbone from a chicken breast, nestled in front of the third cervical vertebrae. Reaching in with a six-inch pair of tweezers, she grasped it and held it steady while I flooded it with hot water.

"Don't sneeze," I said.

"Don't make me laugh," she retorted. "Oh, wait, I forgot—no risk of that. I've heard your jokes before."

I worked the spray back and forth to extend the exposed region, and gradually the unmistakable U-shaped arch of the hyoid bone emerged from the goo. When it was completely free, Miranda bore it to the countertop as if it were a prize. Still holding it with the tweezers, she braced her elbows on the countertop as I swiveled an illuminated magnifying glass into position. She hunched in concentration, studying the bone from every angle. Finally, wordlessly, she pulled back so I could look.

Reaching in with both hands, I slid my fingers over hers onto the tweezers. "Okay, got it," I said, and she let go and stepped back.

The hyoid is an arch measuring an inch to an inch and a half high, and about the same in width. Under the magnifying glass, it looked five times that size. Once upon a time this hyoid had supported the dead woman's tongue and the other muscles she used to talk. Now I hoped the bone itself could tell us how she died.

Attached to the central arch, or "body," of the hyoid are two thinner arches, called the "horns." Normally, the arch's height is roughly the same as its span, or the distance between the tips of the horns. In this case, though, the horns were much closer together. It was easy to see why: where the horns joined the central body, the cartilage looked ripped from the bone, and the body itself was cracked at the midline. I had seen dozens of damaged hyoids in my time, but none so mangled as the one I held now. This young woman had been strangled with crushing force. The story of her death was written in bone.

I straightened and looked at Miranda. She raised her eyebrows, and I gave her a grim smile. "Well, now we know she didn't just crawl in that cave and die on her own," I said. We had just reached a crucial milestone. Before, I had suspected that a murder had occurred; now I knew it. The small, fragile bone I held in my hand not only proved that a murder had been committed, it also told us *how* it happened. A rush of excitement surged through me. I liked to think of it as the wholesome satisfaction of a fruitful scientific inquiry. The truth was, though, it was more like a drug. Other people were hooked on cocaine or cigarettes or runner's high; I was addicted to forensic discovery.

"We'll want lots of photographs of this," I said. "Thirty-five millimeter; use the closeup lens and get in as tight as you can. Take it over to the engineering lab, too, and use their scanning-electron microscope. Besides these visible fractures, the SEM will probably show lots of microscopic avulsion fractures, too, where the cartilage has torn from the bone. We'll need good evidence photos if this ever comes to trial." Miranda nodded. "Okay, let's pry off that pendant and then see what the clavicles tell us."

We returned to the remains on the gurney, and I slid a long, thin spatula beneath the rectangular lump near the top of the sternum. It pried loose with a spackling sound, like cold bacon grease letting go. I gave it an exploratory feel; it was thin and hard, with well-defined edges beneath the irregular layer of goo. Miranda held open a small zip-lock bag; after I'd slipped the object inside, she sealed it, then labeled it with the case number, the date, and the words "necklace/pendant." As she wrote, I unleashed a spray of hot water across the dead woman's collarbones.

They came free with almost no effort. Their lateral ends, where they met the upper arms and shoulder blades to form the shoulders, merged seamlessly with the shafts. Their sternal ends, though—where they joined the breastbone at the top of the rib cage—hung raggedly. The epiphyses—the ends of the bones—were connected to the shafts by a narrow zone of tissue that had not yet fully matured from cartilage into bone.

"So she's still maturing skeletally," said Miranda. "She's not a kid anymore, but she's not fully a woman, either."

"Just like you," I said. She elbowed me in the ribs, hard. "Ouch! 'Skeletally speaking,' that was all I meant. Under the age of twenty-five. *Aren't* you?" I knew she was, but only by a few months. I didn't have many students who would challenge me or tease me, and none who would throw the occasional elbow. Miranda felt free to spar with me, and I liked the confidence and ease that reflected. She'd long since become immune to the lesbian and prostitute jokes about her last name, Lovelady, and she'd turned down countless cops who'd asked her to handcuff and "Mirandize" them. She was smart, strong, tough, and funny, and she didn't take herself too seriously. But she was young enough to be my daughter, and she was my student, to boot.

I cranked up the water pressure a bit. As the adipocere and intercostal cartilage dropped away, the rib cage emerged like some ancient shipwreck being scoured from a sandy seabed. Rib by rib I began dismantling the wreckage, wriggling each bone free of the sternum and free of the vertebra that it joined in the back. As I extracted the bones I handed them to Miranda, who laid them on the table beneath the skull in their proper anatomical position. As the adipocere-clad body departed the gurney piecemeal, a skeleton slowly took shape on the nearby countertop.

When I'd worked my way down the first seven pairs of ribs, I handed Miranda the sternum. She gasped, and I looked up. "What is it?"

"Look at that." She pointed to a neat round hole, dead center in the lower end of the bone. "Was she shot, too?"

I studied the hole. "Well, it sure looks like it, doesn't it?" When I said it, she glanced sharply at me, sensing a trick of some sort.

She studied the sternum more closely, first on the front side of the bone, then from the back. I could see her searching her data banks, trying to match what she saw with something she'd read or seen in my osteology handbook, my bible of bone science. It was in there, all right—a drawing at the top of page 117—but I wasn't giving her any clues. "Well, it's about the right size for a small-caliber bullet—

maybe a twenty-two," she murmured, but she sounded dubious. She glared at the bone accusingly, as if it were guilty of something. "But there are some things that don't fit with that."

"Such as?"

"For one thing, it seems too big a coincidence for a gunshot wound to line up exactly with the midline." I kept my mouth shut. "For another, the hole looks beveled on the front *and* the back sides, and bullet wounds widen only in the direction of the bullet's travel."

"Right," I said. "As the bullet smashes through the bone, the shock wave propagates in the shape of a cone, producing a larger hole at the exit. Like those funnel-shaped holes BB guns make in plate-glass windows—tiny on the outside, big on the inside."

"Spoken like a boy who had a BB gun," she said.

"Hey, a guy hears stories," I said. "Now quit stalling. What else do you notice about this hole, which might or might not have been left by a gunshot?"

"Okay, what looks like beveling on both sides of the bone isn't, really—it's a smooth, undamaged surface. The beveling made by a bullet is rougher, and there are usually fracture lines radiating from the hole."

"Excellent," I said. "So this is . . . ?"

She furrowed her brow. "A foramen?"

"Exactly. A natural opening in the bone. Rare in the female sternum, by the way—ten percent of men have them, but only about four percent of women. That's why you've never seen one before." She grinned, excited by the new nugget of firsthand knowledge. This, too—like the thrill of finding forensic clues—I found addictive. "Okay, let's keep moving. Are you ready for what comes next?" Her grin vanished, and she took a deep breath. "This could be disturbing," I added. She nodded. "If you have any trouble, just take a break and step outside. No shame in that." She nodded again, eyes wide. I took up the sprayer again, but not before turning down the pressure by half.

As the adipocere melted away from the center of the woman's body, I felt a sense of amazement I'd experienced only a few other times in my life. A thicket of tiny, nested bones began to appear, suspended in a paler lump of adipocere—a lump that had once been amniotic fluid and fetal tissue. Our young woman had been pregnant—was pregnant still, in a way—with a baby whose birth, at my hands now, was years overdue. It was a grim, sad delivery I was about to perform.

"We're going to need a two-millimeter screen over the drain please, Miranda." She scurried over to a cabinet and pulled out a disk of wire mesh, which she fitted into the round neck of the drain. I hoped it was fine enough to catch everything.

The tiny vertebrae were like little seed pearls on a string; the body, or centrum, of each vertebra was no bigger than a lentil. On either side of each vertebral body floated the two halves of the neural arch, which would have fused to one another in the first few years of life, then fused to the centrum sometime around preschool or kindergarten age. At the base of the spine nestled the minute beginnings of the hip bones, about the size and shape of baby lima beans. Folded up alongside the spine were the legs: the femur was about the size of the middle bone of my index finger; the tibia was more like a pinky bone. The bones of the feet were so small, they'd have to be screened out with a sieve. Arching at right angles to the axis of the spine and legs were ribs—thin, curving slivers so light and frail they might have come from a quail or a trout. The bones of the skull, which was the lowermost point of the fetal skeleton, were also bird-sized; the occipital, which formed the base of the skull, was no bigger than a quarter.

"Hard to believe we all start out this small and fragile," I said. "Looks like she was just about midway through her pregnancy."

"How can you tell? Who's researched this? Who could *bear* to?"

"A couple of pathologists in Budapest back in the 1970s. They studied and measured one hundred and fifty fetal skeletons, from every stage of development. I don't know why they started, but I guess they bore it the same way we're bearing this right now: bone by bone, for the sake of something more important." We fell silent, and I found myself thinking back to the other fetal skeletons I'd examined.

I'd seen skeletons in the womb only three times before. Two were in Arikira Indian graves in South Dakota. Their village, I knew, had been decimated by smallpox, which was deliberately spread by white fur traders—an early case of biological warfare. In the third case, a pregnant woman's remains were found in some brush beside a rural stretch of Kentucky interstate; the woman, as best the police and I could determine, had been hitchhiking and climbed into the wrong vehicle. In those cases, though, both the mother and the fetus had already skeletonized by the time they were found. Here, the baby's remains were hidden away inside an intact corpse—until I burrowed in to expose them. I felt a brief flush of shame at my intrusion, and then a pang at the reminder of just what a risky venture life can be: a race in which some people never even make it out of the starting gate.

I glanced up at Miranda. Tears were running down her cheeks and soaking her mask. I touched her arm. "Maybe you should take a break," I suggested. She jerked away, shaking her head, and I saw rage flashing through the tears. It was not anger at me, I realized, but at whoever had snuffed out these two lives. "Thanks, I need the help. Let's put these in anatomical order beside the mother's body, head down."

She nodded, then grimly set about reassembling the tiny skeleton as I handed her the bits of bone.

Six hours after we began, we finished. The waxy-looking mummy we'd brought in was now a skeleton, still slightly greasy and smelly, but merely a fading echo of a strong young woman. Beside her was something even fainter: the fading whisper of a baby who never drew breath.

Our knowledge, like the specimens on our counter, was skeletal: we knew this was a young white female of unusual height. We knew that she was pregnant, and that halfway through her pregnancy, possibly around the time she began to show, she'd been murdered—strangled, with no other signs of trauma, at least nothing visible so far. We still didn't know her name, but the examination had told us other things that would help us seek her name. The echoes and whispers from these bones might help us understand why she'd been killed . . . and if we listened carefully enough, they might even suggest whose hands had encircled her throat and squeezed without mercy, leaving a record of violence for us to find.

I looked at Miranda. Her face was drawn; her eyes, which had danced and shone when she'd delivered the X-rays triumphantly, now looked drained and bleak.

"I know," I said, "this one's tough."

She nodded.

"And Miranda?" I waited until her eyes met mine. "Let's keep this to ourselves for a while."

8

ART BOHANAN WAS GLUED to his microscope. Literally, and unhappily.

The fingerprint lab was in the basement of the Knoxville Police Department—a grim beige fortress in a grim black section of the city, surrounded by acres of asphalt and low-income housing projects. The uniformed officer on guard at the front had buzzed me into the elevator and pointed toward the floor. "He's down there. Like always."

The acrid scent of superglue bit my nostrils as I entered the lab in the basement. Art looked up as I walked in. "Hey, you wanna give me a hand here? Squirt some of that acetone on my fingers, would you?" His left thumb and index finger were fastened to the focus knob of a stereo microscope; his right hand gripped the light source. An open tube of super-glue lay on the counter.

"So you're really stuck?"

"Last ten times I checked. You wanna tug for yourself, or you gonna help?"

"Hold on—oh, wait, that's what you're doing already," I teased. "When's the last time you got pantsed? You got a camera somewhere?"

"Great, now I'm supposed to help you humiliate me even further? Thanks."

"Don't mention it."

"Come on, Bill, this light's hot. Durn it, I'm not kidding."

I picked up a small can of acetone and dribbled a bit over the edges of Art's fingers, starting with the ones gripping the metal housing of the light source. "So what's the flash point of acetone? And what's the temp of that light?" As the solvent soaked in, Art's taut skin slowly peeled free. The fingers were an angry red. He rubbed them with a rag, then some hand lotion.

"Thanks a lot," he said. "I owe you." I wasn't sure whether he was thanking me for setting him free or threatening me for dragging my feet about it. Both, knowing Art. I made a mental note to sniff my steering wheel in future before grabbing hold of it.

"Next time you really oughta read the label. That stuff sticks to your fingers."

"Ha-ha. Very funny."

If anybody knew about superglue and fingers, it was Art. Not only was he KPD's senior criminalist, he was one of the nation's leading fingerprint experts. In crime labs all over the country, technicians were using superglue-fuming gizmos to coat objects with sticky fumes that could pick up latent prints. And the gizmos they were using had been designed and patented by my buddy Art. Even the FBI had taken a shine to Art's superglue gizmo, which in forensics is like Michael Jordan taking a shine to your basketball shoe.

Spread on the counter beside the scope was a batch of photos. Most looked to be crime scene photos showing the interior of a car, a battered blue Impala. One, though, was a school portrait of a girl, maybe eight years old. Little girl, big smile. I recognized the photo: I'd seen it in the paper half a dozen times in the past two weeks, which is how long Stacy Beaman had been missing. She was last seen getting into a rusty blue car. The one in the photos belonged to a registered sex offender who'd been seen near the girl's school three times in the days before her disappearance.

I looked at Art's scope. There was a car window crank clamped to the specimen stage. It didn't take a forensic genius to figure out that the crank had come from the passenger door of that rusted Impala.

"You getting anything?"

"Hell, no. Not even a partial. Not from her, anyhow. His, they're all over the place. Not surprising—it's his car—but it's killing me that we missed hers."

"Missed 'em? Sounds like you think they're in there somewhere."

"*Were* in there; aren't anymore. Hell, *she* was in there—three witnesses saw her. We just didn't move fast enough. By the time we got the warrant and got the car, the prints were gone. Vanished into thin air."

He wasn't speaking figuratively. It was a phenomenon he had told me about before, one that had baffled investigators in child abductions for many years: why were children's fingerprints so elusive, so fleeting? It had baffled Art, too, but the second or third time he found himself coming up empty-handed, he had vowed to figure it out. He'd enlisted the brain trust over at Oak Ridge National Lab—he pulled together a team of organic and analytical chemists—plus some parents and kids from a local elementary school. This cobbled-together team had done a research project to ferret out the differences between adult fingerprints and children's prints. Once Art had gotten the ball rolling, it didn't take the chemists long to figure out what was going on. Adult prints are oil-based, they found; kids' prints, on the other hand—before puberty kicks in and activates all those acne-producing oil glands—are water-based. And water evaporates, taking the prints with it. The explanation was simple; the ramifications could be simply heartbreaking.

"How long did it take y'all to get the car?"

"Two days. Which was one day too many. Twenty-four

hours sooner, her prints would've been there. Her prints *were* there."

"Witnesses slow to come forward?"

"No. Lawyer quick to tie our hands. Claimed we were harassing his client."

I had a bad feeling inside. I didn't want to ask, but something in his face dared me to. "Who's the lawyer?"

"Three guesses."

I didn't need three. "DeVriess."

"Good ol' Grease. Your new buddy." He shot me a black look.

"Look, Art, I hate what he does, and I hate how he does it, as much as you do. Most of the time. If he's helping a child predator, he'll burn for that someday. But this stabbing case he's got me working on, it's different. The ME screwed it up, plain and simple, and the DA's covering for him. And if you don't know that, you're not as smart as I think you are." I glared at him, furious that he would tar me with the same brush as DeVriess.

He glared back, then looked away and sighed. "I know. You're right. I understand what you're doing. I respect it. I respect *you*—hell, you know that. It's this little girl—it's tearing me up. I want to kill the son of a bitch that snatched her, and I want to dismember the son of a bitch that kept us from dusting that car until the kid's prints had evaporated."

"I don't blame you for that."

"Sorry I jumped on you."

"Forget it."

He took a deep breath and closed his eyes, then blew it out loudly. As if from another life, the phrase "deep cleansing breath" popped into my head, unbidden and unwelcome. Art rubbed his raw fingertips. "So, aside from the pleasure of my cheery conversation, Bill, what brings you here?"

I reached into my jacket pocket and fished out a ziplock plastic bag and handed it to him. "This."

"What's the story?"

"It was around the neck of a corpse. Is it what I think it is?"

He squeezed the outline gently in every direction: the narrow side, the long side, and the thin edge. "Probably. Was he a veteran?"

"Not a he. A she. And no, I don't think so."

"What's she doing wearing a military dog tag?"

"That's what I'm wondering."

"And whose is it?"

"That, too."

"And you brought it to me because you can't read?"

"Exactly. Also, I'm hoping there might be a print somewhere under that gack."

"Gack—is that one of those technical anthropology terms you Ph.D.s throw around to impress and intimidate us common folks?" I nodded. Art fingered the tag, frowning. "A print. Sheesh—you don't ask much, do you?"

"What's the problem?"

"Well, for starters, we've got to figure out how to remove the gack without removing the print. *If* there's even a print under there. Which I very much doubt."

"How come?"

"The metal may have corroded or oxidized, though dog tags are supposed to be corrosionproof. If the metal did corrode, it's undergone both chemical and physical changes that could destroy or distort the print. And if it didn't corrode, the gack—adipocere, we lowly criminalists call it—will have either absorbed or smeared any prints that might have been there once upon a time."

I nodded glumly. "So what you're saying is . . ."

". . . not a snowball's chance." I'd pretty much expected him to say something like that—he was a criminalist, after all, not a wizard—but until he actually said it, I'd held out some hope. "But still, let's see what we can see."

He laid the bag on a lab table and donned a pair of latex gloves, then slid the ziplock open and extricated the waxy tag. After studying it awhile, he leaned toward a tray of tools and selected a pair of tongs, then rummaged under a counter and hauled up a small torch, the sort a chef might use to caramelize the sugar atop a dish of crème brûlée. Holding the tag by the slightly curved end—where the chain once threaded through—he began playing the torch gently over the adipocere. As it began to melt, the reek of decomp rapidly replaced the acrid fumes of superglue. "Dang, Bill, you might've warned me. Switch on that fan, will you?"

I reached for the switch he'd nodded toward as he moved the fragrant object under an exhaust hood. Then I brought over some paper towels, which I folded and positioned underneath to catch the foul fluid beginning to drip from the lower end.

"Art?"

"Yeah?"

"Couldn't you have just put it in an autoclave, wrapped in some paper towels?"

"Sure. But where's the fun in that? It's not every guy who gets to play with fire on the job."

"Are you never going to grow up?"

"I sure hope not. My childlike immaturity's the only thing standing between me and a major midlife crisis."

Art extinguished the torch and set it down, then withdrew the rectangle from under the hood. It was discolored and slightly bent, but it was a dog tag, all right, its stamped-in lettering still crisp. Art moved to a lab table with an illuminated magnifying glass, just like the one in my decomp room, and studied both sides. "Well, shoot."

"What?"

"As usual, I was right. Unfortunately, in this case. Sometimes fingerprint oils will etch metals, so even after the print itself is gone, there's still an image of it left behind. Not here, though—this tag really is corrosionproof. Wish they made cars out of this stuff."

"So there's nothing there you can work with?"

"Well, I wouldn't exactly say that. We've got somebody's name, rank, and serial number here, which might—just possibly—be considered a clue. It's not your corpse's name, unless she was called 'Thomas,' but—"

"Wait. Did you say *Thomas*? First name or last?"

"First."

"Here, let me see." I scanned the tag, half-expecting to read the last name *Kitchings*—and feeling a mixture of relief and disappointment when I didn't. That would have been straight out of the Twilight Zone. Even the coincidence of the first names seemed odd, somehow: a backwoods sheriff named Tom finds a corpse wearing the dog tags of another guy named Tom. I pointed it out to Art—who had already noticed it on his own, of course. "You think there's any connection?"

"With the sheriff?" Art shrugged. "Still, we know this is somebody who was connected to her somehow, and he'll have a pretty good paper trail, at least while he was in Uncle Sam's army." It wasn't the dramatic revelation I'd been hoping for, but it was a start. "I've got a old pal in Army Records," Art said. "Want me to see what he can find out for us?"

"Sure. Thanks. You need to hang onto the tag?"

"Naw, just get the guy at the front desk to make me a big photocopy on your way out. You keep it with the rest of the evidence. I'd hate to have Da Grease come after me for evidence tampering in a case that's completely outside my jurisdiction."

"So I shouldn't tell him how you tried to destroy this thing with a blowtorch."

"If he gets wind of it, send him over. I'll demonstrate my torch technique on his testicles."

"You really could have kept that little fantasy all to yourself."

"Hey, I'm a generous guy. I like to share."

"I'll remember that. Thanks for the warning. And thanks for the help."

"Anytime."

As I left, I glanced back just in time to see Art relight the torch. I paused to watch him. First he eased the tip of the flame close to his forearm, a look of curiosity on his face. Wisps of smoke began to curl up from the hair on his arm, then suddenly he yelped and jerked the torch back with a rueful, goofy grin. Then his gaze lit on the crime scene photos strewn across the counter. Reaching over, he plucked one from the stack. It was a mug shot of the man suspected of abducting young Stacy Beaman. Holding the photo by one corner, Art brought the torch close. Wisps of smoke curled up, and the man's face burst into flame.

THE PHONE RANG JUST as I was contemplating the structure of the female pelvis, and I jumped, then hissed a curse before putting on my telephone manners.

"Hello, this is Dr. Brockton."

"It's Sheriff Kitchings."

"Hey, Sheriff, I've spent some time going over these remains, and I've got some mighty interesting things to tell you. First of all—"

He cut me off. "Hang on, Doc. I'm not sure we should discuss this on the phone. This could turn out to be a pretty sensitive case."

This was a first. I always wrote up my findings in a formal report, but I'd never yet encountered a lawman who didn't want to know what I'd found out as soon as possible. "Well, shall I just write up what I found and mail it to you?"

"No, sir, I believe we should move a little faster than that. Could I send Williams to get you again? And could you bring the, uh, the *material* with you? The material you've got there in Knoxville?"

I sighed but decided to play along. "Well, it's possible for me to come see you, if you think it's urgent, but I can't bring the, uh, *material* just yet. I need to simmer on that for another day or two, if you catch my drift." After a moment, he allowed as how he caught my drift. "Look," I suggested,

"I've got a class to teach in a few minutes, but I'll be through at noon if you want to send your deputy sometime after that."

"Any chance you could skip that class? Maybe get somebody to fill in for you?"

"Sorry, Sheriff. I don't cut my own class. Besides, it's at least an hour's drive down here."

"Thing is, Williams is already in Knoxville." They must think I had nothing to do but wait to be summoned to Cooke County.

"Well, I can find something to keep him busy for an hour or so," I said. "We've got a few skeletons that need digging up, if he wants to lend us a hand out at the Body Farm. He knows how to find it now."

The sheriff laughed mirthlessly. "I expect he'd just as soon pass on that, but thanks anyhow. I'll holler at him and tell him to get you at noon."

I told him how to find my private office. It was tucked deep beneath the east stands of the stadium, down near the level of the football field. Pretty close to the east end zone, in fact, but separated by layers of concrete and steel and spectators. I'd lost count of the times I'd looked up from a skull or femur to feel the entire structure shaking—another UT touchdown, I knew. Visiting teams didn't score very often at Neyland Stadium, and when they did, there weren't enough fans to rattle the girders. Ten, twenty thousand people couldn't cause much vibration. Ninety thousand hometown fans at a grudge match against Georgia or Florida or 'Bama, though, could set off seismographs clear over in Nashville.

I hung up, pushed back from my battered desk, and walked through a doorway into an adjoining room filled with cardboard boxes, each measuring one foot square by three feet long. Each box contained a cleaned, disarticulated human skeleton.

There was only one way into our skeletal collection, and that was through my office. I didn't want just anyone to have access to the skeletons—it was easy to envision drunken fraternity pranks, macabre Halloween decorations, and countless other student hijinks if word got out that there were hundreds of boxes of bones just lying around for the taking. So while we made no bones, so to speak, about having the collection—took great pride in it, in fact, since it was the world's largest collection of modern skeletons whose age, race, and sex were known—I was careful to keep the collection room locked and to issue keys only to the forensic faculty and graduate assistants.

Threading my way among the gray metal shelves stacked with oblong boxes, I felt like a bookworm browsing in the Library of Congress. There were hundreds of stories recorded in these skeletons—tales of childhood bicycle wrecks, skull-bashing barroom brawls, years of secret domestic violence, decades of gradual decline. To hear a particular story, all I had to do was slide the cardboard box off the shelf, take it to a table, flip open the top, and lift out the bones. Some tales were written in the lurid detail of fractured limbs, cut ribs, and bludgeoned or bullet-shattered skulls. Others were understated, like the sturdy bones of the nineteenth-century black man whose arms and legs and massive muscle attachment points bespoke a life of heavy labor.

I pulled two boxes from the shelves—old friends, in a way, who had helped me teach thousands of students over the years—and removed a few of their bones. Their broad surfaces were smooth as ivory from the touch of countless hands; as I grasped them, they felt familiar and comforting, these pieces of the dead.

Unlatching the battered briefcase I kept in the collection room, I laid the bones on the gray foam padding inside and closed the lid. Then I ducked down the back stairs, emerging beside the tunnel that led to the end zone. Threading my way up a maze of concrete ramps and stairs, I emerged near the rear of McClung Museum, a blocky 1960s building that housed the university's modest assortment of Native American artifacts.

Two hundred seventy faces turned my way when I strode through the door at one side of the lecture hall in McClung. My introductory class—Anthropology 101: Human Origins—was the only course in the department's curriculum not taught in the warren of rooms beneath Neyland Stadium; there simply wasn't room for it anywhere beneath the stands. The museum, whose handful of offices had housed the entire department back when there were only three anthropology professors, now held only the museum's staff. McClung was quiet most of the time, attracting only a smattering of visitors, but three mornings a week, it bustled with the chatter and laughter of freshman and sophomore undergraduates.

Most intro courses were taught by junior faculty or even teaching assistants; in fact, I was the only department chairman I knew who still taught a 101 course. I told colleagues that I thought it was important for an administrator not to lose sight of day-to-day teaching, and that was true. Also true, though, was the fact that I loved being around students as they began falling in love with a new subject. With *my* subject. And—maybe, by extension, just a bit—with me.

Not romantically or sexually, of course. I'd never gotten involved with a student, though occasionally it had taken considerable willpower to resist the urge. During one unforgettable class, during a revival of the miniskirt, I had meandered over to the left side of the lecture hall to make some point or other about the structure of the pelvis. For the first time in my teaching career, I found myself rendered momentarily speechless on the topic. An attractive young coed in the front row, directly in front of me, chose that exact moment to uncross her legs and languidly drape one leg over the arm of her desk. As her skirt slid up her taut thighs and her flawless pelvic structure, it became clear that underneath, she was wearing nothing at all. Astonished, I looked up at her face; she cocked her head, raised an eyebrow, and smiled sweetly. Beating a hasty retreat to the other side of the auditorium, I struggled manfully to salvage my sentence, my lecture, and my composure. This same student appeared in my office a few days later—I'd just handed out midterm grades, and hers was an F. Her lower lip quivered as she leaned toward me across the desk in a low-cut blouse. "Oh, Dr. Brockton, I'll do *anything* to pull up my grade," she breathed.

"Then *study*," I snapped. She dropped the class three days later, but not before turning in a quiz on the bones of the hand and arm, in which she defined *humerus* as "something that, like, makes you laugh."

Today's class—like the day of the migrating miniskirt—also happened to focus on pelvic structure. That seemed fitting, since I'd just been examining the pelvis of the body—the woman—found in the cave in Cooke County. As a teaching aid, I'd brought to class two sets of pelvic bones, one male and the other female, from the skeletal collection I'd been building over the years. Using red dental wax as a temporary adhesive, I reattached the pubic bones to the innominates, or hip bones, and then held them up, first the male, then the female. "Okay, I've noticed some of you carefully studying the pelvises of your classmates. So I'm sure you'll have no trouble identifying the differences between the male and female."

A laugh rippled across the room—a good beginning. "Which is the female, number one or number two?"

"Number two," chorused a handful of voices.

"Very good. How can you tell?"

"It's wider," chirped one girl.

"Cuter, too," added a boy.

"The bones in front come out farther," said someone.

"That's right, the pubic bones project more," I said. "Why is that?"

"Pregnancy?"

"Right, to make room for the baby," I said, "not just during pregnancy, but also—especially—during childbirth." I rotated the pelvis backward by 90 degrees, giving them an obstetrician's-eye view of the bones that frame the birth canal. "You see the size of that opening? That's what a baby's head has to fit through during childbirth. Now compare it to the male's." I held up the narrower pelvis in the same position. "Any of you fellows think you could pop a baby out through there? You better hope you never have to try!" I heard a few murmurs along the lines of "Ouch, man."

Next I showed them the female's sciatic notch—the notch just behind the hip joint where the sciatic nerve emerges from the spinal column and runs down the leg. "See any difference here?"

"Wider." "Bigger."

"Correct. That's another result of the geometry of childbearing: as the female's innominates flare out at puberty, this notch gets wider. Notice that I can easily fit two fingers into the base of this notch, but only one in the sciatic notch of the male? So ten years from now, when you're working a forensic case, and a hunter or a police officer brings you nothing but a single innominate bone, you can tell immediately whether it came from a man or a woman."

One of the girls near the front—Sarah Carmichael, according to the seating chart; she wore sensible clothes and asked sensible questions—said, "But if those changes don't happen until puberty, how can you tell the sex of a child's skeleton?"

"Good question, Miss Carmichael. The answer is, you can't. Before puberty, there's no reliable way to distinguish between the bones of males and those of females. All you can do is tell whether the bones you have are the right size for a boy or a girl of a given age."

Most of them looked puzzled, so I trotted out an example. "When I looked at the child's bones that were recovered in the Lindbergh kidnapping case"—a few heads nodded, but there were blank looks on a lot of faces—"I couldn't say for certain whether they were the bones of a boy or a girl. All I could say was that they were consistent with the bones of a twenty-month-old male—which is how old Charles Lindbergh Junior was at the time he was kidnapped and killed. But the bones would also have been consistent with a twenty-four-month-old female."

Sarah raised her hand again. "In that case, couldn't you do a DNA test on the bones and compare it to the parents?" Sarah's quickness and interest actually made her far more appealing than any temptress in a slithering skirt.

"You couldn't back then, of course—the crime occurred about sixty years before DNA testing became common—but you could now," I said. "The bones have been kept in glass vials; there's even a little bit of soft tissue on some of them still, so there's probably plenty of DNA for a test. But the authorities and the Lindbergh family seem confident of the identification: the clothing matched what the boy was wearing, and one of the feet had crossed toes, a genetic anomaly that was pretty distinctive. So there's really no good reason to put the family through more anxiety this long after the case has been closed." Sarah nodded thoughtfully.

"Let's get back to the pelvis," I said. "I'm going to pass these around. Be careful. I know most of you fellows have never handled a female pelvis before, so this is a good time to practice a gentle touch." That was an old joke; it used to get laughs throughout the room, but something had shifted over the past few years, I'd noticed. The boys would still laugh, but the girls tended to frown now instead. I made a mental note to drop that line from the lecture next year.

As the pelvises made the rounds of the class, I explained how the face of the pubic symphysis—the joint where the two pubic bones meet at the midline of the abdomen—changes with age, and how those changes could reveal a person's age at death. I passed around two additional pubic bones—one from an eighteen-year-old female, the other from a forty-four-year-old—so they could see for themselves the erosion that occurs during a quarter-century of wear and tear.

As the female pelvis reached Sarah, I noticed her rotating it, scrutinizing it from every angle. She furrowed her brow and chewed on her lower lip, concentrating intently. I walked toward her row. "Did you have another question?"

She looked up. "Can you tell just from the bones whether this female—whether any female—has given birth?"

It was a simple, logical, and innocent question, and it blindsided me completely. Visions of Kathleen—in the throes of labor, and then in the throes of death—writhed in my head, mingling with images of the strangled young woman and her sad little fetus. After what could have been either half a minute or half an hour, I became aware of the students' stares.

"Yes," I finally murmured. "Yes. You can."

I stumbled toward the door.

"Class dismissed."

10

BY THE TIME I THREADED my way back to the hallway beneath the stadium, my runaway pulse had slowed to a trot and the ragged edge had left my breathing.

The hallways in the Anthropology Department echo the shape of the stadium above, so where the stands wrap around the end zones, the hallways bend as well. Walking along a dim, curving tunnel that continuously unspools ahead, you get the sensation that you're in some miraculously preserved Minoan labyrinth or some prodigiously dilapidated space station. As I banked toward my office, Deputy Leon Williams came into view, studying a posterboard presentation on nineteenth-century Navajo skulls.

"We're going to make an anthropologist out of you yet," I said.

"Well, it might not be too bad if I could stick to bones like these. I don't have any trouble with 'em when they're clean and dry."

"Yeah, but it's a whole lot more work to dig those up. There are always tradeoffs and compromises, Deputy, even in science."

He waited for me to open my door, but I didn't. "Don't you need anything, Doc—notes or bones or something?"

"No, I'm not quite finished defleshing the skeleton—the skull and pelvis are still simmering in the crock pot. It's pretty easy to remember what I've found so far." He looked eager to hear more, but I wasn't feeling chatty. "Sounds like your boss is in a hurry. Reckon we better get going?"

"Sure thing." He spun on his heel, and I followed him out to the Cherokee, which was tucked between two of the diagonal steel girders supporting the stadium's grandstands. A one-lane strip of asphalt encircled—or would it be "enovaled"?—the base of the stadium, threading between the rows of massive girders and branching, in places, into short, dark spurs of pavement that led into catacombs where I imagined the high priests of the religion of Southeastern Conference football must be entombed.

Williams and I talked UT football for a while, but I could tell he was itching to ask other questions. Finally, as we merged onto the interstate, he broke. "I bet you've had some interesting cases, huh, Doc?"

"Well, they're all interesting to me."

"But what's the most interesting? Or the most unusual?"

"Hard to say." I thought for a minute. "One of the most unusual, I suppose, was the woman in Connecticut whose husband—a former police officer, by the way—killed her and cut her up and burned her body in the front yard."

He whistled. "Sounds like a TV show—*When Good Cops Go Bad.*"

"I'm not sure he was ever a good cop; he may have just gone from bad to worse. There were several odd things about that case. One is that we were never able to figure out what he used to cut her up. Another is that he went to the fire department and got an open-burning permit the day he cremated her."

He hooted, then turned to face me for an unnervingly long time, considering that he was now driving at seventy-five miles an hour. "A permit? Are you shittin' me, Doc?"

"No, I'm not, Deputy. I guess he didn't want to break any really important laws in the course of murdering and dismembering his wife."

Mercifully, Williams refocused his gaze on the road ahead. His voice got conspicuously casual. "Anything weird showing up in our case?"

I paused, searching for the right way to do this. "You know, Deputy, Sheriff Kitchings said this is likely to be a pretty sensitive case, and he seemed worried that the phone line might be tapped. If somebody's tapping your phone, they might have your vehicle bugged, too." Williams looked simultaneously startled and suspicious, though I couldn't tell whether the suspicion was directed in my direction or elsewhere. "I think we better wait till we're someplace the sheriff knows it's safe to talk."

"Good idea." He nodded and smiled. Underneath the smile, though, I noticed his jaw muscles working.

When we left the interstate to snake along the river road, he kept his speed down and his turns gentle. I thanked him for taking good care of me. This time, he smiled in earnest.

"So how'd you end up in law enforcement, Deputy?" It was a question I always like asking officers, because the range of answers—of motivations, of pathways—seemed nearly infinite, and usually fascinating: a family tradition for three generations; a brother who was murdered; an overdose of *Dragnet* reruns; a genuine desire to make the world a better, safer place.

Williams was quick with his answer. "You remember I told you about my granddaddy?" I nodded: the man unjustly jailed, then shot and burned to death. "I wanted to make sure that kind of thing never happened to any of us again. Only way to do that is to be the guy with the badge and the keys." It wasn't the most noble reason I'd ever heard, but I could see the logic of it up here in Cooke County.

We had reached the most tortuous section of the road when Williams slowed and began edging onto the right-hand shoulder of the road, such as it was. "Doc, I'm sorry, but I've got to stop and take a leak."

"We're pretty close to town—you can't wait?"

"No, sir, I don't think so. I drank a lot of sweet tea in the cafeteria while you were in class; too much, I reckon. I do apologize. You just sit tight and I'll be back in one minute."

And with that, he was gone.

He didn't come back in one minute, or two, or even three. To pass the time, I pulled a notepad out of my pocket and began drafting a job recommendation a former student had asked me to write. At last the door swung open. "I was about to send out a search party," I said, my eyes still on my notes. "You must have had a couple quarts of tea with your lunch, Deputy." But it was not the deputy who leaned down and peered at me through the open door. It was a bear of a man, dressed in a camouflage jumpsuit, the tree-bark pattern worn by deer hunters, complete with a camouflage cap.

"Dr. Brockton, I'm real sorry about this, but we got a little change of plans. My name's Waylon. Now, I ain't gonna hurt you. How about sliding over behind the wheel and pulling back onto the road? You're gonna head toward town a piece, then make a turn where I tell you."

"Where's Deputy Williams?"

"Leon? He's all right, don't you worry none about him. He's just kindly . . . *tied up* at the moment, you might say." The big man flashed either a grin or a grimace at me.

I sat. "Would you mind telling me what's going on?"

"Somebody needs to talk to you. In private. Prob'ly won't take a half a hour, then we'll get you back to town so you can go on about your business with the sheriff."

I studied Waylon. He outweighed me by at least a hundred pounds, and I was guessing there was a pistol tucked somewhere in that camo suit. Maybe a skinning knife, too. "What if I say no?"

He sighed. "Look, Doc, ain't no reason we got to have trouble between us. I told you, I ain't gonna hurt you, but I will hogtie you if I have to. Besides, you'll want to talk to this fellow I'm taking you to. I bet he can help you figure out who you pulled out of that cave the other day."

News travels fast in a small town. I cranked the engine and shifted into gear. "You tell me where to go."

He grinned, flashing a smile of scattered teeth, pitted with cavities and flecked with chewing tobacco. "Now you're talking. Once you cross that next bridge, take your first right. It's gravel." We wound along for maybe a mile; during that time, I considered half a dozen escape plans and rejected them all—not because I was hopelessly outmatched, though plainly I was. I rejected them because this homespun mountain man had shrewdly punched the one button—short of threatening my family—that was guaranteed to ensure my complete cooperation: he dangled before me the prospect of a forensic revelation.

We thunked onto a new concrete bridge—obviously a replacement for some predecessor that had washed away in one of the floods that frequently scoured the mountain valleys—and off the other side. "Best slow down a bit—it'll sneak up on you. Right yonder—you see it?"

I did, barely: two mammoth hemlock trees arched over the right-hand side of the highway, and running between them, as if they were some great gateway, a gravel road turned off and disappeared into the forest.

The road was deceptive: unobtrusive, but smooth and well-maintained, free of the ruts and mud holes that plague most gravel roads in the mountains. The Great Smoky Mountains are classed as a temperate rain forest, with up to eighty inches of precipitation a year, so it's a rare mountain road that doesn't have a few wallows and washed-out spots. This one was firm, dry, and well-drained by ditches and culverts everywhere that drainage might be a problem. There were no weeds in its center, either, a sign of frequent traffic or regular grading.

"This is a good road. The county keep it up like this?" I tried to sound offhand.

He swiveled his bearlike head at me. Perhaps I hadn't managed to sound quite as casual as I'd hoped. "Naw," he said. "This here's what you might call a private drive." After a moment, I heard a low, rumbling growl that seemed to shake the entire vehicle. I glanced over to see him chuckling. "Private drive," he mumbled again, and chuckled some more at his wit. Then he flashed me a delighted, speckled smile. *Lord God, what have I got myself into,* I thought, shaking my head. Then I felt myself chuckling, too, at the absurdity of the situation.

But the chuckle died in my throat a moment later when the big man said, "Stop the car right here, Doc." I felt myself freeze up, unable to speak or act. The world seemed to shrink, until nothing remained but a green tunnel, a gray gravel track, and a steering wheel gripped by a pair of white-knuckled hands that might or might not have been my own. Another hand reached in from somewhere and cut the ignition switch. The car drifted to a stop on the gravel, the only sounds the crunch of gravel under the tires and the rush of blood in my head. Then even those sounds were gone, and the tunnel of green faded to black.

WHEN I AWOKE, I felt myself curiously confined. The air was dank and hot and close against my face, depleted of oxygen, yet my arms were cooled by a breeze. The darkness was softened by fuzzy globules of light. As my eyes shifted focus, instinctively seeking some definable shape, the globules sharpened into myriad pinpoints of daylight, viewed through the weave of fabric. My thoughts regained their focus, too, and I recognized the damp, acrid smell of sweat. A pungent camouflage cap was stretched tightly from my chin to my forehead. My arms twitched as if to bat it away, but they would not move. I jerked against whatever was restraining them and began thrashing my head.

"Easy, there, Doc, you're gonna hurt yourself that way," rumbled the deep voice to my left. "We're nearly there, so just sit tight a minute. I told you I weren't gonna hurt you, and I ain't, but they's some things you need not to see, in case somebody was to ast you about 'em later."

I slumped back against the seat and fought to rein in my panicked breathing.

The car stopped, and the cap came off of my face. I shut my eyes against the light, then opened them to see Waylon leaning toward me with a hunting knife. He reached down and deftly flicked the knife against strips of duct tape—printed, like the rest of his ensemble, with a camouflage pattern—binding my wrists to my thighs.

"Sorry I had to do that," he said. "I didn't want to have to fight you to get you here. That wouldn't be healthy for you, and Big Jim wouldn't be none too happy with me, neither."

Big Jim? I could scarcely imagine the immensity of a man that a behemoth like Waylon would refer to as "Big."

He got out of the Cherokee and came around to open the door for me, as if he were some backwoods chauffeur instead of an abductor. I paused, struggling to make sense of it all, then gave up and got out and followed him.

We had parked in a small clearing of grass, surrounded on all sides by kudzu, a vine that is notorious in the South for engulfing trees, barns, broken-down vehicles, and—I'd heard it sworn to be true—even the occasional napping cow. At one edge of the clearing stood a weathered farmhouse, its sides and front porch fringed with vines. More of the ropy tendrils were already creeping onto the roof at the back of the house and spiraling up the mast of a small satellite dish. As I followed Waylon up the steps, he kicked at the vines snaking around the base of the porch. "Damn stuff grows two foot a day in the summer," Waylon said. "Turn your back on this house for a week, and it'd be gone. You'd never find it again."

The side of Waylon's fist tapped the door frame twice, and the house shuddered. "Boss? We're here," he called through the screen door into a dark room beyond.

"Thank you, Waylon. How about keeping an eye on things to make sure we're not disturbed?"

"Yessir." With a swiftness and stealth that belied his size, Waylon slipped off one end of the porch and melted into the kudzu vines hanging from what had once been trees at the edge of the clearing.

The screen door screeched open, and a man stepped onto the silver-gray boards of the porch. "Dr. Brockton, I'm Jim O'Conner. Thank you for coming. I apologize for sending Waylon to shanghai you that way."

I felt an almost electric jolt go through my body. My captor stood perhaps five-five in his cowboy boots; if he didn't take them off to weigh, he might tip the scales at one-forty. If I'd seen him up in horse country, I'd have taken him for a jockey. "You're Big Jim?"

He smiled, a touch ruefully. " 'Fraid so. It started out as a joke, when I was a kid," he said. "Seems to have stuck."

But the name somehow seemed to fit. The small man positively radiated authority and power, from his piercing blue eyes to his whipcord forearms and springy legs. It wasn't the sort of brutish, aggressive force wielded by bullies and cowards; it was the quiet, confident strength of a man sure of who he was and what he could do under almost any circumstances.

"By the way, I've read about a lot of your forensic cases. It's quite an honor to meet you, sir." He held out a sinewy hand. Out of years of reflex, I took it, but I cocked my head and gave him a questioning, dubious look, the one I use on students I suspect of some sort of fraud. He met my gaze openly, like a man with nothing to hide, nothing to be ashamed of, and his grip tightened briefly. Then he nodded slightly, smiled faintly, and let go.

"Please, have a seat. I'll tell you why I needed to see you." He motioned to a pair of oak rockers on the porch, and planted himself in the farther one. I sat, stiffly at first, then found myself rocking in time with O'Conner's slow arcs.

"Cooke County's a funny place, Doc. The most fearless, loyal people you'll ever meet—and the meanest, orneriest sons of bitches on the face of the earth. Being an educated man, you probably know that back during the Civil War—the 'War of Northrun Aggression,' as some of my South Carolina kinfolks persist in calling it—Cooke County stayed loyal to the Union." I nodded, wondering where he was going with this. He continued rocking and talking. "The citizens of Cooke County actually tried to secede from the state of Tennessee. We always got by without slaves, figured other folks could, too. Couldn't see dying for some rich Memphis cotton kings. At one point, a band of Confederate vigilantes came in to teach us a lesson. Never came out again."

He paused to watch a hawk circling above the valley floor. I took advantage of the opening. "I'm not sure I quite take your point."

"Not sure I do, either. Guess I haven't quite stumbled onto it yet. Please forgive me for rambling." He was an oddly courteous kidnapper. "I parted company with the law a long time ago, Dr. Brockton. I won't go into all the reasons; all I'll say is that it was my family that first stood against the Confederacy. That, and it's damned hard to make a law-abiding living in these mountains." I thought I detected something like sadness in his voice and his eyes. "But there's certain lines I've never crossed. One of them is murder. I killed when I was a soldier in Vietnam. After I got home, I swore I'd never do it again. It hasn't always been easy up here, but I've kept that vow for over thirty years." He rocked in silence.

"Exactly what is it you want to talk to me about, Mr. O'Conner?"

"You hauled a body out of Russell's Cave the other day. I suspect I'm being set up to take the fall for that killing. There's some petty politics and some bad blood stretching way back in this county, and I figure this looks like a good chance to settle some scores. No matter what anybody tells you, I didn't do it, Dr. Brockton. I guess all I'm asking is that you keep an open mind. Doubt everything except what you can verify for yourself."

"Including your claim of innocence?"

He considered, then nodded. "Fair enough."

"I'm a scientist," I said. "That's how I work."

He reached into his shirt pocket and handed me a piece of paper. "Here's two phone numbers. Please call me if I can help in any way. Offhand, I don't know who this guy was, but seems like he shouldn't be too hard to track down."

I took a moment to consider whether what I was about to say might compromise the investigation. I made my words and tone as neutral as I could. "So you've also heard that it was a man?"

O'Connor sat motionless for a moment, then turned to face me. "Ah. I'd just assumed. Possibly a woman? Well, that would certainly change the picture. Perhaps ol' Lester Ballard is alive and well in Cooke County."

"Lester Ballard?"

He waved off the question. "Never mind—I shouldn't've said that. Silly and completely inappropriate. Seriously, though, I can think of several men in this county who might *need* killing, and a few more who wouldn't bat an eye at *doing* some killing. But I can't think of any local women who've gone missing recently."

"How about not so recently? Tall? Blonde?"

His brow furrowed for a moment, and then the look of puzzlement vanished, replaced by a realization that was swift and terrible. His gaze—so clear and confident before—was suddenly stricken. He looked away. "Oh, Jesus, no," he breathed, staring out across the valley. "Oh, God, not her." Tears welled in his eyes, then rolled down his cheeks. He made no move to wipe them away, gave no sign that he even noticed them.

I waited what seemed an eternity. "Mr. O'Conner?"

He seemed not to hear, so I spoke his name again, louder. When he answered, he sounded years older and a lifetime away. "Yes?"

"Is Jim your first name?"

"No. Middle."

"Mr. O'Conner—Lieutenant Thomas J. O'Conner—you want to tell me what your dog tag was doing around a dead woman's neck?"

When he finally turned to face me once more, his eyes were as cold and lifeless as the waxy spheres I had washed from the face of the dead woman and rinsed down the drain of the morgue.

11

WAYLON AND I RODE BACK to the highway in silence. He didn't duct-tape me this time, but he did cover my face with his rank cap again, giving me a look of sheepish apology as he doffed it and leaned over to hook it under my chin. O'Conner hadn't spoken another word to either of us; he'd simply waved us away with that dead look still in his eyes. Waylon looked scared, like a child who's seen his parents fighting or his mother weeping.

He left me sitting in the Cherokee, and a minute or so later Williams appeared, rubbing a visible bump on the back of his head. He, too, was silent the rest of the way into Jonesport. We seemed to have adopted a don't-ask, don't-tell policy regarding the last half-hour. I wondered if Williams was too embarrassed to speak of what had happened to him. I also suspected it was more than just coincidence that he'd made his pit stop where and when he did.

Kitchings was pacing his small office when we entered. "Where the hell have you-all been? You shoulda been here an hour ago."

I kept quiet. Williams cleared his throat. "My fault, Sheriff. I pulled off to take a leak down by the river. Slipped on a wet rock and fell pretty hard. Musta been out longer than I thought."

Kitchings studied Williams, who was rubbing his head and grimacing, then turned to study me. "He *was* gone quite a while," I said. "I reckon I fell asleep. Next thing I knew, he was getting back in the car with that goose egg on his noggin." I didn't understand why I was covering for Williams; then it occurred to me that I might actually be covering for O'Conner. I didn't understand that, either. Then again, maybe it was really myself I was covering for, somehow. But what had I done, or what was I thinking of doing, and why?

Kitchings looked disgusted. "Ever time I send him after you, something goes wrong. I don't know which one of you's to blame, but damned if I'll let it happen again."

"Sheriff, the minute we can wrap up this case, I'll be glad to head back to Knoxville for good."

"Yeah. Well. Whatcha got so far?"

"Well, it's pretty much what I thought from the beginning: white female, twenty to twenty-three years, unusually tall—somewhere between five-ten and six feet in stature. Blonde hair, fairly long. No dental work; small, unfilled caries—cavities—in two of her molars and one of her canines. Only sign of skeletal trauma was multiple fractures of the hyoid."

"Fractures of the what-oid?"

"The hyoid."

"What's that mean?"

"Means she was strangled. The hyoid's that small, wiggly bone just above your Adam's apple." I demonstrated, and the sheriff and his deputy jiggled their hyoids from side to side. "Hers was crushed. Pretty sure sign of manual strangulation."

He looked grim. "Anything else unusual?"

"Well, she was wearing a U.S. Army dog tag around her neck." I paused, giving him a chance to process the information. "I took it to Art Bohanan, the resident fingerprint guru at KPD, in hopes he might pick up a print from whoever had his hands around her neck."

Kitchings took in a breath and leaned toward me, his eyes blazing. "And?"

"Nothing."

He exhaled. "Shoot. But was the tag still legible?" I nodded. "What'd it say?"

It was my turn to take a breath. "It said Lt. Thomas J. O'Conner."

Kitchings turned away. "That cocksucking son of a bitch," he whispered. "I am gonna nail his sorry ass to the cross."

I waited. "Sheriff?" He turned. "Any idea who she was?"

I was conscious, at the edge of my field of view, of Williams, motionless but tightly coiled. Kitchings drew in a long breath, let it out, and shook his head. "Hard to say, Doc. Real hard to say."

I was getting that impression. Maybe not so hard to *know*—at least, to insiders—but damned difficult to *say,* at least to outsiders. He was hiding something, I felt sure; I wondered if it was the girl's identity, and if so, why. I turned to Williams with an inquiring look, but the deputy just shrugged and shook his head. I decided to play the card Jim O'Conner had just handed me. "Sheriff, does the name Lester Ballard mean anything to you?"

He looked up at the ceiling, as if the answer might be found somewhere in the peeling plaster. "Lester Ballard? No, can't say as it does. Why?"

"Hard to say. It just sorta came up."

He eyed me suspiciously, sensing some subtext but not sure what it was.

"There's some Ballards over in Union County, I believe, but I don't know of any Lester. I damn sure know of a Thomas J. O'Conner, though."

I nodded. "Sheriff?" He looked annoyed. "What's he like, this O'Conner?"

Kitchings made a face, shook his head. "Smartass. Thinks he's better and brighter than the rest of us."

"Wouldn't be too bright to strangle a woman and hang his name around her neck, would it?"

He shook his head dismissively. But it was clear that he wasn't dismissing the notion of O'Conner's guilt. He was dismissing my question, and he was dismissing me. Just to make sure I got the message, he spun on his heel and walked out, before I had a chance to tell him about the cavewoman's pregnancy. I wasn't entirely sure I'd have told him even if I'd gotten the chance.

12

BY THE TIME I GOT back to campus, night was falling. The autumnal equinox was only a few days away, and the days were markedly shorter. Not so long ago—was it one lifetime, or two?—I'd have hurried home, stopping in my office just long enough to phone Kathleen and apologize for running late. Now, the habitual impulse to call still popped up, but only for an instant: just long enough to remind me that there was no reason to call, no one there to answer the phone.

She'd been gone for two years now, but the ache and the emptiness still cut to the bone.

I sat at my desk, staring into space and time—time long past—for what might have been a minute or an hour. I forced my thoughts back to the Cooke County case: I had an unknown victim—unnamed, at any rate—an unknown killer, and people on various sides of the law who seemed to know more than they were telling. I kept coming back to two names: Jim O'Conner and Lester Ballard. I knew who O'Conner was now, at least superficially. But Ballard, whom O'Conner had mentioned, was a mystery. "Lester Ballard," I said aloud. "Calling Lester Ballard. Come in, Lester Ballard."

A knock at my door made me jump. "Excuse me, Dr. B.?" It was Sarah, my bright 101 student. In one hand she was carrying a briefcase, in the other, a well-worn copy of my osteology field guide, the bone identification handbook I made all my forensic graduate students commit to memory.

I smiled sheepishly. "You're not Lester Ballard."

She laughed. "Not quite. I *am* considered eccentric, but I'm pretty tame compared to him."

"Wait—you've actually *heard* of Lester Ballard?"

"Sure. He's great."

"Great how? He's not a murderer or something?"

"Well, yeah, he *is* a murderer, among other unsavory things, but he's a great character." I might have looked baffled. She definitely looked amused. "Fictional character. He's in a novel."

"A *novel*? Go on."

"Southern lit. The book's called *Child of God*. By Cormac McCarthy, possibly the greatest Southern writer since Faulkner, certainly the greatest writer Knoxville has ever produced. His best-known work is *All the Pretty Horses*; got made into a movie with Matt Damon and Penelope Cruz a few years ago." The name rang a bell, but I hadn't seen it. "Wonderful book, mediocre movie. Most of McCarthy's other stuff is really dark, sometimes bizarre. Like Lester."

"Bizarre how?"

"Well, Lester's a mountain man—a real primitive, backwoods type—who ends up killing some women and hiding their bodies in a cave. Somewhere along the way, he develops a taste for necrophilia. Can't get a date with a live woman, I guess." She giggled, for reasons I couldn't fathom.

"Jesus. You've read this? You *liked* this?"

She nodded brightly. "It sounds really gross, and some of it *is* horrifying. But the weird thing is, even though Lester's a monster, he's kind of charming, too. Funny, and naive, and somehow an innocent at heart, despite his dastardly deeds." I shook my head uncomprehendingly. "Okay, you remember *The Andy Griffith Show,* right?" I nodded. This was familiar ground; I could recite whole scenes of dialogue between

Andy and Barney. "So you remember Ernest T. Bass, the hillbilly who's always throwing rocks through the jailhouse window? Wild, crazy, but not malicious at heart. Lester Ballard is sort of like that, only orders of magnitude beyond. I know it sounds silly to compare a necrophiliac killer to a simpleminded window-breaker, but read *Child of God* and you'll see what I mean."

I wrote down the book's title on my desk blotter. "I see you're doing some other light reading," I said, pointing to the osteology book. "Afraid I'm going to throw in a trick question on the midterm exam?"

"No," she laughed, "it's just that whenever I get interested in something, I tend to go overboard, plunge in headfirst. Actually, I was wondering if you'd sign it for me?"

"Sure," I said. "Why don't you set down your briefcase while I do it."

But it wasn't her briefcase, it was mine, I realized—the one I'd left behind when I melted down in class that morning. I flushed with embarrassment.

"You . . . forgot these today, Doctor B." She lifted the lid, revealing the two pelvises I had been using to demonstrate the differences in male and female skeletal structure.

"You're right, and I hadn't even missed them till now. Thank you."

"You're welcome."

There was a long, uncomfortable silence before she spoke again. "Can I ask you something else about this one?" She held up the female pelvis, still tacked together with red dental wax. "You said it's possible to tell from the bones if a woman has given birth. Can you show me how?"

I took the bones from her. "This woman was in her forties when she died. You can tell that from the erosion in the pubic symphysis, the joint where the two pubic bones meet." I pulled the pubic bones loose from the hip bones and peeled off the wax. "You see how the bone is starting to look a little weathered and spongy here at the face of the joint?" I rubbed the rough surface with my index finger, and she reached in to do the same. Our fingers brushed, and I felt my pulse quicken.

Before speaking again, I swallowed hard. I could feel a stutter building, and I struggled to let go of the panic rising from my chest. "But there's some t-t-trauma, here, too," I said, "from childbirth." I didn't stutter often—hadn't much since I was a child, and my mother took me to a speech therapist—but when I got nervous, it could sneak up and seize me by the throat. I couldn't remember the last time I'd felt this jittery. Sarah leaned down for a closer look, taking my hands in hers to steady the bones and bring them close to her face. I could feel her breath on my fingertips. It was the most intimate touch I'd felt in a long time. "These grooves here and here," I said, "are called 'p-parturition p-pits.' During childbirth, the ligaments sometimes start to pull free of the bones. That can cause bleeding and infection, which carves these small grooves in the damaged regions of the bone. Like I tell detectives, flesh forgets, but bone remembers."

So does the heart. I took a deep breath. "My wife had terrible complications during pregnancy," I said. "Three miscarriages, then a full-term pregnancy that ended in a very difficult labor and delivery. She should have had a C-section, but she wanted so badly to do natural childbirth. It nearly killed her." Sarah looked stricken. "A couple more miscarriages and twenty years later, she died of uterine cancer. That was two years ago. The doctors say there's no connection, but I can't help thinking there was. Can't help thinking we shouldn't have kept trying to have children. Can't help blaming myself for her death. I don't know what to do. I can't . . ."

Sarah turned her face up to mine. It did not look like the face of a student; it looked like the face of a bright and sensitive young woman, her eyes full of compassion. She reached up and laid a hand on my cheek, brushing away a tear with her thumb. Then she leaned toward me and touched her lips to the same spot. I felt a shudder run through my entire body. Then she laid both hands on the sides of my face and guided my mouth to hers. It was a kiss of pity first, I think, or consolation. Comforting and warm. And then it became something else. Her mouth opened, and I felt the heat and urgency of her tongue on my own. Her body pressed against mine—or maybe it was mine against hers—her breasts and thighs and pelvis melting into me, melting the cold that encased me in my grief. I groaned with pent-up sorrow and longing.

I pulled free to catch my breath, leaning back to look at Sarah's face. Over her shoulder, in the open doorway, my eyes caught a flash of movement. Miranda Lovelady stood there paralyzed, her eyes wide with shock or embarrassment or betrayal or some awful mixture of them all. She met my gaze for the briefest instant, her face crimson and contorted, and then she whirled and ran.

Instinctively I went after her, hearing her footsteps but never quite seeing her for the curve of the hallway. I heard the clatter of the crash bar on the stairwell door, and I knew she was gone. Cursing myself for a fool, I turned and retraced my steps to my office. It, too, was empty now—emptier than it had ever felt before.

God. How could I have been so foolish? I'd spent years cultivating a reputation for decency and decorum and professionalism, and I'd just chucked it in the trash can. Not only had I crossed the line with an undergraduate—a girl younger than my own son—I'd done it in front of the one graduate student whose respect mattered most to me. If she chose, Miranda could damage my reputation with the other grad students and the university administration as well. But that wasn't my main concern. My main concern was the look of confusion and pain on her face. I hated to be the cause of that—hated to hurt her. I also hated the notion that there might be a deeper problem with Miranda as well. Had I somehow gotten too close to her, too? Was there something more serious and less appropriate than camaraderie lurking beneath our easy collaboration and rapid-fire gallows humor? Had I crossed a line—a powerful emotional line—during all those hours in the morgue with her?

I thought and fretted about Miranda all the way home. Then, when I was in bed, in the dark, I thought about Sarah: the way her eyes shone at me, the way her mouth felt on mine, the way her breasts and hips pressed against me. For the first time since Kathleen's death, I felt sexually aroused in my wasteland of a bed. For the first time in many months, I slept hard. And for the first time in many months, I awoke hard.

Now what? I remembered a line from Garrison Keillor, whose public radio show UT's NPR affiliate had broadcast for years: "Life is complicated, and not for the timid." *Amen to that, brother,* I thought. *Amen to that.*

13

THE HILLS WERE SHOWING their first signs of fall color as Art Bohanan and I wound along the river road in Cooke County. We had the windows of the UT truck cranked down, and the hum of the tires was punctuated by the crackle of sycamore leaves, the first to spiral down every autumn. I'd brought Art up to date on what I knew about my case, which wasn't all that much. "Anyhow," I concluded, "the sheriff seems to figure O'Conner for the killer, but I'm not so sure. O'Conner doesn't strike me as the Lester Ballard type."

"The *what* type?"

"Lester Ballard."

"Who's Lester Ballard?"

"Art, I'm disappointed in you. Don't you read anything but police reports? Lester Ballard is one of the great characters of modern Southern literature." From a jacket pocket, I pulled a ragged copy of *Child of God,* which I'd found in the used bin at the campus bookstore an hour before. I waved it knowingly. "Lester likes women. Dead women. Keeps 'em fresh in caves."

"Don't we all. So you think there's a connection between that book and this murder? Copycat thing—true crime imitating weird fiction?"

"No, actually, I don't think that. What I *do* think is that Jim O'Conner is mighty smart and well-read to be a murderous hillbilly. I'd bet my salary he knows that woman's name; he sure got upset when he seemed to figure it out. So why won't he tell us, if he's not the killer?"

"So maybe he *is* the killer. Just 'cause he quotes mod-ren South-ren litra-ture don't make him Dudley Do-right."

"I know, but he doesn't strike me as a killer. Call it anthropologist's instinct."

"Lotta anthropologists used to think Ted Bundy was a heckuva nice guy, too."

"Okay, forget it. Judge for yourself. Hey, you said you'd heard back from your buddy in Army Records. What'd he find in O'Conner's military file?"

"Army Ranger. Served with valor and distinction. Led a mission into North Vietnam to rescue a downed pilot. Got a promotion, a Purple Heart, a Silver Star, and a Medal of Honor nomination for it. If he were running for office, his opponent would paint him as a lily-livered coward, but he sounds like the kind of guy I'd want watching *my* back in the jungle."

"Well, you can see if he looks that way, too, in just a minute."

Or maybe not. All of a sudden, the meeting I'd brought us here for was looking problematic. A hundred yards in front of us, the road ended against a solid wall of green. Bluffs closed in on either side of the gravel track. I slowed the truck to a crawl. "Now what?" I asked.

Art shrugged. "You sure this is the way you came?"

"Well, I was pretty sure I was sure. I know we turned off the river road between those two hemlocks. I know we stopped at that big sycamore about a quarter-mile back, so Waylon could capfold me. After that, all I could see was the inside of his hat—but it didn't feel like we made any stops or turns."

"Well, then, I guess we keep going."

"But where? How? It's the end of the road."

"Well, go till you can't go anymore, then we'll figure out where to go from there."

We crept forward. The wall of vegetation ahead was a clotted mass of kudzu vines. As we got close, I noticed that the road didn't actually end at the kudzu; instead, it seemed to disappear beneath it. To the left of the gravel, a small stream tumbled out through a curtain of vines. I looked at Art, and he grinned. "Damn the tendrils," he hollered. "Full speed ahead!"

I idled forward, and the truck nosed beneath the overhanging vines. They writhed across the windshield like some snaky nightmare, then rasped onto the roof, clutching at the mirrors and wipers and antenna with slithering, slapping sounds. The engine began to labor, not from the resistance of the vines, but from a sudden steepening of the road. Overhead, I thought I glimpsed a web of wires or cables—a sort of tensile arbor stretched between converging bluffs to support the kudzu.

After a quarter-mile that seemed to stretch for an eternity, the kudzu tunnel ended at another curtain of vines, and the road emerged into a small, high valley—a hanging valley, I'd heard these called—that opened before us, like something out of Shangri-la. But this was a valley I'd seen before: the valley where Jim O'Conner had watched a hawk surfing on a rising current of air. The valley where I, too, had stumbled into some unseen current, whose force now gripped me and swept me along. As Art and I eased to a stop before the weathered house, I saw a figure sitting motionless in one of the rockers on the porch. It was O'Conner—a slumped, much aged O'Conner. I nodded to Art, and we got out.

I felt the gun's muzzle behind my ear before I heard or saw anything. For a big man, Waylon moved with remarkable speed and stealth. "It's okay, Waylon; thank you, though," murmured O'Conner. "Dr. Brockton, this is an unexpected pleasure. What brings you back this way?"

I held up a cautionary finger at Art, who I figured had a gun in an ankle holster and was looking for an opening to go for it. "Mr. O'Conner, I do apologize for intruding on you. I know people in the mountains value their privacy and their property, and I've just trampled on both of those uninvited. It's just that this murder case has raised some hard questions, which I think maybe you can answer. That young woman who was killed deserves somebody to speak for her, and I can't do it without some help."

He sat silent. I plowed ahead. "I've brought a colleague, Art Bohanan. Art's a Knoxville police officer, but he's not here as a cop, he's here as my friend. Could be yours, too, if you'll let him."

O'Conner turned slightly and inspected Art, who met his gaze openly, with neither fear nor challenge. Then he turned back to me. "No point," he said. "She's gone. Speaking for her won't bring her back."

"No, it won't. But she deserves some sort of justice," I said. "Somebody should be held accountable for her death, even if they're already dead, too."

He shook his head sadly. "I don't think I've got it in me to dredge all this up. Missing or murdered, she's gone. That's it, and with all due respect, it doesn't concern you."

I hated what I was about to do. "That's not entirely it," I said, "and with all due respect, it *does* concern me. There's another victim I have to consider."

He looked away, out across the valley, then back to me. "What other victim?"

I steeled myself. "Mr. O'Conner, she was carrying a child. She was four and a half months pregnant when she was killed."

I heard a ragged intake of breath, the sort of tearing sound that means a heart is being ripped apart. I couldn't face him.

Art spoke up. "Mr. O'Conner, I checked your service records. You shipped out for Vietnam in June 1972. Was she pregnant when you left?"

"No!" O'Conner shook his head dazedly. "How could she be? We never. . . . We wanted to wait. Well, *she* wanted to wait. I never even. . . . Oh, Christ."

Art gave him a moment. "How about when you got home?"

"I never saw her when I got home. She was gone by then. I don't even know when she left—I didn't even know she had the dog tag till Dr. Brockton mentioned it the other day. I sent it to her after I got promoted, but she never wrote back to say she'd gotten it. Her letters just *stopped*. It was like the earth opened up and swallowed her."

And it had.

"How old was she when you left for Vietnam?"

"Twenty-two."

It fit exactly with the skeletal indicators. I wanted to be sure I understood what he'd said earlier. "Mr. O'Conner, are you saying you never had sexual relations with her?"

"Never. She wanted to be a virgin when we got married. It sounds quaint in this day and age, but it was really important to her."

"Would you be willing to provide a DNA sample to prove you weren't the father of the baby?"

He stared at me bleakly. "How's this?" He flipped open a pocketknife and drew the blade across the heel of his left hand. I saw a slit open, then brim with blood. He took a handkerchief from a hip pocket and soaked it in the blood, then held it toward me. I hesitated. "It's okay, Doc," he said. "No AIDS, no hepatitis, no syphilis. Pure as the driven snow." Art produced a ziplock bag from somewhere and sealed the bloody cloth inside, then handed it to me.

During the long silence that ensued, I realized that I had delivered far worse news than I'd expected: not only was the woman he once loved a murder victim, but she'd been pregnant. By another man. A man to whom she'd given her prized virginity. "This must be a shock; I'm sorry." He nodded grimly. "I hate to be blunt, but I don't know any other way to ask this. She must have had sexual relations with *someone*, at least once. Do you have any idea who that might have been? The person who got her pregnant might be the person who killed her. Any idea who that might be?"

He looked up at the sky, and his eyes roamed back and forth, searching for something long ago and far away that didn't want to be found. Then they froze, widened momentarily, and clamped nearly shut, in a look as black and menacing as a summer thunderhead. "Does the sheriff know all this?"

"He knows she was murdered. He knows she was wearing your dog tag. He doesn't know she was pregnant. I'm fixing to go tell him."

There was another long pause, long enough for me to make out the crowing of a rooster somewhere in the distance.

"You're right, Doctor Brockton. She does deserve justice. And so does her baby. Go tell Sheriff Kitchings what you just told me. I'd love to be a fly on the wall when you do."

ART AND I rode in silence down the valley and into the tunnel of kudzu. As we emerged into daylight once more, I spoke up. "Well?"

"He's not the guy that killed her."

My curiosity outweighed the urge to gloat. "What makes you say that?"

"Dog tag's a pretty good alibi, at least on the front end. He had to have sent it to her after he was in 'Nam, 'cause he didn't make first lieutenant until he'd rescued that pilot. Besides, he doesn't strike me as a killer. Call it cop's instinct."

I grinned, until I remembered the menacing look on O'Conner's face. "But he knows who did it?"

"I think he *thinks* he knows."

"The sheriff?"

Art chewed on that awhile, looking troubled. "Chronology's a problem. How old's Kitchings?"

"Forty, give or take a couple years."

"But the evidence suggests she was killed thirty-two years ago. You think little eight-year-old Tommy Kitchings knocked up a strapping twenty-two-year-old, then throttled her when she started to show?"

Not likely, I conceded. "So why'd O'Conner point us at the sheriff?"

"Maybe he figures the sheriff knows. Maybe he figures the sheriff's protecting somebody."

That would explain Kitchings's reluctance to speculate about the victim's identity. But something about that scenario troubled me. It took me a moment to put my finger on what it was. "That doesn't make sense, though. If the sheriff's involved or covering up, why'd he drag me into this in the first place?"

"Good question. Maybe he's *not* connected. Or maybe he is, but he didn't realize it at first. Not till you started pulling on threads and his sleeve began to unravel."

"Hmm. You still got time for an informal visit with one of your law enforcement brethren?"

I saw worry flicker in his face for the briefest of instants, then he flashed me a forced-looking grin. "Damn the tendrils. In for a penny, in for a pound."

The sun was shining on the granite blocks of the courthouse when we parked, but as we walked toward it, a cloud moved in. The stone took on a dark and sinister hue. So did the SUVs and the black-and-gold helicopter parked behind the building. "Uh-oh," I said. "Not a good omen." We were almost to the front door when I caught Art's arm. "Hang on, I'll be right back." I turned back toward a sagging bench under a dying oak tree. The dilapidated bench was inhabited by two equally dilapidated old men, whittling on cedar sticks.

Piles of fragrant shavings lay at their feet, covering their boots to the ankles. I nodded deferentially as I ambled toward them. "Howdy, fellas," I said, raising my voice a few decibels.

"We're just old. We ain't deaf," said one of them.

"What's that?" wheezed the other through a sunken, toothless mouth.

I turned my attention on the first one, who seemed like the better prospect. "You look like you probably know the ins and outs of Cooke County pretty well. Reckon you could help me remember a name from quite awhile back?"

"Well, I ain't senile, either, but I cain't make ye no guarantee."

"Local girl—young woman, actually. Blonde, tall. Real tall. Lived around here in the nineteen-sixties, early seventies. Woulda been twenty or so by then."

"Mister, I got no earthly idea."

His companion wheezed to life. "Hell, course you ain't. You ain't been livin' here but twenty year. You don't know jack shit about Cooke County." He worked his gums together thoughtfully. "Blonde-headed? About six foot? Likely-lookin' girl?" I nodded hopefully, though I couldn't vouch for her prettiness based on the waxen death mask I had seen. His stubbled jaw slid from side to side. "Bonds."

"Excuse me?"

"Bonds. That was that girl's name. I disremember her first name. She was a looker, though, I 'member that real clear. Kindly high-spirited—sorta gal might need a little tamin'— but you could tell the ride would be worth gettin' throwed off a time or two, if you know what I mean."

"You remember what happened to her?"

"Just up and left. Run off, story I heard. Don't know why. Wisht she hadn't of—left a big hole in the scenery round here once she was gone." The memory inspired more gum-grinding.

I thanked him and headed back toward Art, who was waiting on the steps. A wheezy voice called after me. "Sheriff might remember her given name. Ought to, leastwise. She was his kin."

Tom Kitchings was cleaning a rifle when I flung open his door and stormed into his office. He looked up, startled at the intrusion, then startled at the expression on my face. "Easy there, Doc, you shouldn't oughta startle a man holding a gun. What's up? You come to bring me that skeleton?"

"No, I come—*came*—to see why you're lying to me about this case."

He laid the rifle down across the desk and looked up at me slowly. "Hold on a minute, Professor. Those are pretty strong words. You got something to back 'em up?" He looked over my shoulder at Art, who'd followed me into the office. "Who is this?"

"This is Art Bohanan, a criminalist with KPD."

"What the hell is he doing in my county?"

Art spoke up calmly. "Just sightseeing. Just along for the ride."

"Well, sightsee somewhere else. I hear there's a big national park not far from here's got some kickass scenery."

"Maybe we can swing by there on our way home," said Art amiably.

"Best get going, then."

I slapped the desktop with a force that surprised everyone, including myself. "Goddamnit, what's her name, Sheriff? You know damn well who she is."

He reddened, glowering at me. "I haven't finished checking the old files."

"You don't have to check your files. Check your family bible. Last name Bonds. This skeleton is dangling from your own family tree. What happened, Sheriff—she disgraced the family, so she had to be disposed of?"

Kitchings jumped to his feet. "Don't you dare come in here

and insult me and my family. Get the hell out of my office, the hell out of my county, and the hell out of my business."

"The hell I will. This a murder case, and I won't let you sweep it under the rug just because you don't like where it's going all of a sudden."

The sheriff grabbed the rifle off the desk and began to swing it up. Instinctively I grabbed the barrel and wrestled for control. Suddenly the sheriff froze. I looked up to see Art Bohanan standing beside him, one hand clutching a fistful of hair, the other holding a pistol to Kitchings's temple. "Okay, let's everybody take a deep breath and calm down here," said Art. "Sheriff, let go of that rifle." He did. "Bill, set it over there by the door." I did. "Okay, we're gonna just head on back to Knoxville now," Art continued. "We see anybody in the rearview mirror, and I'll be on the radio like a duck on a June bug to the FBI, the TBI, and a couple undercover cops that would make your worst Cooke County badass look like a mama's boy."

Kitchings was panting through clenched teeth. "You listen up, Doctor. I'm getting a warrant for the arrest of Jim O'Conner. I'm bringing him in on a charge of murder, and I'm sending Williams over to retrieve those remains as evidence."

I shook my head. "I'll turn them over to the district attorney, if he subpoenas them, but I won't turn them over to you."

"You'll do whatever the man says," came a voice behind me. I turned to see a younger, slimmer version of Tom Kitchings, wearing a deputy's uniform and a brass bar that read "Orbin Kitchings, Chief Deputy." He was sighting down the barrel of the sheriff's rifle, which was pointed straight at my head. "Put your weapon down," he said to Art. "And I do mean right now." Art kept his pistol at the sheriff's head. "Put it *down,* city boy, or I'll by-god blow his brains out."

The room was so still you could hear a toothpick drop. Finally Art broke the silence. "You can't do it, Deputy."

"The hell I can't."

"You can pull the trigger, but you can't shoot him," Art said levelly. "The chamber's empty. Sheriff was just cleaning that rifle. Might be some rounds in the magazine, but by the time you can lever one in, I'll have two bullets in you and one in the sheriff." I saw the sheriff give a slight nod to his brother, which I fervently hoped was confirmation of Art's empty-chamber theory. "Put it down, Deputy, and step over here with your hands out in front of you."

"Go on, Orbin, do what he says," sighed Kitchings.

Orbin complied.

Kitchings spoke, and he sounded like a different man—a much less certain and much more weary man—than the one who had tried to turn a rifle on me moments before. "I don't know what's going on here, Doc. You're right, she was my cousin. Leena Bonds—Evelina, actually—was her name. She lived with our family for a few years after her folks died, and then she left town. At least, that's what we'd always thought, right up until now. Leena dated Jim O'Conner. Hell, I think she was even engaged to him. In my book—in anybody's book—that makes him the prime suspect."

"Not if he was in Vietnam when she was strangled," I said.

"Do you know when she was strangled?"

"Not precisely. But the dog tag suggests it was sometime after he left for Vietnam."

"So maybe he did it once he got home. Any proof it didn't happen then?"

"Not that I know of. But I suspect a DNA test will show it wasn't his baby she was carrying."

The revelation burst like a bombshell in the office. I hadn't intended to broach the subject of Leena's pregnancy quite that way, but then again, I hadn't expected to find myself in a Mexican standoff with two law enforcement officers, either.

Tom Kitchings sagged backward against a filing cabinet, looking as if he'd been struck. "She was pregnant?"

"Yes. Four and a half months, best I can tell from the fetal skeleton."

The sheriff remained thunderstruck. His brother spoke up. "Hell, there's your motive right there, gents. G.I. Jim comes home, finds out his sweetie's been takin' her love to town—got knocked up in the process—and he goes apeshit. Might have a hard time making murder one stick, but I guaran-damn-tee you we got enough right now to make a strong case for murder two."

"I don't think he did it," I said.

The sheriff hauled himself upright from the filing cabinet, then leaned toward me, both palms flat on his desk. "Nothin' personal, Doc, but I don't give a rat's ass what you think. You may be a fine bone detective, but you're an outsider here. You don't know the first thing about Cooke County or Jim O'Conner and what he might or might not be capable of. I'll be gettin' a warrant for his arrest. I'll be gettin' a subpoena for those bones. And I'll be takin' it real personal if I catch you messin' around in this case any further."

I decided this might be a good time to make our exit. I looked at Art, and he seemed to agree, as he cocked his head toward the door. "Sheriff," I said, backing out of the office, "I'll be on the lookout for that subpoena. Orbin, good to meet you. Y'all have a nice day."

"Remember," said Art, "we'll have one eye on the rearview mirror and one hand on the radio."

As we dashed out the front door of the courthouse, Art said, "Go get the truck and swing around back and pick me up." I started to ask him why, but he cut me off. "Just do it. I'll tell you later."

The tires squealed as I backed out of my parking space. They squealed again when I slammed the gearshift into forward, and again when I slung the truck around the corner to the rear parking lot. Out of the corner of my eye, I noticed the two old-timers had ceased whittling and were staring at me, slack-jawed and mostly toothless.

As I pulled into the lot, I saw Art at the door of the helicopter. As I skidded to a stop beside him, he pocketed a small bottle, then leapt into the truck. "What were you doing?"

"Oh, nothing," he said. "Just buying us a little time." He pulled the bottle back out of his pocket, and I recognized its shape: superglue.

"You superglued their door locks?" He grinned proudly. "The cars? The *helicopter?*" He nodded happily. "They are gonna be *furious.*"

"More furious than when they tried to shoot us?" He had a point there.

Despite Art's stratagem, I wasted no time getting out of town. Careening along the river road, I glanced in the mirror as often as I could without running off the embankment or making myself carsick. "Better get that radio out, just in case," I told Art.

"What radio?"

"The radio you're going to call for help on." I looked at him; he shook his head and held out his empty hands, palms up. "So what was that big line you were feeding them about radioing the FBI and the TBI if they came after us?"

"That, my friend, is called a bluff. A successful bluff, to be precise." I was not nearly as pleased with Art's gamesmanship as he was. "Hey, what was I supposed to say—'Oh, please don't come after us, because if you do, we're screwed'? I'm glad *you* weren't doing the talking at that moment." Chalk up another point for Art.

We rode in nervous silence awhile, until we turned onto I-40 and the mileposts began flashing past at a hundred miles an hour. For once in my life, I was hoping I'd get pulled over by a state trooper. "Art, I'm in unknown territory here," I said. "I've never had a case where I couldn't tell the good guys from the bad guys."

He nodded. "I remember the first time that happened to me. I was still pretty new in homicide when this cocaine dealer gets shot in the projects in East Knoxville. Shot by a rival dealer, the vice cops tell me. But little things about it start to bother me. No other dealer moves in on the territory. The missing coke—supposedly some hot new stuff—never hits the streets in Knoxville. Instead, pretty soon it starts showing up in Memphis. Turns out one of the vice cops ambushed him, sold the cocaine to a dealer he knew in Memphis. Scary when you realize you can't always trust the guys on your own team."

Scary indeed. "So what should I do?"

"Depends. What do you want to happen?"

"I want to find out who killed that girl. I want to do right by her, if it's possible."

He nodded. "Wouldn't have expected anything less. So just do what you always do: speak for the victim, tell the truth, and use your brain. Oh, yeah—watch your back from now on, too."

"That's it? That's all you've got for me, Supercop?"

"Hey, it's all I've got for me, too. Seems to be working okay. So far."

"Such a comfort. No wonder I wanted you with me."

"Damn right. But wait, there's more. I'm not just a comfort and a lifesaver; I'm also a primo evidence gatherer." Art reached into his shirt pocket and pulled out a folded handkerchief, which he handed to me.

"This hanky is primo evidence?"

"Shit, no, Sherlock. Look inside."

I unfolded it. Tucked in the folds was a hank of human hair. "Whose is it?"

"Fresh from the scalp of Sheriff Thomas Kitchings. Remember when I saved your skin back there? I had a pretty good grip on his curly locks while I was holding my gun to his head. Seemed like long as I was there, might as well bring a few strands home as a souvenir. You still got that former student working up at the Pentagon's forensic lab?"

"Bob Gonzales? Yeah, but why?"

"Might be interesting to see if there's any links with your cavewoman or the baby."

"I say again, why? The sheriff just admitted he's her cousin. And you already convinced me that he was too young to have fathered the baby."

"Bill, this is Cooke County. Never say never. You never know what might turn up."

"Whatever you say. You're the primo criminalist. Thanks, by the way, for saving my skin back there."

"Anytime. Except probably not for the next day or two. I'm still working that child abduction."

"Any luck?"

He shook his head. "Nothing. We're three weeks out without a trace, and we've been tailing the bastard for two-point-nine. Unless we've badly misjudged this slimebag, the kid's been dead since the night he nabbed her. We've got the cadaver dogs searching for a body."

I could think of nothing heartening to say.

The sky had clouded as the day wore on, but suddenly—just as we crossed the big bridge over the French Broad River—spokes of sunlight shot from behind a tower of cumulus. Against a purplish-black storm front to the west, the nearer clouds and the forested river banks glowed with such luminescence my heart tightened in my chest. "God's light," my mother had always called such displays.

I wasn't at all sure I believed in God anymore. But I believed this: despite its pockets of darkness, the world can be a beautiful place.

14

I'D BEEN AVOIDING THE calendar for weeks, but I couldn't suppress the memory of the day that had finally crept up on me: September 27, the two-year anniversary of the day Kathleen had died. I'd ushered in the day promptly at midnight, during the first of many hours of fitful tossing. By daybreak I was nursing a screaming headache, and my hand shook as I poured my coffee. When the telephone shattered the silence of the kitchen, I jumped so much I sloshed out half the cup.

"Hello?"

"Hey, Dad, it's Jeff."

Jeff lived fifteen miles and a world away from the tree-lined sanctuary of Sequoyah Hills. He and his wife had just bought a sprawling new house in Farragut, a booming suburb far to the west on Kingston Pike. Having an anthropologist and a social scientist as parents had given him enough ivory tower experiences to last a lifetime, I suppose, for Jeff had majored in accounting at UT, quickly earned his CPA certification, and built a lucrative practice in less than a decade. His two boys, ages five and seven, were already enrolled in a soccer league, and Jeff's wife, Jenny, meshed well with the other affluent soccer moms in Farragut. At thirty-two, my son was successful and happy. And I could hardly bear talking with him.

"Hi, Jeff. I need to keep it short—I'm about to be late for class."

"It's Saturday, Dad. Is UT scheduling classes on Saturday now?"

"I didn't mean class. I meant an exhumation. I have to go exhume a body."

"You okay? You sound . . . strange."

"I'm okay."

"Listen, I just wanted to let you know I'm thinking about you today." I wished he hadn't said that. "How you feeling—really? Don't just say 'fine,' because you don't sound so hot."

"Gee, why could that be? Oh, now I remember—my wife died on this day a couple years ago."

There was a momentary silence on the other end of the line. "I know, Dad. So did my mom."

"Well, you seem to have had an easier time getting over it." My tone was sharper than I meant it to be.

"What is *that* supposed to mean? Is that some kind of accusation?"

"No. Just an observation. You don't seem to be especially grief-stricken."

I heard a deep intake of breath, then a long, forced exhalation. "You are *way* over the line here. I loved Mom. A lot. And when she died, it hurt like hell; sometimes it still does. But you know what, Dad? I cried a lot, and then I faced the fact that she had died, and I decided to carry on with my life. You, on the other hand, seem determined to make some sort of crusade out of wallowing in your grief—you carry it like a cross, you wear it like a crown of thorns, some self-inflicted stigmata. And anybody who doesn't get down there and wallow with you, you think their grief just isn't quite up to the mark, so maybe their love for her didn't measure up, either. And when you do that, Dad, you alienate yourself from the people who love you and wish you well and want you to be happy again."

"I'll be happy again when the time comes."

"No, you won't. Because you resist it. It's like some perverse challenge to you—seeing how long you can milk your misery and loneliness."

"And this conversation's supposed to be cheering me up?"

"I didn't start this; you did. Come on, Dad, admit it—you're hiding from life. You bury yourself in your work, and you immerse yourself in your grief. And those two things are all you do anymore."

"My work is very demanding."

"So demanding you don't have time to call or see your son and your grandkids? So demanding you don't have time to go out to dinner? When's the last time you had a sit-down dinner with a woman? Or with a man? With me, for that matter?"

"It's hard to see you. It hurts."

"And why is that, Dad?"

If I were telling the truth, I would have said to my son, "Because I blame us both for her death. I blame myself and I blame you, whose birth was so hard on her reproductive system." But I was not telling the truth—I could not tell him that truth—so what I said was, "You remind me too much of her."

"Why can't you take some comfort in that—in the fact that a part of her lives on in me?" I didn't even attempt an answer. "Hell, if you still can't handle an evening with me, at least see *somebody*. Preferably a therapist, but anybody would be better than nobody. I bet you haven't had a social engagement since the funeral."

It was true, I hadn't, but I didn't want my son reminding me of it.

"Look, Jeff, I appreciate your concern for my social life, but I'm fine. I'm a grown-up, and I can manage that quite well on my own." It was a transparent lie, so I blustered as I served it up.

"So are you seeing anybody yet?"

15

I WAS HALF AN HOUR early for Billy Ray Ledbetter's exhumation, even though the cemetery, in Morgan County, lay forty two-lane miles northwest of Knoxville, perched on the edge of the Cumberland Mountains.

People in Cooke County tapped the Appalachians for ginseng and moonshine and marijuana. People in the Cumberlands—including the county seat, the unfortunately named Wartburg—ripped open the mountains themselves, raking low-grade coal from strip mines and bench mines, leaving the ridgetops mutilated and the streams choked with debris and acid.

Billy Ray had worked a wildcat mine—an illegal, unlicensed one—until the Office of Surface Mining had found it and shut it down. After that, he mined food stamps and disability checks for whatever he could, spending most of what he got in the county's windowless cinder-block roadhouses. It was in one of them that he and his friend Eddie Meacham had squared off against half a dozen badass bikers. Unfortunately for Meacham, Billy Ray survived his stomping for eighteen days—until the day, in fact, Billy Ray hitched a ride into Knoxville to ask Eddie to take him to a hospital. He never made it there alive, according to Eddie, because upon staggering into Meacham's apartment, he promptly keeled over, crashed into a glass-topped coffee table, and expired.

That, at least, was the story Meacham was telling, and that was the story Burt DeVriess hoped the exhumation and examination would corroborate.

A freshly waxed black hearse idled at the cemetery entrance, its tinted windows pulsing with rock music cranked up loud enough to wake the dead. Parked beside it was a Caterpillar backhoe in a two-tone color scheme of yellow and rust. From the backhoe's cab, Tammy Wynette pleaded with me to stand by my man. I wondered if anyone had ever stood by the poor bastard whose eternal rest we were about to interrupt so rudely.

Native Americans and New Agers alike say it's wrong to dig up a body after it's been laid to rest—it disturbs the spirit of the departed, they say—and I'm inclined to agree. Unfortunately, sometimes the alternative is even worse: letting a killer go scot-free . . . or sending an innocent person to life behind bars. It was the latter misfortune I hoped to avert by disturbing the spirit of the late Billy Ray.

The morning was gray and chilly as half a dozen of us clustered around a sad little grave outside Wartburg. The cemetery was wedged onto a narrow strip of Cumberland ridgetop, shared by a tiny white clapboard church. The crowd that gathered was quiet and grim. Two uniformed Morgan County sheriff's deputies stood guard, as if someone might be interested in making off with a plywood coffin and pauper's corpse that had been deteriorating in the ground for nine months. Knox County prosecutor Bob Roper, still hoping to salvage his murder case against Meacham, stood alongside a Louisiana forensic anthropologist he'd brought in to try to refute my testimony about the impossible wound path. I found myself in the unenviable position of standing next to Burt DeVriess, my nemesis-turned-employer—an arrangement I hoped would prove brief and never to be repeated.

Not present was Dr. Jessamine Carter, the regional medical examiner from Chattanooga, one hundred miles south of Knoxville. She would rendezvous with us—or, rather, with the body—in the morgue back at UT Medical Center once the exhumation was complete.

The lawyers had wrangled about which pathologist should reautopsy the body. Obviously Knox County's medical examiner, Dr. Garland Hamilton, couldn't do it, since the competence of his initial autopsy was the issue on which Meacham's guilt or innocence now turned. Grease had argued that a big-name out-of-state pathologist should be called in—Dr. Michael Baden, for instance, or Dr. Kay Scarpetta—since Hamilton's Tennessee colleagues might be reluctant to contradict him. The prosecutor countered that if the other MEs in the state couldn't be trusted to tell the truth in a difficult case, they should all be fired anyhow—was that what Mr. DeVriess was suggesting? After a few sarcastic exchanges along these lines, both lawyers had finally stipulated that Dr. Carter might possibly be acceptable for the job. Dr. Carter—Jess, I was allowed to call her, since we'd worked together on a handful of cases during the past five years—was a graduate of Harvard Medical School. How and why she'd landed in Chattanooga remained a bit of a mystery to me, but she was widely considered an expert in discriminating between antemortem, perimortem, and postmortem trauma—that is, between wounds inflicted before, during, or after the time of death. If there was enough soft tissue left for her to examine, she might be able to tell whether Ledbetter had bled to death from a bizarre knife wound, one whose trajectory I had been unable to replicate in a corpse.

As Tammy Wynette belted out the final chorus, the backhoe rumbled into the cemetery and followed a deputy's hand signals to Ledbetter's grave. At a nod from Bob Roper, the machine began clawing at the rocky red soil.

The soil was still soft—it takes years for disturbed earth to recompact, and even then, it's never as hard as it was before being disturbed. Anthropologists depend heavily on that property; it's what allows us to find and excavate ancient burials. Early in my career, for instance, I had spent more than a dozen summers excavating centuries-old graves of Arikira Indians in South Dakota, staying just one step ahead of the rising waters of a new Corps of Engineers reservoir. The Arikira graves—circular in shape—lay beneath a foot of fine, windblown topsoil. After a couple of summers of backbreaking manual searching, I did some experimenting and found that a road grader was the perfect tool for exposing the tops of the graves: a series of shallow passes with the grader would gradually remove the foot of topsoil in long, even rows; as soon as it reached the level of the graves, neat circles of fluffier, disturbed earth would appear. The power equipment increased our speed by a factor of ten—delighting our Smithsonian sponsors at the time, and dismaying Indian activists years later.

Crime scene technicians rely on this property of the soil, too. Rather than digging up an entire field or forest where a body is thought to be buried, the technician jabs the ground with a T-shaped probe—a thin steel rod with a handle welded across one end. If the probe resists going in, the soil is probably undisturbed, but if it plunges in easily, the technician knows somebody's been digging there recently. An even higher-tech version of the soil probe is ground-penetrating radar, which we've helped refine at the Body Farm: just by dragging a scanner across the surface of the ground, a skilled technician can tell (by reading magnetic sworls and squiggles that look utterly random to me) the relative density of the soil and can spot areas of disturbance.

The backhoe clattered and bucked as it clawed open the grave. Scoop by scoop, the pile of dirt beside the grave grew steadily. Finally a sharp clatter and scraping sound told us that the operator had reached the top of the concrete vault that surrounded the coffin itself. After a few more scrapes—which set my teeth on edge like a hundred sets of fingernails raking down a hundred blackboards—he raised the scoop and clambered down off the tractor. Retrieving a pair of steel chains from the back of the rig, he snagged four metal hooks into eyebolts on the lid of the vault and tied the chain over the bucket of the backhoe. Once back in the driver's seat, he took up the slack in the chain and hoisted the concrete lid. As it rose from the grave, red clay crumbled off the edges of the concrete. Swinging it to one side, the operator set it on the damp grass, crushing a stray and faded plastic bouquet.

"Doc, how come graves are lined with those big concrete things, anyway?" DeVriess asked. "Seems kinda pointless. I mean, the body's going to decay anyway, right?"

"Sure," I said. "But people—the living, the ones that funerals and coffins and cemeteries are meant to console—don't like to think about that, so they try to postpone it with embalming fluid and stainless-steel coffins and reinforced concrete vaults." DeVriess rolled his eyes and shook his head at the folly. I didn't like that—didn't like his smug, superior attitude—so I went on. "You think it's dumb?" He gave a noncommittal sideways nod. "For the sake of your client, you better hope this vault stayed nice and tight, and that flimsy wooden coffin stayed dry, and the undertaker didn't scrimp on the embalming fluid the way so many of them do. Those might be the only things that can save his neck and save your case." My voice had risen as I spoke, and I noticed several people looking at us. I snapped my mouth shut and moved to the other side of the grave.

The vault had kept out most of the groundwater, but not all. The rubber gasket that ran around the top of the vault's walls must have slipped slightly out of position, for a small loop of it dangled muddily into the vault, showing where the seal had failed. A greasy moat several inches deep surrounded the coffin, which bobbed slightly from the aftershocks of the backhoe's jarring. Perching precariously on the concrete edges, the gravedigger slipped straps of webbing underneath each end of the coffin and worked them in a foot or so, like dental floss slipping down around a giant tooth. After tying the straps to the bucket he hoisted the coffin, just as he had raised the vault lid. As it rose from the grave, a putrid stream of gray water dribbled out of one corner. It continued to drip even after it was settled on the ground, and I was glad I hadn't offered to haul the coffin back to the morgue in my truck. The gravedigger, the hearse driver, and the two deputies heaved the coffin into the back of the hearse, and the small convoy headed back to Knoxville, a funeral procession in bizarre rewind.

16

DR. JESS CARTER HAD offered to let me observe the autopsy, an invitation I accepted eagerly. I wasn't qualified to testify in court about pathology—the medical aspects of disease and trauma, manifested in bodies that were fresher than the ones I usually studied—but I seized every opportunity I could to learn more about it. After all, what separated Jess's work from mine was only a few days of decomposition—or even a few hours, in conditions of extreme heat, or a few saw cuts, in cases of dismemberment. So the more I knew about finding forensic evidence in fresh tissue, the better I'd be able to spot evidence in not-so-fresh tissue. Besides, Jess was a hoot—funny and irreverent, yet also dead serious about the quality of her work. She had a keen wit, a quick scalpel, and sharp eyes, and she wielded them all with equal deftness.

Her red Porsche Carrera was already parked behind the morgue when I pulled in, followed by the Cadillac hearse bearing Ledbetter's sodden coffin. As the hearse backed into the loading dock, the metal door opened and Jess emerged in scrubs, followed by Miranda, whom I hadn't seen since the night she walked in on Sarah and me kissing. Suddenly I wasn't so sure I wanted to be in on this autopsy after all.

They looked up as I approached, so I waved. "Hi," I called to Jess, "welcome to the hornet's nest. You're pretty gutsy to get mixed up in all this."

She shrugged. "Or not too bright. Never did like to take the safe route—usually boring." She gave me a smile. A very tight smile, first cousin to a grimace. "Miranda's been telling me about some of your recent doings. Sounds like you've got a handful of trouble yourself." I looked at Miranda, whose eyes flashed when they met mine. My face flushed, and I turned toward the hearse. Why was that infernal driver taking so long to unload the damn coffin?

I cleared my throat. "Well, I do have an interesting, um, case right now. I'll t-t-tell you about it later. Right now, let me go get changed so I don't keep you waiting." With that, I fled into the morgue, slinking into the safety of the men's changing room. What a mess I'd made of things with Miranda. What an idiot.

When I entered the autopsy room, taking refuge behind a surgical mask, I saw only Jess, scalpel in hand and headlamp on her forehead, leaning over the body. The coffin sat in a corner by a floor drain, still oozing a bit of water, or something. "Looks like you're my diener today," she said.

"What's a diener?" The word rhymed with "wiener," which is what I felt like; it was also the way a foreigner might say "dinner," a realization that did little to ease my apprehension as she and the scalpel turned in my direction.

"Autopsy assistant. German word. Actually means 'servant.' Just so you're clear on the pecking order at the moment." She sounded mad and looked even madder.

"Where's Miranda?" I asked.

"She said she had a lab to teach. Does she? Or does she just not want to be here?" Her eyes glittered above her mask.

"I . . . I don't know. She . . . I guess maybe she didn't want to be here."

She slammed the scalpel down onto the steel table. "Damnit, Bill, this is ridiculous and unprofessional."

"You're right. I'm sorry. I'm very ashamed."

"I respect you and I like you, but that doesn't make me any threat to her."

"I know. I—huh?"

"She's got no reason to dislike me."

"*You*? What are you talking about?"

"That . . . that *girl*. While you were taking your sweet time about changing, she practically started a catfight with me. Like I was here to snatch away her boyfriend or something." Again she slammed the scalpel down on the metal table—it seemed to make her feel better—and again I flinched. "Goddamnit, this is not junior high school."

I had misunderstood utterly, had misinterpreted the tension and angry looks completely. A wave of giddy relief washed over me. I started to laugh, and found I couldn't stop. I laughed so hard my stomach muscles began to ache; my mask grew so wet with tears that I had to rip it off just to breathe.

She stared openmouthed at me. Then, slow and bright as sunrise, a smile dawned across her face. She waggled a gloved finger at me, shook her head, and said, "And what were *you* talking about? *Are* you her boyfriend?"

"No. *No!*" I thought I was starting to laugh again, but I was crying. She laid a hand on my arm and left it there till I got hold of myself. "Oh, God, Jess, I've made a royal mess of things."

"You screwing a student? Hey, it's not like you're the first professor to take a bite out of that shiny apple. Just between you and me, back in my own reckless youth . . ."

I stared at her. "*You?!*"

"Dr. Crowder. Microbiology. And talk about microscopic!" She laughed. "So you and Miss Priss got something going on? That why she bared her fangs at me?"

"No. At least, not like that. It's complicated." She raised her eyebrows quizzically, and so I told her everything: how I came unglued in class; how Sarah came to my office that night to return the bones; how we fell into a torrid clutch; how Miranda reacted to the sight. "Jesus, Jess. I've compromised myself with a student—an undergraduate, at that—and simultaneously alienated my best graduate assistant. I don't know how to fix things."

She fixed me with a stern, no-bullshit look. "Bill, when's the last time you got laid?"

I flushed. "It's been awhile. Not since Kathleen died. A few months before Kathleen died."

She held the look. "So, what, two years or more? That's a long damn time for a man in his prime. And you're around young women—smart, attractive young women, women who look up to you—day in and day out. I'm amazed you haven't thrown some poor lass to the floor and ravished her by now. Jesus, Bill, give yourself a break. Yeah, you kissed a student. Probably as much her doing as yours—take my word for that. And yeah, your timing sucked. Too bad. You want to apologize to one of them, or both of them, go ahead. And then go *on*." Her voice softened. "Bill, Bill. We all make mistakes. Even you. Grieving, lonely, stiff-upper-lip you. And if getting caught in a kiss knocks you off that pedestal your diener's put you on, well, maybe that's best." She leaned closer, right into my face. "Understandable as it is, Bill, it's not healthy for her to idolize you."

I blinked. A lot had just happened: confession, understanding, forgiveness, counsel. "I thought you were supposed to be a pathologist. Sound more like a shrink. A damn good one, by the way."

She smiled. "Nope, just a woman who's been around the block a time or two. If I weren't happily lesbian now, I might take you for a spin myself, try to put a smile back on your face. But enough with the therapy. We've got a corpse to dissect."

She left me with my jaw hanging open—"happily lesbian

now"? Whatever happened to the husband she'd introduced me to at that forensic conference a year or so ago?—and turned her attention to Ledbetter's corpse. The Y incision from Dr. Hamilton's autopsy had been stitched shut with coarse black baseball-style sutures, which Jess cut with a flick of the scalpel. Stuffed into the abdomen was a red plastic biohazard bag; extricating it and laying it on the table, she said, "Well, at least he bagged the organs instead of just dumping them into the cavity. We might as well look at the lungs first, although I'm not feeling optimistic about what kind of shape they're in."

"Nine months is a long time," I agreed. "I'll be surprised if they're not completely putrefied."

"Me too. Looks like our man got the bare minimum of cosmetic embalming—just enough in the neck to keep his face presentable for the funeral. And the organs were already removed and bagged at that point, so they didn't get any formalin at all." She cut the zip tie at the neck of the bag. "Brace yourself—this is going to be pretty ripe." Opening the bag wide, she revealed the contents to our eyes and our nostrils.

The lungs—or, rather, what had once been the lungs—were now a few handfuls of gelatinous gray goo. They had been sliced apart during the original autopsy, and the dissection and decay had combined to render them useless as any source of additional forensic information. "Shit," she said. "And I mean that descriptively as well as editorially." She tied the bag shut again and strode toward a stereomicroscope at a desk against one wall of the autopsy suite. "At least your girlfriend did me one favor before she stomped out of here. She got us the slides." Jess switched on the light source and peered into the eyepieces. "Come take a look."

I took her place at the scope and leaned in, tweaking the focus a bit to compensate for my lack of reading glasses. The field of view was filled with lacy, delicate circles of pale pink; the insides of the circles were nearly opaque brown. "Tell me what I'm seeing."

"Cross-section of the alveolar sacs from the lower right lobe of the lungs. Five microns thick—one two-hundredth of an inch. The water in the tissue has been replaced with paraffin."

"So the pink circles?"

"The business part of the lungs—the sacs where air exchange takes place."

"That was what I figured. And the brown?"

"Blood."

"Perimortem?"

"Nope. Clotted. Definitely antemortem."

"Any way to tell how long antemortem?"

"Top of the head, I'd guess two weeks," she said. "I wish Dr. Hamilton had kept the save jar."

"Save jar?"

"Yeah—a highly technical term for the jar where we packrat-type pathologists sometimes pickle bigger slices of organs in formalin. I've got thousands of 'em—I tend to keep mine for years, at least in forensic cases. But I think Hamilton incinerates the larger sections as soon as he finishes writing the report. Keeps the shelves clear, he told me once. Also makes it harder for somebody else to second-guess him, I'd say."

"What would a bigger section tell you?"

"Maybe nothing, but maybe—if we got really lucky—it might have included traumatized tissue. Which might have lent credence to his stabbing theory—or might have shown what a completely idiotic idea that was."

She leaned closer, practically inserting her head into the cavern that had once housed the rubbery heart and spongy lungs, and played her headlamp over the interior. "The soft tissues inside the body cavity show signs of advanced decomposition," she dictated, "however, the parietal pleural

membrane appears to be intact, showing no sign of a pene-
tration wound on the posterior wall of the chest cavity." She
lifted her foot from the Dictaphone's pedal. "You wanna
help me roll him over?"

We rolled the corpse onto its stomach, or what was once
its stomach, so she could examine the back. A ragged gash,
roughly two inches long and an inch wide, punctuated the
lower left side of the back, just above the hip. Jess teased it
open with the tip of a probe. As she worked the probe around
inside the wound, a muffled grating sound emerged from the
corpse. "Hark," she said, eyes dancing above her mask. "Do
you hear what I hear?" I nodded. "Let's see what we've
found."

Trading the probe for a scalpel, she cut gently at the top
and bottom of the wound to widen it slightly, then inserted a
small spreader to open it. Something glimmered dully deep
within the rotting flesh. Reaching in with a pair of forceps,
Jess grasped and pulled, wiggling gently to help tease the
object from the tissue. "Come to Mama," she murmured as
she worked it free, then, "Eureka." It was a shard of glass, a
quarter-inch thick and two inches long. The end she held in
the forceps was perhaps an inch across; the piece tapered,
over its two-inch length, to a wicked point. "That had to
hurt," she said.

"Meacham said that Ledbetter had collapsed onto a glass-
topped coffee table. That's got to be a piece of it. Could it
have killed him?"

"Don't see how—not right there. It's completely lodged
in the erector spinae—the main group of muscles of the
lower back—so even though it's a bad puncture wound, it
wouldn't have severed any major blood vessels. Eventually
he might have bled out or died of infection, but he didn't.
For all his sloppiness in this case, Dr. Hamilton did get the
cause of death right: it *was* a pulmonary hemorrhage that
killed him. What he got badly wrong were the cause and the

timing of the hemorrhage. This glass was just icing on the cake. In fact, this guy might have already been dead, or close to it, when he hit the coffee table."

"So there's no evidence of a knife wound, Jess?"

"Well, you never know. Maybe the guy stabbed him and then stuck this in there to cover his tracks. Sounds far-fetched, but I still get surprised once in a while. You're gonna check for knife marks on the bone, right?"

I nodded. "Yeah, I wasn't trying to get out of the work. Just trying to make sense of what we're seeing here."

She wrapped up her dictation with a matter-of-fact notation that the remains had been transferred to forensic anthropologist William Brockton of the University of Tennessee for further examination, to ascertain whether the spine or ribs had sustained trauma, then switched off the recorder. "Bill, you want me to save you a little time?"

I wasn't sure what she meant. "What do you mean?" I asked. Reaching to one side of the instrument tray, she picked up a long, straight-bladed knife that must have measured eighteen inches from stem to stern. I vaguely recalled seeing its twin one morning in Panera Bread, where a baker deftly dissected a cinnamon-raisin loaf into perfect slices. "Looks like a kitchen knife," I said.

"Oh, *please,*" she said. "It's a highly specialized implement with a precise medical name: *bread* knife." Her arm extended and then swiftly drew back, and suddenly the corpse's legs and pelvis lay separated from the upper body by a crisp, narrow gap. The one-eighth-inch cartilage disk between the twelfth thoracic vertebra and the first lumbar vertebra had been slit neatly in half.

"Wow," I said. "Remind me never to make you mad."

"Don't ever make me mad," she obliged. "I keep hoping some creep will try to mug me in the hospital parking lot some night, but it never happens."

"Tough break," I commiserated. "But don't give up hope.

You're far too young and beautiful to become embittered by life's disappointments."

"Thanks."

"Say, you think you could do that again, up here between the thoracic and cervical vertebrae?"

"Gee, I dunno," she said, "that mighta just been beginner's luck." I pulled my finger back a split second before the knife flashed again. The head rolled free of the shoulders. "Two in a row—whattaya know?" Jess washed and dried the knife and began shucking her scrubs and paper booties. Underneath, she'd kept on a pair of black jeans, a blue silk blouse, and a pair of square-toed leather boots. "Okay, sport, he's all yours. Have fun." I nodded, already mentally dissecting the rib cage. "Oh, and Bill?" I turned to look at her as she sheathed the blade and tucked it into the belt of her jeans. "Don't forget what I said. Do what you need to do to straighten things with these students. Then cut yourself some slack. And for pete's sake, get yourself laid!" She winked broadly and pushed open the door, leaving me standing red-faced above the disarticulated torso of Billy Ray Ledbetter.

I didn't need to deflesh the entire skeleton, just the thoracic region which Jess had cut free for me. Curling my fingers under the rib cage, I lifted the ripe section of torso and lugged it to a nearby counter, where a mammoth steam-jacketed steel kettle stood waiting. Resting my burden on the rim, I shifted my grip and lowered it in, then filled it to within a few inches of the rim, using a short hose hanging on the wall behind it. I added a splash of bleach from a Clorox bottle—I liked the fresher, green-labeled variety—and what I guessed to be a tablespoon from a jar of Adolph's Meat Tenderizer. The Adolph's would cut the time and the bleach would cut the odor, as well as lightening the bones' caramel color to the shade of aging ivory that lawyers and jurors seemed to prefer. I twisted the thermostat at the base of the kettle to 180 degrees. Below that, the tissue would take too long to soften; any higher, and I'd be risking a nasty boil-over.

As I left Billy Ray Ledbetter to simmer, I realized I'd been doing a lot of stewing myself. I'd kept a tight lid on my emotions ever since Kathleen died—outwardly, at least—hoping that by doing so, I could keep my life from getting messy. Jess's advice, and my own behavior lately, had shown me that I, too, had come close to boiling over. Maybe she was right. Maybe I needed to loosen up. Maybe I did need to get laid.

17

I LEANED OUT THE TRUCK and down toward the drive-through window. "Here you go," said Dolores, handing me the bright yellow plastic box.

"Did I get anything besides the lens cap?"

"Some great shots of your left index finger," she laughed. "Your buddy Art could run those through his fingerprint database for sure." Seeing the alarm on my face, she laughed again. "Gotcha. Not bad, mostly—less gross than usual, which I personally appreciate. Some of 'em, though, looks like you accidentally hit the shutter button before you were ready."

"What makes you say that?"

"Nothing but mud."

I smiled. "Any footprints in that mud?"

"Well, now that you mention it, seems like maybe there were. Is that what you were after?" I nodded.

Dolores had been developing my slides for years now; during that time, she'd seen photos from crime scenes that had made hardened cops lose their lunch. She always seemed interested, but her questions invariably stopped short of nosiness. I didn't mind sharing a few details, because I knew she'd keep anything she saw or heard to herself. In her mind's eye, she seemed to click back through the strip of film. "Nothing but mud in some, but others, you'll probably find something interesting. You must've been shooting at night."

"In a cave, actually."

"I wondered where you'd found all that mud, dry as it's been this month. Always something new with you, Doc."

"Keeps life interesting, Dolores. Keeps old age at bay." I paid, took my receipt, and waved as the drive-through window slid shut and Dolores disappeared into the depths of FotoFast.

Back at the office, I inserted the slides, upside-down, into a carousel tray and snapped the tray onto the Kodak projector. I switched on the projector's lamp and turned out the overhead fluorescent. As the autofocus lens ratcheted in and out, seeking clarity, green and yellow blurs gradually resolved into the ATVs we'd wrangled up the mountainside and into the cave. Sheriff Kitchings's belly flashed up, filling half the screen, as he wriggled through the narrow squeeze. His face was contorted and his teeth were clenched with the strain. I studied him, this man who had asked for my help and then hidden the truth from me. Something about the photo disturbed me. The image—the way he was hoisting his belly—was grotesque, but that wasn't what nagged at me. I stared at his face awhile longer, still unable to put my finger on anything specific, then moved on. The soles of three different boots—the sheriff's, the deputy's, and mine—flashed past. Only then, because I had purposely loaded the three-boot reference photos out of sequence, did my shots of the cave's muddy floor begin.

The first few images showed some hint of foot traffic, but the angle—high, shooting nearly straight down—made everything appear flat and featureless. As the camera angle got progressively lower, shadows appeared and grew, as if the sun were setting in the cave, throwing the contours of the mud into sharp relief, revealing a world of texture. A world of footprints.

The prints reminded me of craters on the moon, seen through a telescope: at full moon, viewed straight-on, the rocky surface appears deceptively smooth. But at other stages, especially when viewed at the terminus—the border between light and dark—the craters and canyons show themselves to be rugged, razor-edged, and forbidding. The cave's craters were made by human feet, not by massive meteorites, but the surface looked almost as pocked and layered as the ancient face of the moon.

Kitchings had told me that he and Williams ventured into the grotto just far enough to determine that a body lay there. Sure enough, two sets of tracks—a lugged-sole pattern that matched the sheriff's boots and a rippled design that matched Williams's—led toward the rock shelf where the body lay. The tracks stopped, and some random, layered trampling suggested shifting stances by both men. Then the tracks reversed direction, leading back toward the camera and in the direction of the grotto's entrance. I nodded to myself; it was what I'd expected to see, based on what they'd told me.

What I hadn't expected to see came in the next slide, which I'd taken by leaning far to the left, beyond the corpse's head, still shooting low. The image that flashed onto the screen made me gasp. A veritable stampede of footprints approached the body from the opposite direction—a shadowy nook in the grotto, as I recalled, which I had taken to be a dead-end crevice. The tracks—lots of them, a dozen or more—departed the same way they'd come. I was dumbfounded. "Jesus," I said out loud, "how many people were in on this damn thing?" Then another thought struck me: could they be morbid sightseers, who had somehow gotten wind of the grisly spectacle in the grotto? But it took only a few seconds to decide that what appeared to be many people's footprints were actually many prints from a single person: layer upon layer of tracks from what appeared to be the same pair of boots. Judging by the soles, the boots were old and worn—work boots, maybe, rather than hiking or combat boots. But here and there along the edge, some of the earlier tracks—ones that were only partially obliterated by later imprints—looked sharper, as if the boots were newer. I felt my mind ratcheting back and forth, like the projector's lens, struggling to focus. Finally I got it: someone had visited the grotto repeatedly, over a long period of time. I'd ask Art to take a look and give me his read on it, but that seemed the only explanation that made sense. The only other possibility was that a crowd of people had trooped in, wearing identically made but differently aged boots. Either scenario was disturbing.

But not as disturbing as what I saw next. It was the final image of the cave's floor, similar to the previous one, but following the tracks even farther toward what was clearly the room's other entrance. At the edge of the mass of identical tracks was one additional set of prints—uppermost, and therefore most recent. Unlike the layers of increasingly worn work boot tracks, these prints showed crisp, practically new soles. Lugged soles. They looked a lot like the soles on the feet of Sheriff Tom Kitchings.

I switched off the lamp and sat in darkness, quiet except for the low hum of the projector's fan. The machine's heat warmed the room, but the picture I had just seen gave me a chill. I was working a case for a sheriff whom I did not know and did not trust. I was in contact with a self-described outlaw—a potential suspect—whom I likewise did not know but, oddly, *did* trust. The solid footing I normally felt underfoot seemed to be falling away on either side, leaving me teetering along a knife-edge ridge, defined only by dark and dizzying drops on either side. For the first time in my career, I began to consider withdrawing from a case. Every internal alarm I possessed was ringing like crazy; the stakes seemed too high, the truth too tainted by secrets that lurked deep within the mountains or the hearts of the clannish people who dwelled there.

I drew a deep breath. Flicking the lamp back on, I clicked to the next slide. She—Leena, as I now knew to call her—lay on the stone shelf, immobile forever now. I was startled anew at the freshness of her waxy death mask, at the remarkable preservation the cave's climate and the body's chemistry had effected. It was odd to think that after years of near-perfect preservation, she existed no more: in examining her, I had destroyed her. It was necessary, but it was sad—all the more so in hindsight, in light of the small life she was nurturing when she died.

I flashed up the other images of Leena, pausing briefly on the best side view of the abdomen. Now it seemed obvious that she was pregnant, but I knew that was only because my mind's eye was superimposing the shape of the tiny skeleton I had extricated from her abdomen. Finally I stopped on a full-frame close-up of her face. For long minutes I studied it, trying to decipher whatever secrets it held. Had her expression held any faint clue that hinted at her pregnancy—some inner smile or worried tension? If so, it had been replaced by a more gruesome expression. Was it terror, or accusation, or just the mechanical distortion of mummification?

"What's your story, Leena Bonds," I murmured, "and who killed you and your baby, and why?"

As soon as I said it, I knew that, come what may, I would not withdraw from this case.

18

I GOT NO ANSWER AT the first number Jim O'Conner had given me, so I tried the second number. "Howdy, Doc," rumbled a deep voice after the second ring.

"Hello? Is this . . . *Waylon*?"

"Shore is."

I was taken aback to get the mountain man instead of O'Conner. "Sorry to bother you on a Sunday morning, Waylon. I was trying to call Jim. How'd you know it was me?"

"You city folks ain't the only ones got Caller ID," he said. "We're gettin' kindly high-tech our own selves, Doc. Hell, I got me a cable modem and high-speed Internet, too." I tried to picture what sort of web sites Waylon might be inclined to surf—hunting equipment? survivalist how-to sites? backwoods personal ads ("broad-minded moonshiner seeks adventurous black sheep for loving relationship")?—then shuddered and strove to banish the images from my mind. "Jim's out of town for a few days. Whatcha need?"

"Listen, Waylon, I'm hoping maybe you can do me a big favor. You know the cave we found that body in—Russell's Cave, I think it's called?"

"Course. Used to play in it when I was a kid."

"Is there any way you could take me there? I need another look around, and I don't want to bother the sheriff or his deputy. If you can't do it, just say so—I know it's a long ways off the beaten track. It took us over an hour by ATV just to get up there."

There was a long pause on the other end, which I figured meant he was groping for an excuse.

"It took you'uns a hour to get there? On ATVs, you say?"

"At least an hour, over a pretty rough trail up the mountain. My legs are still sore; a return trip might just put me in a wheelchair."

He laughed. "Well, Doc, I might be able to help you out. How 'bout you meet me at the Pilot station at the interstate exit in about a hour?"

"How about an hour and a half? I need to stop by my office and get my camera and a few tools." He agreed, and I hung up, hoping I wasn't making a foolish mistake.

I'd expected Waylon to be driving a pickup; what I wasn't prepared for was the sort of pickup it proved to be. A battered rust bucket, sporting a patchwork of Bondo, gray primer, and multihued body panels scavenged from disparate hillside junkyards: that's what I'd expected. The vehicle waiting for me at the gas station made my full-size GMC Sierra look shabby and sissified by comparison. A Dodge Ram 3500, it measured at least a foot longer, wider, and taller than my truck. Waylon owned the Arnold Schwarzenegger of pickups. Twin vertical exhausts, which could have been transplants from a Kenworth semi, flanked the rear corners of the cab. Rear fenders flared widely above dual wheels, tricked out with monster tires on sculpted alloy rims. Waylon ambled out of the minimarket and fished a keyless remote beeper out of one of his myriad pockets; when he clicked to unlock the doors, it sounded as if the locking mechanism on a bank vault were ratcheting open. An air horn beneath the vehicle emitted a locomotive-sized blast. Waylon motioned me in.

I stepped up—way up—onto a running board and hoisted myself cabward with the help of a vertical handrail just aft of the door. Grunting from the climb, I plopped into my seat—a swiveling captain's chair, sheathed in buttery glove leather. The dash and overhead console bristled with enough electronics to make a NORAD technician envious: GPS, moving-map display, satellite radio, CB radio, hands-free cell phone, CD/cassette/AM-FM deck, even a passenger-side DVD screen. A small refrigerator—sized to hold either a case of beer or a haunch of venison—whirred quietly between us.

I swiveled in my seat and surveyed the aft cabin.

"You need something, Doc?"

"No, I was just looking for the hot tub," I said. "You seem to have everything else in here."

Waylon rumbled out a laugh. "I might oughta put me one in. Thing is, if I did, I never would get my girlfriend outta here."

He turned the key, and somewhere beneath us, a sleeping giant of a power plant awakened. "Cummins Turbo Diesel," I'd read on the side of the hood as I clambered up. The cab quivered gently as the engine idled; the rumble bore more than a passing resemblance to Waylon's laugh: low-pitched and muffled, but simple and powerful. "Sounds like you've got some serious horsepower there," I said.

"It'll do. They's actually a gasoline engine with more horsepower, a 10-liter V-10, but it gets shitty mileage. This here's got more torque, anyhow. Tow twenty-three thousand pounds with this rig. Besides, you can't beat a Cummins. Go three hundred fifty thousand miles 'fore it needs a overhaul."

Another pipe, topped with wire mesh and a chrome cap, projected above the hood from somewhere on my side of the engine compartment. "What's that thing sticking up? Looks like a chimney flue."

"Snorkel intake," Waylon said. "You can ford a crick six foot deep in this thing. I've done it. Helps if you got some weight in the bed, though, especially if they's some current. She's one hell of a truck, but once she starts to float, the handling goes all to hell. You don't want to have the windows down, neither."

As he roared beneath the interstate and headed up-country, Waylon half-turned to me. "Doc, I got to do a little financial business on our way back from the cave, so I need to make me a quick stop on the way up. If you don't care to."

The phrasing gave me pause. Where I'd grown up, in Virginia, "I don't care to" was a polite way of saying, "I prefer not to" or even, given a frosty enough inflection, "hell, no." In East Tennessee, though—at least in the mountains—I'd noticed that it seemed to mean exactly the opposite. I wasn't sure how much financial business Waylon could conduct on a Sunday, but I told him I didn't care to stop.

We headed north on the river road for a few miles, then made a left onto an unmarked paved road that disappeared into a wooded valley. A small, mean-spirited brick house hugged the road, centered in a small clearing fenced with chain-link; in the driveway sat a Cooke County sheriff's cruiser. I pointed. "Tom Kitchings live here?"

"Naw," growled Waylon. "His damn brother, Orbin. Sorriest sumbitch in Cooke County." He opened his mouth as if to say more, then clamped it shut.

A quarter-mile up the blacktop, we turned left onto a broad swath of fresh gravel running up the mouth of a small valley. "Right up this holler here's our first stop," Waylon said. We'd barely left the pavement when he halted at a small, glass-doored booth, from which a thirtysomething blonde woman emerged. Clad in snug designer jeans and a short suede jacket, she could have passed for a stylish West Knoxville mom who had been suddenly plucked from a kid's soccer game or the mall and beamed out here to the boonies. Waylon rolled down his window and handed her a laminated card of some sort. She scanned it with a portable bar-code reader, then gave it back and waved us in. High-tech indeed! As she turned to go back into the booth, Waylon nodded at her shrink-wrapped backside. "That there's just about worth the trip, ain't it, Doc?" I didn't want to admit it, but the view was stunning.

The gravel drive soon widened into a huge backwoods parking lot, measuring forty or fifty yards across and at least a football field in length, bulldozed into the floor of the hollow. The lot was crammed with three neat rows of diagonally parked cars and trucks. As we eased up one aisle and down the other in search of a vacant slot, I lost count at 150 vehicles, mostly pickups, bearing license plates from Tennessee, North Carolina, South Carolina, Georgia, Alabama, Florida, Kentucky, even as far away as Oklahoma and Texas. As best I could tell, it was a wholesale auto auction—there was a similar auction lot beside Interstate 75 between Knoxville and Chattanooga—though why this one lay so far off the beaten track was a mystery to me.

At the upper end of the lot was a barn-sized metal building, surrounded by dozens of small garden sheds, battered travel trailers, and a new two-story structure that resembled a small, windowless motel, with dozens of doors giving onto the ground-floor sidewalk and the second-floor balcony. Waylon had finally circled back nearly to the entrance booth to park, so we hiked up the long gravel lot toward the big metal shed, which appeared to be the hub of the complex.

"This is quite an operation here," I said as we trudged across the coarse gravel.

"Yeah, it's been around ever since I can remember," he said, "but it seems to be really expanding under this couple that bought the business a few years ago."

"Are you bidding on one of these vehicles? I haven't seen anything in the lot that holds a candle to that truck you're driving."

"Bidding?" Waylon chuckled. "Well, you might call it that, I reckon."

The metal building seemed to pulse with a cacophony of

yells and whoops. The auction must really be heating up, I thought. A door was set midway along the side. As we approached, I glimpsed a pair of eyes peering out through a narrow slit in the door. The eyes studied me for an uncomfortably long time, with an expression I took to be some combination of suspicion and hostility, then cut in Waylon's direction. Waylon seemed to recognize the irises or pupils through the slit. "Hey, T-Ray, you gonna let us in, or do we hafta just listen from out here?"

A nasal voice slithered up through the slit. "Who's that you got with you?"

"Friend of me and Jim's from Knoxville. He's all right."

"He better be."

Waylon nodded his immense head, though I wasn't sure whether he was offering further assurance that I was, in fact, all right, or was simply acknowledging what seemed to be the other man's unspoken "or else." Maybe both. At any rate, T-Ray's eyes vanished from view, a metal bolt slid back, and the door swung open. "Stay close," Waylon rumbled in my ear, and we stepped inside.

It took my eyes a moment to adjust—not to the dimness I'd expected, but to the glare of fluorescent tubes, practically enough to light Neyland Stadium for a UT night game. Nearly two hundred people jammed the building, some of them standing, others perched on wooden bleachers that ascended nearly to the roof. Big-bellied men and gangly boys, mostly, though I noticed several women and even a handful of girls clustered on the top row of bleachers. The crowd's skin tones ranged from pasty Anglo white to Hispanic olive brown; their attire ranged from overalls and feed caps to hip-hugger jeans, snakeskin boots, Abercrombie sweatshirts, and milky white Stetsons.

A narrow gap bisected the bleachers directly in front of us, and through it, I glimpsed a round enclosure at the center. Waylon began threading his way toward it, and—mindful of his instructions and of T-Ray's unwelcoming eyes—I stuck close.

As we approached the enclosure, I saw that it was a circle about fifteen feet across, dirt-floored and fenced in by wire mesh rising to a height of eight or ten feet. Dust hung in the air like dry, allergy-baiting fog, giving the scene an even more surreal quality than it already possessed. Shouts punctuated the background din: "Hunnerd on the red!" "Fifty on the gray!" "*Call* fifty!" "*Five* hunnerd on the red!" This last cry, in Waylon's booming voice, nearly shattered my eardrum.

Two men faced each other inside the ring. One was a long-bearded ancient who resembled some Old Testament prophet in baggy overalls. The other was a young Hispanic man in a snug brown jumpsuit, monogrammed "Felipe." Leaning toward each other, weaving and swaying rhythmically, the men seemed to be cradling something to their chests. I was still trying to make out what it was when they squatted in unison and then stood back up, now empty-handed. There was a momentary lull in the din, followed by an explosive flurry of wings and feathers, accompanied by bloodcurdling screeches and raucous cheers. "Hit 'im, Red! Hit 'im! There you go!" "Come on, Gray! Stick it to 'im!"

As I watched in horror, two roosters beat their wings in midair, kicking and tearing at each other with their feet as they struggled to hover. I caught the glint of steel blades on their legs, and I knew with sickening certainty that the cockfight I had stumbled into would end swiftly. Cockfighting was illegal in Tennessee, I knew—as it was in every state but Oklahoma, Louisiana, and New Mexico—but in a hardscrabble area like Cooke County, which tended to regard the law more as a challenge than as a code of conduct, it was hardly surprising that it continued.

The birds tumbled to the ground in a knot of feathers and blood. "Hit 'im baby, hit 'im baby, hit 'im baby," chanted a bleached-blonde woman sitting by my right shoulder. "Git 'er done, Red," yelled a man at my left.

In the ring, a third man—cockfights had referees, apparently—motioned to the birds' handlers, who swooped in to disentangle the snarled cocks. The men clasped the birds to their chests again, smoothing their feathers, blowing warm air onto their backs; they even seemed to be pressing their lips around the roosters' combs as if to warm them, though I had no idea whether that was the purpose or whether it was merely some good-luck ritual.

In their first dustup, the red-and-black rooster had looked smaller but quicker and more aggressive; the one called a gray, though (actually multicolored, with an off-white neck and head), looked strong and tough. It appeared to be a classic David-versus-Goliath match—except that in the Bible story, I recalled, David had been armed only with a slingshot and stones. These birds, though, were armed with sharpened steel. On the back of one leg—strapped with a leather band to what must have been the stump of his natural spur—each cock wore a gleaming knife blade, two inches long. Judging by the caution with which the handlers carried the birds, the knives were razor-sharp. "Hang in there, Flea-Pay," a freckled teenager yelled to the Hispanic man, who stroked and blew on the gray rooster.

The handlers began their rhythmic dance again, which I now saw was actually a way of taunting the birds, getting them agitated and ready to fight. As the handlers circled and bobbed and swayed a foot or two apart, the cocks' heads lashed forward at one another, coming close but never quite making contact. Once the birds were sufficiently enraged, the handlers set them down for another round. As soon as he was released, the gray one darted furiously toward the red and leapt up to strike. This time, though, instead of meeting him in midair, the red cock ducked and ran underneath, spun swiftly, and then launched himself at the gray's back, windmilling his feet as he made contact. The crowd gave a collective shout, then fell eerily silent. The gray cock toppled onto his side, panted a few startled, ragged breaths, and died in a small pool of blood. The red rooster shook hard and fluffed himself, then strutted over to the body of his fallen rival and pecked at the lifeless body. Next, placing one foot on the gray's head, he swelled his chest, threw back his head, and crowed triumphantly. As if in reply, the crowd—except for the few dejected-looking losers who had bet on the gray—let loose with a cheer equally primal. A teenager sauntered past, holding a cardboard food tray. It was filled with fried chicken strips.

Waylon leaned toward me and yelled, "That red'un sure is game, ain't he? I b'lieve that's his tenth win this year."

Upset by the animal carnage and the human brutality, I yelled sarcastically, "Yeah, too bad I didn't get a chance to bet on him."

Waylon either didn't notice the sarcasm or chose to ignore it. "If we'da got here a minute sooner, you coulda. I had me a hunnerd on him. Tried to lay five, but didn't get no takers. Easy way to make a hunnerd, though."

"Tell that to the dead one," I said.

He swiveled and studied me, then nodded. "I reckon it does kindly depend on where you're at in the peckin' order, don't it?"

"So this was the financial business you needed to do— putting a bet on a cockfight?" He nodded.

"This ain't for me, Doc, and it ain't just for fun. I got a cousin in a bind. Quickest way I know to raise some money for him."

"Does Orbin Kitchings know there's a cockfighting pit a stone's throw from his house?"

Waylon spat in the sawdust on the floor, which absorbed blood and spittle with equal efficiency. "Know it? Hell, he's a damn regular. Gets a percentage of the take. Bets big, too. If he wins, he's real quick to collect. If he loses, you can figure on hell freezing over 'fore he'll pay up. Folks try not to bet with him on account of that, 'cept he pressures 'em, if you know what I mean." I was starting to get the picture, and it was a deeply disturbing portrait of Cooke County's chief deputy. "Listen, Doc, I got to speak to this fella over yonder. Won't take but just a minute." He reached into a pocket and extricated a small, round container, the size and shape of a tunafish can. "Here, have a little dip while you wait." He popped off the lid and I caught the moist, pungent aroma of tobacco. I looked down, amazed: in all my years in East Tennessee, I had never before been offered a chew; now, suddenly, I was face to face with a wad of tobacco while standing ringside at an illegal cockfight. What next, I wondered—moonshine? hookers? animal-sex acts? Waylon saw the uncertainty in my eyes. "You ain't never dipped before?" He sounded incredulous. I shook my head. He held the container closer and smiled encouragingly, a stray strand of depleted tobacco wedged between his upper incisors.

A man leaned down from the bleachers above my head, evidently taking an interest in our exchange. "Go on, buddy, give 'er a try."

Waylon looked up. "Oh, hey, Rooster."

Rooster nodded to Waylon, then resumed meddling. "Go on, it'll perk you right up. You look like you could use some perkin' up."

What the hell, I thought, and reached in with my thumb and forefinger. I snagged a pinch of the soft, shredded leaf and brought it slowly toward my mouth. Waylon laughed. "Shit far, Doc, that ain't near enough. Git you some more." I reached in and doubled the size of my pinch. "Aw, hell, that ain't gonna do nothin'. Go on, grab you a hunk." Embarrassed, I reached in a third time, scooping with my middle finger, too. This time my hand emerged clutching a ragged wad of Copenhagen the size of a cotton ball. Waylon winked in approval, then tugged open his lower lip—mercifully empty at the moment—and pointed, showing me the spot to cram it. When I did, carefully tamping in the loose ends, he beamed. "Doc, we'll make a good ol' boy out of you yet," he said. "Don't you go nowheres; I'll be right back." I nodded, afraid of the harelip sounds and the slobbery mess that might emerge from my swollen lower lip if I spoke. Waylon gave me a final appraisal and felt moved to offer a final word of advice. "Just blend in."

With that, he threaded his way through the crowd, moving with surprising grace. On the opposite side of the ring, he bent to confer with a wizened bantam rooster of a man whose creased face resembled distressed leather. The man reached into a pocket and pulled out a thick roll of bills; he peeled off one and handed it to Waylon. Waylon leaned down and spoke urgently, but the man shook his head stoically.

Just then another pair of handlers stepped into the pit, accompanied by a new referee. The handlers had numbers on their backs, I noticed; these two were numbered 29 and 57. If the entrants' numbers started with one and ran sequentially, this cockfight was blood sport on a scale worthy of ancient Rome. And if the betting that was cranking up again for this match was typical—dozens of bets of twenty dollars, a handful more at forty and fifty and a hundred, even one at a thousand—some serious money was changing hands here. Was it possible that the sheriff himself didn't know this was going on? Or—and this seemed more plausible—were Tom Kitchings and his deputies all being paid to look the other way?

In the pit, the new pair of handlers was beginning the warm-up dance. Anxious to avoid witnessing another death match, I turned away and edged toward the side wall. My mouth was filling with saliva; I didn't have anything to spit into, so I swallowed, and nearly gagged. My head was beginning to hum just a bit, which surprised me, as I hadn't had the tobacco in my mouth more than a minute.

A handful of men parted as I drew closer to the wall, and I saw what they were gathered around. Inside a smaller, square pit, a battered and blood-smeared white bird—one eye gone and a wing dragging in the dirt—crawled in circles, trying to escape a rooster that remained largely undamaged, with the exception of a mangled left leg. The upright bird hopped gamely after his adversary, but he hadn't quite figured out how to leap, strike, and recover with just the one good leg, so he was reduced to pecking at his foe's remaining eye and tugging at the tatters of comb. Each time he got a beakful of comb, he would yank himself off-balance, falling onto the downed rooster. This spectacle, though less bloody than the knife fight I had witnessed in the main pit, seemed worse, somehow, for the prolonged suffering. I was appalled, but I found myself hypnotized, unable to turn away. I watched the handlers part the birds three times, stroking and breathing them back to life each time, restoring them from a glassy-eyed stupor to a brief resurgence of life and rage. Finally, on the fourth try, the hopping cock got it right: the long, curved spike on his good leg sank deep into the belly of the white bird, which squawked feebly and then flopped lifeless. "She-it," spat his handler, reaching down to hoist the dead bird by the splayed wing and then tossing him into a trash barrel beside me. The other handler leaned down, too, seized the victor by the head, and gave his bird a brisk, neck-snapping spin before heaving it, too, into the trash barrel. It caught the rim, hung there briefly, then plopped onto the cock it had killed only moments before.

Suddenly the shed began to spin in a blur of nicotine and nausea, blood and feathers and feed caps. Something in the Copenhagen or the carnage was conspiring with my Ménière's disease to bring on the mother of all vertigo attacks. Staggering back against the metal wall, I grabbed for the closest support I could find: the rim of the trash barrel, half-filled with dead roosters. Bracing myself on my forearms, I leaned down, my face inches above the barrel's rim. Just as I felt myself spinning down into darkness, I began to vomit. Half-conscious, I kept on vomiting long after my stomach was empty, long past the point where the violent heaves produced only trickles of tears from my eyes and commingled strings of bile and snot and tobacco juice from my nose and mouth. "Just blend in," I reminded myself absurdly, and with that parting thought, I felt my brain fade to black as my body tipped forward, headfirst, toward the mound of lifeless roosters.

19

I FOUND MYSELF RIDING IN Waylon's truck. I had been vaguely aware of the big man carrying me through the cockfight shed, parting the crowd like Moses at the Red Sea. Cap-topped faces, gap-toothed and disgusted, had loomed into my field of view, then swiftly disappeared into a fog of nausea and semiconsciousness. Some indeterminate time later, I felt the rumble of pavement beneath wheels. Occasionally I would rouse myself enough to retch; at those moments, a plastic dog bowl materialized beneath my chin, attached to a mammoth paw that I realized must be Waylon's hand. "Sorry," I would murmur. "Thank you. I'm sorry." Then I would slump back into oblivion in my posh captain's chair.

Eventually the fog began to lift. I sat up, looked out the window, and saw that we were now parked at the Pilot station at the interstate exit, right beside my truck. For the first time in what must have been hours, I felt hopeful about the prospects for a return to civilization and good health. Moving slowly and carefully, I opened the door to clamber out of the cab, then turned to ask a question that had been gnawing at me ever since my head started spinning back at the cockfight. "What's *in* that stuff, Waylon? I thought Copenhagen was just tobacco, but something in there hit me like a freight train."

Waylon held up a finger to pause the conversation, then got out of the truck and came around to my side. Reaching up with his tree-trunk arms, he lifted me down like a child, and began walking me around the parking lot. "Dip is just tobacco, Doc, but they pump up the nicotine somehow; I don't know how. You don't hear much about it, but nicotine packs a pretty good wallop, you get enough of it. A lipful of dip is worth ten unfiltered Camels. It'll knock you on your ass if you ain't used to it. Hell, I knowed that; I shoulda thought about it before waving that tin under your nose."

I shook my head. "I'm a big boy, Waylon. Didn't have to take it." The walking was helping, but I still felt woozy. "When I was a kid, my granddaddy used to smoke a pipe. Prince Albert. Never liked cigarette smoke, but I loved the smell of Granddaddy's pipe. Whenever he came to visit, I would beg for a puff on his pipe. He'd always say, 'No, it'll make you sick,' but I'd plead and whine and wear him down. Sure enough, I'd get sick every time. But nothing like this, man. I'm amazed this stuff is legal."

"Wouldn't matter if it wasn't. People get hooked on it, they'll get ahold of it anyhow. Just like moonshine or weed or chicken fights. Scary thing is, I see kids ten or twelve year old already doing a can a day. Gonna be losing their lips and tongues time they's forty." He scratched his chin. "I got me a late start, and I'm what you might call moderate. Figure my mouth won't fall off till about sixty-five."

The image almost pushed me over the edge again. I concentrated hard on another question that had been nagging at me. "Waylon, that first day you took me up to meet Jim— how come Leon Williams, the sheriff's deputy, helped you shanghai me?"

Waylon rubbed his chin, and I heard a sound like coarse sandpaper rubbing on rocks. "You want the short answer or the long 'un?"

"Give me the long 'un, if you don't care to."

"First I'll give you the short 'un: bullshit walks, money talks. Deputy sheriffs in Cooke County don't make too much. Leon's probably pulling down about twenty thou a year, which ain't what it used to be. So he's open to a little extry income, if the deal ain't gonna get him thowed in jail hisself."

"So how much extra income did he get for handing me over to you the other day?"

"Hell, you was pretty cheap, Doc. Couple hunnerd, I think."

"That *is* cheap. Should I be insulted?"

"Naw, that weren't about what you was worth; that was about how bush-league Leon is. If Orbin had-a been carrying you 'stead of Leon, he woulda charged ten times that much."

I wasn't sure whether that made me feel better or worse. "What's the rest of the answer?"

"Well, they's some history between Leon's people, the sheriff's people, and Big Jim. Some of it goes way back—some bad blood about fifty, sixty years ago between the Williamses and the Kitchingses."

"I might've heard something about that. Leon's grandfather dying in a shootout or a fire at the jail. Is that the thing?"

"Right. He'd been arrested by Tom's granddaddy, who was the sheriff way back then." Williams hadn't told me that piece of the story. "So if Leon gets a chance to thumb his nose at a Kitchings behind his back, he's probably gonna do it. Nothing big; he's just disrespectin' Tom to feel better about his own self and his people."

"And where does Big Jim fit into all that?"

"Well, he's got a little history with the Kitchingses, too. He ain't never quite forgive 'em for standing between him and that girl. And they ain't never quite forgive him, either, for I don't know *what*—maybe just for bein' a better man than what they are. Sometimes a real good person just rubs you the wrong way, you know?" I nodded; I did know. "Well, Jim—I think he's that person for the Kitchingses."

By now my head had cleared, and my stomach and I seemed to have reached an uneasy truce. I checked my watch; I had been unconscious or asleep for three hours in the truck as the big man kept vigil over me. The afternoon was waning, and my trip to the cave would have to wait. I thanked Waylon for watching out for me, said good-bye, and pulled onto I-40, heading into a blood-red sunset that kept me in mind of fighting cocks and feuding clans all the way back to Knoxville.

When I got home, I showered and fell into bed. Before drifting off, though, I made up my mind, and dialed the phone number I'd pulled from my Rolodex the day Tom Kitchings pulled a gun on me.

20

THE JOHN J. DUNCAN FEDERAL Building is a cube of pink granite and black glass in downtown Knoxville, occupying a unique nexus in the city's geometry of history, power, and knowledge. On one side it faces the old Tennessee Supreme Court building; on another side it flanks the *new* Tennessee Supreme Court building (which, for its part, now occupies the *old* post office . . .). One corner of the cube backs up to the main public library; the opposite corner has been rounded off to form an entrance, at the corner where the two Supreme Court buildings approach one another. Inside its gleaming granite and glass, the Duncan Building houses three federal agencies that strike fear into the heart of East Tennessee's assassins, mobsters, and deadbeats: the FBI, the Secret Service, and the Internal Revenue Service.

Steve Morgan, an agent with the Tennessee Bureau of Investigation, met me at the building's entrance and gave me a crushing handshake. Steve was one of my former students. He had majored in criminal justice, but he took enough anthropology to acquire a solid grasp of the human skeleton and the basic techniques of forensic anthropology. He landed a job with the TBI straight out of undergraduate school. "Thanks for helping," I said as he held the door for me. "Sorry to call you at home on a Sunday night."

"No problem," he said. "Glad you did." As he led me toward the security checkpoint just inside the main lobby, I noticed a pair of handcuffs on the back of his waist, and I couldn't help smiling at a memory from Steve's student days. One of my favorite teaching techniques in Osteology 480—my upper-level bone course—was to place a few bones inside a "black box." The box was designed to allow students to reach in and touch the bones, but not to see them. The idea was that it's important to know the bones not just by sight, but quite literally by feel. I still remember the class one April morning—April 1, 1994—when Steve somehow managed to rig a pair of handcuffs inside my black box. The first student to reach inside—an attractive coed to whom Steve had handed the box with mock gallantry—was instantly manacled. To get her out, we had to unscrew the corners of the wooden box. As he was unlocking the cuffs, Steve asked her out on a date; two years later, they got married. I catch up on them—they have three stair-step kids by now—every year or so, whenever I run into Steve in a courtroom or at a crime scene. I have a sneaking suspicion that my Osteology class wasn't the only time handcuffs have figured in their relationship, but I'm afraid to ask. I'm afraid he might actually tell me.

I had brought along my TBI consultant's badge—I'd had one for years, ever since the agency's director issued it to me in exchange for free scientific work—and I asked Steve if I should show it to the guard at the checkpoint. "Only if it makes you feel good," he said. I noticed that Steve wasn't wearing his shield clipped to his belt, as he normally did; instead, clipped to his shirt, he wore a laminated plastic tag with his photo and name. "The feds aren't impressed by TBI credentials—in fact, I think the security guard actually laughed the one time I showed him mine." After unloading my pockets and making it through the metal detector, I handed the guard my driver's license, which he scrutinized for a long time, checking me closely against my photo. Then, once he was satisfied that I was indeed the person that both the TBI agent and I claimed I was, he waved me on. Steve led me to an elevator.

"So why are we meeting in the federal building?" I asked once the doors had closed on the two of us. "Last time I checked, the TBI office was over on the north side of town."

"It is. But we're not the only ones interested in this." He didn't seem inclined to elaborate, so I didn't press him.

The elevator doors opened on the sixth floor, opposite a big FBI logo. Steve led me to a receptionist sitting behind bulletproof glass, like a convenience store clerk in a bad neighborhood. She slid a form through a small slot at the bottom of the glass, and once I'd signed in, she buzzed us into a mazelike warren of offices that claimed the entire floor. After several turns in either direction, we entered a conference room occupied by half a dozen or so state and federal law enforcement types—I could tell by the dark suits, serious ties, and conservative haircuts. They were seated around an oak table worthy of King Arthur. Steve introduced them quickly; I'd met one of the FBI agents, Cole Billings, on a forensic case a few years before, but I didn't know the other Bureau man and woman, nor the DEA guy, nor the second TBI agent, as best I could recall, though that one—Brian Rankin—looked vaguely familiar. Clearly I'd been invited to a breakfast of champions. The League of Justice.

The female FBI agent—Special Agent Angela Price—seemed to be running the show. "Dr. Brockton, first of all, let me express our appreciation for your time today. Second, I need to stress that everything discussed in this room today stays in this room. That probably goes without saying"—I gave a nod—"but I'm saying it anyway." I nodded again, just to be sure I was on record as a good listener and cooperative fellow.

"It's been awhile since I worked with an interagency task force," I said. "Last time was probably fifteen years ago, with Agent Billings here—the Fat Sam kidnapping and murder case." Billings smiled at the memory of the bumbling counterfeiter, who'd been bilked by a slicker counterfeiter and had turned ineptly vengeful.

Price frowned, shook her head slightly, and held up a finger. "This is not a task force, Dr. Brockton, simply an informal joint investigation. Depending on what we turn up, we could ratchet this up to a task force, but that would require a lot more predication—evidence of wrongdoing—and a lot more paperwork. For now, we're just trying to get a handle on what's going on up in Cooke County."

Price recapped some relevant Cooke County history. Back in the early 1980s, a joint FBI–TBI task force—the full-fledged version—spent two years investigating corruption in Tennessee sheriffs' departments. They found a lot of it: more than one-quarter of the state's sheriffs were indicted and sent to prison. It had been an embarrassing time for Tennessee's sheriffs' departments in general, and for Cooke County's in particular: the sheriff at the time had been caught running both a brothel and a cocaine-trafficking ring (complete with its own private airstrip). He ended up getting a fifteen-year sentence in federal prison.

Price finished her history lecture. "That was twenty years ago—a long time between housecleanings. Not surprisingly, the dirt seems to be building up again."

"I'm shocked, shocked," I said with mock indignation.

She ignored the joke. "We've been monitoring some things in Cooke County that seem to point to an increase in a whole host of illegal activities," she said. "As you may know, the Marijuana Eradication Task Force and the Tennessee Highway Patrol work together on surveillance flights to detect pot cultivation. There seems to be a substantial increase in cultivation in Cooke County over the past two years, an increase that's not been matched in any other counties in the state. We have additional information suggesting a rise in harder drug trafficking, gambling, and prostitution."

"Sounds like one-stop shopping for all your vice needs," I said. The familiar-looking TBI agent grinned slightly, and suddenly I realized why he looked familiar. I'd never *met* him before, but I'd *seen* him before: twenty-four hours earlier, at the cockfight in Cooke County. What had Waylon called him? Rooster, that was it. I recalled my conversation with Art about the perils of being unable to tell the good guys from the bad guys. My palms began to sweat and my mouth went dry as cotton.

Price was still talking; I willed myself to concentrate on her words, though I was still staring at Rankin. "When Agent Morgan said you'd called him to express concerns about the conduct of the sheriff's department in the homicide case you're working, it occurred to us that you might be able to shed some indirect light on whether there's official protection or involvement in any of these various criminal enterprises."

Rankin's eyes were locked on me like laser beams. I opened my mouth to speak, but seemed unable to get any words out. My brain was reeling with possibilities. What if the official corruption wasn't limited to the sheriff's department? What if it extended into the TBI—indeed, even into this very task force? Clearly I was in way over my head. "I . . . I . . ." I licked my parched lips with a thick, pasty-feeling tongue.

Rankin cocked his head. "Doc, you look a little dry in the mouth there. Can I get you some water?" I nodded my head nervously. "Or maybe you'd prefer a little dab of this?" He slid something that looked like a hockey puck across the oak table toward me. I caught it, picked it up, and turned it over in my hand. It was a can of Copenhagen. My stomach began to churn. "Go on, buddy, give 'er a try," Rankin intoned, in the thick, good-old-boy accent he'd used at the cockfight. "It'll perk you right up. You look like you could use some perkin' up." As he finished quoting himself, he grinned broadly and winked at me.

Bewildered, I scanned the other faces in the room. The other agents seemed to be studying their notepads intently, but I thought I detected some twitching mouths and twinkling eyes. Suddenly Cole Billings choked back a snort, and it hit me: these guys—these straightlaced, straight-arrow, suit-and-tie agents—were teasing me. At first I felt a wave of indignation, but it was quickly replaced by a profound sense of relief. Rankin must have been working the cockfight undercover; hell, he'd probably even been wearing a wire, making it conceivable—likely, even—that all these agents had heard the audio of my retching into the barrel. As I pictured that, I couldn't help but yield to the absurdity of it myself. Sliding the can of tobacco back to Rankin, I drawled, "Hell-far, Rooster, I done give up on dip, but if you'uns got any shine, I wouldn't care to take me a swig or two."

The League of Justice erupted in laughter. As soon as I could make myself heard, I added, "Okay, you've got me dead to rights—I broke the law. I'll talk. Just promise you'll go easy on me." Several of the agents were wiping their eyes. I decided maybe it was time to switch gears. "Seriously, tell me how I can help you," I said to Price. "Then maybe we can figure out if you all can help me, too."

"With the recent rise in cultivation, Cooke County now leads the state in marijuana production," she began, as briskly as if she were launching a PowerPoint talk. "In addition, there's an alarming rise in methamphetamine labs in basements and trailers up there. We have it from a well-placed source that the sheriff's office is shielding drug traffickers, possibly even extorting protection money from them. If that's true, we can prosecute that as racketeering." I nodded, remembering a case in which the Justice Department had once categorized the Chicago Police Department as "a criminal enterprise." My ears pricked up when Price added, "We've also heard—not just from your phone call to Agent Morgan—that in the homicide case you're working, the sheriff might be guilty of obstruction of justice, conspiracy, possibly even murder. What are your thoughts on that?"

"Well, let me back up a ways." I briefed the group on my involvement in the case, starting with the recovery of the body from the cave. When I described being shanghaied by Jim O'Conner, I was interrupted by a flurry of questions about the man; I gathered that O'Conner had managed to fly beneath their radar up to now. His secret road and kudzu tunnel seemed to excite them most. Did I see other vehicles? Any tracks from heavy trucks? Signs of marijuana cultivation, processing, or distribution? Containers or odors that might suggest methamphetamine production?

I answered "no" to all of those questions. "This guy is interesting, and unusual," I said, "and he admits he's had some illegal business ventures in the past. But he was a war hero, and I don't think he's a killer." The war hero status seemed to carry some weight. "The sheriff wants to charge him with the murder," I conceded, "but then again, the sheriff has an old ax—a family feud sort of ax—to grind with O'Conner, so it's possible that's clouding his judgment."

I finally circled back to Price's question about the sheriff. "Sheriff Kitchings certainly seems to know more about this case than he's letting on," I said. "He hedged and stalled and even lied outright when I asked what he knew about missing females. When I finally confronted him about the victim's identity and his family's connection, he pointed a rifle at me. If wishes were bullets, I might not be here today." Several questions about the armed confrontation ensued, which I answered as matter-of-factly as I could. "I don't know whether he's intentionally obstructing justice," I went on, "or whether he's just behind the curve and reacting badly to the discovery that his family might have some involvement. That's why I'm here today. I'd like to know what the TBI and the FBI can do to find out whether he's guilty of more than confusion and a hair-trigger temper."

She glanced at the other federal agents. "Unfortunately, Dr. Brockton, I'm not sure the FBI can get involved in that case, although we certainly have an interest in it."

"Why not," I asked, "if he's obstructing a murder investigation? Isn't that a federal crime?"

She shook her head. "Not necessarily. You have to look at the original, underlying crime—in this case, homicide. That's a state crime, so it would be a matter for the local prosecutor or the TBI."

"I've got no problem with the TBI handling it. After all, it was Steve that I called in the first place." I turned to Morgan. "Who's the TBI got up in Cooke County these days besides Brian 'Rooster' Rankin here? Anybody I know?"

Steve shifted uncomfortably in his seat. "We're kinda in between right now. We just pulled the guy who'd been up there for years. We weren't sure he was quite as . . . *vigilant* as he ought to be. Haven't assigned anybody new yet. We wanted to focus on the undercover angle for awhile first."

That was disappointing news. "Well, you ought to have one hell of an animal cruelty case. Gambling, too. What additional evidence would you need to charge the sheriff with obstruction?"

He winced. "That could be difficult, Doc. Although we could gather evidence, any criminal charges would need to be filed by the Cooke County DA or—more likely—by a grand jury. Taking it to a grand jury covers his ass, if there's any fallout either way. Unfortunately, a Cooke County grand jury—the folks who elected Tom Kitchings by a landslide, you may recall—probably wouldn't indict him. If they did, and the case went to a jury trial, he'd have a pretty good

chance of being acquitted. Kitchings is a very popular sheriff up there."

I stared at him. "So you're saying that even if he's
guilty—even if you *know* he's guilty—the TBI might look
the other way?"

Steve squirmed in his seat like a student who didn't know
the right answer. "Thing is, Doc, in cases like this, you get
one shot. If you don't win—if a grand jury votes not to indict, or if you lose the case at trial—that makes the sheriff
much more powerful. He becomes virtually untouchable at
that point, and he knows it. So then you're really screwed."

This was not going at all the way I'd hoped. "So what am I
supposed to do, then? Just shrug my shoulders and figure that's
the way things work in Cooke County?" I looked from one
face to another, but no one at the table would meet my gaze.

Finally Price spoke up. "No, Doctor, you're supposed to
do your job to the best of your ability, and trust us to do ours
to the best of our abilities. Believe me, we don't like to see
public officials break the law any more than you do. But we
have to work within congressional statutes and FBI protocols. Sometimes those feel like impediments. But they're
part of the American justice system, which beats the hell out
of any other system I know of."

It appeared I'd overstepped. "I didn't mean to imply—"

She cut me off with a wave of her hand. "Not necessary,
Doctor. We understand your frustration—we share it, in
fact—and we do appreciate your help. Please keep your eyes
and ears open; tell us about any illegal or suspicious activities
you observe. As I say, our hands might be tied on the homicide case, but you never know—we might learn something
that would give us some leverage with another witness, somebody who *could* corroborate federal offenses." I nodded.

Price glanced at her watch. "Anything else?" I shook my
head. "Well, we don't need to take up any more of your time,
Dr. Brockton; I'm sure you're busy." I was, but not too busy

to notice that I was being dismissed. "Do let us know if something else crops up."

"Sure," I said. "Although I can't imagine what more could crop up at this point."

"You'd be surprised," she said, and gave a quick nod to Steve Morgan.

"I'll run you back downstairs," said Steve, hastily rising from his seat at the Round Table.

On the way back down, we made awkward small talk: Ashley, his oldest, was starting ballet lessons; Justin, the middle child, played T-ball last summer and was a solid hitter but not much of a fielder; Christian, the toddler, fell off the porch and blackened both eyes, earning Steve and his wife suspicious stares from strangers for a couple of weeks, until the shiners faded. We shook hands in the lobby and I said good-bye to the security guard, who gave me a reluctant tip of the head. As I reached the main door, I consulted my watch, then turned back to check the time on the wall clock above the elevator. Both read five minutes to ten. And, as I'd suspected, Steve Morgan had not moved from the spot where I'd left him.

I fiddled with my watch briefly, waved good-bye to Steve, and walked out into the crisp fall air. I went as far as the next corner—out of the line of Steve's sight—then crossed the street and ducked into the old Supreme Court parking lot, which was bordered by a hedgerow sparse enough for me to see through without being seen from the entrance of the federal building.

At one minute to ten, a man sauntered up to the granite cube, and Steve Morgan stepped out to greet him. Agent Price's last words had been prophetic: I was surprised; shocked, even. The man who went inside the federal building with Steve was a Cooke County deputy sheriff: my old pal Leon Williams.

21

"WHAT, NOW I'M SUPPOSED to be psychic? I don't know what it means," said Art, taking a sip of sweet tea between bites of his sandwich. He had answered my panic-stricken call from outside the federal building and agreed to meet me for lunch at Calhoun's On the River, which boasted the best barbecue in town.

"Even if you don't know, you can at least help me think through the possibilities," I insisted.

"Okay, you tell me what you think the possibilities are," he said, "and I'll give you my considered opinion."

"Scenario A," I began.

He interrupted. "We've moved from possibilities to scenarios already?"

I glowered. "Scenario A: Williams contacted the feds because he knows the sheriff is protecting the cockfights and the gambling and the drug trafficking, like Price said." Art chewed his pulled pork thoughtfully. "B: Williams contacted them because he thinks the sheriff's hiding something or protecting someone in the murder case." Art ruminated some more. "C: The feds hauled Williams in because they think he's involved in something illegal, and they're leaning on him to cooperate." Art stroked his chin slowly. I tried to wait him out, but couldn't. "So which is it?"

"Could you run those scenarios past me one more time?" He took another bite.

"Come on, Art, this is worrying me."

"Well, I'm not sure I buy A or B," he said, his mouth still full. "The fact that Williams may have helped Waylon shanghai you that day makes me wonder who the deputy is really working for. C is possible, I suppose, though I'm not sure the feds would risk hauling a cooperating witness all the way to Knoxville—how's he gonna explain being gone half a day? There's also D and E to consider, too."

"D and E? What are those?" I asked.

"D: Williams thinks *you're* obstructing justice, and he's there to squeal on you."

"*Me*? How could I possibly be obstructing justice?"

"By protecting Jim O'Conner."

"What? I'm not protecting Jim O'Conner. I'm just point-ing out some things that suggest his innocence. Things they don't want to see, maybe because they've got a grudge against him, or because he's just a handy scapegoat. Protect-ing O'Conner? I can't believe you'd say that."

"Hey, don't get your drawers in a wad," Art said. "*I'm* not the one ratting you out."

"You really think that's what Williams is telling them?"

"No, not really. Just trying not to overlook any possibili-ties."

"Great. Thanks a heap. And E? I can't wait to hear E."

"E is 'none of the above.' Maybe Williams is working some angle of his own that we haven't even thought of yet. Maybe he wants to be sheriff himself, figures he'd have a lot easier time getting elected with Kitchings behind bars. All I'm really saying is, we have absolutely no way to know what he's telling them, or why. So you need to keep doing exactly what you've been doing: learn all you can, tell the truth, watch your back. And trust no one."

"Including you?"

"Well, that's how most cases start out," I said. "That's why we need sheriffs and detectives and forensic scientists."

"Aw, hell, that ain't what I mean. I'm talkin' 'bout the misery of hisery. I mean, mystery of history. Family history. I b'lieved for thirty years that Leena run off. Been told that for thirty years. Somewheres; nobody knew where. We didn't talk about it—it was one of them things you just knew you wasn't s'posed to talk about." He paused, and I heard a swish and a swallow. "You got family, Doc?"

I said that I had a son—a die-hard UT fan, and a big admirer of Kitchings's college career—and that my wife had died two years ago.

"Goddamn, Doc, I'm sorry to hear that. Real sorry."

"Thanks. I still miss her. A lot. Not much to do but carry on." A pause. "You ever been married, Sheriff?"

"Naw. Engaged once, back when I was a big football star. She was a cheerleader and a sorority girl. Memphis debutante, too. Heady stuff for a redneck from Cooke County. She busted up with me right after I busted up my knee. Thing is, she kinda spoilt me for these Cooke County girls, you know what I mean?" That was a shame, I said; life gets mighty lonely without a wife. He seemed to mull that over for a while. When he spoke again, I wasn't sure whether he was still thinking about love or was broaching a new subject. "People in Cooke County don't have a lot, Doc," he said. "A few of us got halfway decent jobs, but most folks up here live hand to mouth most of the time. Hell, the Kitchings clan been living hand to mouth near as long as I can remember. Maybe that's why family's so important to us. Even when your back's to the wall—'specially when your back's to the wall—your family'll stick by you. Thick or thin."

"Right or wrong?"

"Right or wrong. That's the code. They's your blood."

I thought about that. Would my son, Jeff, stick by me, right or wrong? What if I disgraced him—what if I were fired for misconduct with an underage female student? Would Jeff, my blood, follow the code? What about Art, my closest friend? He'd certainly stuck his neck out for me today. Would I do the same for him, if push came to shove?

"Must be nice to know you can count on that."

"Mostly." He paused. "Not always."

"I can see how it might complicate things for a sheriff sometimes."

I heard another swallow, though it didn't seem to be preceded by the sound of a swig. "Ever'thing seems tangled up right now, Doc. See, Leena—she was family, too. She was blood, too. Seems like somebody needs to stick by her, if you know what I mean."

"Yes, it does. Her baby, too—seems like that baby could also use some good folks in its corner."

Liquid gurgled into the sheriff's mouth. "Doc, you ever raise your head and look around and wonder what happened?"

"How do you mean?"

"Wonder how the hell you ended up where you're at, dealing with the shit you're dealing with? 'Scuse me." I waited for him to continue. "This sure ain't what I pictured for myself, you know? Man, back when I was playin' ball, I had my ticket out of here. I was gonna shake the dust of Cooke County offa my cleats." Even from my brief time in his jurisdiction, I could imagine how thrilling that prospect must have seemed. "And then I got sent sprawling back home. Crawling back home." He exhaled loudly. "Hell of it is, I been trying to do a good job. Which ain't always easy to do up here. Lots easier to do a bad job, you know? Now, I ain't even sure what a good job is anymore."

"Well, don't give up. Maybe it'll get clearer before long. Like your coach used to tell you, look for daylight and run like hell."

"Did he say that?" He pondered. "Daylight. Yeah. Maybe." He drew another long breath, like he was winding up to something. "Doc, I trust you, and that's more'n I can say 'bout a lot of people. I was outta line when I tried to shoot you, and I 'pologize."

"Thanks."

"You just do the best damn job you can, you hear?"

"I will. You too, Sheriff."

"Awright. We'll see you, Doc. You better get some sleep."

Amazingly, I did.

23

MIRANDA WAS LAYING THE last of Billy Ray Ledbetter's ribs on a tray when I walked into the bone lab. The torso had simmered for a day and a half in our biggest kettle, a steam-jacketed vat nearly the size of a frontier-era bathtub. The kettle wasn't the only thing simmering, judging by Miranda's face. She looked away when she saw me. *Keep things light and breezy,* I told myself. "Anything interesting?"

She flushed. "I'll let you decide for yourself." She shoved the tray along the counter in my direction and headed for the door. So much for light and breezy.

"Miranda, wait." She paused, her hand on the knob. "Please. Come talk to me about this."

"You don't need me to tell you anything about this. You don't need a pathologist, either. Hell, an undergraduate—a goddamn *undergraduate*—could tell you the story on these ribs."

She wasn't making it easy. "I don't mean what's wrong with the ribs. I mean what's wrong with you and me."

She turned. "You and me? There is no 'you and me,' Dr. Brockton." She turned the knob and cracked the door.

"Miranda, wait. Look, I made a mistake. I'm sorry I did, and I'm sorry you saw me make it."

"Yeah. Me, too." She shoved the door open furiously. It banged against the doorstop outside and careened back into her, catching her on the forearm. She yelled in pain. "Ow, shit! Oh, goddamn! Oh, son of a bitch. Oh, oh, oh!" I started toward her, but she saw me coming and shouldered on through the door to get away. The heavy steel door slammed shut behind her.

Yeah, Einstein, that went well, I sneered at myself. What a screwup. I plopped onto an ancient stool and laid my forehead on the counter. Closing my eyes, I took three deep breaths and tried to calm my mind by focusing on the sounds around me instead of the turmoil inside. Somewhere in the bowels of the structure, the ventilation system thrummed. Outside, beyond the maze of girders and concrete pilings, a weed-eater buzzed relentlessly, then gave a strangled cry and died. Moments later, the ventilation system fell silent, too. In the sudden quiet, all I heard was a deep groaning, the sound of an animal in pain. I looked out the lab's wall of windows for the source of the sound.

Miranda sat crumpled on the concrete steps outside the stadium, her purse and backpack a few steps below her. Hunching over, she clutched her right arm to her chest, sobbing from somewhere deep inside. I hurried outside. As I got close, I noticed that the ulna—the forearm bone that runs from the elbow to the wrist—had a lumpy kink that hadn't been there sixty seconds earlier. The bone was broken; things just kept getting worse.

"Miranda, you're hurt. Let me take a look at that." I laid a hand on her shoulder.

She shook it off. "Don't touch me. Just leave me alone."

"No. Until I get you to a doctor, I'm not leaving you alone."

"Look, I'm a big girl, okay? You don't have to take care of me. Besides, I wouldn't want to make you late for your next babysitting session."

"Miranda, I made a mistake. I've never done that before, and I'll never do it again. I'm sorry, but I'm only human."

"But . . . why *her?*" And she began to sob anew.

Jess was right. I had been blind and careless. "Oh, Miranda. Listen to me. You've already got the best of me, don't you understand? If we tried to have more, we'd end up with nothing."

She raised her head and stared at me with anguished eyes. "You don't know that. Why do you say that?"

"Miranda, I love working with you. It's my favorite part of my job, and my job is the only bearable part of my life these days. When we're in the lab together, I don't feel thirty years older than you. I feel young and smart, and connected to a person I like and admire enormously. But if we were together in a different way—in a relationship, in a bed—our thirty years' difference would hit us like a ton of bricks. Sooner or later you'd feel sorry for me, and then you'd feel trapped by me, and then you'd start to despise me. And that would kill me. It would absolutely kill me."

Something in her face softened a bit. "Oh, bullshit, how could I ever despise you? I worship the damn ground you walk on."

"Not so much. Not lately."

"Don't be stupid. Of course I do. I'm just . . . so . . . *furious* at you for messing around with . . . with some *child!*"

"Temporary insanity. Point taken. A never-to-be-repeated mistake. She is, after all, a whole five years younger than you. But just for the record, in the eyes of the law, I believe she's an adult." A low growl emanated from Miranda's throat, which I took to be a good sign—too much feistiness in it for a suicide candidate. "She's smart, too, for an undergraduate." The growl ratcheted up a few decibels. "And fairly easy on the eyes . . ." An elbow—her left elbow—shot out and caught me in the ribs. "Ow. Not as smart or fetching as you, of course, but then again, who is?"

"Damn you, why can't you just let me stay mad?"

"Well, judging by that arm, it's not so good for your health."

"Oh, that. I did that on purpose. So I could file a worker's comp claim. I'm tired of being your defleshing slave."

"You're saying you needed . . . a break?" She groaned at the pun. "By the way, if you really want to sound professional, you should use the German term, *diener*." She rolled her eyes. "Come on, let's get you over to Student Health and get that ulna set."

"Okay. No, wait. First I want to show you something on these ribs." I helped her up from the steps, picked up her things, and held the door for her, seeing as she was wounded and all. Back in the lab, she made a beeline for the tray of bones and picked up a rib with her left hand. "Look at this," she said, pointing with her right index finger. "Yow!" She laid the curved, ivory-colored bone down on the counter and pointed with her left hand. It was easy to see what she was excited about.

The bone—rib seven or eight, I guessed from the size— was a comma-shaped arc roughly ten inches long. Its curve was asymmetrical, though that wasn't the odd part: ribs arc sharply near the spine, but the curve flattens out near the sternum. There's a slight sideways warp to the curve, too, which keeps the bones from lying flat on a desk or examination table. With all those compound curves, students sometimes have trouble telling which way is up on an individual rib, until they learn to look at its cross-section. In cross-section, the rib is shaped like an upside-down teardrop; in other words, the rounded part is the top surface. The lower, more pointed edge is a bit lopsided—it's actually slightly concave on its inner surface, to make room for the artery, vein, and nerve that nestle beneath each rib. The architecture and engineering of the human body never cease to amaze me.

What had gotten Miranda excited enough to ignore her throbbing arm was a region about midway along the shaft of the rib. A ring of thicker material, maybe half an inch wide and an eighth-inch thick at its midline, encircled the rib. Several other ribs in the tray had similar features. "Recently broken," she said proudly. "But already healing. Definitely not perimortem."

She was right; it couldn't have been broken at the time of death. "Got a guess on how long before death?"

She swung the lamp with the built-in magnifier down over the bone and switched on the doughnut-shaped light. "Well, the hematoma at the break would have turned into this healing callus within a week to ten days, so I'd say the fracture occurred at least a couple of weeks prior to death. But the callus is still more cartilaginous than bony, so it's got a ways to go yet. Just a guess—I'd need to search the literature to pin it down—but I'd say this break was two or three weeks antemortem."

"Would you say it's consistent with injuries sustained in a barroom brawl eighteen days before death?"

She swiveled her head to look at me. "Well, *yeah*. Would you say our friend *participated* in a barroom brawl eighteen days before he died?"

"Got the shit kicked out of him, according to the defendant, who also came out a little the worse for wear. Happened in one of those windowless cinder-block beer joints in Morgan County that practically shout, 'Enter and die!' Couple other locals corroborate the story. Apparently Mr. Ledbetter here got stomped by some bad hombres wearing combat boots."

She laid down the first rib and picked up another. "Here's the really interesting one. See the callus? Not a nice, neat ring around the bone. I've never seen one shaped like this." Neither had I. The patch of new bone was long and irregular; instead of encircling a cross-section of rib, it extended for several inches in a lumpy, wavy path. "Weird, huh?" I nodded. "Must be a comminuted fracture, with multiple fragments," she went on. "But that's not all. Look at the distal end of the break. Something's missing."

I leaned closer to the lens. Sure enough, extending beyond one end of the healing callus was a gouged-out groove in the underlying bone. "I'll be damned," I said. "Looks like a piece splintered off."

Miranda nodded excitedly. "So where's the missing piece?"

"Maybe somewhere in the right lung," I said.

"Exactly what I was thinking," she grinned. "Let's go see."

"No. *I'll* go see," I said. "*You'll* go get your arm fixed."

She made a face, then brightened. "This is a great case!"

"Yeah. I'm mighty glad to have your help. Good work, Miranda. Thanks." I caught and held her eyes. They glistened and filled—damn, was she going to cry again?—and then she smiled and nodded briskly. *Thank you, God,* I thought, and nodded back.

I let her out at the service entrance to the health service. We were regulars there, what with our frequent trips for quick X-rays when we didn't want to drive clear across the river to the morgue. Miranda hipped the door of the truck shut and waved me on with her good arm.

I crossed the river—our own River Styx, one of my colleagues had once joked, but that made me death's boatman, and I wasn't sure I liked the label—then threaded behind the hospital and angled in beside the morgue's loading bay. Punching the combination code for the adjoining door, I hurried inside. My first stop was the X-ray room. I found Ledbetter's file and clipped his films to a light box. His ribs were a mess: six ribs on the right side were fractured, three of them in two or more places. The seventh rib—the last of the "true ribs," so-called because they joined the breastbone, while the "false ribs" below them did not—had one of the worst comminuted fractures I'd ever seen; it looked like one end had been fed through a KitchenAid garbage disposal before being patched back together with Bondo. I couldn't believe Dr. Hamilton's autopsy report had failed to mention the injuries—and I couldn't believe I'd neglected to check the X-rays weeks ago. I studied the multiple bone fragments, which were denser and paler on the negative than the healing callus, trying to determine if any of the pieces were so displaced as to have pierced the lung. It was hopeless: the ribs themselves could easily have blocked the camera's view of any wayward fragments, unless the fragments happened to align with the intercostal spaces. I'd have to revisit the corpse.

I swung open the heavy cooler door and switched on the light. Ledbetter's remains—what remained of them—were on a gurney in a far back corner, wedged behind two other bodies. One was an immense young white woman who filled the gurney's flat surface almost entirely, the dimpled flesh of her hips and thighs lapping up the rim around the table's perimeter and drooping over the edge. The other was her exact opposite, an ancient, scrawny black man.

Ledbetter's decapitated head lay on its right side, propped in place by folded-up paper pads. Three inches of neck still clung to the head; below that, a messy eighteen-inch swath of stainless steel gurney divided the neck from the pelvis and legs.

The bag of organs wasn't on the gurney.

I jockeyed the two other corpses out of the way and looked closer.

Up close, it still wasn't on the gurney. Or under the gurney. Or anywhere in the same room with the gurney.

Damn. I raced out of the cooler and down the hall, sticking my head in every door along the way. In one of the autopsy suites, a young pathology resident of indeterminate gender was bending low over a body, the gooseneck light pulled down close. When I barged in, the resident straightened abruptly, whacking the light. "Son of a bitch," moaned a strangled voice, still of indeterminate gender.

"Sorry," I called, beating a hasty retreat.

I made my way up the long hallway toward the front desk, a part of the morgue where I seldom ventured. The receptionist sat behind a bulletproof glass window. On the other side was a small waiting room, which was entered—generally by grieving family members, arriving for the grim task of identifying a son or daughter, sibling or spouse—from a corridor in the hospital's basement. The morgue was, by design, as far off the beaten track as possible. People had to work pretty hard to find it, and once they found it, things generally got a lot harder for them. Then there were the other people who might come in the front way—the ones the bulletproof glass had been put up to defend against: the pissed-off brother of a guy who'd been shot by a cop. The boyfriend in a love triangle, trying to make sure that the ME's autopsy wouldn't find a bullet from the wife's purse gun inside her dead hubby. Far as I knew, the glass had never been put to the test, but then again, its mere presence might have deterred some borderline crazies.

As I approached the desk from the morgue's inner recesses, I struggled to dredge up the name of the young woman perched there. She was the latest in a long line of short-lived receptionists. Short-tenured, anyway. Tiffany? Kimberly? Tamara? As I got closer, I decided I hadn't even met this one yet. That meant the last one had come and gone in less than a month.

"Good morning, young lady, I don't believe we've met," I said, extending my right hand to introduce myself. We both noticed my purple rubber glove at the same instant. "You really don't want to shake my hand right now. I'm Dr. Brockton."

She shook her head and sighed. "Hi, Dr. B., I'm Katie. We have met. Twice. You're looking better, by the way."

Okay, perhaps we had met after all. What was wrong with my memory, and what had been wrong with me last time she saw me? I didn't have the time or the heart to pursue either question. I asked if she'd seen the morgue tech I needed, hoping I wasn't too late. "Joey? I think he's doing a burn." *Not good*, I thought. I spun on my heel and sprinted down the corridor that led out one side of the morgue, where the medical waste incinerator was tucked into an out-of-the-way angle of the hospital complex.

Joey Weeks, the lowest-ranking morgue assistant, stood beside the incinerator's open hatch, a gurney parked beside him. I saw him toss a bag into the burner, then grab another off the cart. "Wait!" I yelled.

"Hey, Doc," he said as I skidded to a stop. "What's up?"

"Joey, I'm looking for some tissue that came from an exhumation a couple of days ago."

"Exhumation? Oh, you mean that one autopsied by Dr. Carter from Chattanooga? The guy that ain't got nothin' between the head and the waist? That's creepy, man."

"Yeah, that's the one. You know anything about that? There was a biohazard bag with some tissue in it with the body in the cooler."

"Sure. Dr. Hamilton told me it was waste. Said to incinerate it. Probably going up in smoke right now."

Hamilton? "Damn."

"Problem?"

"I was hoping to take one last look at something."

He motioned toward the cart. "Well, I got a few bags left here. Maybe it's not too late. Let's take a look. Do you know the number?"

I racked my brain. "It had two autopsy numbers on it—the original was from last year, but I don't remember what came after the 'A-2004.' But Dr. Carter added a number when she looked at it the other day, A-2005-125, maybe."

"Can't be too many with double numbers. If it's here, we'll find it."

We checked the cart. It wasn't there, and my heart sank. Then I noticed the bag still dangling from Joey's right hand. If I'd arrived a second later, it would have gone up in flames.

I bore the putrid organs before me with both hands, like the crown jewels on a velvet pillow. It wasn't so much a gesture of reverence as a stance of caution: the bag had been punctured and was dripping steadily. Entering the decomp lab, I laid my prize on a countertop and sliced open the top. The contents slithered and plopped out onto the absorbent surgical pad.

I fished out the remnants of the heart, stomach, and intestines first, then what I believed to be the liver, then various other organs that were more or less recognizable as themselves, or at least as something other than lung. That left a mound of lung tissue, which looked like a chocolate pudding gone terribly wrong in the making.

The most efficient way to do this was also the messiest. Picking up the nearest blob of tissue, I began to squeeze, squishing it through loosely clenched fingers. Nothing. I repeated the process with half a dozen other lungish-looking blobs. Still nothing. I scooped up the last of the blobs and gave it a hard, frustrated squeeze . . . and when I did, something sharp jabbed the heel of my hand. It was a shard of bone, an inch long, a quarter-inch wide, and tapering to a wicked point. It had nicked my glove; I hoped it hadn't also broken the skin. I rinsed it off, set it in a small pot to simmer, and then cleaned and disinfected my hands. The skin appeared unbroken, but I still gave it a pretty thorough marinade in Betadine.

Just as I was drying off, the door opened and in walked Miranda, sporting a bright orange fiberglass cast. She pirouetted, angling the cast in all directions. "UT orange," I said. "Very sporty."

"Thought it might get me a close-up on ESPN at the football game next weekend," she said. "Any luck with our friend here?"

"Yeah, barely. Pure, blind, last-second luck." I fished the bone fragment out of the pot with some tongs. She whistled appreciatively. "It wasn't a knife that punctured his lung and made him bleed to death—it was a piece of his own rib."

"And that happened eighteen days before he collapsed and died?"

"Assuming it splintered off during the stomping he took in that bar fight."

"So the guy you're helping . . ."

". . . was helping his pal fight off the gang who did this. Unfortunately, he just happened to be on hand when Billy Ray finally collapsed. I'm sure DeVriess won't have any trouble getting Dr. Carter to testify to that effect."

I thought I saw a frown when I mentioned Jess Carter, but I didn't pursue it. "You, Dr. Carter, and Grease," Miranda said. "Strange bedfellows."

"Very strange," I agreed. I couldn't help wondering if she meant more by "bedfellows" than just courtroom allies, but I let that slide, too. I wasn't touching that one with a ten-foot pole. A pole of any length, for that matter.

and brown, nestled deep in a matrix of mottled gray mortar. The building appeared to have been created by geologic action rather than human hands. The double doors set into the front were stout wood, silver with age; their black hardware was forged iron, the hammer blows still visible on its surface. A pair of metal license plates was nailed to the doors: "Jesus Is Coming R-U Ready?" asked one; the other read "Heaven or Hell—Where Will You Spend Eternity?"

"Friendly crowd," I observed. I tried the iron latch, but the door seemed to be bolted from the inside somehow.

"Behold, I stand at the door and knock," deadpanned Art, striking a Jesus pose. He rapped on the wood. "Ow! Looks like oak, feels like ironwood. Let's see what we can see through a window."

The windows were miserly—few, small, and high— minimizing the temptation, I supposed, to admire the trees instead of heeding the sermons. Luckily the stonework made it easy to climb the wall. Art and I hauled ourselves up a few feet and peered through a grimy pane. There wasn't much to see: a dozen backless benches, a scattering of ragged hymnals, a battered upright piano, and a lopsided wooden lectern. "Now I see why they call it 'primitive,'" I said. We clambered down and began circumnavigating the little building.

A wide, well-worn path ran alongside the church, then led to the base of the bluff out back. The pathway ended at a natural rock basin, waist-deep or so, filled with clear water. The surface rippled slightly in the center, where water from a fissure welled up continuously. At the back of the pool, the water gurgled over a lip in the basin and disappeared into an opening in the cliff. "Now I see why they call it 'Cave Springs,'" Art said. "Handy for baptisms, huh?"

"Very. Okay, your spelunking friend was right—hard to miss." The opening in the rock wall was an oval about eight feet high by four feet wide. A grate of rusting bars blocked the entrance, supported by iron hinges pounded into the rock; a stout padlock hung from the hasp. "Dang," I said. "Now what?"

"Pray," said Art as he moved to study the lock. I heard a jangling of keys, then the click of a lock popping open.

"Hey, how'd you do that?"

"God provides," he intoned, looking heavenward as he slipped a master key back among its fellows and dropped the key ring into his pocket.

We made a quick trip back to the truck for flashlights, jackets, Art's headlamp and evidence kit, and my camera, then returned to the opening. Despite the rust on the grate, the hinges turned easily and silently. I noticed a liberal coating of grease on the pins. "Be nice to know who greases the hinges and carries the keys," I said.

As we entered the mouth of the tunnel, a cool wind fanned our faces. I sniffed the air, wondering if I might pick up a faint whiff of decomp or adipocere, but I knew that if I did, it would be emanating from my imagination, not the cave itself. Just inside, once the harsh daylight began to fade behind us, Art knelt down, his flashlight angling low along the dirt floor. "Look familiar?"

I crouched, and felt a chill that had little to do with the cave's temperature. "See all those? Those are the same work boot prints as in the slides." He played the beam slowly back and forth, and I clutched his arm. "There—that's the sheriff's track, or one just like it." Just as in the photos I'd taken in the grotto, the crisped lugged prints were superimposed over the worn tracks. At least, in the closest set of prints. But as Art played his beam farther along the cave floor, he let out a low whistle.

"This place gets more traffic than a bathroom in a sports bar," he said. "Looks like whoever owns that beat-up old pair of boots has been back one more time since your friendly neighborhood sheriff was in here." Sure enough, here the worn prints were clearly uppermost, smashing the lug marks nearly flat.

"So whoever it is, he knows that somebody else knows."

"Maybe. Probably. But that's not all." Art wiggled his flashlight beam slightly to the right of the layered prints. "Somebody else has been here, too."

I studied the area he was illuminating, but I couldn't see any more prints. I leaned closer, but all I saw were what appeared to be vague smears in the mud. I looked at Art in puzzlement.

"That one was smart enough to cover his tracks," Art said. "Maybe dragged a board or something along behind him to wipe 'em out. Lot of work."

Art snapped open his evidence kit and took out a small headlamp, which he snugged into place, then removed a big ziplock bag. The bag was half-filled with a white powder that I recognized as dental stone, a stronger, harder cousin of plaster of paris. "What say we grab some casts?" said Art. "Just for kicks. So to speak."

"You are the sole of wit," I said. "I'll take some pictures, too."

From a plastic squeeze bottle, Art squirted a stream of water into the bag, zipped it shut, and began to knead the mixture through the plastic. "This is some kind of mess we're stirring up here, Bill," he said. This time he wasn't joking.

"I know. You wanna just pack up and forget about it?"

"Naw, too late for that—hate for this dental stone to go to waste." The mixture looked a lot like pancake batter, though I wouldn't want to bite into a cake of it once it was hard. "Besides, you've got me curious now. You wanna bail?"

"Guess not. Still can't stop thinking about that girl and her baby."

"Okay then." He dribbled the goopy mixture into four individual prints—two from each boot—as well as a short section of the obliterated track. "First time I ever tried to match a sawmill print," he said. "These'll take thirty minutes to set up. Meanwhile, you wanna see where these tracks go?"

"I've got a pretty good guess. Let's see if I'm right."

Hugging the wall of the passage so as not to disturb the other tracks, we followed the trail. It didn't go far: barely two hundred yards from the entrance, the tracks veered sharply to the left and through a cleft in the tunnel wall. It was so narrow, Art and I had to plant our feet on the walls and straddle through to avoid trampling the sets of footprints. As the cleft opened up, I saw that we had emerged right where I'd thought we would: in the narrow end of the crystalline grotto. Directly ahead of us was the foot of the stone bench where Leena's mummified body had lain. "Son of a bitch," I said. "Every time I decide he's okay, I find out the sheriff's playing more games with me. Hauled me up a damned mountainside, when he could've just dropped me off at the front door." I remembered the hours I'd spent straddling the ATV, and the days of sore muscles. "Obviously he wanted me to think she was way out in the middle of nowhere."

Art's headlamp bobbed assent. "Looks like it. Reckon how come?"

"Something he didn't want me to know about the front entrance, maybe."

He nodded again. "That'd be my guess, too." He played his light across the stretch of floor between us and the bench. "That the same way it looked last time you saw it?" There was a mass of tracks in the room now. Amid the jumble, I could make out my own prints coming in from the opposite side, along with those of Tom Kitchings and Deputy Williams. I could see them departing, too. But ours were no longer the uppermost set of tracks: the work boots trumped us all. Heading into the grotto from where Art and I now stood, they approached the now-empty shelf, then turned and followed partway out the other side of the room before doubling back toward us and the church.

"You know what this means?"

"Yeah," I said, with a queasy feeling in my gut. "He's been here within the past week."

"Yeah. So not only does he know that *somebody* knows, he knows that *several* somebodies know. Place like this, won't take much asking around to find out that you're one of those somebodies."

Suddenly there was a muffled thud, followed by the clatter of falling rock. A cloud of dust shot through the crevice, filling the grotto, sending us into spasms of coughing. I put my arm across my face and tried breathing through my shirtsleeve; Art pulled his face inside the neck of his pullover shirt, turtlelike. We stood stock-still, and gradually the clatter and the dust subsided, leaving behind a silence that was close and menacing. A silence like death.

The rubble extended all the way up to the cleft in the grotto wall.

"Just a guess," Art said, "but I'd say somebody knew we were here."

It didn't take a forensic genius to realize we'd have little hope of digging our way out through the rubble blocking the entrance by the church. "Guess it's a good thing I know the back way after all," I said. We headed for the opposite side of the grotto, but then I stopped to snap photos of the new footprints on the floor. "Not that I'm feeling real confident I'll ever get to use these in court," I muttered, "but I'm getting pissed off now."

"Yeah, this is getting personal," Art said. "Those were some of my best plaster casts ever. That one of the board? I was gonna get a trip to a forensic conference outta that one."

"Easy come, easy go," I said. "So the good news is, I

know how to get out of here. The bad news is, the road is three or four miles down a rough trail, and that's nowhere near the truck. It might take us—"

A bright flash split the darkness, accompanied by a sharp crack. The floor shook, and rocks began raining down around us. Art grabbed my jacket and yanked me backward just as a stalactite plunged downward and shattered on the floor where I'd been standing. I jumped, then cursed. A lot.

"Bill, you okay?"

I nodded, shaken. "You?"

"Still taking inventory. So far, I count a knot on the head and a couple bruises, but nothing broken." He paused. "Hey, Bill? That four-mile trail you called the bad news? I think that was actually the good news. Back when there *was* some good news."

We picked our way across the fringe of jagged rock surrounding us, making our way toward the cave's back door, or what used to be it. The pile of debris grew steadily higher. Within a few yards the rubble reached clear to the roof, sealing off the passage completely.

I felt a tide of panic rising fast. I couldn't seem to get my breath, no matter how deeply I breathed. My head began to swim. As if from a distance, I heard Art's voice. "Bill? Bill! Listen, Bill, you need to calm down." He sounded strangely normal, not like a man struggling for oxygen. "Bill, you're hyperventilating. You need to breathe slower or you'll pass out." I fought the urge to gasp, but it was stronger than I was. "Try breathing through the sleeve of your jacket—maybe that'll help." I felt his hands on my arm, bringing my sleeve up to my face. The fabric slowed the flow of air. As I labored to breathe against the resistance, I felt my respiration slow, my head begin to clear. Finally my breathing seemed under control again, and I dropped my arm.

"Sorry," I said. "Thought we were running out of air."

"Not yet. We've got plenty still. Probably starve to death first."

"Damnit, Art, this isn't a joke. We're in a tunnel that's blocked by tons of rock. Even if we could clear it, which I doubt we can, there might be somebody outside just waiting to kill us."

"Might be," he agreed. "But no sense getting all worked up about it, seeing as he'll have to wait awhile for us to get within range. Let's figure out what to do."

"I'm open to suggestions."

"Okay, let's see what our resources are. We've got two flashlights and one headlamp. A camera. A gun. An evidence kit, which probably doesn't help us much at the moment. You got any food or water?"

"Pack of gum," I said. "Sugarless, so there's no energy in it. We got water flowing in the cave, though." I pointed my light in the direction of the subterranean stream, which we now knew originated at the springs behind the church. But the stream was gone, leaving only a muddy bed behind. The first of the two cave-ins must have blocked it.

"I've got a Snickers bar and a bottle of water," said Art. "If I can just pull off that loaves-and-fishes trick I read about in the Bible, we'll have bushels of leftovers. Oh, this might help—the map Methuselah the Caver faxed me."

"What good's that gonna do? We already found the cave. Unfortunately."

"It's not a map *to* the cave, Smarty Pants, it's a map *of* the cave. The interior. The part where we happen to be trapped like rats. Or bats."

"But we're sandwiched between two cave-ins, with nothing in the middle but fifty yards of tunnel and that damn grotto." Art studied the map silently. "Face it, Art," I said. "We're sealed up in here. No way out."

Art aimed his headlamp straight into my eyes, blinding

me. "You're just gonna give up?" he said. "Me, I'm not ready to throw in the towel." With that, he spun and began picking his way back through the debris, back toward the grotto.

"Art, wait. Slow down."

"You hurry up." He kept moving, his lights sweeping every square foot of the tunnel's walls and ceiling. But his pace slackened slightly.

I caught up with him in the grotto, just in time to see the beam of his light point upward at the grotto's ceiling and disappear into a circular opening about the diameter of a beach ball. "Aha!" he said.

"Did you know that was there?"

"Not until I checked the map. Back there when you were busy kissing our asses good-bye."

"Sorry. Does it go out?"

"Don't know."

"What's the map say?"

"Says 'Unexplored.' Guy who made the map used to be pretty hefty. I'm guessing the word 'Unexplored' shows up on most of his maps."

"So maybe it leads to another entrance—but maybe it just meanders around inside the mountain for a while and then peters out?"

"Maybe. Do I need to get all hardass with you again, or are you feeling optimistic and exploratory?"

"Let's go."

That proved easier said than done. The opening was about ten feet overhead. Even if I stood on Art's shoulders, I doubted I could reach it. I was about to suggest we start hauling in rocks from the tunnel—we certainly had enough debris to build a big pile—when Art clambered up onto the stone shelf and began studying the wall above, playing his light across the surface from various angles. "Hand me that case, will you, Bill?"

I stared at him, dumbfounded. "You found some evidence up there?"

"No, genius. I need something to stand on."

I handed it up, and he stood the rectangular case—a glorified tackle box, basically—up on end. Reaching slightly up and to one side, he grabbed a small knob of rock with his left hand. With his right, he stretched straight up and jammed two fingers into a narrow vertical crack in the wall. With a grunt, he levered himself up off the box, the toes of his hiking boots somehow latching onto projections I hadn't even seen. Once he had both feet up off the evidence kit, he extricated his fingers from the crack, reached a foot higher, and inserted his entire right hand into the crack. As first one foot, then the other, sought purchase on the wall, I saw him strain. His left hand lost its grip and he slipped, smacking against wall and dangling by his right hand, still wedged tightly in the crack. He cried out in pain, and his feet frantically scrambled against the rock. Instinctively I climbed onto the stone bench, took his boots in my hands, and hoisted upward with all my strength. With agonizing slowness, his boots reached the level of my chest, then my shoulders; finally, I found myself standing with my arms fully extended, quaking with the effort. Just as I was about to gasp out a warning about my strength failing, I felt the load lighten, and then he was gone, his legs disappearing up through the opening in the roof of the grotto.

I kept expecting him to reappear, and when he didn't after a few moments, I felt the panic returning. Finally, his head popped back into view. "Damn, that was tough. Thanks for the help. I thought for a minute there I was gonna leave that hand behind."

I was still panting, partly from exertion, partly from fear. "No problem. Anything encouraging up there?"

"Come see for yourself."

I considered the rock wall facing me. "Hell, Art, I can't climb this. I can't believe you could."

"My wife gave me some visits to a climbing gym last Christmas. I think she was hoping I'd get hooked on climbing and fall off a cliff somewhere."

"Well, unless there's a ladder up there you can send down—or unless you want to trade places and push me up— you might have to go on without me after all."

"And break up this winning team? No way. How big's your waist?"

"Thirty-four. No, more like thirty-six these days. What's that—" A glimmer of understanding began to dawn on me. "How 'bout yours, Slim?"

"None of your business. But throw me your belt and we'll see if we're fat enough." I took off my leather belt, refastened the buckle to make a hoop, and tossed it upward. Art snagged it, then disappeared. When he reappeared, he had fastened the tapered end of my belt into the buckle of his own. As he lowered one end of the linked belts, I saw that they added up to a good six feet long. "Let's hope that buckle holds," he said. "The rivet looks pretty stout, but then again, so do you."

Art sat on the lip of the circular opening, bracing his feet on the opposite edge. Wrapping a loop of leather around one wrist, he gripped the strap with both hands. "Try to feel for footholds," he said. "I'm not sure I can deadlift you all the way up." I nodded, climbing onto the evidence kit. Standing on tiptoe, I could reach just enough of the strap to take a turn around one wrist, as Art had done. He nodded. "Ready?"

"Ready. No, wait. Shouldn't we bring the evidence kit?"

He considered this. "We've got bigger problems now than evidence gathering. Besides, I don't think we can—you're gonna need both hands to get up."

"Yeah, but we might need to stand on it again. Lucky you're trapped with a Ph.D." Stepping down off the case, I bent down and unlaced both of my hiking boots. Splicing the two laces together gave me a piece of cord nearly ten feet long. I knotted one end to the case's handle and hitched the other to one ankle. Then I climbed back up, put my flashlight in my pocket, and took hold of the dangling belt again. "Heave-ho," I said, and he did.

Much grunting and scrambling later, I felt one of Art's hands grasp first one wrist, then the other. He hauled me through the opening and landed me like some giant fish, thrashing and gasping. I undid the loop of belt from my now-purplish hand, fished out my light, and set it beside me, pointing upward. As I reeled in the evidence kit, I surveyed my new surroundings. We were in a disappointingly small chamber, narrow and low-ceilinged. I looked at Art. "You sure this is progress?"

He was wearing his poker face, but I thought I saw a trace of a smile at the edges of his mouth. "Let's take a look around, see what we see."

It didn't take long to spot what he was smiling about. "Okay, I see footprints going around that bend in the wall. But do they go anywhere besides a dead end?"

"What do you think? Study the tracks, Sherlock."

I did. "Okay, I see prints going in both directions. But the last ones are leading away from here."

"Which means . . . ?"

"This must go somewhere."

"Bingo. Unless, of course, we find Injun Joe's shriveled corpse wedged in a cul-de-sac up ahead."

"Or Lester Ballard's lying in wait to have his way with us."

"Lester? I thought Lester only had a thing for the female body."

"These days," I said, "you never know. Forensics makes for strange bedfellows."

25

WE DIDN'T FIND INJUN JOE or Lester, but it wasn't long before we came to a cul-de-sac, or at least a crevice we couldn't fit through. The tracks we'd been following led straight through it, so it wasn't as if we'd missed a turn or side passage. There were none to miss in any case—we'd kept one pair of eyes on the tracks and another on the walls and roof of the passage. From the opening in the top of the quartz grotto, it led here and *only* here. It had seemed to be sloping upward, too, which had given us hope that we were slanting toward the surface. For all we knew, at this moment we might be standing within a hundred yards of an exit—but it might as well have been a hundred miles.

"Well, one thing's for sure," said Art glumly. "We know these aren't the sheriff's tracks. At least, not unless he passed through here about eighty pounds ago."

"So now what? Do we go back down and try to dig our way out to the church, or do we dig for the back door, or just stay here till we get skinny enough to squeeze through?"

"I don't know anymore, Bill. I'm out of ideas."

I studied the crevice more closely. The problem wasn't actually that we were too fat, although it wouldn't have hurt either of us to lose twenty pounds. But fat could be squeezed through almost any opening, given enough effort, as Sheriff Kitchings and his ample belly had demonstrated the day we recovered the body from the grotto. Our problem wasn't flesh, it was bone—the unyielding dimensions of our skeletal structures. If there wasn't room, there wasn't room.

I studied the geometry of the crevice. Its widest point—located about waist-high—was roughly ten inches across. The slot tapered gradually above and below that point; down by my knees and up by my chest, it narrowed to barely six inches across. Maybe, just maybe, if we went at it sideways, we could worm our way through in the center.

I bent from the waist until my chest was parallel to the floor, then rotated my trunk until my shoulders were aligned vertically, like the slit. Easing forward, slowly and awkwardly, I inserted my head in the slot. It would clear, though by an uncomfortably small margin. I tend toward claustrophobia, so the idea of wedging my body into the narrow crack—which led into unknown darkness—was only slightly more appealing than remaining trapped where we were. *Think, man, think,* I told myself.

I knew my cranial dimensions—I'd measured my head countless times in undergraduate classes, demonstrating how to use a pair of calipers. From the center of my eyebrow ridge to the back of my skull, my head measured 187 millimeters, or seven and a quarter inches. The width, on the other hand, was only 165 millimeters, or six and a half inches. Either way, there was no risk of getting my head stuck, I knew. The real problem would come lower down, with my chest. I'd have to rotate my shoulders to slide them through the vertical slot, and I wasn't at all sure the opening was big enough for my rib cage. "I wonder if babies have to problem-solve like this to fit through the birth canal," I muttered, "or if they're just squished out by uterine contractions and plenty of slime."

"I'd feel better about our chances if we had a big jar of Vaseline to grease you up with," Art said. "But I took that out of the evidence kit last night so I could fry up some chicken. Clean forgot to put it back."

Claustrophobic or not, I couldn't procrastinate any longer. Bending over, I easily threaded my head through the gap. My shoulders and arms passed through easily enough, too, once I'd twisted my trunk ninety degrees. Now for the chest; if I could manage that, the pelvis and legs should be simple. "Okay, Art, I might need your help in a second here," I grunted as I wriggled forward. I'd barely squeezed past my collarbones when I ground to a halt. Panic gripped my chest as tightly as the rock did. "I don't think I can make it," I said, wriggling back out.

"Try exhaling as much as you can," Art suggested. "That'll make your rib cage contract."

"Make me asphyxiate, too," I said.

"Not if I can push you on through."

"What if you can't?"

"Well, if you're sure you won't fit, just click your heels together three times and say 'There's no place like home,' and I'll yank you back real fast."

"And what if I won't budge? I won't last more than a minute or two if I can't breathe and you can't get me loose."

"I'll get you loose. Count on it."

I tried to visualize it, but all I could see in my mind's eye was a pair of alternating images: one was my head, shoulders, and arms wiggling frantically on the far side of the crevice; the other was my legs kicking desperately on the other side, as Art pushed and pulled in vain. The disjoint halves of me were like images from a cartoon, or an old-fashioned television set whose vertical hold was wrong by half a screen. Finally I forced the images from my mind and made my shaky voice as calm as I could. "You think this is our best chance, Art?"

There was a long silence. "Yeah, Bill, I do."

"Okay. Once I get my head and shoulders through, count to three while I empty my lungs, then lift my legs and push like hell."

I took off my jacket and tossed it through the crevice; that took a whopping tenth of an inch off my girth, and I knew the margin between success and failure might well be that narrow. I considered shucking my shirt, too, but knew I'd leave a lot of skin on the rocks if I went through bareback. Taking a long, deep breath, I held it for a few seconds, squeezing my chest and abdominal muscles tight, putting as much pressure on my lungs as I could stand without blacking out. By forcing more oxygen into my blood, like a pearl diver, I could go longer before needing a breath.

Or so I hoped.

After four or five seconds I pursed my lips and blew hard, until my lungs felt completely empty. Then I sealed my lips, worked my cheeks and jaw like a bellows, and managed to draw a bit more air from my chest up into my mouth. I quickly forced that out my lips, then repeated the maneuver twice more. By now I felt on the verge of imploding. I thrust myself into the opening, willed myself to contract within myself, and wriggled as best I could while Art lunged forward, gripping my legs.

I felt myself slide forward an inch, two inches . . . and then I stopped, wedged tight. My rib cage was pinned in a vise, and the vise's grip felt deadly. Desperately I struggled to knock my heels together, the signal for Art to pull me back, but something—maybe the rock, maybe Art—had my legs immobilized. Oh God, what a way to die, I thought as I began to suffocate.

Then came a sensation like a locomotive slamming into my knees. I opened my mouth in an involuntary scream, but there was no air to carry it. My chest and spine ground forward, and I thought I heard something crack, and then I found myself lying in a heap on the floor, my shirt hanging open, its buttons smashed and torn off. I felt battered, maybe even partly broken, but I was on the other side. And I could breathe. I closed my eyes, took in a huge, agonizing, delicious breath of air, savored it greedily, and let it out with a loud groan.

When I opened my eyes, I winced. A blinding light was shining directly into them from just inches away. From my side of the crevice, not Art's. "Hello, Doc," rumbled a familiar voice. "Looks like I got here just in the nick of time."

I shielded my eyes and stared up at the big man looming over me. It couldn't be coincidence that brought him here. I had been far too trusting of Waylon and his homespun routine, I realized; he'd just been stringing me along, biding his time, waiting for the perfect moment to strike. I didn't know if he was acting on his own, or on Jim O'Conner's orders, but I knew our luck had run out.

"Hello, Waylon," I said flatly, too defeated even to plead. "Guess you're here to take care of us, huh?"

"Well, you might could call it that. Just doing my job, really."

"Right," I said. "Nothing personal, just business, is that it?"

"Let's quit jawin' about it, Doc, and just get you and Art to a better place as quick as we can."

"A better place? You talking about heaven? Give me a break, Waylon. If you're fixing to kill us, at least spare us the Sunday School euphemisms."

"The whats? Fixin' to *kill* you? What the hell are you talkin' about, Doc? You done hit your head in this cave?"

"You're not here to kill us? Then what are you doing here? What about the explosions, the cave-ins?"

He set the light down on a shelf, pointing at himself. As usual, he was dressed head to toe in camouflage. He held his arms out, palms up, I guess to show he was unarmed, though I knew there were probably several weapons tucked into each of his many pockets. "Big Jim ast me to keep a eye out for you, make sure you didn't get into any trouble you

Waylon led us a hundred yards up a gently sloping tunnel; for the latter half of the trek, an irregular oval of light grew larger and brighter. "Uh-oh," said Art from behind me.

"What? We're almost out."

"We're ascending toward a bright, white light. Last time that happened to me, they had to hook jumper cables to my heart. Maybe we weren't as lucky in that second cave-in as we thought."

"If we were dead, we'd be climbing a big marble staircase."

"Marble? We're inside a mountain in Cooke County; I'm guessing the afterlife's a little more rustic here, too."

Before I could think up a retort we emerged, squinting and blinking, into the glare of the late September afternoon. Overhead, the sky shone electric blue; around us, the dogwood and tulip poplar leaves blazed red and yellow. Scrambling up out of a small sinkhole, we angled along a hillside for perhaps a quarter-mile, then scrambled down one end of the bluff behind Cave Springs Primitive Baptist Church. The church looked just as we'd left it, just as it probably had for the past fifty years or more. Beside it, though, my truck bore a fresh coating of limestone dust.

Waylon's truck was parked beside mine. It looked freshly washed. Unless he'd somehow scrubbed it after the explosions, Waylon was telling the truth: by the time he'd arrived, the cave's entrance had been blasted long enough for the dust to settle.

"Let's get the hell out of Dodge," said Art.

"Wait a second—I've got an idea. You still got your forensics kit?"

"Are you kidding? After that big production you made of hauling it up by your bootstraps, I knew I'd never hear the end of it if I left it behind. Why?"

"Come with me."

I led him back to the cave's entrance. Just as I'd expected, there in the mud beside the spring was a fresh set of boot prints. They led into the mouth of the cave, vanishing beneath the fresh rockfall.

"Eureka," said Art as he knelt down and set about taking a cast from the clearest of the several prints. "Look familiar?" They didn't, but it could have been a familiar pair of feet inside an unfamiliar pair of boots.

I studied the surrounding area. As far as I could tell, the tracks led into the cave—but didn't lead back out again. "You think he's still in there? Got caught in his own cave-in?"

Art shrugged. "Maybe. Kinda hope so. But maybe he slipped out the back before setting off that second blast. Or maybe he's coming out the same way we just did."

I shook my head. "Doubt it. If he'd been in there with us, seems like he'd've come after us. Anybody that's packing explosives is surely carrying a gun, too. He'd have shot us before we climbed up out of the grotto. The thing I can't figure out is, why not just shoot us in the first place?"

"Too suspicious. Cave-in could be passed off as an accident. Bullet holes are harder to explain—might bring an angry mob of vigilante UT professors up here hankering for vengeance. If the cave-in plan had worked, though, our bodies might be buried under a hundred tons of rock. We might go down as 'missing, presumed dead' or some such." I was beginning to grasp Cooke County's colorful reputation among my law enforcement colleagues. "Hey, you want your laces back? Or do you like the freedom of movement you get with your feet sliding around inside those boots?"

I'd clean forgotten. Taking the laces from Art, I used the rear bumper of my truck as a prop as I relaced my boots. As I retied the laces, I glanced once more at the church's rock sign, and I saw something I hadn't noticed earlier. Beneath the church's name, in paint so faded I could barely read it, was a line of script. I called to Art and pointed. Over my shoulder, I heard his low whistle of amazement.

"I'll be damned," I said.

"Possibly," he agreed. "But I don't think you'll be the only one. There might be a Kitchings or two down there to keep you company by the fire."

The faded line read, "THOMAS KITCHINGS, SR., PASTOR."

26

THE SKULL ROCKED GENTLY back and forth with each step I took. I had cradled the occipital on a doughnut-shaped cushion and lined the sides of the box with bubble wrap, so I wasn't worrying about damage, merely noticing the movement. I found myself counting the slight, rhythmic bumps, like the clicks of some macabre pedometer. *Now there's a moneymaking idea,* I thought, *the Brockton SkullDometer—the perfect gift for the forensic anthropologist who has everything.* Other ludicrous marketing slogans began popping into my head: "Two heads are better than one." "Give the gift that keeps on giving—throughout the extended postmortem interval." "Don't stop—I'm gaining on you!"

Normally I don't take skeletal material from open forensic cases to class, but today—fresh from the cave that had entombed Leena, and had nearly swallowed me—I was completely preoccupied with the Cooke County woman. As I counted the bumps within the box, I hoped that going over the case in class might spark some new insight.

The lecture hall was nearly filled by the time I entered, even though it was still several minutes before class time. One student who was not in her customary seat this morning, though, was Sarah Carmichael. My heart sank. I had hoped that we'd be able to pretend nothing had happened in my office that recent night. Actually, what I *really* hoped was that I had dreamt it all, but I knew that wasn't so. Still, I had told myself, if we could just ignore the whole thing, maybe it would fade into a dreamlike memory. No such luck, the empty front-row seat told me.

I set the box on the desk at the front of the auditorium and carefully removed the bones, balancing the skull on the cushion and laying the hyoid and sternum in front of the mandible. "I have good news and bad news today," I announced. "The good news is, you get to play forensic detective. This skull belongs to a recently discovered homicide victim, case number 05-23, and we're looking for the killer right now." There was a general stirring and murmuring throughout the room. I had their attention.

A wary voice drifted down from the back. "What's the bad news?"

"The bad news is, our murder victim here is the subject of a pop quiz. Go ahead and put your name on a piece of paper." The murmurs gave way to scattered groans and a few whispered curses. "Don't get excited," I added, "it's only three questions, and they're purely for extra credit. You get one point added to your midterm average if you can tell me both the race *and* the sex of this individual; you get another point if you can tell me the manner of death—in other words, how was this person killed? If you've read the chapter on the cranium and didn't miss class last week, these should be easy for you." Judging by the expressions on the sea of faces in front of me, some of them had done the reading and stayed awake during the lecture, while others suddenly wished they had. Several students leaned forward and began scrutinizing the skull from afar. Others flipped open their texts and began scanning pages. At the back of the room, I thought I saw the door open just a crack.

"I expect a lot in this class," I went on, "and it's not because I like to trip you up, or keep you too busy to party. It's because mastering this material could be a matter of life and death someday. Our dead friend here, for instance: I don't know who committed the crime, or why, or exactly when. And until we can figure those things out, somebody's getting away with murder."

The mood in the classroom had turned dead serious. "I can't pass this around, and I can't let you touch it," I said. "It's forensic evidence, so it has to be protected from damage or contamination. But if you'll line up and file past, you'll see everything you need to see to answer those three questions. Jot your answers down quickly. For question number one, just put 'M' for 'male' or 'F' for 'female.' For question two, put 'C' or 'N' or 'M,' depending on whether you think it's Caucasoid or Negroid or Mongoloid, and for three, just put one word that describes what you think caused the death. Hand me your paper as you head back to your seat."

A boy at one side of the room—a quadrant from which I'd heard snores on more than one occasion—raised his hand. "Did you say Mongoloid?" I nodded. "Man, that's harsh. Why would somebody kill a retard?"

The room erupted in groans. I checked the seating chart. "Do your reading, Mr. Murdoch!" I thundered. "In physical anthropology, 'Mongoloid' refers to peoples of Mongolian descent—Asians and Native Americans." He slumped in his seat.

I motioned to the first row, and they formed a line to one side of my desk. As the students scrutinized the bones—student by student, row by row—their faces were alive with curiosity, wonder, sometimes sadness and even reverence. I was so intent on watching their reactions that I stopped keeping tabs on the line, so I was surprised when the last student filed past. I was doubly surprised to see that it was Sarah. She must have slipped in the back door after the line had formed.

She didn't meet my eyes as she approached; I wasn't sure

whether to be worried or relieved by that. The fact is, none of the other students had met my eyes, either: they were all focusing exclusively on the skull. The only difference was, I hadn't shared a passionate and inappropriate kiss with any of them since the last class.

Sarah lingered over her paper, scrawling considerably more than the letters "F" and "C" and a one-word description of a murder. When she handed me her paper, I saw it bore several lines of script, but I was afraid to risk reading it while standing in front of 270 students. The last thing I wanted to do was fall apart in front of them again.

"Okay, how many of you said this was a male?" A few hands shot up, Mr. Murdoch's among them. He looked around furtively. "Small features, sharp upper edge to the eye orbit, no external occipital protuberance at the base of the skull: class, what does that tell us?" The rest of the students called "female" in unison. "The mouth structure is vertical, rather than having teeth and jaws that jut forward," I said. "What's the race?" The chorus of "Caucasoid" was less robust, and I thought I heard a "Negroid" or two. "Caucasoid," I said. "Remember the pencil test: if a pencil or a ruler can touch both the base of the nasal opening and the chin, it's Caucasoid; if the teeth slant forward too much to allow that, it's probably Negroid. Mongoloid peoples have flatter cheekbones and shovel-shaped incisors, Mr. Murdoch." He wasn't the only student looking chagrined, though.

"Now, the hard one: manner of death." I held up the sternum, pointing to the small, round foramen. "How many said gunshot?" Nearly everyone in the room raised a hand proudly. I wagged a finger and shook my head, smiling. "That was a trick question. One of my best graduate students almost got fooled by that hole in the sternum." I explained how to tell the difference between a foramen and a gunshot wound, and then I pointed out the fractures in the hyoid. "Did anyone guess strangulation?"

One hand went up in the back row. It was Sarah's. "Well done, Miss Carmichael," I said. "You've got the makings of a good forensic anthropologist. I hope you'll stick with it." She reddened and ducked her head, but she nodded. When class ended, though, she was out the back like a scalded cat.

Walking back to class, the box tucked under one arm, I unfolded Sarah's quiz paper. Beneath her answers to the three quiz questions, she'd written two things. I stopped at the top of the department's exterior staircase to read them. "P.S.," read the first one, "She has no lateral upper incisors. Genetic?" Golly, she was sharp! I went on to the second addition. "P.P.S. I was deeply moved by your story and your sorrow," it said. "I'm embarrassed by what happened next, but I'm not actually sorry."

I laughed out loud. "Okay, then neither am I," I said. Two passing students gave me a sidelong glance, then looked quickly away. *The nutty professor,* I could feel them thinking. I didn't care. I practically danced down the maze of ramps and stairs leading to the base of the stadium, then took the steps to my office two at a time. When I saw my door, though, my euphoric bubble burst.

The steel frame bowed outward into the curving hallway, while the metal door itself bent inward. Just above and below the knob, the pea-green paint hung in slivers from two spots where a wrecking bar had pried open the door to my office.

Heartsick, I stepped inside. The filing cabinet hung open, its locked drawers also mangled by the pry bar. Forensic case folders lay strewn across the floor, examination reports and field notes and newspaper clippings commingled like some mass grave of moribund murder investigations. Sorting and refiling the mess would take hours, if not days. A single folder lay atop the cabinet. I knew without looking which report it would be: 05-23. Leena Bonds.

When I repacked the skull, sternum, and hyoid in a small

hatbox for the trip up to class, I had left the big box containing the rest of her skeleton sitting on my desk. That box, like the scores of others lining the shelves in the adjoining room, measured three feet long by a foot in cross-section. It would be hard to miss. And now, as I whirled to look, I saw that her box was missing. "Damn," I muttered, setting down the student papers and the hatbox. "Damn." Then a flood of relief washed over me as I realized that all was not lost. Leena's skull and hyoid—the key to her identification and her manner of death—were safe in the hatbox. Whoever had come looking for them had gone away frustrated. He hadn't left empty-handed—the theft of the rest of her skeleton was a bitter loss—but I still held the trump cards, if the case ever came to trial. Thank God I had taken her to class.

Using my handkerchief, I picked up the handset of my phone and dialed the campus police. "This is Dr. Brockton in Anthropology," I told the dispatcher. "Someone's just broken into my office and files. They've also stolen some skeletal material." The dispatcher promised to send an officer right away. "Tell him to park at the east end zone access portal," I told her. "There's a stairway that leads from there straight up to my office." She read the directions back to be sure she had them right. "The stolen material is part of a murder case," I added. "I'll need to call in some outside cavalry, too. Just so you know." She promised to give the responding officer a heads-up.

My next call was a quick one to Art. I told him what I thought I should do, and he concurred, so I pressed the switchhook, pressed "8" again for another outside line, and dialed the number on the business card I fished from my wallet. "FBI," snapped a no-nonsense male voice. I identified myself and asked for Agent Price. "One moment, I'll see if she's in," he said, swiftly parking me on hold.

Ten seconds later, Angela Price picked up. "Dr. Brockton, how are you?" Price's voice was crisp but cordial. "You're not calling with a field report from another cockfight, I hope?"

"No, I'm calling from my office at UT. Somebody's just broken in and stolen the postcranial skeleton from my Cooke County murder case."

"Postcranial?"

"Everything below the skull, or nearly everything. Luckily, I had the cranium and the hyoid bone—the bone from her throat that shows she was strangled—in a classroom with me. So those are still safe, for the moment."

"What would you like me to do, Dr. Brockton?"

"Well, you said to let you know if anything else cropped up, and this sure counts as cropping up in my book. Does this merit sending the Bureau's crime scene wizards over to take a look? Just informally, of course. I'm also wondering if you folks could take temporary custody of the skull and hyoid for me, too? It's easy to get into a professor's office, but I can't imagine somebody breaking into the FBI's evidence vault."

"Hang on a second." She, too, was quick with the "Hold" button; must've been emphasized in the curriculum at Quantico. I hung in limbo for several minutes. Just as I was about to hang up and redial, she picked back up. "I'm not trying to dodge you, Dr. Brockton, but Steve Morgan, your former student? He already knows his way around that labyrinth over there. He's on his way now, and some TBI evidence techs will be right behind him in a mobile crime lab." She must have sensed some disappointment on my end of the line. "We just don't have either the jurisdiction or the resources right now, and TBI does. Can you understand that?"

"I reckon I'll have to." I regretted the petulance of that as soon as I said it. "Sorry. Yes, of course."

"Do you feel safe there?"

It hadn't even occurred to me to worry about that. "Yes, I

think so. Thanks for asking. A UT officer should be here any minute. In fact—yes, there's his car now."

"Good. Keep in touch. Don't give up on us." She rang off without another word, and I met the campus cop at the door. He looked young enough to be a student himself; his gun was drawn and his hand was shaking. When I explained that a TBI team was on the way, his big eyes got even bigger. Mercifully, he holstered the trembling weapon, then scurried back to his patrol car and returned with a roll of crime scene tape. With it, he fashioned a big X across the open doorway. When Steve Morgan arrived ten minutes later, he eyed the crime scene tape and sized up the eager young cop. "Anybody been in here besides Dr. Brockton?"

"No, *sir*," said the young patrolman, all but saluting.

"Good work," smiled Morgan. "We'll take it from here. Thanks."

The young man's face fell. "You don't need me here?" Morgan looked surprised by the question, maybe faintly amused. I felt bad for the UT officer, but he wasn't ready to slink away just yet. "I, um, was sort of hoping to watch—to *observe*—how the TBI works a crime scene."

Morgan smiled. It hadn't been all that long since he was standing in my office apologizing for classroom hijinks. "Now that I think about it, Officer, if you've got time to stick around and control the perimeter here, the TBI would be much obliged."

The lad practically trembled with excitement as he fished out his radio. "Unit Three to Dispatch," he blurted. When the dispatcher responded, he snapped to attention, as if she could see him. "TBI is requesting officer assistance at the scene."

"Copy that," drawled the dispatcher, not nearly as impressed as he'd hoped. "Holler when you're done. We're starving, and we need somebody to make the deli run."

It wasn't long before two TBI techs arrived, light sources and evidence kits in hand, and began surveying the room methodically. Morgan and I stepped out into the hallway, but I leaned into the doorway to watch the techs at work. When they turned on the ultraviolet lights, purple prints showed up on every surface. Most of them were mine, I knew, and probably the rest belonged to graduate students. "Excuse me, sir," said one of the techs, "can you tell me where this door leads?"

"Sure, it leads to the skeletal collection room."

He wiggled the knob—it was locked, I knew from checking it myself—and inspected the frame for signs of forced entry. Finding none, he turned his attention back to my desktop.

Morgan cleared his throat to get my attention, then began a litany of questions—when had I left my office, how long was I gone, who knew my class schedule, how many different exits could the thief have taken, did I see anybody or anything suspicious, and so on, and so on. Finally, when he'd exhausted my factual knowledge, he asked the question that had been hanging in the air all along: "So who do you think might have done it?"

"Well, my first thought is the sheriff, of course. I still think he's afraid of where the murder investigation is leading."

"Has he ever been here before?"

"No, but it wouldn't be hard to find out where it is."

"Yeah, but that's only half the battle," said Morgan. "This office isn't exactly easy to *get* to. You're tucked away about as far from the rest of the Anthropology Department as you can get without burrowing clear under the AstroTurf."

"Makes it easier to hole up and concentrate," I said defensively.

"I'm not criticizing; just thinking out loud. Is there anybody who *has* been here before that might have an interest in stealing that skeleton?"

"Well, there's the sheriff's deputy, Leon Williams."

"A deputy?" Morgan sounded dubious.

"You asked, and he's been here before. He could have come to fetch it for the sheriff." Suddenly I remembered Art's Scenario E, the unknown possibility: "Or he could be working some angle we don't even know about. Maybe he's setting up the sheriff for a fall?" The more I thought about it, the surer I was that this was Williams's handiwork.

" 'Scuse us," Morgan said to the UT policeman, taking my elbow and steering me into the stairwell. He checked the flight of stairs above and below the landing where we stood, then leaned close to me and spoke in a near whisper. "Listen, you didn't hear this from me—if it got out that you did, I'd be in deep shit with Agent Price—but I guarantee you Williams was not the one who broke into your office and took those bones."

"You can't be sure of that."

"Yes I can," he hissed.

"How?"

"Because he's spent the last two hours in a roomful of FBI and TBI agents, that's how."

I had to admit, it was a pretty good alibi.

"Then it's got to be the sheriff. Or maybe his brother. Orbin doesn't seem the sort who would shrink from a little breaking and entering. Can't you guys *please* get some sort of surveillance going on them?"

He checked the stairs again. "The paperwork's in motion even as we speak," he whispered. "Office, homes, vehicles. Should be in place within a week." He gave my arm a sharp squeeze. "Remember, we did *not* have this conversation."

I nodded, grateful that we hadn't.

27

STILL AGITATED AFTER THE TBI crew left, I phoned Jim O'Conner to tell him about the theft of the bones. He sounded shaken and angry. "Listen," I said, "I wonder if you could give me some more background on the Kitchings family. I can't help thinking at least one of them is behind this, but I can't figure out which one, or why."

"I don't think we should talk about this over the phone," he said. "Drug seizure money up here has bought all sorts of fancy equipment in the past few years." I'd ridden a top-of-the-line ATV and had seen the helicopter parked behind the courthouse, so I knew what he was talking about. "Electronics, too," he said. "I don't say anything on the phone I'm not willing for anybody in the county to hear."

"Okay," I said. "It's one-fifteen now. I'll need to hit a drive-through on the way up, but I could be there by two-thirty."

"Let me send Waylon to meet you at the exit."

"I don't know about that," I said. "Last time Waylon picked me up, I ended up headfirst in a barrel of dead chickens, covered in blood, vomit, and tobacco juice."

He laughed. "Makes a hell of story, doesn't it?" I had to admit it did. "And he helped get you out of the cave," he reminded me. Despite misgivings, I agreed to give Waylon one more chance at chauffeuring.

He rumbled to a stop in the gravel lot beside the Pilot sta-

tion as I wolfed down the last of my lunch. As I hoisted myself up into his cab, he flashed me a grin. "Howdy, Doc. You
don't look any the worse for wear from your spe-lunkin'.
Glad we ain't put you offa Cooke County for good."

"I'm back. But no more cockfights—and no more
Copenhagen."

I heard a wheezing sound coming from Waylon's direction; it built to a snicker, then exploded into a booming,
truck-shaking roar of laughter. He pounded the steering
wheel with one mammoth fist, then wiped tears from his
eyes with a camouflaged shirt sleeve. "Doc, I wisht you
coulda seen yourself pitching over into that trash barrel. I
b'lieve that's the funniest damn thing I ever saw. That, and
the look on all them fellas standing around as you was
keelin' over. If I had me a video of that, I bet I'd win the ten
grand on that TV show for funny videos."

First the TBI, then O'Conner, now Waylon. Apparently I
was never going to live this down. My only consolation was
that my colleagues and students at UT hadn't witnessed the
debacle. "Well, if you hear of somebody else who caught it
on tape, I'd probably pay ten grand myself, just to take it out
of circulation." Waylon looked thoughtful, doubtless searching his memory banks in hopes of dredging up a video.

Halfway toward O'Conner's place, Waylon turned off the
river road onto a narrow track of dirt. "Way-*lon*," I said,
"this isn't the way."

"I just got to stop by and see my cousin Vern real quick.
He's the one I was bettin' on the cockfight for. Come on,
Doc, this won't take but a few minutes."

"Oh, no, you don't," I said. "I've been down this road with
you before."

"Naw you ain't," he said. "The cockfight was over by
Gnatty Branch. This here's Laurel Branch."

"You know what I mean. No more side trips!"

"Hell, Doc, don't make me feel worse'n I already do. It's

real important—if I don't do this, Vern's gonna have his ass in a sling big-time. No joke—this is a genu-ine family emergency. Besides, we're already here." We lurched to a stop and Waylon shut off the mighty diesel.

I looked out the windshield. There wasn't much "here" here: a rutted turnaround, from which a narrow footpath led into the woods. Waylon got out and headed down the trail. "Hey, wait up," I called. Fifty yards down the path, I was surprised to see trees posted with Keep Out and No Trespassing signs. Running beneath them were shiny strands of barbed wire. Waylon pressed down on the top strand and stepped over the fence, then motioned for me to follow.

"Waylon, I think whoever put up this fence and these signs means business."

He laughed. "Oh, he means business, but he don't mean *us*. We's family."

The trail angled through a stand of pines—all dead, decimated by a pine beetle infestation three years before—which bore additional menacing signs. I looked at Waylon doubtfully, but he just grinned and motioned me forward. As I neared the edge of the pine thicket, Waylon slowed, then stopped. "Doc, watch your step here—be sure you don't catch that war."

"War? What war?"

"That war about a foot off the ground there, couple steps ahead."

I looked where he was pointing. A taut monofilament line—invisible unless you happened to catch a glint of sunlight through it—stretched across the trail about knee-high. To my left, it was wrapped around the trunk of a dead pine; to the right, it disappeared into a pile of deadfall. Looking closer at the deadfall, I detected two small dark circles, rimmed in bluish-black metal. "Waylon, is that what I think it is?"

He nodded. "Double-barrel Remington twelve-gauge. For them that can't read."

Waylon was already moving down the trail, so I high-stepped over the trip wire, very carefully, to keep up with him. "What are we doing here, Waylon, and why's your cousin Vern so antisocial?"

"He's got a note comin' due that I got to help him with. He's a small farmer, you might say, and he don't like people gettin' in his crops or messing in his business."

"But he's not gonna mind us? Or *me?*"

"Naw. I'm blood, and long's you're with me, you're awright. Matter of fact, he's heard about you, kindly wants to meet you. Duck your head, Doc. *Duck,* damnit!"

I ducked, just in time to avoid getting snagged by a series of triple-ganged fishhooks, suspended at various approximations of eye level, from more monofilament line. I guessed the reasoning was, if you didn't read the warning signs, you didn't need your eyesight. I renewed my vow never to travel with Waylon again, even if it meant walking back to Knoxville.

The trail followed the hill's contour lines, and now it arced through a small hollow strewn with boulders, ranging in size from television sets to trailer trucks. As we approached a narrows hemmed by rocks, Waylon stopped again. "You see them leaves in that low spot yonder?" I nodded. "You're gonna wanna jump clean over them. Got it?"

"Got it. Why do I want to do that?"

"So you don't get bit by them copperheads curled up right there."

Looking closely, I could just barely make out the fat, mottled shapes of three copperheads coiled on the bed of leaves. "How'd you know they'd be there?"

" 'Count of them fishhooks in their tails. Keeps 'em close to home, you know?"

"Fishhooks? You mean they're staked out in the middle of the trail? Damn, Waylon, how many more booby traps between us and Cousin Vern? And what if he's rigged up some new ones you don't know about?"

"This here's the last 'un, coming in this-away. And Vern ain't rigged up no more, 'cause he ain't the one rigs 'em." He said this with a mixture of matter-of-factness, modesty, and the proprietary pride of an artist displaying his handiwork. I should have known.

We wound down the hollow, which gradually widened into a small bowl. At the center, there appeared to be a sunlit clearing, though as we got closer, I saw that much of it was occupied by small trees, ten or twelve feet tall. At one edge of the opening stood a small cabin—more of a hut, really—with a wisp of smoke curling up from a rusted flue. Suddenly I understood: the clearing wasn't a thicket of small trees, but a patch of huge marijuana plants, some of them with stalks as thick as my wrist. Of course—why else would a trail in the woods be booby-trapped with shotguns and copperheads? This lush, blue-green foliage waving in the breeze was the linchpin of Cooke County's underground economy.

While we were still a hundred yards away, Waylon gave a piercing whistle. A deep baying emanated from the hut, and a rickety screen door screeched open and then slapped shut. Loping toward us on legs nearly as long as mine was a huge red hound, lop-eared and goofy-looking. The beast charged up to Waylon and reared up like a stallion, then placed immense paws on his shoulders. He stood eye to eye with Waylon and licked him square on the mouth. Waylon laughed, making no effort to dodge the dog's slobbery tongue.

After he'd had his fill of kissing, the dog dropped to all fours and trotted over to sniff my crotch. Luckily, the smell didn't inspire him to French-kiss me. "Best keep him and your girlfriend apart," I said. "One of them's liable to get jealous."

Waylon thumped the dog's rib cage. "This here's my *buddy*. Hard to believe it now, but a year ago, he could fit in the palm of my hand. Not much of a coon hound, turns out, but he's a real sweet dog, ain't you, Duke?" As if in answer, Duke slobbered happily on Waylon's palm.

The door screeched again, and a skinny, stunted echo of Waylon slouched toward us. "Hey, Vernon," Waylon called. "I got the Doc here with me. He's that genius bone detective I was telling you about."

Vernon nodded hello. I nodded back. "You'uns ain't just come from a chicken fight, is you?" Vernon snickered at his own humor, and I shot Waylon a baleful look.

Waylon fished a wallet from somewhere. "Here's two hunnerd. I thought I'd be a little flusher, but I didn't make out as well last Sunday as I planned."

That was my fault, I realized—if I hadn't collapsed at the cockfight, Waylon could have stayed longer and wagered more.

Vernon took the money and shook Waylon's hand. "I 'preciate you. I hate to ask, but we're still having a bad time with Ralph. He's my least-un," he explained to me. "He's pale as a ghost, he won't eat, and he's got blood in his pee and his shit—'scuse my language, Doc. Waylon, he don't look good at all. We're afraid he ain't gonna make it."

With good cause, I thought—it sounded like the child might have leukemia, but I hesitated to bring up the subject. Maybe I could talk about it with Waylon later.

Waylon clapped Vern on the shoulder, then folded him in a bear hug, almost completely enveloping the smaller man. A muffled sob issued from the vicinity of the big man's chest. "It's gone be all right," Waylon said. "Y'all just hang in there; everthing's gone be all right. Listen, I got to get the Doc over to Jim's."

In the distance, I became aware of the staccato thudding of a helicopter heading our way. Waylon's head snapped up.

"Shit, let's go, Doc," he said. "We got to be out of sight before that chopper sets down."

He bounded off the trail and scampered behind a tangle of fallen pines. I followed as quickly as I could, hoping we weren't venturing into a different zone of booby traps. I heard a rustle behind us, and looked back to see Duke, the hound, following us.

Once we were hidden, Waylon's hand resting on Duke's collar, we dared a look back toward Vernon's hut. A sleek, black-and-gold Bell JetRanger settled into the edge of the clearing amid a whirlwind of leaves and dust. On the helicopter's side was a five-pointed star and the words "Cooke County Sheriff." As the turbine engine spooled down, Orbin Kitchings emerged from the cockpit and strode toward Vernon, utterly unconcerned about the rotor still freewheeling above his head.

Out of the corner of my eye, I saw Waylon fiddling silently with something, but I paid it no heed until my nostrils caught a familiar and dreadful aroma: he had opened a can of Copenhagen, and I was directly downwind. I fought back the urge to gag, forcing myself to focus on the figures arguing in the clearing. As the noise from the engine and the prop died, I began to make out their conversation. "But that's all I got," said Vernon, his voice high and tight. "I ain't playin' games, that's ever cent I have in this world. My boy's been sick and I ain't got no money till this crop comes in. Just come back then."

Orbin spat. "Shit, Vernon, it ain't worth my time and fuel to come out here for this. I told you five hundred." *Damn,* I thought, *if only the TBI had already bugged the helicopter.* Maybe they'd have it done by his next trip.

"I know, Orbin, and I tried, but I just ain't got it till I get this crop in. Weather stays good, I'll get another week's growth. That's an extry couple thousand. You got to cut me some slack here."

There was a pause. "*What* did you say to me?"

"You . . . you got to work with me, Orbin." Vernon's voice quavered. Sensing his distress, the dog squirmed, but Waylon held tight to his collar.

I saw the deputy backhand Vernon, but it took a fraction of a second for the sound to carry to us. "You listen to me, you little pissant. I don't got to do *nothin'* with you. I don't got to give a rat's ass about you or your snotty-nosed sick kid or your crippled grandmother or any other sob story you got. And you can cry all you want to, but it don't make a damn bit of difference to me. Are we clear on that?" I saw Vernon's head nod slightly. "I can't hear you. Are we clear?"

"Yes. We're clear."

"Good. When I come back in two weeks, that harvest moon better be shining, and you damn well better have me a thousand dollars in your hand."

"I . . . I just give you two hunnerd, Orbin. Means I'll owe you eight hunnerd next time."

"Shut the fuck up. Penalty for late payment. Thousand dollars, and be grateful I ain't rattin' you out to the DEA or burning you out my own damn self."

Beside me, I heard Waylon draw in a long, angry breath, then exhale slowly through his mouth. His breath, warm and redolent with tobacco, wafted directly into my face. With a sense of impending doom I clenched my jaws tight, but there was no holding it back this time, and I began to vomit. Up came the Kentucky Fried Chicken I'd consumed at eighty miles an hour. Right behind it came the mashed potatoes, biscuits, and gravy. Duke yanked free of Waylon's grip and began slurping up my lunch. As my retching and coughing continued, Orbin's head snapped in our direction. "What the hell is that?" demanded Orbin. "Vernon, you got somebody over there waitin' to bushwhack me?" Waylon clapped a hand over my mouth, and Vernon squawked a desperate denial. "I swear I'll shoot you both, you son of a bitch." I could hear angry footsteps crashing toward us.

"Wait," Vernon yelled. "It's just my dog. He ate a dead coon this morning—been thowin' up all day. Duke, come here, boy. Duke! Git over here!" Vernon's command was directed as much at us as at Duke. Waylon reached down, tore the dog from my spattered lunch, and flung him away from us. Duke stumbled out of the brush and loped into the clearing. "There you are, Duke." Vernon sounded a little less scared. "You still sick, buddy? I hope you done learnt your lesson 'bout eating roadkill."

Crouching behind the fallen pine, I heard Orbin shout. "Hey! Git, dog! *Git,* goddamnit!"

"Aw, he ain't gonna hurt you," said Vern. "He just wants to—"

"Git!" I heard a dull thud, the sound of a boot hitting flesh and bone. A yelp of pain and confusion split the air. I peered over the trunk.

"Damn you, Orbin Kitchings, you had no cause to kick my dog."

I saw the deputy strike Vernon again, knocking him flat this time. When he did, it was as if a circuit was completed deep within the dog's instinctual brain. The gentle, dopey hound began to roar and snarl, lunging and snapping at the deputy. Orbin launched a series of flailing kicks, which the dog met with flashing jaws. Suddenly the big dog hurtled backward, twisting in midair, as the crack of a gunshot reached us. Duke crumpled to the ground, and after a moment's shock, Vernon scrabbled over and threw himself onto the animal's body, sobbing. The deputy stood over him, the gun pressed to Vernon's head now.

Beside me, I felt Waylon stir and start to rise. His face was purple with rage. I grabbed his arm, but he shook me off and stood, drawing a pistol from his combat pants. I scrambled up and hissed in his ear, "No, Waylon. He'll shoot Vernon. Then he'll shoot us."

Waylon turned a murderous gaze on me. "He's got to die,"

he muttered. "I'm gonna kill that black-hearted, bottom-feeding cocksucker."

"You *can't!*"

"You watch me, Doc."

"Wait," I whispered. "Do you want Vernon to die? Even if you could hit him from here, you can't be sure he won't pull the trigger."

Waylon clenched his jaw and glared furiously from me to the deputy and back again. Crouching down again, he propped the pistol on the fallen tree trunk, taking careful aim at Orbin. He held so still I wasn't sure he was even breathing. The deputy stepped away from Vernon, but he kept his gun pointed directly at the man on the ground. "Vernon, you stay where you're at, and not another damn word out of you. You have that thousand when I come back in two weeks, or I'll shoot you like a dog, too." He backed away and climbed into the chopper, the gun still pointed out the open door. Only when the engine had spooled up did he withdraw the gun and slam the door. Seconds later he was gone, leaving behind a vortex of dry leaves and fresh grief.

28

O'CONNER POURED WAYLON ANOTHER shot of whiskey—his third, by my count, and I was counting pretty closely, as I was depending on Waylon for a ride back to my truck. "I know you want to," O'Conner said for the hundredth time, "but killing him won't help. It'll ruin your life, and Vern's too." Waylon just snuffled and shook his bearlike head.

"What turns a man into something like that," I asked O'Conner, "all mean and hateful inside?"

O'Conner shrugged, as if he had no clue, but I was reasonably sure he possessed some insight, so I waited him out. Finally he spoke. "Well, Cooke County alone—the hardscrabble life that requires a man to break the law or break his back just to get by—is enough to harden anybody," he said. "Anybody predisposed to it, at least."

"But this goes way beyond hardened," I said.

"Well, then there's the Kitchings family itself—sort of the Cooke County of families."

"How so?"

"Well, you haven't had the pleasure of meeting the matriarch and patriarch yet," he said, "but they're about as warm and nurturing as those copperheads on the trail to Vern's. A copperhead mostly wants to be left alone—he won't generally come after you—but provoke him, and you'll get a nasty dose of poison."

"But the father's a minister, isn't he?"

"He is, but you've got to remember what kind of church he's in. Primitive Baptists—'Hardshell Baptists,' they're also called—are about as flinty as Christians get, in my experience. Their faith is the washed-in-the-blood, fire-and-brimstone variety. Not as keen on the touchy-feely, love-thy-neighbor part of the gospel. Most of the time, they're pulled in pretty tight—don't tolerate drinking, dancing, or card-playing; take a pretty dim view of movies and television; don't much trust a woman who cuts her hair or wears pants or makeup. Funny thing is, though, on Sunday, this tamped-down, thou-shalt-not crowd completely cuts loose, working themselves up into a frenzy of righteous enthusiasm."

I nodded. Cultural anthropology was full of studies of religious ecstasy; that variety of spiritual experience cuts across virtually all nations and cultures, including highly conservative groups. Even Pentacostal churches that practice snake-handling and speaking in unknown tongues—practices at the far end of the Christian spectrum—were based on ecstatic, trancelike states.

"I heard Reverend Kitchings preach a few times in my youth," O'Conner went on, "back when I was courting Leena, trying to make a good impression on the family. Sitting in that cold stone building, I would just marvel at the transformation this tight-lipped, tightassed puritan would undergo once he got fired up. He'd get into this preaching rhythm that was almost hypnotic, more incantation than sermon. He'd punctuate every sentence with a 'Praise God!' or a 'Hallelujah!' instead of a period. Go hell-for-leather till he'd run out of breath, then give this final, quacklike gasp, then draw in another huge breath and let fly again. I reckon he's still at it these days. You should go hear him; I bet you'd find it fascinating."

"I probably would," I agreed. "How about the mother? How would you describe the family dynamics?"

"Well, I'd say the reverend is a big fan of St. Paul—'Wives, submit to your husbands'; that sort of thing. I don't think she's had an easy or pleasant life with that man. Pretty hard for the sons, too."

"In what way?"

"Well, let's just say that if it took a liberal application of the razor strop to keep his boys on the straight and narrow path to salvation, the reverend was just doing his Christian duty." He said this with a grim look that told me he had probably witnessed a Kitchings flogging or two firsthand.

"But why did Tom and Orbin turn out so different," I asked, "if they both came from that same harsh environment? Not to let Tom off the hook—after all, I'm pretty sure he's derailing this murder investigation—but he doesn't seem to be a bad guy at heart. Unlike Orbin, who seems truly bad to the bone."

"Damn right," growled Waylon. "Meanest sumbitch on the face of the earth."

O'Conner smiled slightly. "I'd say you're a pretty shrewd judge of manflesh, Doc. He *is* bad to the bone. Not sure why. I mean, why do some abused children grow up to be serial killers, while others grow up to be compassionate doctors and teachers and social workers?"

Ah: the Problem of Evil. I'd spent a lot of fruitless hours pondering that conundrum. "I guess it would've been hard to be Tom's little brother," I ventured.

"Real hard," O'Conner said. "Still is. The halo's slipped some by now, but Tom Kitchings was Cooke County's golden boy. Didn't get a huge amount of nurture and affirmation at home, but to the rest of the county, Tom was practically a god. Led the high school football team to two state championships, then led UT to a couple, too. Good-looking, pretty smart, and really personable. Orbin, less so." Judging by my two brief encounters, O'Conner was giving Orbin a huge benefit of the doubt there. "Be easy to turn hateful if you found yourself being measured and found wanting your whole life. Hell, even now, Orbin's still playing second fiddle to Tom. Sort of the age-old story of Cain and Abel, isn't it? Orbin can either bash his brother's brains out, like Cain did, or he can use weaker folks like Vern as his whipping boys. Been doing it just about all his life."

O'Conner's armchair analysis made a lot of sense. "So would you guess Orbin's flying solo when he puts the squeeze on pot farmers and cockfighters, or is it possible Tom's in cahoots with him?"

He frowned. "Don't know. When he was younger, Tom would never have stooped to that. But when he was younger, he had a lot more choices. He's had some big disappointments to reckon with, and you never can tell whether somebody's going to walk out of the valley of the shadow as a bigger person or a smaller one."

As he said it, I found myself wondering whether I was seeing a bigger or a smaller Jim O'Conner than the one who'd courted Leena Bonds. Then I found myself wondering whether he was seeing a bigger or a smaller Bill Brockton than the one who'd lost Kathleen. I remembered my last phone call with Jeff, and I knew the answer. I vowed to call him and apologize.

"Hell, that's enough of my cracker-barrel psychology for one day," said O'Conner, draining the last of his whiskey. "Let me get Waylon to take you back to your truck."

"You sure Waylon ought to be driving?"

"Hell, Doc, I could drive that stretch of road with my eyes closed," said Waylon.

"He's not kidding—I've seen him do it," O'Conner laughed. "It'd take another three drinks before Waylon started to feel that whiskey, and even then, he'd be a better driver than you or I stone-cold sober."

With some misgivings, I climbed into the truck with Waylon. I rolled down the window and called to O'Conner, "Will you *please* make him promise not to drag me into any more adventures along the way?"

He laughed. "You hear that, Waylon? Straight to the Pilot station; no stops. All right?"

Waylon nodded. "No stops," he said.

It never occurred to me to extract a promise to drive with the headlights on. Halfway along the river road, Waylon flicked off his lights, leaving us careening along in utter blackness.

"Waylon, stop!" I yelped.

"Cain't," he said. "I promised—no stops."

"Then turn your lights back on!"

"You b'lieve now?"

"Believe what?" Had something in our discussion of religion struck a nerve in Waylon?

"B'lieve I can drive this with my eyes closed."

"Yes, for God's sake. Now turn on your headlights."

He did. As the beams shot through the blackness, I saw that the big truck was tracking dead-center in the right-hand lane, halfway through an "S" curve, as if it were on rails.

"Waylon, you're going to turn me into either a believer or a dead man."

He laughed. "Well, either way, you won't feel scared no more."

29

THE GUARD AT THE John J. Duncan Federal Building was the same stony-faced sentinel who'd been keeping watch over the lobby the last time I was here. This time, I was determined to get a smile out of him. I checked his name tag. "Morning, Officer Shipley," I said cheerily. "I'm Bill Brockton, from UT. I'm going up to the FBI's offices again." He nodded ever so slightly. "You doing all right today?" He looked startled.

"Just fine, sir." He said it stiffly, but it was a start, at least.

"Glad to hear it. By the way, did you read the paper this morning?" He nodded warily. "Did you see that story about the recently declassified CIA case?"

"Uh, no, sir, I don't believe I saw that one."

"You'll appreciate this, being familiar with federal agencies," I said. "You remember back when President Jimmy Carter got attacked by that wild rabbit?" He looked puzzled, so I decided to refresh his memory. "Carter was fishing in a pond down in Georgia, and this big bunny came swimming out toward his boat in a threatening manner, hissing and gnashing his teeth. Remember that?" He nodded, and I could tell he wondered where this was going. "Well, according to this new report, the CIA sent double agents—undercover squirrels and chipmunks—scampering throughout the forest to gather every scrap of intelligence they could about this foiled rabbit assassination plot. After spending months on analysis and millions in payoffs, they still couldn't catch this killer rabbit. The reason, it now turns out, is the CIA itself had been infiltrated . . . by a mole." He looked at me without expression. "Get it—a mole?" I grinned and nodded encouragingly.

I saw pity in his eyes. "Yes, sir, I'm afraid I do get it." He shook his head sadly. "That," he said, "has got to be the *worst* joke I've ever heard." He continued to take the measure of the joke's lameness, and when he'd finished, he finally cracked a smile.

"There," I said triumphantly. "You're a tough audience, but I knew I could make you smile."

"Don't quit your day job," he said, waving me toward the elevator.

Up on the sixth floor, I tried the CIA joke on Angela Price and the rest of the federal and state agents. They liked it about as much as Shipley had, so I decided to hold the FBI joke I'd prepared as an encore. "Okay, a lot has happened since I saw you last," I said. First I told them about what I'd seen in the pot patch just twenty-four hours earlier; then I recounted what happened in the cave; finally I circled back to the sheriff's drunken phone call. "I don't get it," I said. "Maybe it was just the liquor talking, but he sounded like a man who's trying to do the right thing."

Price looked dubious. "Well, I'd be happy to be convinced of that. But it'll take a lot more than a sloppy drunk crying into the phone to persuade me. I'd give more weight to the theft of the bones and the explosions in the cave."

"Yeah, the phone call rang a bit hollow to me after that, too," I admitted, "although we don't know for sure the sheriff was involved in those. Or in his brother's shakedown operation, either."

The DEA agent—I had never really gotten a fix on his name—leapt in and began asking questions about the pot patch: who was the farmer, where was his patch, how big, and so on. Some things I could answer, but others—the location, Vern's full name, the number of plants—I didn't know. "I'm sorry I'm not more help on the specifics," I said. "I was a ways off, I was sick as a dog, and I was scared out of my wits. Not at my most observant." I hesitated. "I'm not sure I should say this next part, but I feel sorry for Cousin Vern. He's obviously struggling, he's got a sick kid, and Orbin shot the man's dog out of pure spite. Looked like it just about broke Vern's heart. I don't know how much leeway you have in cases like this, but if there's any way to give that guy a break somehow, it seems like the humane thing to do."

An awkward silence followed my plea. Finally Price spoke up. "Well, Doctor Brockton, it's a good thing you became a scientist rather than a law enforcement officer or a prosecutor. If we let everybody who's got a sad story off the hook, we wouldn't make many arrests. Still, if it makes you feel better, I'll remind you that the focus of this informal investigation is corrupt officials, not small-scale pot farmers. And we do have some discretion in how we deal with small fry who help us land bigger fish. Beyond that, we can't promise anything."

I nodded. "Fair enough. I appreciate that. And I'll certainly encourage anyone who can to cooperate as fully as possible. Mind you, I haven't seen anything that suggests that *Tom* Kitchings is involved in extortion. However, sick and scared as I was out in the pot patch, I saw enough to testify that Tom's brother—who is also his chief deputy—is crooked as a dog's hind leg."

"Is he taking bribes, or is he extorting money?" The question came from a man who had slipped into the room right after I'd started talking. Price introduced him as David Welton, the in-house lawyer for the FBI's East Tennessee field office.

"Well, he put a gun to the man's head and promised to kill

him if he didn't come up with a thousand dollars in two weeks. I'd sure call that extortion."

Welton was taking notes now. "And he was in uniform when he did this?"

"Hell, even his helicopter was wearing a uniform."

The lawyer looked at Price. "Sounds like we've got him on both Hobbs and colorful law," he said. She nodded.

I looked from one to the other, bewildered. Welton explained, "The Hobbs Act outlaws robbery or extortion that interferes with commerce. It was passed back in 1946 to keep the Teamsters Union from taking over the trucking industry." I appreciated the history lesson, but I wasn't sure whether I was getting less bewildered or more. "Marijuana cultivation isn't *legal* commerce," he went on, "but I think we can make the case that in Cooke County, it's *established* commerce. A pillar of the underground economy, in fact." I was beginning to see his reasoning, but could it really be possible that Orbin's crime was obstructing drug trafficking? "By the way," he added, "speaking of pot patches, if your friend Vern has booby-trapped his, the way a lot of these backwoods guys do"—I felt a rush of panic on Waylon's behalf but tried not to show it—"he could be looking at ten years in federal prison for that alone." I made a mental note to warn Waylon at the first opportunity.

"So tell me about colorful law," I said. "What's that?"

"Excuse me? Oh, color *of* law. The 'color of law' statute is something we've found useful in prosecuting corrupt law enforcement officers. Basically, it says that if a public official deprives a person of their rights under what's called 'the color of law'—that is, using their position and power to commit the crime—it's a federal offense. By swooping down in that helicopter and committing assault, extortion—hell, even shooting the dog, which probably falls within the technical definition of 'taking'—this chief deputy has stepped way over the color-of-law line."

Price nodded. "So maybe we haul in Sky King, hold a ten-year sentence over his head, and get him to turn witness against big brother?"

"Maybe," cautioned the lawyer, "but be sure you do it right. As a law enforcement officer, the deputy's considered a highly sensitive source. You'll need to bring headquarters into the loop before you do it. Probably means you need to create a formal task force." Price frowned, and I recalled her earlier description of the mountain of paperwork involved.

"Excuse me," I interjected. "Do you mind if I ask a couple more things?" Price frowned but assented. I turned to Morgan. "Steve, did your TBI techs find anything at my office? Any prints? Any other evidence that might point to the sheriff—or rule him out?"

Morgan shook his head. "As we expected, mostly your prints. Some we haven't ID'd yet—probably students—but definitely not the sheriff's or either deputy's. Your prints on the doorknob were smeared, which means that whoever broke in was wearing gloves."

"Can't you get a search warrant and go look for the skeletal material?"

"Look *where?*" he said. "The sheriff's office? His house? His brother's house? The other deputy's house? The sheds at the cockfight pit?" He shook his head, the former student now reprimanding his professor. "We can't just go fishing all over Cooke County for it, even if we wanted to. Any judge in the state would hand me my head if I asked for a multiple-choice search warrant."

I hesitated; this was not going quite as well as I'd hoped. But I had to ask one more question. "There's another thing I'm wondering about. Concerned about." I'd promised Morgan to keep our stairwell conversation to myself, but I hadn't made any such promise about what I saw from the bushes after my first meeting here. I looked at Price. "The last time I was here, I saw a Cooke County sheriff's deputy coming in as I was leaving." Price looked daggers at Morgan; he reddened, eyes locked on his notepad. "I assume Deputy Williams is another one of your sources for this investigation. Does that mean I can consider him one of the good guys? It sure would be nice to know that kind of thing."

Price's voice rang like case-hardened steel. "Dr. Brockton, this investigation is a matter of strictest confidence—or *should* be, at any rate." She shot another glare at Morgan. "You are not, under *any* circumstances, to speak with *any* person about *any* matters under discussion in this room. I thought I made that clear at our first meeting."

"You did. I just assumed—"

"*Don't*," she snapped. "Don't assume anything, about anything or anyone. If you do, you could jeopardize this entire investigation, you could jeopardize your own safety, you could jeopardize the lives of other people. Is that one hundred percent clear this time, Dr. Brockton?"

"Yes, ma'am," was all I could muster. She spun and left the room, and with that, it seemed, the meeting was adjourned. I got a few awkward glances and head nods as I walked out, but not much more. Morgan silently escorted me past the glassed-in receptionist and as far as the elevator, then left me without a word.

Down in the lobby, Officer Shipley gave me a smile and a wave as I stepped off the elevator. "Hey, Doc, you hear the one about the CIA interviewing people for an assassin's job?" I held up a hand to fend him off, ducked my head, and got out of the federal building as quickly as I could.

30

JUST SEEING CAVE SPRINGS Primitive Baptist Church gave me the willies all over again. Even the mortar between the stones seemed to ooze menace.

I swung the truck wide in the parking lot so I could glimpse the opening of the cave. The heavy steel grate remained in place—secured with a shiny new padlock, which seemed odd, since the cave-in had left the tunnel impenetrable anyhow. Although it was midday, I switched on my headlights and flipped to the high beams. Within the blackness of the opening, the light grazed the fringes of the rubble pile that had nearly entombed Art and me.

Circling back to the other side of the parking lot, I parked the truck near the house that adjoined the church. Art and I had guessed that this was the parsonage, where Reverend Kitchings and his wife lived. Most Knoxville ministers these days lived miles from their churches, in upscale suburbs where they blended invisibly with the doctors and lawyers and accountants, but I suspected Cave Springs had more in common with nineteenth-century Knoxville than twenty-first-century Knoxville, and that the pastor—"shepherd," the word originally meant—still hovered close to his flock. I wasn't sure I'd catch Reverend or Mrs. Kitchings at home, and if I didn't, I'd have made a long drive for nothing, but it

seemed risky to phone ahead and announce my arrival—
either to the couple or to their two excitable sons.

The house reminded me of my grandparents' home, a
simple wooden farmhouse built in the 1920s. A broad covered porch ran the full width of the front of the house. The
angle of the roof changed, the slope lessened, where the tin
flared above the porch. A dormer window broke the roofline
above, letting light into an upstairs bedroom or, judging by
my grandparents' house, an attic crammed with musty furni-
ture and fading mementoes. I wondered if any of those mementoes were of Leena.

The wooden steps had once been gray, but now the
paint—where paint remained—had turned the murky color
of used mop water. The ends of the porch's floorboards projected an inch or so beyond the joist that supported them;
each weathered end tilted and warped with a mind of its
own, giving the edge of the porch the appearance of a
mouthful of crooked teeth.

Two rockers—a high ladderback and a lower, spindle-
backed one—flanked the front door on either side. The rockers of the ladderback were worn and blunted at their tips,
suggesting years of vigorous rocking. The other chair's
rockers were worn in exactly the opposite pattern, ground
nearly flat in their central region.

The screen door was slightly ajar, having sagged enough
over the years to drag across the floor, etching a pale, paint-
less quarter-circle to mark decades of comings and goings. I
imagined some of them: The family headed to church every
Sunday, Tom and Orbin first as toddlers, then as rambunc-
tious boys, then as sullen teenagers. A procession of troubled parishioners—philandering spouses and injured
parties, problem drinkers, delinquent youths. A movable
feast of roasts, stews, casseroles, cakes, and pies, tasty
enough to offset the long hours and low pay that define a
country parson's life.

I tugged open the screen door, adding my own modest mark to the history etched on the floor. The door's rusty spring screeched at exactly the same hair-raising pitch my grandmother's screen door spring once wailed. My knock on the front door rattled the pane of glass, whose glazing putty was shrunken and cracked with age.

There was no response, so I knocked again, then closed the screen door so as not to seem too pushy. After a pause, I heard slow, creaking footsteps. A lace curtain was pulled back a fraction of an inch, then released, and I heard the click of an old-fashioned lock being opened. An elderly woman frowned at me through the dusty screen.

"Yes?"

"Are you Mrs. Kitchings?"

"Yes, I am."

"I'm sorry to bother you, ma'am, but I was hoping I might talk to you for a few minutes. My name is Dr. Bill Brockton, and I'm up here helping your son Tom with a case."

"What kind of case?"

"Well, it's an old case that's just now come to light. The death—the murder—of a young woman I'm told was your niece."

"Oh, yes—Evelina. Tommy told me Leena had been found. Strangled. After all these years. What a shame."

"Yes, ma'am. Would you mind if I come in and talk to you about it?"

"Well, I'd have to think about that. Tommy's the sheriff, and I done told him everthing I know. She just run off one day. We never did know why at the time. Tommy says you figgered out she was expectin'. I reckon that explains it. We never did see her again. That's all I can tell you."

"Mrs. Kitchings, I know it's been a long time, and it might be hard to remember details, but if you wouldn't mind a few questions, you might just remember something that will help us." The flimsy screen door was like an impenetrable force field between us. "Would you mind if I come in for just a few minutes?"

She shook her head. "Not meaning any disrespect, Doctor, but my husband ain't home, and I don't let strange men in my house when I'm alone."

"I'm not quite as strange as I look, and I promise I don't bite." She was not amused. "Tell you what—it's a nice day; how about if we sit out here on the porch in these rocking chairs?"

She frowned, but she pushed open the screen and stepped onto the porch. I headed for the ladderback chair, to leave the smaller one for her, but she reached out a bony hand and stopped me. "That-un's mine," she said. "You can sit in Thomas's there." She settled into the big chair and launched a series of huge, swooping arcs.

"You sure do get the good out of those rockers," I said.

She never wavered. "Rock your troubles away, that's what my mama always told me."

"Does it work?"

"Don't know. Ain't never tried *not* rocking. Gives you something to do while you worry, leastwise. Keeps you legs strong, too."

I laughed. "Reckon I better buy me a rocker when I get back to Knoxville." I tried to find a rhythm in the spindle-backed chair, but I'd no sooner get some momentum in one direction than I'd hit the flat spot heading back the other way and grind to a halt. "I think maybe this one needs a tune-up. I can't seem to get up a head of steam."

"Thomas, he ain't much for rockin'. He kindly goes through the motions, but his heart ain't in it."

"What's he do with *his* troubles?"

"Prays 'em away. Preaches 'em away. Coon hunts 'em away. Everbody's got their own ways."

"Tell me about Leena."

Her white hair bobbed up and down with her arcs. "Leena

was my sister Sophie's girl. Leena was a Bonds, not a Kitch-ings, but she was still my blood kin. Her daddy was one of them Bondses over to Claiborne County." She seemed al-most entranced by the rhythm of the chair. "Leena come to stay with us when her mama and daddy died. Our boys, Orbin and Tom, was three and five then. Sometimes she was real good with 'em, sometimes not. Leena was what you might call high-spirited, which ain't far removed from mule-headed. But she was good-lookin', just like her mama, I'll give her that."

"Tell me about her mama—Sophie, you said her name was?" The old woman gave an oversized swing of her head. "Sophie was your sister?" Another big nod. "Older or younger?"

"Younger. Three years? No, four." She looked down at the spotted hands clutching the arms of the rocker. "Sophie al-ways was the pretty one of us two. I think Thomas really fancied her, but when she took up with Junior Bonds, Thomas started courtin' me. Reckon he figured if he couldn't have Sophie, he'd make do with me." I recalled what O'Conner had told me of the preacher's sternness, and I felt sorry for the woman who had been his second choice in a wife.

"How'd Leena's parents die?"

"House fire. Chimney caught one night after they was asleep. Leena jumped out the window, only thing saved her. Sophie and Junior wasn't so lucky."

"How old was Leena then?"

"Thirteen, fourteen, maybe. Leena was kindly a late bloomer, but when she finally started to blossom, she was a beauty. If they was a church social or a wedding or even a funeral, you couldn't fight your way through the boys around her."

"Was one of those boys Jim O'Conner?"

She cut me a quick look. "Well, sure. He weren't the

biggest feller around, but he was good-lookin', and he had a lot of gumption. Like a little banty rooster, struttin' around the barnyard, but somehow you didn't mind it." She smiled, briefly and sadly. "He was real sweet back then. He's turned a mite hard since, but I can't say as I blame him. Maybe all of us do, once we get some hard lessons in the way of the world."

She paused—verbally and physically—and I waited awhile before asking my next question. "Mrs. Kitchings, were she and Jim O'Conner sweethearts? Serious sweethearts?"

She began rocking, and nodded. "Yes. Yes, they was. They was talking about getting married once he come back from Vietnam." She put the stress on "Nam," making it rhyme with "ham."

"And how did you feel about that?"

"Oh, I thought that would be all right. I liked Jim, and I could tell she was crazy over him. Not too many girls up in these mountains gets a man like that. It's pretty slim pickins, and you take what you can get, or else you make your peace with being a old maid." It sounded like she was talking about herself now. "I wanted Leena to have a good life and a good husband."

"So you and your husband gave them your blessing."

There was a momentary hitch in her rocking, but she quickly found the rhythm again. "Well, we would have. I cain't say Thomas had took the same shine to the O'Conner boy what I had. Thomas was like a daddy to that girl, so for him, no fella was ever going to measure up."

I knew what I needed to ask, but not how to ask it. "Did he try to discourage her? Or him?"

Her pace quickened. "They mighta been a discussion or two. Thomas has always spoke his mind straight out. Not one to mince his words. He could be right sharp, and he said some strong words about the O'Conner boy to her once."

"And how did Leena respond?"

"Why, that girl lit into him like—" She ceased rocking and turned a suspicious eye on me. "Why you asking me these things? That's thirty years ago, and we ain't never seen her since. Not since she got herself in trouble and run off. Never heard from her, neither—not so much as a by-your-leave or fare-thee-well or thankee-kindly. That girl made her bed, and I don't know who she laid in it with, but it weren't us. So good riddance, I say."

Inside the house, a phone began to ring. It was a harsh, metallic jangle, the likes of which I hadn't heard in years. I expected to hear an answering machine pick up, but the phone rang without ceasing. The longer it rang, the more nervous I got about who might be calling Mrs. Kitchings, and what might ensue if she said she was talking to me. She began worrying at the fabric of her housedress, and I could tell she was about to answer the phone. I didn't want to risk staying through the conversation, so I pushed myself up from the flat-rockered chair. "Sounds like somebody really wants to talk to you. Reckon I should let you go do it."

She looked startled at the swiftness of my departure. It was customary down South to spend a half-hour or more saying good-bye, but I myself had never embraced the extended leave-taking, what I called the "Southern good-bye." I thanked her for her time and hustled down the stairs.

She hesitated at the screen door, as if to make sure I was really leaving. As I turned back to wave, I noticed something I'd missed earlier. A faint path led from the back of the house, which probably contained the kitchen, a back door, and a utility porch. The path hugged the treeline at the base of the hill, and it led straight to the blasted entrance of the cave.

31

DISTRICT ATTORNEY BOB ROPER looked like he hadn't slept in three days. Burt DeVriess looked like he'd just won the lottery. We were convened in the chambers of Judge Barr to review the exhumation results. "Gentlemen, let's proceed," said the judge. "This is most unusual, but given that Mr. Roper asked for this conference, and Mr. DeVriess agreed, I'm willing for us to have an informal discussion about this case. I've got a hearing in ten minutes, so we need to cut straight to the chase."

DeVriess was happy to oblige. "Your Honor, I think the exhumation results speak for themselves," he crowed.

"Then why are you talking, Mr. DeVriess? Kindly be quiet." I suppressed a grin, or at least tried, halfway. "Dr. Brockton, I've read your report, along with Dr. Carter's; thank you for your quick and thorough examination." I nodded, figuring I shouldn't speak unless asked to. "Mr. Roper, have you read the report?" Roper nodded miserably. "And what is your response? Does your forensic anthropologist take issue with Dr. Brockton's conclusions?"

Roper hedged. "Your Honor, much as we respect Dr. Brockton and Dr. Carter, there is other evidence in this case that strongly corroborates the state's case."

The judge pounced on him. "Such as?" Roper drew a deep breath, like a man about to take a long swim underwater, but the judge cut him off. "For God's sake, Bob, cut your losses. The ME blew the autopsy and you know it. Unless Dr. Hamilton has something on you that could ruin your career or wreck your marriage, just bite the bullet and drop the charge. It's embarrassing, but not as humiliating as losing in court would be. I can pretty much guarantee that you won't win this one, and you lay yourself open to a malicious prosecution lawsuit. On the other hand, if you drop the charge and apologize to the defendant, you look like the good guy. You get to talk about how truth and justice have prevailed, and you get to celebrate the vindication of an innocent man. It's the best damn deal you can walk out of here with."

Roper swallowed hard; it was a big dose of medicine he was being handed. "Your Honor, in light of new evidence, the state respectfully withdraws the charge, apologizes to the court and to the defendant, and thanks Dr. Brockton and Dr. Carter for bringing important exculpatory facts to light in this case."

The judge smiled. "There, that wasn't so bad, was it? You file the paperwork and I'll order the defendant's release. I'm also ordering his record expunged. Unless, of course, defense counsel has some objection?"

DeVriess smiled a smug smile. "Well, Your Honor, the defense was eagerly anticipating a jury trial . . ."

"Just shut up, Grease," snapped the judge as he stood and strode toward his courtroom, "before I change my mind." DeVriess reddened, Roper brightened, and I smiled to myself.

The rest of us stood to leave by way of the door to the judge's outer office. Roper shook my hand with a rueful smile. "Bill, you did the right thing, unfortunately for me."

I clapped his shoulder with my left hand. "Don't take it too hard, Bob. You based your case on the autopsy report; not your fault it was bad. The one who's got something to answer for is the medical examiner. I wouldn't be surprised if the state tries to yank Garland's medical license over this. It's not his first screwup, you know."

"I know. But it's his last screwup on a case for me—I've already made arrangements to contract out my autopsies to Dr. Carter and her staff down in Chattanooga." I'd heard as much already from Jess, but I acted as if it were news, and welcome news, coming from the DA. "Bill, if the state moves to pull Dr. Hamilton's medical license, I hope you'll testify as candidly in Nashville as you did here."

I nodded. "I won't like it, but I'll do it."

"Thanks," he said. "He needs to be put out to pasture. If this case helps bring that to pass, I guess it's worth the humiliation." I was glad to hear him looking ahead. "Thanks for what you did, Bill. I didn't enjoy it, but I do appreciate it."

DeVriess leaned in. "Hey, how about sharing the love? I'm the one that cried foul."

"Go to hell, Burt," said Roper. "Bill, I look forward to working with you again. *With* you. Okay?"

"Okay," I smiled. "See you." He nodded and started down the marble hallway. "Oh, and Bob?" He looked back. "Thanks for what you said about Kathleen the other day. It's been rough, and I'm not good at talking about it, but it helps to hear from folks who care." He smiled and walked away.

"Bastard," muttered DeVriess. "Dr. Brockton, I've got somebody who really wants to meet you." I had a class to teach, I protested, but he persisted. "This'll just take a second, and I think you'll be glad." I relented, and he led me away from the judge's chambers office and into a part of the court building where I'd never been before. A uniformed guard buzzed us through a security door; DeVriess opened a door marked "Dock" and led me into a bare white room. A scrawny man in faded jeans and a white shirt rose from a plastic chair. "Eddie, I want you to meet Dr. Brockton. Doctor, this is Eddie Meacham, the man whose name you just cleared. The man who just got his life back."

Meacham stared as if I were some alien species, then flung himself at me and wrapped me in a bony hug. I patted him on the back a few times, then extricated myself so I could breathe again. Meacham made several attempts to speak. Finally he whispered, "Thank you. Thank you." That was all he managed to get out. But it was enough. I nodded, moved myself, and backed out of the room.

DeVriess had been right—I was glad. Glad I'd met his client; glad I'd taken the case—taken the bait that Grease, pervert-protecting bastard that he was, had lobbed my way that day over lunch. Miranda was right: "Strange bedfellows indeed," I murmured as I pushed open the courthouse door and stepped into the early October sunshine.

32

I WAS STILL BASKING IN the glow of the sunshine and Meacham's gratitude when a man fell in beside me on the sidewalk. "Think you're pretty smart, don't you?" he hissed. I stopped in midstride and turned toward him, and found myself facing Dr. Garland Hamilton. "Think you're hot shit, don't you?"

"Hello, Garland," I said to the medical examiner whose credibility I had just destroyed. "I'm sorry this played out the way it did. It wasn't personal, you know."

"Wasn't personal? Wasn't *personal?* You sanctimonious son of a bitch. It's sure as hell personal to *me*. Try losing *your* career and *your* reputation, and then tell me it's not personal." He jabbed a finger into my chest to punctuate his words. "You have destroyed me. And I take that very, very personally."

I took hold of his finger; he yanked it away in fury. I wanted to punch him, but I knew that absolutely no good and probably lots of trouble would come of it—lurid headlines and a huge lawsuit. "Look, Garland, *you* botched the exam, not me. If I hadn't pointed it out, somebody else would have."

"Bullshit," he said. "You and Jess Carter put your heads together and came up with a perfect scheme to get me out of the way. Ironic, isn't it—turns out I'm the one who really got stabbed in the back in this case." I just shook my head; there was no point trying to argue with him. "Jess has wanted to take over the forensic center here ever since she got divorced," he continued. "Did she screw you, Bill? Is that how she got you to help her screw *me* over?"

"Not true, Garland. Dr. Carter and I have never had anything but a professional relationship."

"Dr. Carter and I," he mocked. "You make me sick."

"Frankly, Garland, I don't give a damn," I said. "There's nothing between Jess and me, never has been, never will be. She's happily lesbian, in case you didn't know."

He snorted. "Yeah, right. Tell that to the guy I saw her wrapped around in the bar of the Hilton last week in Chattanooga."

I tried not to be surprised at that. "Good-bye, Dr. Hamilton." I turned and began walking away.

"Don't you walk away from me," he yelled. "I'm not finished with you!" I kept walking. "Do you hear me? I'm nowhere *near* finished with you!"

33

THE PHONE ON MY desk jangled, startling me from a daydream that mostly involved Miranda, Sarah, and Jess Carter, with occasional nightmarish interruptions by a deranged medical examiner hell-bent on revenge.

"Dr. Brockton?"

"Yes."

"This is David Welton." I struggled to place the name. "The FBI's district counsel."

"Oh, yes. Sorry."

"No problem. Listen, I may have some good news for you."

"I can always use some."

"Angela Price and I were talking about your Cooke County homicide case. As you know, we're up against a sort of catch-22 on obstruction of justice, and that's frustrating."

"Frustrating for the FBI, or frustrating for me?"

"Both. Despite what you may think, Price is a dedicated agent, but she has to work within fairly strict protocols. Also, there's a lot more politics involved in law enforcement than most people realize, especially in places like Cooke County. Nearly everybody up there is related to everybody else in some way or other, and they have their own notions of justice, as you're painfully aware."

"Right. And even the TBI can't touch them, sounds like."

"Well, that's a little cynical, but it is true that an obstruction case would be really tough for the state to win up there."

"That doesn't sound like the good news you mentioned."

"Sorry, I'm just getting to that," he said. "We might have more options than we thought. I was trying to figure out some creative way for us to turn this into a federal offense, and I remembered a pretty creative maneuver the Bureau used a few years ago to prosecute one of our own guys." He had my attention. "The name JJ Smith mean anything to you?"

"No, 'fraid not. Should it?"

"If you worked for the Bureau, it sure would. JJ Smith was an FBI agent in Los Angeles who was handling Chinese spies."

"Their spies, or our spies?"

"Exactly. Thereby hangs the crux of the matter," he said. "Or the crotch of it, you might say. Smith was giving one of his female assets, code-named 'Parlor Maid,' some very special handling. They would meet and have sex, and sometime in the course of those encounters, she would take classified papers from his briefcase, copy the information, then relay it to Beijing."

"Sounds like Mata Hari," I said.

"Very like. There's a name for a female spy who uses her charms to seduce sources and obtain secrets. She's called a honey pot."

"Hmm. My grandpa used to call my grandma that. Although the only secrets he had were the bottles of Jack Daniels he had tucked away in the barn, and I'm pretty sure she never seduced those away from him."

"Well, then, your grandma wasn't as shrewd as this Chinese agent, 'cause she plucked JJ Smith like a turkey. We were having one hell of a time building an espionage case against him, though. The thing we finally got him for was mail fraud."

"Which spelling of the word are we talking here?"

He laughed. "The mail fraud statutes make it a crime to use the U.S. mail, radio, telephone, or other communications over an interstate carrier to commit fraud. And fraud is defined very broadly—so broadly, it can include simply depriving a person of what's called the 'intangible right of honest service.' In JJ Smith's case, having hot sex with a Chinese spy, on the Bureau's clock and at taxpayer expense, hardly counts as 'honest service.' Sounds like grasping at straws, but it worked."

"Sort of like Al Capone eventually serving time, not for murder or bootlegging but for tax evasion?"

"Exactly. If Plan A doesn't work, switch to Plan B."

"And how does this relate to Sheriff Kitchings? We send Price up there in something by Victoria's Secret?"

"Whoa. If she ever even *suspected* you'd said something like that, you'd need emergency admission to the Witness Protection Program."

"Sorry. The 'dishonest service' charge just seems a little vague."

"It is," he conceded. "That's why I'm hoping to relegate that strategy to Plan B."

"Does that mean you've got a Plan A?"

"We'll see," he said. "I'm looking at a map of Cooke County right now. Think you can steer me to the cave where the woman's body was found?"

I described the route east from Knoxville on I-40, directing him to the Jonesport exit and then taking him along the winding river road. "Okay, about six or eight miles upriver, look for a right-hand turn that heads up into the mountains," I said.

There was a pause. "Okay, got it. Now what?"

"Go three or four miles up that, then look for a road to the left. Cave Springs is another mile up that road."

"Hang on. Let me make sure I've got this. Yes, I see it." I could hear the excitement rising in his voice. "Bingo," he said.

"What is it?"

"The law giveth, and the law taketh away. If a crime is committed on federal land, it can be prosecuted in federal court. Doesn't make the *crime* federal—your Cooke County murder is a state crime, and always will be. But if it happened on U.S. land, we can make a federal case out of it."

Somewhere in the back of my mind, I knew that. Years before, some of my students were arrested for consuming alcohol in Great Smoky Mountains National Park—four of them shared a bottle of wine at a picnic beside Abrams Falls—and the entire Anthropology Department had shown up in federal court to lend moral support. I was vaguely familiar with the legal framework he was erecting here, so I hated to bring it crashing down. "Listen, I'm not sure I gave the directions quite right," I said, hoping to let him down easy. "The body was found eight or ten miles *north* of I-40. The national park is all way to the *south* side of the interstate. I hate to say it, but it looks like we're stuck with Plan B."

"Your directions were fine, Dr. Brockton," he said cheerily. "Cave Springs Church is shown on this map. And it's just inside a beautiful green strip of federal land."

"But the national park—"

"I'm not talking about the park, Dr. Brockton. Your victim's body was found a mile inside the boundary of Cherokee National Forest."

"You're sure?"

"I'd stake my orienteering merit badge on it."

"Hot damn," I said. I could already hear the hoofbeats of the federal cavalry. "Hello, Plan A."

"Hello, Plan A," he echoed. "There is one thing you need to understand, though, Dr. Brockton."

"What's that?"

"Plan A: it won't happen overnight."

"Oh, I understand. These things can take weeks, even months, can't they?"

He didn't say anything for a long time. "Dr. Brockton, you're not going to want to hear this. The average duration of an interagency task force involving undercover agents is two years, start to finish."

"Two *years?*"

"Two years."

I thanked Welton for his interest, wished him happy hunting, and laid the receiver to rest, along with my hopes for Plan A.

My hand had scarcely left the receiver when the phone rang again. It was Peggy, the Anthropology Department secretary. She sounded upset. "Did you take my spare keys again?"

"No, why?"

"They're not in my desk drawer."

"They'll turn up," I said.

"You're the only one who ever takes them."

"When did you notice they were gone?"

"Last week," she said. "It was the same day someone broke into your office. You don't think . . . ?"

I did think, and I got a very bad feeling.

I hung up the phone and unlocked the door to the skeletal collection room. Accessible only through my office, the collection room housed all our forensic specimens—row upon row of metal shelves filled with cardboard boxes like the one stolen off my desk last week. Flipping on the fluorescent lights, I began scanning the shelves. The foot-square ends of the boxes presented themselves like books in a library—a library of murder mysteries, all of them carved in bone.

Whoever had pried open my office had not broken into the collection room—of this I was certain, for a TBI technician, the university police officer, and I had all checked the door, finding it undamaged and securely locked. Or maybe carefully *re*locked, I now realized.

As I reached the section of shelves containing the most recent years' cases, my knees went weak. There was a one-foot-square gap in the boxes, and I knew without even checking which box should have been there.

Billy Ray Ledbetter's bones were gone.

With a heavy heart, I called Steve Morgan's TBI pager and reported the additional theft to him. "This complicates the picture," he said, echoing my own thoughts exactly. It might mean that the theft of Leena's bones was just a smokescreen, and the mangled outer door was just for show. It might also mean that Dr. Garland Hamilton, a disgraced and very angry medical examiner, hadn't been making idle threats when he confronted me outside the courthouse.

"Did you steal a blind man's cane recently?" asked Morgan. "Rob a church collection plate? Take candy from a baby? Kick a nun? I gotta tell you, I haven't seen this much bad karma in one place since Bernie Kerik's nomination to head Homeland Security imploded in a half-dozen scandals."

"When it rains, it pours," I said miserably. "I'm on the hot seat. I'm wearing a bull's-eye."

"Bullshit," he said, but he promised to send the crime scene techs back to comb the collection room. We both knew they'd come up empty-handed.

34

THE KUDZU TUNNEL TO Jim O'Conner's hideaway was becoming as familiar to me as my own driveway. I had phoned an hour before with news of the additional bone theft, along with a discouraging reassessment of our prospects for recovering Leena. "I was pretty sure she was somewhere in Cooke County, in the hands of somebody who wears a badge," I said. "Now I have no idea who's got her, where she is, or whether we'll ever get her back."

He took the news more calmly than I'd expected; he even tried to console me over the loss. "Well, I hope you recover the bones, and I hope you nail whoever took 'em. But remember, those bones aren't Leena. They're just what's left of what used to be her, a long time ago." This from the man I'd sent reeling, not once but twice—first with the news of her discovery, then with the bombshell about her pregnancy. He was a remarkably resilient human being. "Listen, if you've got the time, come up and see me," he said next. "I've got something to show you. As an anthropologist, you'll find it interesting; might cheer you up." That was all he would divulge over the phone.

On the drive up, my mind raced with the possibilities. Had he found something that shed light on Leena's death, on the identity of her killer? His phrasing puzzled me, though: "as an anthropologist"—what did that mean? Had he unearthed some clue or piece of evidence from three decades ago? Some groundbreaking article about cave burials? Why would I be more interested in whatever it was as a scientist than as a guy who'd been dragged all over the hills of Cooke County—and underneath a few of them, too?

When I pulled up in front of the vine-draped farmhouse, I noticed that the kudzu seemed to have swallowed another foot or two all around the edges. O'Conner seemed unconcerned, though. He was sitting in the same rocking chair where I'd first met him. He lifted a hand in greeting, but continued to rock in big, easy arcs.

As I mounted the sagging steps to the porch, O'Conner reached over and pushed down on the arm of the rocker beside his, setting it into motion. I synchronized my timing, then eased down into it. I found my rhythm matching his.

"Hey." I said, "Why aren't you in jail? The sheriff said he was gonna arrest you days ago."

He chuckled. "They're watching my house in town. They don't know about this place yet."

After a minute, he reached into his shirt pocket and took out a photo and handed it to me. Its corners were unraveling and the colors had faded with age, but there was no mistaking the pretty blonde girl smiling at the camera. It was Leena.

"She sent me that while I was overseas. Last letter I ever got from her." I studied her face; she looked almost like I'd imagined her, but there was a trace of sadness or fear in her face that I hadn't expected. Perhaps things had already started to unravel for her, too. Or maybe I was just imagining things in hindsight.

"Mind if I borrow this and make a copy? I'll take good care of it."

" 'Course not. Anything that helps. Any headway on the case?"

"Not really. Not unless you count the break-in and the cave-ins as headway. There might be some disgruntled students who'd consider an attempt on my life to be a step in the right direction, but it doesn't shed any light on the murder."

"Maybe not directly. But somebody's mighty nervous. Afraid there's something more you're about to find out, or about to figure out."

"Well, I wish I were as smart as someone seems to think I am."

"Answer's bound to bubble up soon. You've just got to let it simmer for a while." He stood up. "Speaking of simmering, how about a cup of tea?"

"Sure, if you're having some, too."

O'Conner disappeared through the screen door, then emerged a minute later and handed me one of two pottery mugs, handmade, imprinted with the outlines of lacy ferns. "Nice mugs," I said, remembering some of what Kathleen had taught me about shapes and glazes. "Local potter?"

He smiled. "Local as you can get. Made 'em myself. Everything you're holding in your hand came off this property—the clay, the ferns, the spring water, the honey, even the tea."

"You're a regular one-man biosphere."

"I like being self-sufficient when I can. Meeting your own needs for food and utensils seems satisfying at some deep level, at least to me. Helps keep a man honest, somehow."

For a reputed outlaw, O'Conner was quite the renaissance man: philosopher, potter, beekeeper, tea farmer. I took a sip of the steaming brew and swirled it in my mouth, startled—it wasn't like any tea I had ever tasted. Underneath the honey, there was a bitter, rocky tang to it. It tasted somehow of mountains and leaves and roots and springs. "That's interesting. I think maybe I like it, but I'm not quite sure. What is it?"

He bowed slightly, acknowledging the slight compliment. "Ginseng. 'Sang,' most folks around here call it. Makes you smarter, healthier, hornier, and more virile, if five millennia of Chinese and Native Americans can be believed. Those UT coeds better watch out for you tomorrow, Doc." Visions of Sarah and Miranda flashed into my mind, and I felt myself blush. "See," O'Conner said, "it's working already."

I laughed, despite the embarrassment. "Well, I don't feel any *smarter* yet."

"That doesn't kick in till the third or fourth cup. It's tea, Doc, not a miracle potion."

We rocked and sipped. Across the valley, a swirl of thick mist crept up the hillside. As it met the morning sun, which was slanting over the ridge behind us, the mist grew soft and wispy around the margins, then gradually faded to nothing. "Doc, you think we humans are anything more than a passing wisp of fog ourselves?"

He wanted to talk about mortality? "All depends on how you look at it, Jim." I pointed across the valley. "Before it evaporated, that scrap of fog drifted across that stand of hemlocks about halfway up that hillside. I'd say those trees will grow a little extra because of that. Maybe some ferns down around the base of those trees will, too. Dry as the weather's been lately, it might be this morning's fog that keeps those ferns alive. Next time a potter needs some fronds to press into a clay mug"—I wagged my cup for emphasis—"they'll be right there waiting for him."

I took another sip, and found the taste growing on me. "I've had students tell me, years after they graduated and went on to work for medical examiners or police departments or museums, that I had a big influence on their career path. I think we all leave an imprint on the world, and on the people we cross paths with, sometimes in ways we don't fully understand." I traced the imprint of a fern. "I know my wife left a hell of a mark on me. When she died, it felt like a tree got uprooted from my heart. Still does, sometimes."

He looked away, and I guessed he was thinking of Leena.

"Jim, as an anthropologist, I'm curious: what did you want to show me? Not just your pottery, I'm guessing."

"Not just the mugs, but they're not completely irrelevant. You ever done any research on what a premium we humans put on finding the magic elixir, Doc? The biochemical fuel additive, you might say, that's going to fix things for us? Mind-numbing things like alcohol and pot? Octane boosters like cocaine or meth or Ecstasy?"

I nodded. "It is interesting. Not just humans, though—animals, too. Elephants gorge on fermented fruit to get drunk. So do orangutans and chimpanzees. Wouldn't be surprised if there's some pothead chimps somewhere in some California commune. I haven't made a study of it, though."

"I have, sort of," he said. "Not so much scientifically as financially. People will pay a lot of money for something that makes 'em feel good, or look good, or last longer in the sack. There's people up here in Cooke County that ain't got a pot to piss in, as my daddy used to say. But some of 'em trade their food stamps for pot or meth. Lotta money to be made in supplying what they demand."

I thought about the questions the FBI and DEA agents had asked about O'Conner. "Some people think you might be doing some supplying," I said. "Hard not to wonder what goes up and down such a good gravel road that's so carefully camouflaged."

His eyes took on a brittle glint, and I wondered if I'd struck a nerve. "You're right; trafficking in exotic substances is a tradition in these hills. Maybe even a birthright. My daddy tended a whiskey still for twenty years. When I was a kid, one of my chores was to split the oak he burned to cook the mash." He shook his head. "Damned thing ended up killing him—getting him killed, anyhow, which amounts to the same thing." He peered into his mug, swirling the liquid. "Over in 'Nam, I smoked a lot of dope; lots of guys did harder drugs. When we weren't out on patrol—hell, sometimes even when we were—we'd be high as kites. Helped make it bearable, though I swear I don't see how any of us made it out of there alive." He drew a deep breath. "When I came home, I started growing marijuana. Selling it."

He fell quiet, and I felt my opinion of him begin to sink. "Funny thing, though, Doc. Didn't take real long to decide I didn't like what I was doing, or who I was becoming." My opinion stopped its freefall and hung, suspended. "Cooke County's a tough place, Doc. Folks up here have a hard row to hoe even when they've got their shit together. Turn 'em into stoners and you pretty much guarantee they won't never amount to nothing, if you'll pardon the triple negative. Didn't seem the neighborly thing to do."

I smiled. "I agree. Not everybody does, though."

"Not everybody can afford to. Some people don't have the skills or the opportunity to do anything but raise pot and draw Social Security. I can't run anybody else's life; my own's about as much as I can handle. I don't worry much about what's legal and what isn't, but I don't want to make my money off marijuana."

"So where does that leave you? A rebel without a cause? An outlaw farmer without a cash crop?"

Just like that, a sunny grin broke across his face. "Like I said, I think you'll find this interesting." Taking me by the arm, he led me into the house, through a sparely furnished front room and a surprisingly modern kitchen behind, then out onto the back porch, which was shrouded in kudzu. From beneath the foliage, I saw something completely invisible from the exterior of the house: the back porch was the entrance to another tunnel of kudzu. The residential version of the camouflaged driveway.

"What's this, your escape tunnel?" He didn't answer; he just kept pulling me along, off the porch and through a trellised, arborlike structure that ran for maybe fifty yards. Then it opened out, and I found myself in an immense open space, the size of several football fields, that was dotted with a grid of telephone poles. The poles supported a network of cables, and the cables supported acres and acres of kudzu canopy, which filtered the light and tinted everything. It almost seemed we were in a dome beneath the sea, so green and otherworldly was the space. At our feet, stretching across what must have been half the valley's floor, were neat rows of plants, knee-high, bearing fuzzy leaves shaped like pointed teardrops. Atop each five-leaf cluster was a knot of red berries.

I gave a low whistle. "Gives new meaning to the word 'greenhouse,'" I said. "Whatcha growing under all this kudzu? Doesn't look much like Cousin Vern's pot plants."

"Sang," he said. "Ten acres of ginseng. Street value of about three million dollars, if I harvest it right now. Four million if I wait a year. Five, the year after that."

I wasn't following him. "Street value? You talk like it's illegal. Is it?"

He laughed. "Sorry; old habits die hard. It's perfectly legal to cultivate ginseng, but this is unlike any other cultivated sang on the planet."

"How so?"

"Ginseng 101," he said. "All ginseng is not created equal. There's a huge market for sang, mostly in China. They've been cultivating it there for centuries. But your true Chinese connoisseur turns his nose up at their domestic crop. American ginseng—*wild* American ginseng, mind you, what's known as black ginseng—that's the cream of the crop. Early Jesuit missionaries made a fortune shipping black sang to China; so did the Astors of New York. Even Daniel Boone sold it by the boatload." Clearly he had done his homework.

"Ginseng grows great up in the Smokies," he went on. "Likes a north-facing hillside with lots of shade, soil with just the right pH, a particular blend of trace minerals. Some of the best patches actually have names—'the sugar bowl' and 'the gold mine,' for instance. High-grade patches, even ones inside the national park, are considered heirlooms, a family's patrimony. The locations of those patches are closely held secrets, and some old-timers wouldn't hesitate to shoot somebody they caught raiding 'their' patch. Couple park rangers got ambushed and killed a few years ago over near Fontana Lake, on the North Carolina side of the park, during a crackdown on poachers."

"I remember reading about that. I hadn't realized park rangering was such a risky occupation."

"Lotta mountain families still hate the government for taking their land to make the national park. And they're by-God gonna keep digging sang." He shook his head. "Thing is, over the long haul, it's not sustainable. Takes ten or fifteen years for a wild ginseng root to reach its peak; takes only a couple hours, with a forked stick or a screwdriver, to dig up hundreds of 'em. Whole hillsides in the park look like they've been ravaged by root hogs."

"But if it can be cultivated," I said, waving at the proof stretching out before us, "why don't people just grow it instead of poaching it?"

"Several pretty good reasons, actually. First, ginseng is pretty damned finicky. I've been trying to grow it for a dozen years now, with help from some pretty good botanists, and I'm just starting to get the hang of it. Second, it's not like marijuana, which can give you a huge profit in just one growing season. You have to leave ginseng in the ground for four years, minimum, before you can harvest it, and during that time, it's not generating a dime of income. The main reason, though, is the price differential."

O'Conner reached into a deep side pocket of his gray cargo pants and pulled out a root, which he handed me. "Ginseng, I presume?" He nodded. The root had four branches, which corresponded remarkably well to the placement and proportions of the arms and legs of the human form. It looked, quite literally, like a stick figure.

"You can see why the Chinese and the Indians both named it 'man-herb,' can't you?"

"I can. Only thing missing is the head."

"Look at the texture." I studied the root; it was smooth and fleshy, rather like a carrot or sweet potato. "That's from Wisconsin, which produces most of the cultivated ginseng exported to China."

"Wisconsin? The 'Eat cheese or die' state?"

He laughed. "That Wisconsin root there weighs about a quarter-pound; it's worth about five bucks." He fished around in another pocket, and handed me another root. This one was slimmer, darker, and nubbier, with rings or constrictions encircling it from its neck down to the tips of its four branches. "That's wild black sang. Waylon dug that; we probably don't want to know where."

I hefted it; it weighed about the same as the other, maybe a hair less.

"That one'll fetch two hundred dollars," he said. I looked from one to the other, trying to see how one could be worth forty times more than the other. O'Conner took them from me. "The wild's more potent, or at least it's perceived to be by the people who buy it."

"Ah, the magic of the free market," I said.

He nodded. "Doesn't take an MBA to figure out that poaching this root in the wild gives a damn good return on an investment of zero. Of course, the poachers aren't counting the environmental costs, or the occasional fine or murder."

I pointed to the cultivated root. "But you've figured out a way to get rich on these at five bucks apiece?"

O'Conner bent down and plucked up one of his own plants. He brushed off the dirt, which seemed an odd mixture of black loam, white Styrofoam granules, and mucilaginous goo—"hydrophilic gel," he said as he wiped the root and his hands on the leg of his pants. "Slimy as snot, but it cuts my irrigation costs thirty percent." He handed the plant to me. It was nubby with constrictions.

I blinked in confusion. "What—you're transplanting wild seedlings?" He laughed and shook his head. "I don't understand," I said. "You grew this here?" He nodded. "But it looks just like the wild one."

"Bingo. I'm not cultivating twenty-dollar-a-pound ginseng here, Doc; I'm growing thousand-dollar-a-pound wild sang. If it looks like wild sang and quacks like wild sang, it'll sell like wild sang."

If his entire ten acres looked this authentic, the audacity and the brilliance of his plan were breathtaking. "How come you can grow roots like this, but the cheeseheads up in Wisconsin can't?"

"I'll tell you, Doc, but then I'll have to kill you." Seeing my expression, he snorted and gave me a reassuring pat on the back. "Like I said, I've had some help from some good botanists. We found a way to shock the plants, chemically and thermally, at regular intervals during the growing season—not enough to really hurt 'em, just enough to make 'em pucker up in those constriction bands. Sort of like subjecting new wood to bleach and buckshot for that weathered, wormy look. Adds a year to the time required to get a mature, man-shaped root, but that extra year will pay for itself ten times over when we harvest."

"You tested this on buyers yet?"

He grinned. "That's where I was part of last week. Product testing. Not just buyers, but chemists, too. The chemists say it's every bit the equal of wild black ginseng. The exporters say they'll take all I can bring 'em."

Suddenly all the secrecy made sense. "So the kudzu camouflage and the hidden road—you're keeping the operation hidden so nobody knows it's cultivated?"

He nodded. "Plus the kudzu creates the shade the ginseng needs. I figure my cover's gonna get blown within a few years, but by then, I'll be millions of dollars ahead. Besides, even if I have to come down some on the price eventually, I'll still be way ahead of the cheeseheads. I mean, look at what they're producing." He pointed scornfully at the smooth root in my hand. "It's like a supermarket tomato—the right size and color, but a sorry substitute for the vine-ripened real deal. Eventually, Cooke County Black Ginseng—I've trademarked the name already—will become the Vidalia onion of ginseng. People will always pay a premium for it, because it'll be the best there is. If the marketing and business plan work like they're supposed to, we'll create a hundred jobs within two years. Maybe help reduce the poaching in the Smokies, too, which would be something to feel proud of."

"You do defy expectations, Jim," I said. "The hillbilly stereotype may never be the same."

But O'Conner wasn't listening to me. He'd suddenly taken a step to one side, cocking his head toward the house, then he cupped both hands behind his ears to catch more of whatever sound he was seeking. "Well, damn," he said to himself, and ran for the kudzu tunnel.

By the time he disappeared through his back door, I could hear it myself. "Damn," I echoed, and began running, too.

By the time I reached the front porch, the faint sound had become the distinctive, rhythmic, and ominous beat of a helicopter rotor. Unless I missed my guess, the helicopter would be piloted by Chief Deputy Orbin Kitchings.

O'Conner, one hand shading his eyes, stared toward the mouth of his hanging valley. Judging by the way the sound ricocheted off the ridges, the helicopter was flying low and closing fast. Suddenly it rose into view, climbing up out of the gorge at the lower end of the valley, almost as if emerging from the earth itself. Black with gold trim, it was unmistakably the sheriff's JetRanger, and it was headed straight for us.

O'Conner cursed again. I was just opening my mouth to say something reassuring and probably wrong when a crack split the air. "My God, somebody's shooting," O'Conner said, and his head spun toward the ridge angling alongside the house. I saw sparks fly from the chopper's tail boom as another shot rang out. "Top of the ridge," he said. "That's a high-powered rifle. Those aren't warning shots—somebody's trying to bring him down."

As if the pilot had heard him, the chopper halted in midair, then veered sharply to the left and began weaving toward us in violent zigs and zags. Orbin had been an army pilot, I remembered. I hoped he recalled enough of his combat training to outmaneuver the sniper.

Wheels began turning frantically in my head, and I flashed back to my pot patch excursion with Waylon, and to the rage he'd shown when Orbin shot Vernon's dog. "We need to find Waylon," I said urgently. "Where's Waylon?" Suddenly, magically—mercifully, even—Waylon's truck stopped in front of the porch. O'Conner waved frantically and pointed toward the ridge just as another muzzle flash erupted. Without a word, Waylon roared to the treeline, then leapt from his truck and sprinted up the mountainside.

As bullets continued to slam into the chopper, the aircraft wove and dodged toward the spot the shots were coming from, as if Orbin wanted to confront his assailant face to face. Sparks flew as a bullet glanced off the main rotor. Suddenly a spiderweb of fracture lines painted the front windshield, and the plastic bubble burst. The helicopter seemed to leap up in surprise, then pitched forward and rolled to the left, plummeting toward the valley floor.

When it hit, it collapsed with surprisingly little resistance, the remainder of the Plexiglas windows shattering, the metal tail boom crumpling like cardboard tubing. The impact was followed by near silence—a few groaning aftershocks, little else. For some reason I was expecting alarms and sirens, so the quiet seemed eerie and wrong. Then, as O'Conner and I ran toward the wreckage, came the searing rush of intense flame. Within seconds fire engulfed the cockpit, making our approach—and his survival—utterly impossible.

O'Conner shielded his face, peering into the flames. "Jesus. What a godawful mess. What the hell is going on here, Doc?"

"I wish I knew. Just when I think things can't get any worse up here, they do. I've heard a lot of bad things about Cooke County over the years. I didn't realize they were all understatements."

O'Conner took out a satellite phone—the nearest cell phone tower was several ridges away—and dialed the sheriff's dispatcher. He told her the sheriff's helicopter had just crashed and burned and that the pilot was dead. He gave directions, including a description of the kudzu tunnel, which the dispatcher asked him to repeat. Prompted, he gave his name. But he did not say that the helicopter had been shot down, and he did not stay on the line, as I could hear the dispatcher instructing him to. "When they get here, tell them about the shots. I don't think it's wise for me to be here when Tom Kitchings finds his brother dead in my front yard." He turned and trotted toward the house.

I was about to go after him when Waylon emerged from the woods and stumbled across the clearing toward me. "Got away," he gasped. "Some boot tracks heading down the back side of the ridge—they's a old logging road down there. Heard a ATV leaving about the time I got to the top. Sorry." He bent over, hands on knees, to catch his breath. "Did find this, though." He fished a knotted bandanna from a pocket and untied it, revealing five brass shell cases, about two inches long, shaped like miniature artillery rounds. "Winchester thirty-thirty," he said. "Hunnerd-fifty-grain load; muzzle velocity 'bout twenty-four-hunnerd feet a second. Same ammunition used by half the deer hunters in this county."

"Waylon, did you touch these?"

"Nossir. Picked 'em up with my hanky here."

"There might still be fingerprints on them. Hang onto them till the sheriff and his folks get here. Then make sure somebody gives you an evidence receipt for them."

For the first time since I'd met him, Waylon suddenly looked nervous. "Doc, the sheriff might take these better coming from you than from me," he said. I frowned, puzzled. "He's gonna be out for blood, and it might not be good for my health if I was to be the one to give him these. Can I turn 'em over to you, and let you give 'em to him?"

"Sure." I took the bundle from him and retied it. Then I pulled a small notepad from my back pocket and scrawled two makeshift evidence receipts. I signed and gave one to Waylon; I tucked the other away for later, to be signed by whoever I gave the brass to. "Keep that in a safe place," I said. He nodded.

I looked around for O'Conner, but he was nowhere in sight. "Sounded like Jim was going to make himself scarce for awhile," I said.

"Sounds like a good idea. Them Kitchingses don't like me all that much, but they's a whole lot less kindly disposed toward Jim."

"You think they'll find him?"

"Not if he don't wanna be found. Hell, he was a Army Ranger, and he grew up in these hills. He could stay hid and live off the land for the rest of his life, if he wanted to."

He was probably right. "Hey, Waylon?"

"Yeah, Doc?"

"I'm glad it wasn't you up there shooting."

A half-dozen expressions crossed his face in quick succession. "So am I, Doc. But then again, I ain't, too. You know what I mean?"

I knew what he meant.

35

WILLIAMS ARRIVED JUST MINUTES after the emergency call, the strobes firing atop his black and white Cherokee. He skidded up to the front porch, then caught sight of the smoldering helicopter in the field below and careened down to where Waylon and I stood. He leapt out and stared at the wreckage, then whirled to face us. "What happened here?" he demanded. Without waiting for an answer, he drew his revolver and pointed it at Waylon. "Put your hands up and get over here to the vehicle." Waylon blinked in surprise, but slowly raised his arms.

"He had nothing to do with it," I said. "He was pulling up in his truck when the shooting started. He was running up the ridge toward the shooter when the helicopter came down."

Williams wheeled on me. "And what the hell were you doing here? And what kind of secret operation is O'Conner running? And where the fuck is he?"

"I'll be glad to tell you everything I know," I said. "You willing to put down the gun? Makes it hard for me to concentrate, being afraid you might accidentally shoot an innocent bystander who also happens to be a witness."

Williams glowered. "I'm not so sure he's just a witness, I doubt very much that he's a bystander, and I'm damn certain he ain't all that innocent." But he holstered the weapon anyway and allowed Waylon to lower his hands while he told what he'd seen when he reached the ridgetop. When Waylon told him he'd found the shell cases, Williams held out his hand. "Here; let me have them."

"I ain't got 'em no more. I give 'em to the Doc."

Williams turned to me, his hand still extended. "Sure," I said. "Why don't you finish with Waylon first, and then you and I can discuss all this in private."

After a few more questions, the deputy allowed Waylon to go. "Don't even think about leaving town," he warned as Waylon climbed into his truck. Waylon nodded. As he drove away, I breathed a sigh of relief.

I gave Williams my account of the events, starting with my tour of O'Conner's camouflaged ginseng farm and ending with the crash. "Waylon did his best to catch the shooter," I said. "Those shell cases could be important. And it might help to get some pictures or a cast of those footprints." Williams looked thoughtful. "Here are the shell cases." I removed the knotted bandanna from my shirt pocket. He reached for it, but I pulled it back. "Deputy, would you mind signing this receipt?" I fished out my handwritten note: "Received from Dr. Bill Brockton: Five brass cartridge cases in red bandanna, recovered from ridge above Orbin Kitchings murder scene."

Williams reacted as if I'd spit in his face. "You think I'm gonna forget I've got shells from the gun that killed Orbin Kitchings? Think I'm gonna throw this ratty bandanna in the washing machine or the trash can?"

"No, not at all," I said. "Things get intense anytime an officer is killed, and this is the sheriff's own brother. An aggressive defense lawyer could completely destroy the value of those shell cases if we don't document every link in the chain of evidence. I'd hate to see Orbin's killer go free because we didn't keep good records."

Williams nodded curtly, snatched a pen from his pocket,

and signed the receipt. I handed him the small bundle. "The TBI crime lab might be able to get some prints off those," I said. "Maybe the guy forgot to wipe 'em clean as he loaded."

He looked surprised. "Thanks, Doc—I'm not sure I'da thought of that. Much obliged." He tucked the packet into the shirt pocket of his uniform and rebuttoned the flap. As he raised his eyes from his chest, I saw his gaze lock onto the end of the valley. A black Ford Expedition was rocketing up the gravel road. It swerved across the field, lurching to a stop beside us, and Tom Kitchings leapt out.

Before I could stop him, the sheriff rushed to the blackened cockpit. There he came face to face with the charred remains of his younger brother. Tom Kitchings let out a loud groan, and then another. Then he clutched his chest, sank to his knees, and toppled to the ground, unconscious.

I was no medical expert—I was the doctor who lost every single patient, after all—but I was pretty sure the sheriff had just suffered a coronary. That meant time was of the essence. We had only sixty minutes—the so-called "golden hour"— to prevent serious cardiac damage. After that, I knew, his blood-starved heart muscle would start to die. "We've got to get him to the hospital right away," I said.

"I'll call for an ambulance," said Williams, reaching for his radio.

"Too slow," I said. "We're half an hour outside of town here. By the time they get here and get him back to town, he'll suffer permanent damage. We've got to get him to a cardiologist within an hour."

"Goddamnit, Doc," he shouted, "we ain't *got* a cardiologist out here."

"No, but we can get him to one faster than we can get him back to town. Call your dispatcher; get 'em to patch us through to LifeStar."

LifeStar—UT Medical Center's air ambulance service— had two helicopters based behind the hospital, within sniffing distance of the Body Farm. It took less than a minute for the dispatcher to patch Williams through to LifeStar's flight coordinator. The deputy described the sheriff's symptoms and asked if they could send a chopper. "What's your location?"

"We're in a small valley six or eight miles southeast of Jonesport," said Williams. "Brush Creek Mountain is directly to our west, and—"

"Wait wait wait," said the coordinator. "Anybody there got a GPS unit?"

"Oh. Yeah. Affirmative," said Williams. He pulled a handheld Global Positioning System receiver from a pouch on his belt and powered it up. The display showed signals from four orbiting satellites. "Stand by for coordinates," said Williams. As he began rattling off numbers, I looked over his shoulder at the display. "Latitude three-five-point-niner-five-three-five degrees north. Longitude eight-two-point-seven-niner-six-eight degrees west."

As the dispatcher read the coordinates back for confirmation, I realized something was wrong. I tapped his shoulder to get his attention, but he shrugged me off in annoyance. I tapped again, harder. "LifeStar, stand by," he snapped, then whirled to confront me. "What the *fuck*?"

"You transposed two numbers in the longitude," I said urgently, pointing at the display. "You said 'point seven nine'; the display says 'point nine seven.'" I did some quick math in my head. "That's almost two-tenths of a degree. They're going to land ten or twelve miles from here, somewhere over in North Carolina."

Williams looked ready to explode. He radioed the flight coordinator to correct the number, and the coordinator read the revised longitude back. "Readback is correct," said Williams. I reached to take the radio from him. He relinquished it with a look of supreme annoyance.

"How soon can they be in the air?" I asked.

"Thirty seconds ago," said the coordinator. "Should be landing in about twelve minutes."

"Wow, that's great. Anything we can do for the patient here in the meantime?"

"Stand by." The radio was silent for nearly a minute before the LifeStar dispatcher came back on. "The flight nurse says keep him quiet, feet elevated. If he's conscious and you can round up an aspirin tablet, give him one to chew. That'll thin his blood a little, maybe help restore some flow to the coronary artery."

"Will do," I said. "Signing off now. Thanks for the help."

"It's what we're here for."

I handed the radio back to Williams and sprinted to the back of my truck, where I always kept a first aid kit. Somewhere among all the bandages and wet wipes, ointments and surgical gloves, I knew there was a packet of aspirin. The profusion of tiny containers was maddening. Finally I found it: a single foil pack containing two aspirin. With trembling fingers, I tore open the foil. Both pills popped out, skittered across the truck bed, and began rolling toward the gap in the tailgate. As the first pill rattled down into the recesses of the bumper, I lunged desperately, snagging the other just as it reached the opening. My own heart was pounding now.

Kitchings had regained consciousness by now, so Williams and I propped him against one wheel of the Jeep. As he chewed, grimacing from the acidity of the pill or the pain in his chest, I told him about the shooting, the crash, and Waylon's pursuit of the shooter. He quizzed me closely about the shell cases—how many? "Five," I said. What caliber? "Waylon said thirty-thirty. Long, like a hunting cartridge. Your deputy has 'em in his pocket." Kitchings looked at Williams and held out his hand.

Williams fished out the bandanna, untied the knot, and placed the nest of cartridges in the sheriff's upturned palm.

"Careful; there might be prints on them," I said. Using a corner of the fabric, the sheriff carefully lifted one shell and studied its flat base. His face—already a mask of pain and anxiety—did not change expression. "Yep, Winchester thirty-thirty," he grunted. "Leon, that mean anything to you?"

"Hell, Sheriff, there's gotta be a hunnerd thirty-thirty deer rifles in Cooke County alone coulda fired those, and a few hunnerd more in spittin' distance." Kitchings nodded grimly, retied the bandanna, and fumbled with the button on his shirt pocket. "Sheriff, I was gonna take them back to the office and get 'em off to the TBI crime lab. Like the doc here says, might be some prints on there. Maybe some ejector marks or firing pin impressions in the TBI ballistics database, too." The sheriff tucked the bandanna into the pocket. "Sheriff, with you goin' to the hospital and all, I don't think it's a good idea for you to be carryin' evidence off with you. Gonna break the chain of custody; hell, they might even get lost." Williams reached toward the sheriff's pocket, but Kitchings knocked his hand away.

"Goddamnit, Leon, I ain't dead yet," he growled with surprising force. "I am still the damn sheriff of Cooke County, and I am taking custody of these damn cartridges." Just as Williams opened his mouth to argue, an orange and white helicopter skimmed over the ridge and dropped to the valley floor. The instant the wheels touched ground, the flight nurse and paramedic were out the door with a litter. Ignoring the deputy and me completely, they set it on the ground and laid the sheriff down, snapping a safety belt across his hips and another, loosely, across his chest. Then they called us in to help. The four of us hoisted the stocky sheriff, bore him to the chopper, and slid the litter through the double doors. Even before the doors slammed shut, the two turbine engines were spooling up.

Through the window, I glimpsed the nurse starting to rig an IV bag. But it was only a glimpse. The helicopter leapt off the ground and banked westward with the speed of a combat aircraft. As it vanished behind the ridge, I checked my watch. Twenty-three minutes, give or take one, had elapsed since the sheriff sank to the ground. If the first hour was golden, I hoped that made the first half-hour platinum. In any case, if speedy diagnosis and treatment were as crucial as the cardiologists claimed, Kitchings should be back on the job within a few days.

But I wasn't sure whether that was a good thing or a bad thing. I also wasn't sure I'd ever see those cartridge cases again. I turned to Williams. "Deputy, once the dust settles and the sheriff's back on his feet, you might ought to get him to write you an evidence receipt for those shells."

"You bet, Doc," was all he said. But the expression on his face—a swirl of anger, frustration, and fear—spoke volumes more. Trouble was, I couldn't quite catch hold of the meaning.

36

HEADLIGHTS DANCED ACROSS THE mangled JetRanger as a vehicle bumped across the field toward the wreckage. I wondered which group was arriving first: the TBI agents or my forensic assistants.

I had reached Miranda on the satellite phone Jim O'Conner left with me. Today was a tough time to be rounding up a forensic team. Not only was it Saturday, it was the Saturday that fell smack in the middle of UT's four-day fall break. Normally, even on weekends, the hallways and offices beneath the stadium were crawling with Anthropology students; today, apparently, they were as scarce as virgins at a fraternity party. Miranda had called back after a half-hour to say she'd completely struck out in her efforts to round up two more grad students. "Call Art Bohanan," I told her. "He doesn't know bones, but he's good at bagging evidence and taking crime scene photos. And try Sarah Carmichael."

"Who's that? Don't know her."

I squirmed at the question. "She's in one of my classes. The campus operator should have a listing for her."

"Sarah Carmichael. Is she a master's or Ph.D. student?"

"She . . . she's an undergraduate, actually."

There was a long pause. "Has she taken Osteology?"

"Not exactly. No. But she's practically memorized the field handbook on her own."

Another pause, even longer. "Is she who I think she is?"

"Probably. Yes. Look, it's the student you saw me kissing, okay? I'm sorry; I know it's awkward, and I hate to drag her into this, but if you can't find anybody else, she might be the best we can do. She's smart, she knows the basics, and she'll do fine recording data and filling in the inventory of skeletal elements." The inventory of skeletal elements was a fancy name for an outline drawing of the human skeleton. In field-work like this, I always assigned one student to color in, with a pencil or pen, the outline of each bone as it was found. Basically, it was like a page from a Halloween coloring book, and the only places where staying within the lines was difficult were the hands, feet, and skull. Besides being faster and easier than writing down the names of bones, the diagram showed me, at a glance, what we'd found—and what was missing. I was confident that Sarah would have absolutely no problem filling it in accurately.

"We don't need her help," said Miranda. "We can do this without her."

"No we can't, Miranda. Your right arm's in a cast, remember? You can't ID bones and write things down and bag evidence with a broken arm. Call Sarah."

Despite the thousands of miles up to the communications satellite and back down, I could hear Miranda's angry breathing; in my mind's eye, I even saw her nostrils flaring. "Damnit," she finally said, "you ask one hell of a lot, you know that?"

"I do know, and I am sorry. But I'm not asking for me. I'm asking for the dead guy in the helicopter here, and his brother the sheriff, who just left in an air ambulance, and their mother and father, who don't even know yet that one of their sons has just been killed. It's a complicated death scene, Miranda, and I need help. Especially yours. Please."

Two hours after that angry exchange, the department's pickup came jouncing across the valley floor, with Miranda at the wheel, Art riding shotgun as navigator, and Sarah folded into the jump seat behind them. I motioned them around to the front of the helicopter, so the headlights illuminated the smashed interior. "Wow," Miranda said as she hopped out, her orange cast practically glowing in the dark. "That kudzu tunnel is incredible. So *Tuscany*—the whole grape arbor effect—with a big ol' East Tennessee twist." She seemed relaxed and happy. Was it the adrenaline rush of a field case, or had she somehow bonded with Sarah on the drive up? Either way, I was relieved. "Three years and fifty death scenes, and this is the coolest." She unlatched the window on the cap that covered the bed of the truck and began unloading gear one-handed.

Art waved hello and gave a big wink, which must have been code for something, but I had neither the time nor the privacy to ask him what it meant. Then Sarah extricated herself from the cramped jump seat. The smile she gave me still looked awkward, but the embarrassment in her smile couldn't hold a candle to the excitement in her eyes. Perhaps I hadn't bungled things forever after all.

The two hours it took them to reach the scene had seemed like an eternity. The fact was, though, even if they'd arrived sooner, we couldn't have started excavating the chopper until the wreckage had cooled, and it still felt almost too warm to touch.

I had just finished introducing my helpers to Williams—I was surprised Art hadn't met the deputy already, on one of the Cooke County visits he'd made with me—when Art pointed toward the mouth of the valley. "Bill, did you order pizza?"

A Crown Victoria eased into the valley and idled across the field toward where we stood. I knew it wasn't pizza, unless Domino's had begun recruiting drivers from the ranks of active TBI agents.

Williams and I had almost come to blows over calling in

the TBI. As soon as the rotor wash from LifeStar had settled,
I had pulled out the satellite phone to call them. "Hell, no,"
the deputy said, when I told him what I was doing. "I'm in
charge here, and I say no." It was true that with the sheriff
incapacitated and the chief deputy dead, Williams was the
ranking law enforcement officer on the scene—and in the
whole county, for that matter. But he was a commander without subordinates, and he seemed unsure how to proceed.
When he balked at the TBI, I suggested the Tennessee Highway Patrol instead, but he said no to them as well. "Well,
somebody's got to take jurisdiction," I snapped. "We're not
on federal land, so we can't call in the feds. Seems like our
best bet is your new pals at the TBI."

I hadn't meant to say that; it just slipped out in the heat of
the moment. Williams went ghostly pale, then angry red; my
attempt at an explanation—that I'd been returning a library
book to the downtown library, and happened to see him talking with Steve Morgan on the steps of the federal
building—sounded lame even to me. "Look," I'd finally
said, "somebody just shot the sheriff's brother. You don't
have the resources for a big investigation. Call in some rein-
forcements. It's your best hope for catching whoever did
this." He still looked unhappy, but he didn't stop me from
making the call.

The front doors of the Crown Vic opened in unison. A
grim-faced Steve Morgan emerged from the driver's side;
Brian "Rooster" Rankin exited the passenger side. His cover
now thoroughly blown, Rankin had traded his feed cap and
overalls for a sportcoat and silk tie.

Williams and Morgan nodded awkwardly to one another,
in the way of people who know each other but hate to acknowledge it—like two ministers bumping into each other at
a strip club. Rankin, on the other hand, made a point of introducing himself to Williams, which told me that the
deputy had not met Rankin at the federal building. That

made sense—he was still working undercover, after all. As Rankin shook his hand, Williams's face betrayed a potent mix of confusion, shock, and fear. When I saw that, I knew that Rankin—the undercover version—must have rubbed elbows with the deputy in some unsavory or illegal context.

The two agents huddled briefly with all of us, first getting a brief recap from me, then asking Williams a few questions—where and when he'd learned of the shooting, when he'd arrived, and so on. Excusing themselves for a moment, they got back into their car, where they conferred in low, earnest tones. When they rejoined us, Morgan seemed to have taken charge of things. "Here's how we'd suggest proceeding," he said, in a tone that didn't actually invite feedback or questions. "I'll stay here with Dr. Brockton and his team as they excavate the chopper. Agent Rankin will ride back to the courthouse with Deputy Williams to get more background, go over the dispatch logs, and review any pertinent files."

"I ain't leavin'," said Williams. "This is a Cooke County crime scene, I was the first officer on the scene, and that makes me the incident commander here."

The TBI agents glanced at each other, then Rankin beckoned to Williams. "Leon—*buddy*—how's about you come chew the fat with your ol' pal Rooster fer a minute?" He pointed toward Leon's Jeep, and they got inside. This time the voices—the deputy's, at least—got pretty loud. Then, to my surprise, the Cherokee's engine fired up and the vehicle fishtailed angrily across the field, taking the deputy and the undercover agent out of the valley.

Morgan flashed me a sunny smile. "Interagency cooperation," he said. "It's a wonderful thing." I waited, hoping he might enlighten me about the leverage Rankin seemed to have with Williams, but he didn't. "Don't let me keep y'all from your work," he said, looking toward the helicopter.

We started by mapping the crash site. I asked Sarah to

sketch the main features of the scene as Art and Miranda plotted the coordinates of key landmarks. The advent of handheld GPS receivers had greatly simplified the job of scene mapping—with the push of a button, it was now possible to pinpoint the latitude and longitude of a body and even superimpose it on an onscreen map—but I wasn't quite ready to dispense with old-fashioned maps and measurements quite yet. Batteries run down, displays burn out, circuit boards fail, even satellites go on the fritz. Besides, most GPS units have a one- to three-meter margin of error, meaning—in the worst-case scenario—that I could go back to a death scene six months later, stand or dig exactly where the gizmo indicated the body had lain, and be off by up to ten feet any direction. If you're troweling for a missing hyoid bone, a twenty-foot circle—three hundred square feet—is an enormous area.

One obvious and unambiguous landmark for our coordinates was the house—specifically, the southwest corner of the front porch, the closest point to the wreckage. Art shot a compass reading to the center of the cockpit, calling out "255 degrees." Sarah drew an arrow and noted the bearing on her map, then, when Art unspooled a long tape measure between the corner and the chopper, she added "87.5 feet" beneath the compass reading. For the second landmark, they chose a large hemlock tree, standing alone beside the small stream that ran the length of the valley floor before plunging into the kudzu tunnel. The chopper lay 74 feet, on a heading of 128 degrees, from the base of the hemlock. So unless the house were destroyed and the tree cut down, we'd be able to pinpoint the crash site with precision and certainty for years to come, GPS or no.

One advantage of the crash, if such a word could be used, was that most of the remains were contained within the shell of the cockpit. I had worked several crashes in the Great Smoky Mountains during my years in Knoxville. Those aircraft—a couple of propeller planes and a military air-refueling tanker jet—were traveling horizontally at high speeds when they hit; as a result, wreckage and body parts were scattered over hundreds of yards of hillside. Orbin's helicopter, though, had dropped nearly straight down, so while there was considerable trauma to his body—first from the force of the crash, then from the fire—at least there was no scatter.

The helicopter had hit sideways, which also made the excavation easier. If it had impacted right-side-up, the engine and rotor would have crushed the cockpit, forcing us to cut or pry our way in. As it was, I could lean into the cockpit, which remained largely intact, through the windshield opening.

As I stepped up to the JetRanger's vacant windshield opening, I was choked by the smell of burned flesh. I knew that by the time I finished, my clothes and even my hair and skin would reek of the unforgettable smell: seared and foul but with a disturbing and sickening undertone of sweetness, too. Best just to get on with it, then. I leaned in and found myself face to face with the gaping skull of Orbin Kitchings.

The skull was propped against the door frame and the edge of the seat. The seat's upholstery was gone, its charred frame and springs smashed flat on the left side by the impact. Orbin's eyes—what had once been the eyes—had been reduced to blackened cinders within their orbits, looking more like chunks of charcoal than windows to the soul. But then, from what little I had seen, Orbin's soul had a lot of blackness to it.

Most of the skull's soft tissue had burned away, yet the mandible remained precariously attached at the hinge of the jaw, giving the mouth a gaping, ghoulish, shrieking banshee look. It was slightly reminiscent of Leena's, I realized—and then I realized that it was more than just slightly reminiscent. Like her, Orbin Kitchings had no lateral incisors in his upper jaw. And as I studied Orbin's teeth, another image flashed suddenly into my mind: the photo of Tom Kitchings, squeezing through the narrow part of the cave, his clenched teeth bared in a grimace of effort. "I'll be damned," I breathed. The gene pool in Cooke County was a remarkably small and shallow body of protoplasm.

Orbin had died strapped into his pilot's harness. The harness's nylon webbing had been consumed by the inferno, but Orbin, or what was left of him, remained at the helm of his ruined ship, looking like some pilot of the damned. Several of my students had researched the effects of fire on flesh and bone over the years, and I'd once watched one of them burn a human head in a barbecue grill. After only several minutes on a bed of hot coals, the skin across the forehead had split open and peeled backward. Judging by the gradations of calcination and color on Orbin's skull—hues ranging from the ashy-white frontal bone to the caramel-brown occipital at the back of the skull—the deputy's scalp had let go of his cranium only gradually, scalped in slow motion by some sadistic fire god.

We might be able to remove most of his body from the wreckage in one piece. If so, that would make the excavation far quicker and simpler. I didn't want to risk damaging the skull, though, so I reached into my tool case and removed a scalpel. Tilting the skull gently backward with one hand, I worked the blade back and forth with the other, severing the burned remnants of ligamentous tissue and spinal cord. As I lifted the skull, I backed out of the wreck and turned to show the skull to my teammates.

Art whistled when he saw the hole at the center of the forehead. It measured nearly an inch in diameter; the edges were jagged, and fracture lines radiated from it like crooked spokes in a mangled wheel. "That's a big entry wound," he said. "Bullet must've mushroomed some when it hit the windshield. Damn good shooting, too," he added. "Or incredibly lucky. I bet Orbin was looking the shooter right in the eye when he pulled the trigger. Talk about staring death in the face."

"If he'd been Keanu Reeves in *The Matrix,*" said Miranda, "he coulda dodged the bullet."

"If he'd been Christopher Reeve in *Superman,* it woulda bounced right off," I said.

"If he'd been Superman, he wouldn't have been flying a helicopter," Sarah pointed out.

"That's right," chimed in Art. "And he'd've used his telescopic vision to spot the guy. And his heat vision to burn him up."

"Enough, already," I said. "These complex forensic hypotheses are making my head spin."

I handed off the skull to Miranda, then leaned back in to determine whether how much of the body remained intact. The arms and lower legs, not surprisingly, had burned off— thin, cylindrical, and surrounded by oxygen, they were always the first to go in a hot fire. Some of those bones lay on the warped metal of the pilot's door; others were fused into a bizarre aggregate with the Plexiglas that had shattered, then melted, then cooled and hardened into a lumpy black mess.

His ribs were almost completely exposed, except at the back, where they joined the vertebrae. There, the seat's padding and leather had protected the flesh from the fire during its first several minutes, as it had beneath the buttocks and backs of the thighs. It would be an awkward, two-person job to wrestle his torso out through the windshield opening. "Miranda, y'all get a disaster bag open on the ground here," I called out. "Art, are you gloved up?"

"Yeah," he said, wiggling his fingers in a pair of purple gloves, "I've got the gloves on, but I couldn't find my matching handbag anywhere. Whatcha need?"

"Come help me wrestle him out of here, would you?"

"Love to."

As soon as Miranda and Sarah had unzipped the white

bag and laid it open at my feet, I reached through the cockpit's left side and slid my hands beneath the torso's left hip and ribs. Art leaned in through the opening on the right, levering his hands behind the right shoulder and hip. "On three," I said. "One, two, *three!*" As we grunted with the strain, the charred torso lifted free of the seat and door frame and lurched toward the windshield opening.

"Hang on a sec; I've got to shift my grip," said Art, and with that, I found myself bearing the torso's entire weight—admittedly, considerably reduced from what it once was, but still a hefty load for a middle-aged academic stooped at an awkward angle.

"Hurry, I can't hold him long," I gasped.

"Okay, got him; let's go," Art said, and I felt my burden ease.

As we maneuvered the torso out the opening, a femur snagged on the windshield's center post, throwing me off balance. I stumbled backward, into Miranda's arms. The body cartwheeled downward, thudding onto my feet. "Damn," I said.

"Good thing we aren't EMTs," said Art. "If he weren't dead already, he would be now. Either that or speed-dialing his lawyer."

I tugged the bag's sides up around the torso, then zipped it closed. "Let's each grab a corner," I said, "and go ahead and get this into the truck." Distributed among the four of us, the weight was surprisingly light—no more than twenty pounds apiece.

Miranda and Sarah reached the back of the truck with their end of the bag first. "Let's set it down here on the tailgate, then climb inside and slide him in," said Miranda. They scampered up and inside the low cap over the bed a lot more gracefully than I could have. "Oh, to be young and nimble again," I said, lifting and sliding my corner toward them.

"Oh, to be tenured and tended by assistants," shot back

Miranda. In the dark interior of the cap, Sarah coughed back a laugh.

"It'll never happen," I said, "if you piss off the department head and he flunks you."

"He wouldn't dare. I've been propping him up for the last two years. He'd be lost without me."

"True," I said, "but I'm grooming your replacement right now."

"I don't think so," said Sarah. "The pay's lousy and the hours stink. So do the patients." They emerged and hopped down from the truck.

"Ooh, that's a new one," I said. "Let me just retreat to my work while I compose a witty retort." I went back to the cockpit to begin extricating bones that had separated from the corpse. The first one I pulled out was a humerus. "Looks like the impact tore his left arm off," I said to Miranda. "Do you know how I can tell?"

Miranda studied the bone as Sarah inked in the outline of the bone on the element inventory. "Well, one end is all black, and the other is gray," said Miranda. "I assume that's a clue?"

"Is that what you call differential burning?" asked Sarah, leaning in.

"Right—very good," I said. Miranda raised her eyebrows, then smiled in grudging admiration. "See the humeral head," I went on, "where the arm joins the shoulder? It's completely calcined; that gray color means all the organic matter has been completely incinerated, leaving nothing behind but the minerals. Look at how fractured it is." They both studied it intently. "Be careful with it—it's very fragile, like bones that have been cremated. The distal end, at the elbow, is sort of caramel colored, which means it didn't burn nearly as much. Because . . . ?"

"Because there was still soft tissue shielding it for a while," said Miranda quickly. She handed off the humerus to

Sarah, who placed it in a brown paper evidence bag, which she labeled and numbered.

"Exactly." I reached into the cockpit and pulled out a pair of bones, still attached to one another at the lower end. "Looks like the left tibia and fibula have that same pattern of differential burning, so the impact probably tore off his lower leg as well." I handed out the leg bones for them to inventory, examine, and bag. "And the left femur has some midshaft calcining; that means the muscle probably split open from the force of the impact." As I held out the femur, Art leaned in to take close-up photos of the burn pattern. The flash seared my eyes. "That's okay, Art," I said, "I didn't really need those retinas to work here."

"Sorry," he said. "I've heard you can ID bones with your eyes closed, so I figured you weren't looking. This differential burning you're talking about—is it forensically significant?"

"Not in this case—we already know how he was killed, because I saw it. So did two other people—three, actually, counting the shooter. But suppose we found these bones in a burned-out house. In that setting, the differential burning would be important—it would probably mean that the body was traumatized or dismembered before it was burned. Not exactly an accidental fire, then—more likely arson intended to conceal evidence of a murder."

After the first few bones, and the first few minilectures, we got into a quiet, efficient rhythm. Without even looking or turning or speaking, I'd hand pieces out to Miranda, who would verbally ID them. As Sarah got busy inking the bones on the skeleton diagram, Art took over bagging and labeling. Soon the ground was covered with brown paper bags, like some gruesome, cannibalistic picnic lunch.

I had gradually worked my way down to the pedals near the pilot's floor bubble, or what had once been the floor bubble. "Hey, Art," I called as I began extricating a handful of calcined foot bones, "I know the pedals on an airplane work the rudder, but what do they do on a helicopter, which doesn't have a rudder? They don't control the throttle, do they?"

"Naw," he said, reaching around me to point at a twisted metal tube mounted in the center of the cabin floor, "throttle's built into the stick here, which is called the 'collective' in a chopper. The pedals control the tail rotor, which works like a rudder, in a frighteningly complex way. To yaw—pivot—to the left, the pilot mashes the left pedal, which actually causes the tail rotor to shove the tail boom to the right. I tried to fly one of these contraptions once."

"And?"

"And like the Lyle Lovett song says, 'Once is enough.' Most complicated hand–eye, brain–machine coordination I ever tried to do. I'd get one thing almost right, and in the process, I'd get two or three other things wrong enough to turn us upside-down or sideways. Flight instructor actually kissed the ground when we got back down alive."

Something caught Art's eye, and he took another look into the cockpit, pointing at a rectangular object. "Bill, mind if I reach in and grab that box?" I shook my head and stepped aside. Art leaned into the cockpit and extracted a charred rectangle, not much bigger than a cigarette pack, and laid it on the ground beside him. Then he leaned back in, peered around, and emerged with a larger metal case as well. He took both objects to Sarah and gestured with the smaller one at an evidence bag. She held it open as he tucked them inside.

"How do you want me to label this?" she asked.

"Label it 'RF unit' and put a question mark after that," he said.

He looked thoughtful for a moment, then walked to the back of my truck and ran his hands along the underside of the rear bumper. "Eureka," he said, and yanked something loose. It, too, was a small metal case, with a wire dangling from one end.

I stared at it. I didn't recognize it, and I'd looked under my bumper many times, retrieving the spare key I kept there in a magnetic case. "What's that?"

"A beacon."

"What kind of beacon?"

"An RF beacon. Somebody put a radio frequency transmitter on your truck." I was still playing catch-up. "Like those radio collars biologists put on the wolves in Yellowstone." Art pointed to the helicopter wreckage. "See those metal prongs sticking up from the roof of the cockpit? That's a directional antenna array, which picks up the signal from this transmitter here. The boxes I found in the cockpit are the receiver and control unit. They pick up the signal from the beacon and compute your direction and distance. Orbin was tracking you, Bill."

"Why would Orbin want to track me?"

"Well, maybe the sheriff and his boys figured you might lead 'em to O'Conner. Or maybe this was Orbin flying solo, so to speak, and he wanted to settle up with you for that day we got the drop on him and his brother. From what you told me about his visit to Cousin Vern's pot patch, he wasn't the type to forgive and forget."

"The thought of Orbin tracking me like an animal gives me the shivers," I said.

"Yeah, me, too," he said. "But I'd say you got the better end of the deal. And now we know why Orbin showed up here right after you did."

Steve Morgan didn't say a word. But the TBI agent didn't miss a syllable of the exchange between Art and me.

37

I PARKED IN MY USUAL spot under the streetlight behind the Regional Forensic Center and let myself in the back door with the keypad combination lock. It was nearly midnight now, and my back and neck ached from leaning into the helicopter's cockpit for three hours straight. The morgue looked deserted, though in fact it was never unattended. If I'd rung the loading bay doorbell, a video camera would have swiveled in my direction after a few moments, and a groggy morgue assistant would have buzzed me in. But since the assistant was probably a pathology intern—and therefore desperately short on sleep—I'd let myself in, and I moved through the hallways as quietly as possible, lest I disturb a much-needed nap.

Once in the basement of the hospital itself, I caught an elevator up to the seventh floor, which housed the cardiac care unit. The night duty nurse at the station smiled broadly when she saw me. "Hi, Dr. Brockton; good to see you," she beamed. "What brings you up here at almost midnight? You must be scouting for likely donors." We shared a laugh at the joke, which I heard some version of almost any time I crossed from the catacombs of the dead to the wards of the ailing.

"Not tonight," I said, "but if you get any hot prospects for me, give me a call. Actually, I wanted to check on one of your new patients, Sheriff Tom Kitchings, who came in on LifeStar a few hours ago."

"He's a popular guy," she said.

"Oh?"

"A gentleman was here earlier, right before I came on shift, and one of his deputies just left. I'm surprised you didn't bump into him in the elevator."

Williams? It had to be Williams, since Orbin was over in the osteology lab with Miranda, getting simmered and scrubbed clean. My mind was racing with scenarios. Had the deputy come out of concern for his boss? Had he heard that we'd found the tracking beacon on my truck—and had he known it was there? Had he reclaimed the cartridge cases from the shooting, and if so, why?

"If he'd bumped into me, he'd have been lost," I said. "I came up from the morgue on the service elevator. I'm surprised he was here, though. This is right on my way home, but it's a long trip for somebody from Cooke County."

"A wasted trip, too," she said. "The sheriff's asleep—I gave him a good dose of Ativan when I changed his drip at eleven. The deputy said he just wanted to get an update on his condition, so I went over the chart with him. He asked if he could look in on the sheriff and just sit with him a few minutes. I said he could, long as he didn't wake him up."

I was bone-tired and raw-nerved, so maybe I was just feeling paranoid, but something about that scared me. "Have you been back in the sheriff's room since the deputy left?"

"No, that was only five minutes ago. Why?"

"I don't know; I'm just jumpy. Mind if we go check on him?"

She looked exasperated, but she left the duty desk and glided down the hall, easing into a room. Kitchings was sawing logs, half-sitting in the angled hospital bed, an IV in his left arm and a bundle of EKG leads snaking out the top of his hospital gown. A heart monitor flashed steadily at seventy-two beats a minute, and his chest rose and fell at about one-quarter that rate. The nurse flashed a thumbs-up sign. "He's fine," she whispered. "He had a very small clot—he probably collapsed more from the stress than from the clot—and he got to the cath lab really quick. A little Roto-Rooter of the artery, and he's good as new. Probably go home tomorrow." I was amazed at the cheery prognosis— when he keeled over, I pretty much wrote him off as dead. The nurse turned to go, and held the door for me, but I thought of something. Tapping my wristwatch, I held up five fingers and cocked my head in a questioning manner. She shrugged, put an index finger to her lips, and left me alone with the snoring sheriff.

As soon as the door closed, I tiptoed over to the wardrobe where I guessed his clothes were stored. Sure enough, his uniform—rumpled and stained—hung in the cabinet. His gun belt and empty pistol dangled from a hook at the back. I felt the left shirt pocket, then the right. Both empty. I searched the pants pockets—also empty. Then I noticed a small plastic bag sitting on the floor of the wardrobe. The bag was heavy; it clattered as I picked it up and set it on the rolling hospital tray parked beside the window. Rooting through the bag in the semidarkness, lit only by the heart monitor's display and the building's exterior floodlights, I saw the sheriff's badge, his keys, his wallet, some loose change, a pack of sugarless gum, and the bullets from his gun. But I did not—on my first, my second, or my third survey of the contents—see the sweat-stained bandanna in which Waylon had knotted the cartridge cases that might have led to Orbin's killer.

38

IT WAS THE LEAD story in the morning paper, which thudded onto my doorstep only a few short hours after I'd left the sheriff's hospital room. "Little Stacy's Body Found," read the headline; the subhead added, "Convicted Molester Charged with Murder." The girl—missing for nearly a month—was found by cadaver dogs in a drainage ditch at an abandoned textile mill, a few blocks from the suspect's seedy house. Hidden beneath old tires, rotting carpet, and other debris, the body was decomposed beyond recognition. But since Stacy Beaman was the only eight-year-old missing at the moment, it took only moments for an assistant ME to match her teeth to the dental X-rays already on hand and awaiting just such a grim discovery.

As I was turning the page to finish the story, the phone rang. "Hey," said a glum voice that I'd known—even as I was reaching for the receiver—would be Art's. The suspect had been arrested twelve hours earlier, while Art was helping me bag bones in Cooke County.

"Hey, yourself," I said. "How you doing?"

"Some good, some bad."

"Glad they found her. Glad they got him. Sorry it turned out this way."

"Yeah."

"How's the case against the suspect?"

"Better than we expected. The crime scene techs found some hair and fibers on the body we think we can link to him, and we're hoping we'll find traces of semen—God, would you listen to me, 'We hope we find some semen'? Also, we've got multiple witnesses, other kids' moms, very credible and sympathetic on the stand. All of them put him near the school the day she disappeared. If your pal . . ." he trailed off, then began again. "If DeVriess doesn't manage to bar testimony about the guy's prior record, I don't see how any jury in the land could fail to convict. But then again, I don't see how any lawyer in the land could aggressively defend this guy, either. Clearly there's a lot that's beyond my feeble powers of comprehension."

"Mine, too," I said, hoping to deflect his rage at DeVriess. "I admire how hard you guys worked to find her and make the case. I'm sure her family appreciates it, too. Or will, when they're able to."

"Yeah, that'll keep 'em warm at night." He sighed. "You know, Bill, sometimes I despise this world and the vermin who infest it."

"I know. There's evil out there, that's for sure, and you've seen more than your share of it. But there's good, too—try not to forget that."

"The good sure seems to take a back seat sometimes. My mama wanted me to be a dentist—'Almost as prestigious as a doctor,' she said, 'and the hours are a lot better.' Maybe Mama knew best."

"Are you kidding? Standing around all day with your hands in other people's slobber? Besides, people positively *adore* cops compared to how they feel about dentists."

He laughed—faintly, but it was something. "You're right, the slobber factor is a deal-breaker. Saying 'Rinse and spit' ain't near as glamorous as yelling '*Freeze,* asshole!'—or so the daughter, Leena, is going to have some DNA from the maternal side and pass it along to her baby. As I say, that part's exactly what you'd expect."

"But there's something else you *wouldn't* expect?"

"Well, maybe I should have, this being Cooke County, Tennessee. But no, I never saw this one coming."

"Damn it, Art; what is it?"

"Besides being Sheriff Tom's cousin, Leena's baby was also gonna be his kid brother."

Suddenly Faye was the last thing on my mind. I wanted to be sure I wasn't misunderstanding. "In other words, according to the DNA profile . . ."

". . . which Gonzales said was a rock-solid match . . ."

". . . the baby's father . . . ?

". . . was Tom Kitchings Senior. The Reverend—or *not-so-Reverend*—Thomas Kitchings."

I floored the gas pedal, and the truck careened around the on-ramp and up onto I-40 East.

Even with the windows rolled up, I had trouble hearing Art's question over the buffeting of the wind. The truck was doing ninety-five, and a gusty autumn wind was whipping out of the north, ripping red and gold leaves from branches, driving purplish clouds before it, their tops curling like ocean breakers. "You're *sure* this is a good idea?" he shouted.

"Sure I'm sure," I yelled, with more confidence than I felt.

"So tell me one more time why we're charging back toward Cooke County like Batman and Robin? Talk slow—last time you explained it, you lost me on one of those hairpin turns of logic."

Sheriff Kitchings was up on the seventh floor of UT hospital, I repeated. His chief deputy was slewing around in a sooty box in the back of my truck. The one other Cooke County officer involved in the case was doubtless chatting with a roomful of TBI and FBI agents, explaining the disastrous turn their investigation had just taken.

"So what you're saying is, the utter collapse of law and order makes it a good idea for us to go riding back into the jaws of death? That's your compelling argument?"

That pretty much summed it up. "But this new DNA evidence sheds a whole 'nother light on the case," I argued, "and nobody knows it. And nobody knows *we* know it but us."

"Your powers of reasoning are unique in all the world," he said, shaking his head. "Not to mention your way with grammar."

"Grammar, schmammer. Don't you see? Old man Kitchings gets her pregnant, then he kills her to cover up the pregnancy. Maybe she never even tells him she's pregnant—probably scared to. But then she starts to show, and he knows the scandal will get out and ruin him. Hard for a preacher to hang onto his flock if they know he's committed adultery, incest, maybe even rape."

Art raised a hand like a student with a question. "He would appear to have vaulted to the top of the suspect list, I'll grant you that. It's your next step—that we're the perfect pair to confront the killer—that I'm not sure follows, exactly."

People had a way of disappearing and dying suddenly in Cooke County, I pointed out. That, he retorted, was precisely why he didn't think we should be headed there, given that we'd very nearly disappeared and died once already. "But what if Kitchings Senior—or somebody else up there—gets wind of the DNA results some other way? What if he vanishes, runs away, or turns up dead? We'd never know the truth."

"And you think he's going to 'fess up to us, after all these years, just because we're such swell guys?"

"If we show up and confront him with this, catch him off guard, I think he's a hell of a lot more likely to 'fess up, or at least reveal something, than he is if we don't."

"Don't show up, or don't catch him off guard?"

"Either. Both. With the sheriff and Williams out of the way for the moment, the coast is clear. And maybe, if we drop the DNA bombshell, we can shock the reverend into admitting something." Art turned his head and looked out the window. I knew my argument was weak. I knew it wasn't logic that was compelling me back to Cooke County today. I reached into my shirt pocket and removed the photo of Leena that Jim O'Conner had given me. I handed it to Art. "There's something in her face that reminds me of Kathleen thirty years ago. Kathleen when she was young. Not just young, either—Kathleen when she pregnant. She'd put on some weight, and her face had rounded out a little . . ." I trailed off; it sounded foolish.

"So somehow this is about Kathleen now?"

"No. Well, maybe. Not her, exactly. More about me, but me trying to set things right with her, somehow."

"Come on, Bill, when are you going to let yourself off that hook? It's not your fault Kathleen died."

"You can tell me that till you're blue in the face—I can tell myself that till I'm blue in the face—but that doesn't seem to change how I feel about it. Maybe this will."

"And if it doesn't?"

"I don't know, Art. I'll jump off that bridge when I come to it."

He sighed. "Well, don't forget to set fire to it as you're climbing over the rail." He slipped the picture of Leena into his own shirt pocket. "Okay, then. Let's just pray we can persuade the good reverend that confession really is good for the soul."

I'd pretty much quit praying two years before, but I decided this might be a good time to give it another try.

39

THE STONE WALLS OF Cave Springs Primitive Baptist Church and its blasted tunnel sent a chill of remembrance through me, and I found myself rethinking the wisdom of our errand. I was just about to say as much when Art tapped my shoulder and pointed toward the house next door. Sitting motionless in his weathered, flattened-out rocker was a seventy-year-old version of Tom Kitchings. His hair was white, his face was craggy and leatherlike, but his underlying bone structure and the distinctive cast of his eyes confirmed him as the sheriff's father, as surely as any DNA test ever could.

I swung the truck across the gravel parking area, stopped near the worn path to the front steps, and got out, followed by Art. We stopped at the foot of the stairs. The stormfront was moving in; big oaks thrashed like saplings, their leaves whirling across the yard.

I raised my voice over the roar of the wind. "Reverend Kitchings?" The man neither spoke nor moved. "Reverend Kitchings, I'm Dr. Bill Brockton. This is my friend Art Bohanan. We're from Knoxville. Your son Tom asked me to help him on a case up here."

He raised his upper lip and spat a wad of tobacco juice down into the yard. The wind caught and shredded it into vapor. "You done it?" he called.

"Excuse me?"

"I said have you done it? Have you helped?"

"Well, it's a tough case, but I'm trying my best."

He spat again, upwind of me this time, and I felt a fine mist strike my face. "Mister, I had me two boys 'fore you started helping. Now I got one. How 'bout you quit helping and git out of here 'fore somethin' happens to my other un."

I glanced at Art. He raised both eyebrows at me, which seemed less helpful at the moment than I'd have liked. This interrogation business wasn't as easy as I'd imagined. "Mr. Kitchings, I am sorry about Orbin, I truly am. I've lost a wife, so I can imagine some of the pain you must be feeling. But I can assure you, I didn't have anything to do with his death."

"The hell you didn't," he shouted. "You come up here and started sticking your nose where it don't belong, started stirrin' up things you got no bidness stirrin' up, and you can *assure* me? Get off my property, or I can assure *you* I'll whup your ass, doctor or not."

Art finally spoke up. "Reverend? About those things the doctor's been stirring up. You afraid of what might float to the top? You maybe got something to hide, Reverend? Maybe some dirty little secret from about thirty years back? A little bit of dirty linen involving your niece, maybe?"

Kitchings stood up. He held out a bony arm and pointed a crooked finger toward the horizon, toward Knoxville. The hand trembled—with rage? Or just with age?

"What was that girl's name?" Art persisted, "Gina? No, Leena, that was it, wasn't it? She was a mighty good-looking girl, wasn't she, Reverend? Tall. Blonde. Spirited girl, folks say, with a real spring in her step." Art started up the steps. "I've got a picture of her right here." Art reached into his shirt pocket and fished out the photo, studying it closely. "Yes sir, she was a beauty. She favored her mama a lot, didn't she, Reverend? Sophie? The sister you really wanted to marry."

The old man raised his other hand, held both hands out before him now, no longer pointing, but shielding himself, palms facing outward, as if to fend off some looming collision or dreadful specter. "Don't you come any closer. You keep that away from me."

Art kept climbing, step upon step, slowly turning the picture and holding it out toward Kitchings. The old man shrank back, like a vampire confronted by a crucifix. "Must have been real hard for you when the girl moved into your house," said Art. "So young, so pretty. So much like the woman you were still in love with, even after you married the homely sister." Kitchings was shaking his head slowly from side to side, but his eyes were locked on the picture. "I bet you dreamed about her at night, didn't you, Reverend? Prayed about her in the daytime, dreamed about her at night." Art was almost to the top step. "Then she took up with that O'Conner boy. Is that what pushed you over the edge, Reverend? Knowing you were about to lose her, too? Knowing another man—a man from a family you hated—was about to pluck that young woman you'd been watching ripen on the vine all that time?"

Art stepped onto the porch, brandishing the picture at arm's length like a weapon. I flashed back to the image of him holding the photo in the KPD forensics lab, the flaming photo of the suspect in his abduction case, and I marveled at the power he was able to invest pictures with. Maybe the Native Americans are right: maybe the camera *does* capture a bit of the soul.

"You forced that girl, didn't you, Reverend, when you realized she was gonna marry Jim O'Conner? She was a virgin, but you knew that, didn't you? That was part of the temptation, wasn't it?" Kitchings was backed up against the front wall of the house now, his head thrashing from side to side as if the words were backhanded blows to the face. I thought back to Art's reenactment of Jack Nicholson and

Faye Dunaway—she was my niece; she was my lover; she was my niece *and* my lover. "Did she cry, Reverend? Did she beg you not to, or was she too proud to plead? How'd you do it? Did you hit her? Hold a knife to her throat and a hand on her mouth?" As Art advanced relentlessly, the old man began to slide down the wall, his knees giving way beneath him. "And when you spilled your seed inside her, Reverend—inside your own *niece,* Reverend—did you ask her to forgive you? Or did you just pray to God you wouldn't get caught?" Kitchings was crumpled at Art's feet now, his breath coming in ragged sobs. "And four months later, Reverend—when her pregnancy started to show—what did God say when you put your hands around her throat and started to squeeze?"

"No," he whispered. "Oh, Lord God, no."

I was holding my breath, and the two men on the porch were motionless. Even the wind seemed breathless, for there was an eerie, electric silence, as if the very cosmos were hanging in suspense, waiting for what would come next. And in that sudden silence I heard the unmistakable click of a shotgun being breached open, then snapped shut.

"All right, Mister, you just step back right now," twanged a flat female voice I recognized from my interview with Mrs. Kitchings. The screen door screeched open against its rusty spring, then slapped shut as she stepped out of the house and onto the porch. "Get your hands up," she told Art, motioning with the shotgun. "You, too," she said, waving the shotgun's gaping twin barrels at me.

I stood frozen, too dumbfounded to move. She raised the gun to her shoulder. Her mouth pursed into a prunelike grimace. Fire blasted from one of the barrels, and I felt a searing wind roar past my right ear. Behind me, I heard my truck's windshield shatter. "I said put your hands up. Next shot takes your head off. One. Two."

I raised my arms.

"Now botha you get over there to the end of the porch. Go on, now."

I mounted the steps, as if toward a gallows, and moved to the far end of the porch. Art came and stood beside me.

The old man struggled to his feet and limped to his wife. He reached out his hand for the gun, saying, "Vera—" The barrel caught him squarely on his right cheekbone. The front sight raked across the flesh, tearing a ragged gash that began to ooze blood. He staggered back against the porch rail, one hand pressed to the cheek. "Vera . . ."

"You shut up. Get over there with them two."

"Vera, listen to me."

"No. No! You listen to me for once, you sorry sack of shit, and you get your ass over there with them two." Kitchings sagged, then shuffled over beside me. "I been chokin' down poison for thirty years on account of you, Thomas Kitchings, and I done had my fill of it. No more; no more. This ends right here, right now. I ain't gonna take no more, and I ain't gonna lie no more. This mess done ruint our lives. It's done kilt Orbin, and it's about kilt Tom, and I don't aim to let that happen. Enough is a damn 'nough."

Art cleared his throat. "Mrs. Kitchings, if you'd please put that shotgun down, I know we can talk about this calmly."

"I don't want to talk about this calmly," she said. "I been calm way too long now. I been calm my whole life, and look what it's got me." She looked around, as if surveying the wreckage of her life; then she shook her head fiercely, her eyes blazing.

"Mrs. Kitchings, I know things look bad right now, but it's not hopeless," Art persisted. "With a good lawyer—Dr. Brockton here knows some fine ones—your husband could plea-bargain. If he made a deal for manslaughter, he might be out in two or three years."

She stared at Art as if he were a madman. "Plea-bargain? Manslaughter? What the hell are you talking about?"

She shook her head and spat, then took her hand off the trigger momentarily, fishing another shotgun shell from a pocket of her apron without taking her eyes off us. She broke the breach open to reload the barrel she'd fired at my windshield. I glanced at Art—the reloading didn't strike me as a good sign—and noticed a slight tensing of his muscles. She fumbled with the shell, glancing down at the barrel. She took her eyes off us for only an instant, but that gave Art an opening. Springing forward, he grabbed the end of the barrel and wrested it from her grasp. She flung herself at Art, but her husband stepped between them and wrapped his arms around her in a bear hug. She fought for a moment, then sagged in his arms. I stood motionless, my hands still high in the air, too stunned to lower them.

"That's real touching," came a voice from the far corner of the porch. "Y'all gonna kiss and make up now?" Leon Williams stepped into view, a lever-action hunting rifle cradled in the crook of his right arm, the barrel angling across his chest. "Howdy, Doc. Art."

I dropped my aching arms. "We sure coulda used you here about five minutes sooner," I said, stepping toward him. Art reached out and laid a hand on my arm. Williams raised the rifle and thumbed the hammer back. "Put 'em back up, Doc. Art, you wanna just lay that shotgun down real careful and slide it over this way with your foot?"

Art shook his head in disgust, the shotgun hanging open and useless in his left hand. He bent down and set it on the boards, kicking it to Williams, who set one foot on the stock. Art's voice surprised me with its steadiness. "This is kinda snowballing on you, isn't it, Deputy? How many more people you plan to kill?" I stared at Art; he stared at Williams's rifle. "Not too bright to bring the same rifle you shot Orbin with, Leon. That's a Marlin 336, isn't it? Shoots Winchester thirty-thirty ammunition, if I'm not mistaken. Be easy for ballistics to check it against the bullet Bill dug out of Orbin's brain last night." There was no bullet in Orbin's brain, only a melted blob of lead in the floor of the chopper—Art was ad-libbing again—but Williams suddenly looked nervous.

"By the way," Art said, "what kind of bullet was it that killed the previous sheriff, fellow who died in that drug bust shootout a few years back? Was that a thirty-thirty, too, Leon? You been gunning for the sheriff's job for a while now?" The deputy's jaw muscles were working furiously. "Don't you think you better cut your losses and make a deal while you've still got a chance?"

Williams shook his head. "I didn't ever have a chance," he said. "Not a real one. Not in this county; not with these people always running things." He waved the barrel toward Mr. and Mrs. Kitchings. "This man's daddy locked my grandpa in the jail on a trumped-up charge and let him burn to death in there." He took a step toward the old couple. "Who made y'all the lords of Cooke County? Tell me—who? Your people been treatin' my people like we was dirt for as long as we can remember. And we remember back a long damn way."

The old man had looked stooped and broken ever since Art had come after him. Now his spine straightened and fire flashed from his eyes. "You don't remember back near as far as you ought to, then. You start feeling proud, you just recollect the Civil War and the damn Home Guard. Your people was galloping around, waving rebel flags and stealing food and burnin' barns and killin' folks that was just trying to stay alive. Struttin' around like y'all was doing your patriotic duty. Well, bull*shit*. If y'all been treated like you was second-class, it's nothin' but what you'uns deserve. You was common back then, and you're common now. Just . . . *common*." He spat out the word with such loathing and contempt that it somehow became the nastiest slur I'd ever heard.

It must have sounded nasty to Williams, too, because I saw his teeth clench and his nostrils flare. The barrel of the hunting rifle jerked in the minister's direction. I opened my mouth to shout—a warning, a protest, a formless shriek, I'm not sure what—but before I could, the deputy's finger clenched and the gun roared. Reverend Kitchings gasped and crumpled to the floor, slipping from his wife's feeble grasp. Everyone stood frozen for a moment, and then I heard a high, keening wail coming from Mrs. Kitchings.

As Williams jacked the rifle's lever to load another round in the chamber, Art lunged for him. Williams swung the rifle, and the stock caught Art in the cheekbone. He staggered and sank to his hands and knees.

I looked away, appalled and sickened. And that's when I saw it: a small, dark dot on the southern horizon. The wind was booming again from the north, drowning out the sound, but I'd seen enough helicopters in the past few days to recognize another one. Whose it was, or how it happened to be swooping toward us, I had no idea. But I prayed the wind would mask its approach until someone inside could get off a shot at Williams. But would they, even if they had a chance? My heart sank as I realized that the deputy—the one person in a law enforcement uniform—was probably the last person another officer would fire on. I looked back to the porch and down at Art—still on his knees—and noticed his eyes flick toward the horizon and register a sign of hope. He'd seen it, too.

All I could think to do was stall for time, distract Williams for a few crucial moments. Maybe once the chopper landed, we could shout for help, shout out an explanation of some sort—if nothing else, as we were gunned down ourselves, maybe one of us could shout that it was Williams who had shot Orbin and the reverend. "I don't see how you expect to get away with this," I said loudly. "You'll have to kill all of us, and the TBI's going to find that mighty suspicious."

He shook his head scornfully. "Naw, they're just gonna find it real tragic," he said. "I'd warned you to stay away from Mr. and Mrs. Kitchings here. Crazy with grief, blaming you for the death of Orbin, Reverend Kitchings here blasted y'all with both barrels. If only I'd arrived thirty seconds sooner." As he said this, he stooped and reached for the shotgun with his left hand, keeping his right hand on the trigger of the rifle, which was cradled in his arm. "When the reverend reloaded and aimed at me, I had no choice but to shoot him." He paused to compose the next lines of his story. "Imagine my surprise when his wife grabbed the shotgun as he fell, and then *she* turned on me. Broke my heart to have to shoot an old woman, but what else could I do?" He looked from the rifle to the shotgun and back again, as if considering which murder weapon to employ first. He seemed to reach a decision, for he set the shotgun back down, raised the hunting rifle to his shoulder, and aimed at Mrs. Kitchings.

The chopper was tantalizingly close now—no more than a hundred yards—and I knew he'd hear it any second. His finger tightened on the trigger. "No!" I shrieked desperately. "I don't want to die! Don't kill us! Please don't kill us! No, no, no, no!" He hesitated, staring at me in confusion and annoyance, then shifted his stance and turned the barrel toward me. But it was the wrong gun—he was planning to shoot Art and me with the shotgun—and he hesitated.

At that moment a Bell LongRanger bearing FBI markings dove toward the parking lot. Even before it slammed down, a door burst open and a figure leapt out and sprinted toward the house, bellowing. Williams spun, astonished. "Gun!" shouted Art. "Up on the porch! He's got a gun!"

Despite twenty years, forty pounds, a knee injury, and a mild heart attack, Tom Kitchings still ran with the power and determination worthy of a halfback. Williams began to fire. The sheriff dodged and juked as if he were headed for the goal line in Neyland Stadium, and I saw something of the speed and agility that had once electrified fans by the thousands. Williams levered off two quick shots, but Kitchings was still churning, still closing the distance, when Art launched himself at the deputy and knocked him to the porch. Williams struggled beneath him, but Art drove a knee into his solar plexus, knocking the wind out of him, then wrenched the rifle free with a finger-snapping yank. Scrambling to his feet, he jammed the barrel against Williams's temple. "Give me a reason," Art gasped. "Give me any little reason to shoot you. Come on, do it!" Williams slumped, limp and defeated.

Tom Kitchings half-vaulted, half-fell up the steps and onto the porch. "Hey, Sheriff, that was some run," I said. "Looks like you haven't lost your form after all." He ignored me and sank to his knees beside his dazed mother and his dead father.

"Oh, Mama," he cried. "Oh, Mama, what's happened to us? What has happened to this family, Mama?" He was gasping and sobbing.

She wrapped her arms around him. "Terrible things," she said. "God's judgment. We brought it down on our own selves. We did. Ever one of us but you."

He choked on the words. "Oh, Mama, I tried. I tried so hard to make good."

"You did. You done real good. You always made me proud. You just keep on, no matter what."

"It's too late, Mama. Too late."

"No it ain't. You got a good heart, Tommy, and you're all I got left in this world. You got to keep on making me proud."

"I can't, Mama. I'm shot. I'm shot, and it's bad." Only when he said the words did I notice the bloom of crimson spreading across the back of his khaki shirt. He sagged against her, then slid to the porch, and just like that, he was gone.

Two more men thundered up the porch steps, weapons drawn: Steve Morgan and "Rooster" Rankin. "TBI," shouted Morgan, "don't move!" But he and Rankin were the ones who froze as they surveyed the carnage at their feet: two men dead, a third facedown with a rifle barrel to his head, an old and broken woman weeping beside the bloody corpses of her husband and son.

Art never shifted his gaze or his aim from Williams. "Police officer," he called out. "Arthur Bohanan, KPD. This is Dr. Bill Brockton, state forensic anthropologist. This deputy here has committed at least three murders."

"It's okay, Art," said Rankin. "It's Agent Rankin and Agent Morgan. We know all about this asshole's handiwork now. Let me just get in there and cuff him, if you don't mind." Rankin knelt and yanked Williams's hands behind his back, then jerked him to his feet, dragging him down the stairs and shoving him toward the chopper.

Morgan must have seen me struggling to piece together what had brought him here in the company of Tom Kitchings, the man I'd accused of obstructing justice. "Sheriff Kitchings called TBI headquarters last night from his hospital bed, so Rankin dropped by to talk to him right after he finished getting the runaround from Williams."

"The *sheriff* called *you?*"

Morgan nodded. "He got suspicious when Williams got to the crash scene so fast, and he knew Williams had a thirty-thirty he was pretty fond of. So he gave us the brass from the bullets that killed Orbin. I stopped by the Cooke County firing range last night on my way back to Knoxville to collect some of the deputy's spent cartridges out there. Ballistics worked through the night comparing tool marks on the shells. Perfect match. Soon as we saw that, we figured we'd better hotfoot it up here before somebody else got shot."

"But how'd the sheriff come to be with you in the helicopter?"

"He checked in with us as he was leaving the hospital, so we did a quick touchdown at the LifeStar base and picked him up. Lucky for you we did. He figured you'd be poking around again, figured you'd start with his father, and figured Williams might try to get you out of the way."

"He figured right," I said. "Looks like I should've given Sheriff Kitchings a lot more credit than I did, for brains and for integrity."

"It wasn't easy for him. He also figured his dad was the one that killed the pregnant woman."

"He missed that one, but not by much. Did he say how he found her body in the first place?"

"Anonymous letter," said Steve. "Had to've been from Williams. Guess the deputy found out about the old man's spelunking, followed him into the cave one day, and figured he could use Leena to bring down the sheriff and his family."

I shook my head and took a deep breath, exhaling hard. "It worked well," I said. "Terribly well."

I looked down at Tom Kitchings, sprawled on the porch in his uniform and his congealing blood. He'd once had so much potential; he'd been on a path that led somewhere important, or at least somewhere glamorous, until his fate took a turn and spun him back to the hills of Cooke County. Where he ended up certainly wasn't glamorous, but maybe, in some tragic, Southern Gothic way, it *was* important. In the end, he had lived up to his potential after all—he died living up to it. His death was a waste and a shame, but at the same time, there was something noble, even redemptive in it. He had given his life for Leena and her baby, I realized, and given it for me, too. The stone church caught my eye. "Greater love hath no man than this . . ." I said.

". . . that he lay down his life for his friends," finished Art. "And he wasn't even convinced we were his friends." He turned to the TBI agent. "Could we give you our statements later?" Morgan nodded. "Can y'all take a statement from Mrs. Kitchings? I believe she's got some things to get off her chest." Morgan nodded again. "Bill, what say we go home?"

We eased down the ridge from the church to the river road, slowly threading the curves to I-40. We even crept along the interstate, flashers blinking. A funereal pace seemed fitting, given the bloody events we'd just witnessed.

Besides, thanks to Mrs. Kitchings and the shot she'd fired across my bow, my truck had no windshield.

Eyes streaming and cheeks flapping in the wind, Art yelled, "Why do dogs like to stick their heads out into the wind?" I shrugged, squinting into the gale. Even at forty, the wind was hair-pulling and skin-chapping. But the view—the mountains blazing crimson and gold all around—the view out that unobstructed opening was the best I've ever had.

For the first time in a long while—two years, I suddenly realized—I could see color and light and beauty clear to the horizon, with nothing in the way.

Epilogue

DRY LEAVES SWIRLED AROUND my boots as I scuffed across the corner of the hospital parking lot toward the gate of the Body Farm. Slate-colored clouds scudded above the hills and skeletal trees, and streamers of morning mist spooled downstream along the river that separated the main campus from the Body Farm.

Unlocking the outer padlock, I swung the chain-link gate wide, then opened the inner lock. The steel chain clattered through the holes bored in the wooden modesty fence and clanked to the ground as the inner gate lurched open. In the central clearing, the grass was brown and wispy, gone to seed; red-orange maple leaves lay atop the stalks, and others hung in midair, suspended in spiderwebs. All in all, the morning was remarkably gray, chill, and bleak, but I took that not so much as an omen of the season that lay ahead as a summation of the events that had just transpired—the strangled mother and her never-born child; the fiery crash and cremated deputy; the tragic end of a once-promising athlete and officer and, with him, the end of a proud blood-line, in a county where old bloodlines and old feuds carry great weight. With the burial of the various Kitchings dead, both the recent and the long-dead, and the murder charges against Williams, I hoped all the feuds and scores might soon be considered settled, at least as settled as such bloody events allowed.

A new body lay at the far edge of the clearing, a white man whose already large abdomen was beginning to bloat and swell. Mounted to a sturdy post a few feet away were a motion sensor and a night vision camera. No one had ever studied the interactions of nocturnal predators and human corpses, so one of my grad students had set up the wildlife surveillance as a thesis project. Judging by the first night's photos of raccoons and rodents, we had the makings of a season's worth of Animal Planet documentaries. Kneeling down beside the corpse, I checked his ankle tag. It identified him as 68-05: the sixty-eighth corpse donated to the Body Farm in 2005.

His face was beginning to wrinkle. Laugh lines around the eyes suggested frequent happiness in his life, but they were tempered by worries etched into his forehead. I thought of the lines by Gibran—"The deeper that sorrow carves into your being, the more joy you can contain." Had he been loved? Probably, judging by the laugh lines. Had he suffered loss? Hard not to, in half a century or so of living. His bones, eventually, would shed some slantwise light on his life, revealing whether he'd labored hard, building strong bones with prominent muscle attachment points, or had lived a life of sedentary ease; whether he'd escaped serious injury for five decades or had crashed through life breaking arms, legs, ribs, ankles, clavicles. His file, across the river in my office beneath the stadium, would give me basic details—cause of death, next of kin, and so on—but it would shed little light on the Big Questions: Who had this man really *been,* deep down, and what kind of life had he lived?

For that matter, I wasn't sure I could answer those questions about myself. Who was I, deep down, and what kind of life was I living? Teacher, researcher, forensic consultant. Widower, father, son. Sedentary academician, unscathed—

skeletally speaking, at least—by life's rough-and-tumble. The descriptors didn't seem to add up to much.

My inward inventory was interrupted by the crunch of tires on the gravel at the entrance. A Jeep Cherokee, bearing the familiar insignia of the Cooke County Sheriff's Department, eased to a stop in the clearing. The front doors opened, and two khaki-clad officers emerged. "Your secretary told me you'd be out here," said a familiar voice. "Couldn't pass up a chance to see the place at last."

I rose and shook hands with Jim O'Conner. "Hey, Sheriff. I heard about the special election; congratulations. You look good in that uniform. So do you, Waylon." The burly mountain man had traded in his camo for a deputy's uniform, the largest I'd ever seen. Waylon flashed me a tobacco-flecked grin. *Some things never change,* I thought.

O'Conner adjusted his gun belt and struck a tough-cop pose, then laughed. "Feels kinda funny still—I'm tempted to arrest myself for impersonating an officer. Been a long time since I wore a uniform; back when I got out of the military, I swore never again. Just goes to show: never say never."

"I never do," I said. "By the way, I didn't get a chance to talk to you at the service, but I thought it was nice, considering. It was generous of you to pay for the three Kitchings funerals, in light of your history with the family. Sweet of you to put up a headstone for Leena next to her parents, too." The TBI had never found Leena's postcranial skeleton, despite turning the sheriff's offices and every Kitchings residence inside out. What little we had of her—the skull, hyoid, and sternum—had been buried in a small ceramic urn that Jim O'Conner had made from clay he dug from one of his mountains.

"You think we'll ever find the rest of her?" O'Conner asked.

"I don't know, Jim. At first I thought Tom or Orbin took

her, then I figured it was part of Williams's scheme to impli-
cate the sheriff for obstruction." He nodded; either scenario
would have been credible. "Now, though, I suspect they were
stolen by Knox County's medical examiner—*former* medical examiner—along with another skeleton. Maybe he took
Leena as a red herring. Or maybe just to get even with me. I
haven't heard the last of him, he says, and I'm afraid he's
right. But if we ever recover Leena's missing bones, you'll
be the first to know."

"I've bought the cemetery plot on the other side of hers,"
he said. "I hope I don't need it for a while, but Cooke County
sheriffs do seem to die prematurely and violently."

"I'm betting you'll be the exception to that rule, Jim."

"Hang onto that thought. Listen, I wanted you to hear this
from me face to face. Leon Williams and his lawyer—some
slick Knoxville guy named DeVriess—just cut a deal with
the U.S. Attorney." I grimaced at the mention of DeVriess,
but I supposed if I were in the deputy's bloody shoes, I'd
hire Grease, too. "Leon's pleading guilty to second-degree
murder in Tom's death and first-degree in Orbin's; in return,
he avoids a possible death sentence. He's also confessed to
shooting the prior sheriff during that drug bust three years
ago. Apparently he'd been plotting against the Kitchings
clan and aiming to be sheriff—pun intended—for quite
awhile."

"Any chance of parole?"

"None."

"Good."

"The prosecutor's also talking plea bargain with Mrs.
Kitchings," he added. "I figure she'll end up doing only a
couple years for second-degree or manslaughter. She doesn't
seem to care what her sentence is. She's got nothing and nobody left to come home to when she does get out."

I nodded. "Sounds about right. I figure Williams deserves

whatever an ex-cop gets in prison, but Mrs. Kitchings has already suffered about as much as a human being can bear."

He agreed. "There's one other thing I want you to know. I appreciate what you did for us up there; what you did for me, especially."

I held up a hand. "Don't mention it. I hate to think of Kitchings pinning Leena's murder on you—or Williams framing you for Orbin's death."

"You saved my neck in a couple of ways," he said. "But I'm not just thanking you for keeping me out of prison. I hadn't realized how much emotional shrapnel I've been carrying around ever since I lost Leena. It still hurts—hell, feels like somebody's just stomped on my heart all over again—but I think maybe this time it'll heal, sooner or later." He wiped his eyes. "I never did stop loving that girl, Doc; it damn near killed me to think she'd stopped loving me. I like to think now that she didn't, after all."

"She died wearing your name around her neck, Jim. I'd say that's pretty convincing proof." How odd, to hear myself quoting a line from Grease.

He drew a deep breath and forced it out through pursed lips. "Part of me'll always grieve for what happened to her—and for my inability to protect her from it. But at least I know the truth now."

"And the truth can set you free," I finished the thought. "If you let it."

"I think I will." He looked into me. "How 'bout you?"

I took a breath. "I'm trying."

He nodded. "Good. You deserve to be at peace, too."

"Thanks," I said. "Mostly I am now. Except when I'm looking over my shoulder for a vengeful medical examiner. Listen, I hope we can stay in touch. Maybe keep tabs on each other's progress. Form our own twelve-step program for griefaholics."

"We can try," he said, "but we might have to hold the meetings by telephone for a while. Me and Chief Deputy Waylon here got us some cockfightin' and pot-growin' and meth-cookin' scoundrels to track down, don't we, Waylon?"

Waylon frowned. "Let's not be too hasty about them cock-fights. TBI might want to keep workin' 'em undercover." O'Conner snorted, but Waylon seemed unfazed. "Doc, Cousin Vern says to tell you 'hey.' Wanted you to know he's gettin' into a new line of farming—raising sang 'stead of weed, up at Jim's place. The sang don't grow near as fast, but it's a mite safer." I felt safer myself, knowing Waylon didn't need to booby-trap the ginseng operation.

"Vernon's got quite a gift for horticulture, too," said O'-Conner. "I think Cooke County Black Ginseng is going to make a big splash next fall over in China."

Waylon fidgeted in his uniform. "Vern's boy's doing real good since you got him in to see that doctor at Children's Hospital, too." I nodded, glad that what I'd diagnosed as leukemia had proved to be merely salmonella poisoning plus a kidney infection. "Oh! and he's got him a new pup, too—another redbone hound. Sweet little thing—named her Duchess in memory of Duke."

I smiled. "You give Cousin Vern my best," I said. "If you don't care to." Waylon nodded and clapped me on the shoulder, nearly sending me sprawling. "Hell no, I don't care to."

O'Conner caught Waylon's eye and nodded at the Jeep. "We better head on back," he said. "I'm afraid to leave the county for more than an hour at a time. I'm not sure I'll be back this way until I get another deputy hired and up to speed, so don't be surprised if you don't see me for a while. On the other hand, probably won't be long before some unidentified, varmint-chewed, vermin-infested body turns up in some backwoods hollow or chop-shop junkyard. We are talking Cooke County, after all."

"Well, I reckon I could find my way back to your neck of the woods if duty calls," I said. "And you know where to find me. Either under the stadium or out here communing with the dead."

He grinned and nodded. We shook hands again, and he climbed back into the Cherokee and backed out the gate.

I checked my watch and realized I should be going, too. I was expected at Jeff's house for dinner in a couple of hours, and it wouldn't do to show up reeking of corpses. Besides, after I got cleaned up, I'd need to swing by the Hilton to pick up Jess Carter, who was back in town to do another autopsy. "My God, is this a *date*?" Jeff had asked when I asked if I could bring her along.

"I don't know," I said. "She might still be happily lesbian."

He laughed. "That could make a difference, Dad. You might want to find out at some point."

"I intend to, son," I said. "Should be interesting." He concurred.

As I swung the gates shut and snapped the locks onto their chains, I looked up at the barren branches ringing the facility. Above them, a narrow ray of sunshine threaded a gap in the clouds. The light caught and backlit the wing of a buzzard. The bird was gliding effortlessly, patiently above the Body Farm, riding the wind, the scent, and his own mysterious yearnings.

He might not fully comprehend why he was drawn to delve into the messy details of death. But delve he did—with grace and gusto.

I couldn't help but admire that.

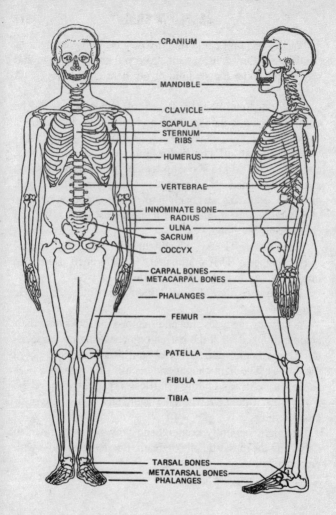

CRANIUM

MANDIBLE

CLAVICLE
SCAPULA
STERNUM
RIBS
HUMERUS

VERTEBRAE

INNOMINATE BONE
RADIUS
ULNA
SACRUM
COCCYX

CARPAL BONES
METACARPAL BONES

PHALANGES

FEMUR

PATELLA

FIBULA

TIBIA

TARSAL BONES
METATARSAL BONES
PHALANGES

Reprinted from *Human Osteology: A Laboratory and Field Manual* (Fourth Edition), by William M. Bass. © Missouri Archaeological Society, Inc., 1995.

THE SKULL

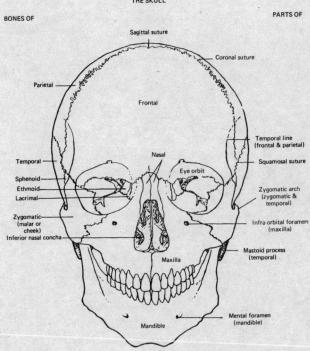

BONES OF

PARTS OF

- Sagittal suture
- Coronal suture
- Parietal
- Frontal
- Temporal line (frontal & parietal)
- Squamosal suture
- Nasal
- Eye orbit
- Temporal
- Sphenoid
- Ethmoid
- Lacrimal
- Zygomatic arch (zygomatic & temporal)
- Zygomatic (malar or cheek)
- Infra-orbital foramen (maxilla)
- Inferior nasal concha
- Mastoid process (temporal)
- Maxilla
- Mandible
- Mental foramen (mandible)

THE SKULL

BONES OF

PARTS OF

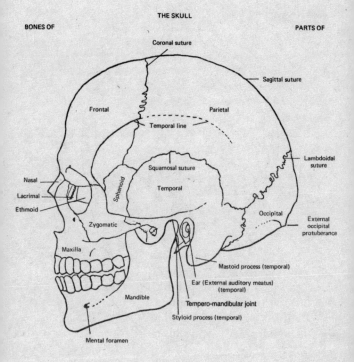

Coronal suture

Sagittal suture

Frontal

Parietal

Temporal line

Lambdoidal suture

Nasal

Squamosal suture

Lacrimal

Sphenoid

Temporal

Ethmoid

Occipital

Zygomatic

External occipital protuberance

Maxilla

Mastoid process (temporal)

Ear (External auditory meatus) (temporal)

Mandible

Tempero-mandibular joint

Styloid process (temporal)

Mental foramen

Acknowledgments

Some novels are pure fiction; others are fiction that is built on a foundation of facts. This book is of the latter type. Although the story is fictional, the science is factual, and some of the places and events described here contain a sizable kernel of reality. Many of the real-world forensic cases my graduate students and I have examined during the past thirty-five years have occurred in East Tennessee, where this story is based. It would be impossible (or at least foolish) to write a story that was not shaped and colored by those experiences.

So many people contribute to a story like this, it's impossible to acknowledge everyone by name. First and foremost, this book could not have been written without Jon Jefferson, a fine collaborator and eager student of forensic anthropology. I also want to thank my hundreds of graduate students, the many local and state law enforcement officers I've worked with, the members of the media who have produced accurate accounts of our investigations, and the thousands of loyal readers who are interested in my work and my stories. We hope you enjoy reading this book as much as we've enjoyed writing it.

—WMB III

Truth is not only stranger than fiction, it's much easier to write, I now realize. Thanks to the many people who have helped me navigate the new territory of fiction. Arthur Bohanan—the real-life Art—gave us gracious and good-humored permission to borrow his name, his reputation, and a few of his accomplishments, in return for nothing more than a promise to call attention to the urgent need for more research on finding ways to detect children's fingerprints. Thanks, Art—that's a promise we're privileged to keep. Dr. Jim Corbin, of the North Carolina Department of Agriculture—a pioneering scientist in the fight against ginseng poaching—answered numerous questions about 'sang; lest his reputation suffer, I'll hasten to absolve him of all blame for the fictional liberties I've taken on the subject of cultivation. For helicopter and air ambulance research—on the ground and in the air—I'm indebted to the flight crews of Smoky Mountain Helicopters and the University of Tennessee Medical Center's LifeStar air ambulance program. Thanks also to Dr. Sandra Elkins of the Regional Forensic Center; to Dr. Ed Uthman, via his website and emails; and to Lynn Faust, John, and Rick.

Many members of local, state, and federal law enforcement agencies were kind enough to answer myriad questions. Among them: KPD firearms examiner Patty Resig; sheriff's deputy (and K9 trainer extraordinaire) Art Wolff; District Attorney General Al Schmutzer; Assistant District Attorney Marsha Mitchell; Assistant U.S. Attorney Guy Blackwell; DEA agent Tim Wilson; TBI agent Greg Monroe; and half a dozen members of the FBI's Knoxville district office—Special Agent in Charge Joe Clark, Assistant Special Agent in Charge Tim Cox, Special Agents Gary Kidder, Beth O'Brien, and Robert Gibson III, and Chief District Counsel James Van Pelt.

Thanks also to my stepsons (and firearms consultants), Adam and Lee Robinson; to our energetic and capable literary agent, Giles Anderson; and to our intrepid editor at William Morrow, Sarah Durand.

As ever, working with Dr. Bill Bass remains a great pleasure, an amazing education, and a high honor.

—*JWJ*

Turn the page to travel inside
the University of Tennessee's
Anthropology Research Facility,
aka the "Body Farm,"
to meet the legendary Dr. Bill Bass
and to get a sneak peek
at the next Body Farm novel,

FLESH AND BONE...

Meet Dr. Bill Bass:

Dr. William M. "Bill" Bass is one of the most famous forensic anthropologists in the world. When he arrived at the University of Tennessee in 1971, forensic science was in its infancy. But with the founding of the Research Facility (the Body Farm) in 1972, the field grew by leaps and bounds. On three acres of land, dozens of donated human remains lie exposed to the elements, enabling Dr. Bass, other forensic scientists, graduate students, and law enforcement personnel to study postmortem change, and since the research program began in earnest in 1981, crucial discoveries have been made in the determination of time of death and manner of death.

For a video tour of the Body Farm, visit *www.JeffersonBass.com*.

For more information on the Body Farm, visit: *http://web.utk.edu/%7Eanthrop/index.htm*.

And to read more about Dr. Bass's life, career, and the groundbreaking work being done at the Body Farm, read *Death's Acre* or log onto *www.deathsacre.com*.

Q&A with Dr. Bass:

What is forensic anthropology?

Forensic anthropology is the application of the traditional
tools and techniques of physical anthropology—skeletal
analysis, mainly—to criminal cases, especially murders.
Forensic anthropologists are often called on to help identify
murder victims. If the police already have a pretty good idea
who the murder victim is, a forensic anthropologist might
look at dental records or medical X rays and try to match
them to the victim to confirm the identification; if the victim
is a John or Jane Doe, we'll start by determining the victim's
age, race, sex, and stature, so the police can crosscheck
missing-person reports or ask the public for leads that might
help identify the victim. We also detect and interpret signs
of skeletal trauma—ranging from gunshot wounds to bludg-
eoning fractures to knife marks on ribs. And these days,
thanks to the research we've done at the University of Tennessee, we also play an increasingly important role in determining time since death.

**What made you decide to go into forensic
anthropology?**

It was an accident—literally. I was majoring in psychology,
working on a master's degree in counseling, at the University of Kentucky. Just for fun, though, I was taking an anthropology class, too. One day my professor asked me if I
wanted to go with him on a forensic case—a woman had
been killed and burned in a highway accident, and he'd been
asked to identify her body. I went along and found it absolutely fascinating. It was like a light bulb went off above

my head. That was the "aha"—that was the moment when I knew what I wanted to do for the rest of my life. I went home, talked to my wife, and changed my major to anthropology. It was the best move I ever made.

What is the "Body Farm"?

That's the nickname for the scientific facility I set up at the University of Tennessee in 1980 to study human decomposition. Officially, it's called the "Anthropology Research Facility," but thanks to a bestselling Patricia Cornwell novel that featured the facility, it's much more widely known as the "Body Farm." At the time I created it, it was the world's only facility of its kind, and although modest efforts have been made recently to start a similar facility elsewhere, the Body Farm remains unique.

What is its purpose?

Its main focus has always been to observe and understand the processes and timetable of postmortem decay, primarily to improve our ability to determine what's called "time since death" in murder cases. In recent years, though, the facility has played an increasingly important role in developing or testing new forensic technologies, and also in training law enforcement groups like FBI agents, crime scene technicians, and cadaver dogs and their handlers. It's a unique scientific resource—you can do research there that can't be done anywhere else in the world.

Why is "time since death" so important?

When I'm called to a murder scene, the first question the police ask me is nearly always "How long has this person been dead?" It's crucial to know when the crime was committed, because that can really help narrow the search for a suspect—or can help rule out potential suspects who had alibis at the time the victim was killed. Now, if the body's fresh—no more than a day or two old—a medical examiner can generally pin down the time since death to within a matter of hours. But if the body's badly decayed—for instance, if it was dumped in the woods and lay there for weeks or months before being found by hunters—determining time since death requires detailed knowledge of the stages of decomposition, the role of temperature and humidity, the extent of insect activity in the corpse, and so on. Those are the kinds of variables we've spent decades researching at the Body Farm.

What kinds of research have you conducted to understand time since death?

Our early research projects were incredibly simple, because we knew almost nothing about decomposition rates. We put bodies out at the facility and watched to see when various limbs fell off. It sounds silly, but nobody knew even those rudimentary things. Gradually we got more and more specific with our research questions: How does the decomp rate compare in sunshine versus shade? In cool weather versus hot weather? In a shallow grave versus on the ground? In water? Inside a car? What effect do other variables have—clothing, body weight, and so on?

What happens to the skeletons after a body has finished decomposing?

Their contribution to forensic science is far from over at that point. Once the research project is finished, we clean off the bones, measure them, and enter the skeletal data in a forensic database created by my colleague, Dr. Richard Jantz. The database is the heart of a computer program called "ForDisc," which is short for "Forensic Discrimination." Using the ForDisc software, which is now in use all over the world, an anthropologist who's been brought into a forensic case can enter a few skeletal measurements from an unknown crime victim or even a partial skeleton—for example, the length and diameter of a femur, or thighbone—and the computer can predict, with amazing accuracy, the race, sex, and stature of the person that femur came from. Over the years, our data bank and our skeletal collection has grown tremendously. Today, I'm proud to say, the William M. Bass Research Skeletal Collection is the world's largest collection of modern skeletal specimens, and it's a tremendous asset in helping forensic anthropologists and police pinpoint the characteristics and narrow down the possible identities of unknown murder victims.

Where do the Body Farm's research bodies come from?
Our research bodies come from three sources. One source is Tennessee's network of medical examiners. If a body that comes through a county medical examiner's office ends up going unclaimed—either because the person is never identified or because no one ever shows up to claim the body—the ME might send it to us for decomposition research or for addition to our skeletal collection. The second source is family members of people who die—folks who know about our research and donate their loved one's remains to help advance the cause of science. The third source is people who will their bodies to us, signing donor consent forms in advance.

What's up-and-coming in forensic science?

Current and recent research projects at the Body Farm include:

Chemical products of decomposition: Using sophisticated analytical equipment, a research scientist from Oak Ridge National Laboratory is analyzing the hundreds of chemical compounds released as bodies decompose. To date, he has identified more than 400 individual compounds. He has also developed a prototype portable instrument that can detect airborne traces of some of the most prominent of these compounds—a step toward a handheld device that could be used to locate murder victims and mass graves in human-rights cases.

Biochemistry of adipocere formation: Adipocere—a latin word usually translated as "grave wax"—forms when a body's fatty tissue decomposes in a moist environment: on drowning victims, for instance, or bodies buried in damp basements or hidden in caves. (Adipocere figures prominently in the murder victim whose discovery in a cave triggers the action of *Carved in Bone.*) One current research project is studying the biochemical stages and compounds involved in adipocere formation, as a step toward developing a time-since-death "clock" that could interpret specific chemical ratios in a corpse's adipocere to determine how long since death occurred.

"Divining" for corpses: Surprising as it sounds, an age-old folkloric technique for locating groundwater—called "divining," dousing, or "water-witching"—is getting a high-tech investigation as a technique for locating buried bodies. Most people who divine for water use a forked, green stick, which—properly wielded—will purportedly twitch when it's carried over groundwater. A remarkably similar phenomenon seems to occur with angled metal wires in the proximity of decaying corpses: the wires twitch, cross, separate, or swing from side to side. One theory currently being investigated by an Oak Ridge National Laboratory research scientist is that as a body decomposes, chemical changes transform it into something akin to a giant battery, whose electromagnetic field affects the wires. Once the mechanism is understood, it—like the chemistry of decomposition gases—could be harnessed to create a sophisticated portable body detector.

Effects of taphonomy on decomposition rates: In a long-term study just completed for the FBI, Body Farm researchers placed corpses in various settings that replicate common murder scenes—inside a car, in a house, in shallow graves, submerged in water, and on the surface of the ground—to compare the decomposition rates and study specific changes in the corpses' hair. Daily weather readings and photographs provided a detailed comparative record. As the researchers expected, the corpses laid on the ground decomposed fastest, because they were most accessible to insects. Slowest to decompose were the bodies buried and immersed in water. Comparative studies like this help forensic scientists refine their estimates of "time since death" when decayed bodies are found at murder scenes.

Another riveting trip
into the heart of forensic science—

FLESH AND BONE

Coming in hardcover from
William Morrow in February 2007.

WE HAD PREPARED the body in the morgue, so I knew what to expect, but even so, I took a sharp breath when I folded back the flap to expose our subject. The blond wig had shifted a bit, sliding down over the face and concealing much of the trauma I'd inflicted, but what remained visible was strong stuff. According to Jess, most of the bones of the victim's face had been shattered by blunt-force trauma—she was guessing something fairly big, maybe a baseball bat or a metal pipe, rather than something smaller, like a tire iron, which would have left sharper, more distinctive marks in the bone. I couldn't bring myself to whale away on a donated body with such violence, so I'd settled for cutting through the zygomatic arches—the cheekbones—and the lower jaw in several places with an autopsy saw, then smearing a liberal amount of blood on the skin in those areas to simulate the bleeding that perimortem trauma would have induced. Miranda, being more skilled in the art of makeup, had applied base and rouge to the cheeks, plus violet eye shadow and a pair of long false eyelashes. I doubted that the makeup would affect the decomp rate, but I didn't want to throw any unnecessary variables into the equation.

Procuring the leather corset that we'd cinched around our subject's torso had proved far easier than I expected. Less than twenty-four hours before, Miranda had spent five minutes Googling and websurfing, then demanded my UT credit card. A few more keystrokes and she announced, "Done. One extra large bustier arriving at 6 A.M., First Overnight, thanks to the efficient teamwork of FedEx and Naughty&Nice.com." I foresaw some red-faced explaining to the UT auditors once the American Express bill arrived, but such was the occasional price of original research.

"Have you got the rope," I asked, "or do I need to go back to the truck and get it?" Miranda was wearing a black jumpsuit that bristled with pockets.

"No, I've got it," she said. She reached down and unzipped a big pocket just above her left knee and fished out a package of nylon cord and a big, military-looking pocketknife. With one twist of her thumb, she flipped open a wicked serrated blade.

"Whoa, that's some serious cutting power," I said. "What is that, a six-inch blade?"

She snorted. "Do men really believe that's what six inches looks like? Try three and a half." With the tip of the blade she deftly flicked off the package's plastic wrapper, then unspooled about six feet of cord—or was it three and a half?—and cut it with a swift stroke. "You wanna tie his hands while I do his feet?" I took the piece of rope and began to bind the corpse's wrists in front of him. Miranda sliced off another length of cord and lashed the ankles together. The rope snagged on the fishnet stockings as she cinched it taut above the stiletto heels. "I've never understood the appeal of crossdressing," she said, "either for the guys who do it or for the people who go to drag shows. But I also can't understand how anybody could get so enraged about it that they'd beat a guy to death for putting on a wig and some slutty clothes."

"Me neither," I said. "The one thing I understand, after all these years and all these murders, is that there's a lot I don't understand about human nature."

Once our stand-in was trussed up like the Chattanooga victim, the next task was to tie him to the tree. "Jess said his hands were up over his head," I remarked, half to Miranda and half to myself. "Hard to get 'em up there without a ladder, though." I spied a low branch. "Maybe if I throw a rope over that limb, we can use that like a pulley to hoist him up." Miranda whacked off another length, which I tossed across the branch where it joined the trunk. Then I tied one end to the wrist bindings, and together we hauled on the line. The nylon cord was thin, so it bit into our hands as we pulled. Once we had him upright, though, the friction of the rope on the branch helped support his weight.

"You think you can hold him," I asked, "while I fasten his legs to the tree?"

"Yup," said Miranda, taking a turn of rope around one hand.

Kneeling at the base of the tree, I pulled the feet close to the trunk and began tying them there. A yellowjacket circled my still-sweaty face, and with one hand I waved it away. Suddenly I heard a sharp exclamation—*"dammit!"*—followed by a slapping sound. Then: "oh, *shit,* look out!"

With a thud, the corpse toppled forward, draping himself over my head and shoulders and knocking me flat. Wriggling like some giant bug, I lay trapped at the base of the tree, pinned by the garishly dressed corpse. "I am *so sorry*," Miranda said, and then she began to snicker. But the snicker died suddenly, and I soon saw why.

A pair of rattlesnake boots, topped by black leather jeans, entered my peripheral vision and planted themselves a foot from my face. I knew, even before she spoke, that the snakeskin boots were coiled around the feet of Dr. Jess Carter. After a moment, her right toe began to tap, slowly and, as best I could tell, sarcastically.

"Don't let him get you down, Brockton," she finally said. "I think you can take him. Best two out of three?"

"Very funny," I said. "Y'all mind getting this guy off of me?"

Jess reached down and grabbed the rope around the dead

man's wrists; Miranda seized a leg. Together, they gave a heave that rolled the corpse onto his back beside me. I regained my feet and as much of my dignity as I could. Jess winked at me with the eye that Miranda couldn't see. I would have blushed, but my face was already red.

"This wasn't one of the questions you asked me to research," I told her, "but I'm thinking maybe more than one person was involved in the murder. Pretty tough to tie his arms that high on the tree without some help."

"I see what you mean," she said, "but the forensic techs couldn't tell. Ground's pretty rocky around there, and we had a dry spell for a couple weeks, so nothing useful in the way of footprints."

"I'm sorry I wasn't in town when he was found," I said. "My secretary said you called right about the time my plane was taking off for Los Angeles."

"Damned inconsiderate of you to help the LAPD with a case," she said. "We may need to fit you with one of those electronic ankle monitors to make sure you don't leave Tennessee."

"Can't do it," I said, pointing to my faded jeans and work boots. "It would spoil my fashion statement."

"Nonsense," she said. "Word is, Martha Stewart's coming out with a designer line of corrections apparel and accessories. I'm sure the Martha anklet will look fabulous on you." Jess handed me the rope. "Shall we try this again?" This time, once we'd hoisted the subject upright, I took the precaution of knotting the rope to the branch immediately. I tied off the legs, and Jess pronounced herself satisfied with the positioning.

"The strange thing is, the head and neck were in better shape than I'd expected," she said. "Lots of trauma, but not much decomp, considering how much blood there was to draw the flies. That would lead me to think he wasn't out there all that long, except there was almost no soft tissue left on the lower legs."

"You think maybe carnivores did that? Coyotes or foxes or raccoons?"

"Maybe," she said, "but I didn't see a lot of tooth marks. I'd like you to take a look at him, though, see if maybe I missed something."

"Sure," I said, "I could probably come down to Chattanooga later in the week. One thing I was wondering about, though: Why are you even working the case? I checked the map, and Prentice Cooper State Forest is across the line in Marion County, isn't it?"

She smiled. "I bet you were a whiz at map-and-compass back during your Boy Scout days, weren't you?" I grinned; she was right, even if she was just joking. "Cops got a report of an abduction from the parking lot of Alan Gold's one night a couple weeks ago. Alan Gold's is a gay bar in Chattanooga. Has the best drag show in East Tennessee. A female—or female impersonator—fitting the victim's description was seen being forced into a car and speeding away. We're working on the theory that the crime began in Chattanooga." She paused briefly, as if considering whether to say something else. "Besides," she said, "Marion County is rural and has a small sheriff's office. They just don't have the forensic resources to work this."

"Makes sense," I said. "Okay, I think we're ready to let nature take its course here. We'll check this guy every day, track the temperatures. The forecast for the next fifteen days—if AccuWeather can be believed—calls for temps about like what you've had in Chattanooga over the past couple weeks. So the decomp rate here should track the victim's pretty closely. Once this guy's condition matches your guy's, we should know how long he was out there before that poor hiker found him."

Jess took another look at the corpse tied to the tree. "There's one more detail we need to make the re-creation authentic." I look puzzled. "I didn't tell you about this," she said. "You were already skittish about the trauma to the head and face, so I figured this would send you clear over the edge." Reaching down to her belt, she unsheathed a long, fixed-blade knife from her waist. She stepped up to the body, yanked down the black satin panties and stockings we'd tugged onto him, and severed his penis at the base.

"Good god," Miranda gasped.

"Not hardly," said Jess. "I'd say this was more the devil's handiwork." She took a deep breath and blew it out. "Bill, you sure this guy is clean?"

I struggled to speak. "Well, I can tell you he didn't have HIV and he didn't have hepatitis. That's all we screen for, though. I can't promise he didn't have syphilis or a case of the clap."

She eyed the penis. "I don't see any obvious symptoms," she said. With that, she peeled off her left glove, dabbed her bare thumb on the severed end of the organ, then carefully rolled a print onto the shaft. As Miranda and I stared in disbelief and horror, she pried open the corpse's jaw and stuffed the penis into the mouth.

"There," she said. "*Now* it's authentic."

Available Now
From *New York Times* bestselling author

JEFFERSON BASS

"[A] unique corpse, solid science, quirky humor and a lovable protagonist." —*USA Today*

CARVED IN BONE

Large Print

978-0-06-112127-2 • $24.95/$32.95 Can.

Read Jefferson Bass in e-book. Download to your laptop, PDA or phone for convenient, immediate, or on-the-go reading. Visit www.harpercollinsebooks.com, or other online e-book retailers.

HARPER **LUXE**   HarperCollins e-books

Imprints of HarperCollinsPublishers
www.harpercollins.com

Visit www.AuthorTracker.com for exclusive information on your favorite HarperCollins authors.

Available wherever books are sold or please call 1-800-331-3761 to order.